Attack of the Angry Legend

Stranger in the Shadows

Planet of Joy

Cover design by Gerald Lee Monks
Cover illustration by Marcus Mashburn

Copyright © 2016 Pacific Press® Publishing Association
Printed in the United States of America

Attack of the Angry Legend originally published in 1996.
Stranger in the Shadows originally published in 1998.
Planet of Joy originally published in 1999.

The author assumes full responsibility for the accuracy of all facts
and quotations as cited in this book.

Additional copies of this book can be obtained by calling toll-free
1-800-765-6955 or by visiting http://www.adventistbookcenter.com.

ISBN 978-0-8163-6158-8

February 2016

Attack of the Angry Legend

Charles Mills

Pacific Press®
Publishing Association

Nampa, Idaho | Oshawa, Ontario, Canada
www.pacificpress.com

Dedication

To Dorinda,
Heaven's response to my lonely heart

Contents

Chapter 1

Huggin' and Smoochin'

Joey Dugan blinked several times and squinted, wrinkling his nose slightly.

"What's the matter with you?" Wendy asked, studying the lanky form sprawled across the wicker chair at the far end of the porch.

The boy pointed to the east. "I thought I saw something in the mountains."

Wendy turned and surveyed the towering summits looming against the night sky. Stars sparkled and shimmered in the warm, late spring air, forming a diamond-studded backdrop to the dark vista.

Joey shrugged. "Guess I was just imagining things. Nothin' up there now."

"Maybe you saw Monty," Wendy suggested.

Her companion laughed. "Oh sure. Like I can see a mountain lion from here. Even a hawk would need glasses for that one."

The girl leaned forward in her chair, causing it

to squeak softly. "What did what you saw look like?"

"Settle down, Wendy," a man's voice called from nearby. Mr. Hanson stretched tired muscles and smiled over at his youngest daughter. "Don't want to gear up that overactive imagination of yours."

"It was a light," Joey said, staring into the darkness beyond the dim glow of the big way station. "Kinda moved a little and then was gone."

Wendy gasped. "A UFO! That's what you saw!"

"Here we go," Mr. Hanson sighed, lifting his hands. "Next thing we know, Wendy will be dragging little green men in for supper."

"Are we expecting company?" Grandma Hanson called from the doorway as she stepped out onto the broad veranda. "I can have Grandpa pick up some extra groceries tomorrow when he's in Bozeman."

"No, Ma," Mr. Hanson said with a chuckle. "We're not having company, unless a spaceship from Mars just landed in the mountains east of here. In that case, you might want to stock up."

"Spaceship? Mars?" Grandma Hanson frowned. "I don't know what to feed an alien."

"Just feed 'em what you feed Joey," Wendy offered. "He's an alien."

Joey was about to respond when his hand shot out. "There. Look! Two thirds of the way up Freedom Mountain. Do you see it?"

The group stumbled to their feet and hurried to the railing. "Hey, yeah," Wendy breathed. "There's a light up there. Kinda dim. And it's moving slowly."

Grandma Hanson turned and headed for the door. "I wonder if Martians like tomato stew."

"*I* like tomato stew," Joey called over his shoulder.

"There, you see?" Wendy snickered. "That proves it. Joey *is* an alien just like I said."

"Is it on the logging road?" Grandpa Hanson asked, adjusting his glasses and peering into the night air.

"I don't think so," Joey responded, moving a few paces to his right for a better look. "There aren't any roads on that part of the mountain. Tar Boy and I have ridden every inch of it. All that's up there are a few deer trails."

"Oh great," Mr. Hanson moaned. "First we had a mountain lion who eats whole-wheat bread and cheese, now we've discovered a white tail who hikes around with a flashlight. What's next, raccoons with cellular phones?"

"What would you say to a raccoon if one called?" Grandpa Hanson asked, returning to his comfortable chair by the big window.

Joey turned. "I'd say, 'Take off that mask and let everyone know who you are.'"

Wendy pointed. "The light went out again. Weird." She shuffled back to her chair. "It's like someone, or some*thing*, is moving across the mountain. But why would anyone be up there so late at night? They could fall off and hurt themselves."

"Not if they knew where they were going," Joey countered. "Remember which mountain that is."

Wendy thought for a moment. "You mean Plenty?"

"Why not?"

Mr. Hanson rubbed his chin. "Isn't it too early? Red Stone usually didn't arrive for another month."

The group fell silent for a moment, remembering their old Indian friend who used to travel from the Crow reservation in the prairie to the mountain they called Freedom. His stories, spoken beside the crackling cooking fire in his cave, had thrilled the inhabitants of Shadow Creek Ranch for several years.

Then, just last summer, he'd gotten very, very sick and almost died. Only the quick action of Joey and the old man's great-granddaughter Plenty had saved his life.

Now Red Stone lived with his family in Pryor, where he could only gaze at the mountains beyond the reservation and dream about days gone by.

"I miss him," Wendy said softly. "He was my friend."

"Yes he was. And *is*," Mr. Hanson offered. "Didn't you get a letter from him last week?"

The girl nodded. "He can't write too well anymore. His words are gettin' kinda squiggly. But he says he often thinks about us and his mountain. I sent him pictures of the ranch and stuff, but I know it's not the same as being here."

The light on the mountain appeared again and then faded. "Maybe he came back," Wendy said, brightening.

"No," Mr. Hanson said quietly, "he can't. That has to be Plenty up there."

Joey settled once again in his chair. "I wonder if she's finished fighting the entire White population of Montana. She really has this thing against anyone who's not Native American. In the past, every time I went up for a visit, she'd meet me with arrow feathers pressed against her cheek and the pointy end aimed at my right ear. Plenty's archery champion for the whole state of Montana, you know."

"Interesting girl," Grandpa Hanson said with a grin. "Wouldn't want to cross her, though. She's a warrior in the true sense of the word."

Mr. Hanson yawned broadly. "Well, I've had enough mysterious lights and Indian talk for one evening. Think I'll head for bed. Got an important case pending tomorrow. My law partners in New York will expect me on-line first thing in the morning. See ya at breakfast."

"G'night, Mr. H," Joey called.

"Sleep tight, Daddy," Wendy whispered, giving her father a gentle squeeze and big, wet kiss on his cheek. "If those *are* aliens up there, I'll protect you."

"I feel so safe now," the man stated, turning for the door.

Grandpa Hanson waved his own farewell and

vanished through the doorway, leaving Joey and Wendy alone on the veranda.

"Good ol' Plenty," Joey sighed, gazing into the distant darkness. "I wonder if I'll survive the summer."

Wendy giggled. "I think she likes you."

The boy gasped. "What? Plenty? Every time she sees me, I get the feeling I should be reviewing my will."

"So she shoots arrows at you. Big deal."

"Big deal? What if her aim is off a few inches? What if she decides the world could stand to have one less White man in it?"

Wendy shrugged. "Yup, she likes you. I can tell."

"You? Little Miss I'm-never-going-to-get-married-because-men-are-useless? *You* can tell if Plenty likes me?"

Wendy shrugged. "My friend Merrilee said men need women to take care of them and that we shouldn't beat 'em up or anything. She has a point. Men are good for doin' heavy lifting, earning money, and stuff like that. Who knows, maybe someday I'll even fall in love, if the guy's strong enough and has a big bank account."

"Well, Wendy Hanson," Joey said, his eyes wide in surprise, "I never thought I'd hear those words coming out of your crooked little mouth."

"Hey," the girl asserted, "love and romance can be a real good thing if you know how to make it work for you."

Joey shook his head slowly. "I don't think that's how you're supposed to approach the subject. Wrangler Barry told me that love should be something beautiful for both the guy and the girl."

Wendy snorted. "Wrangler Barry and my cotton-headed sister are full of mush. They think love is walks in the moonlight and stupid junk like that. No, sir. I want facts. I want to know what I'm getting into. I want things in writing."

With that, Wendy spun around and headed into the Station, chin held high.

Joey chuckled to himself and sighed, then glanced across the wide lawn to the footbridge where two shadowy figures stood in the moonlight. He smiled to himself. Seemed Barry and Debbie were also doing some research on the subject of love, a science they'd been studying a lot lately.

Lifting his gaze, he watched the mysterious light move slowly along a ridge and disappear over the crest. *So,* he mused, *Wendy thinks Plenty likes me. Well, if she does, she sure has a dangerous way of showing her affection.*

Shaking his head, he went inside. For now, his mind was centered on the big container of fresh-squeezed orange juice he knew was hiding in the cold recesses of Grandma Hanson's refrigerator.

The breeze ruffled the surface of Shadow Creek as Wrangler Barry slipped his arm around the slender waist of his companion. He cleared his throat. "Uh, Debbie?"

"Yes."

"What're you doin' tomorrow afternoon?"

"Cleaning my bathroom."

"Oh."

"Why?"

The young man tapped his walking cane on the boards of the bridge spanning the quietly bubbling stream. "I was kinda thinking that maybe we could go on a picnic."

"Oh, that certainly sounds like more fun than cleaning my bathroom."

"Well, you see, there's something I want to ask you."

"There is?"

"Yeah. It's kinda important."

"It is?"

"Yeah. So I thought we could go on a picnic up to Papoose Lake and, you know, sorta sit around, enjoy nature, talk."

"What are we going to talk about?"

"I don't know. You, me, us."

"Well, which one?"

"Us."

"OK."

"The two of us."

"I kinda figured as much."

"You did?"

"Yeah." The girl snuggled closer to him. "I like talking about us."

"You do?"

16

"Yeah."

Barry smiled. "Good. Then tomorrow we'll talk about us all afternoon."

"OK."

"Just you and me. Us."

"Fine."

"No one else can come, especially Wendy."

Debbie grinned. "OK. No Wendy."

"Just . . . us."

"Got it."

"All afternoon."

"Three, four hours of just us together. I look forward to it."

Wrangler Barry tightened his grip on her. "I love you, Debbie Hanson."

"I know."

"And you love me, right?"

"Right."

"Good. Then tomorrow we'll talk about us for a whole afternoon. Just you and me. Just . . ."

"Us?"

"Yes."

"OK."

The moon slipped behind a stray cloud and hid its face from the couple as they sealed their footbridge conversation with a gentle kiss.

☆ ☆ ☆

Breakfast dishes clanked in the soapy sink as Grandma Hanson and Lizzy Pierce dug resolutely into their morning ritual. Six-year-old Samantha stood nearby, dishrag in hand, ready to do her part as soon as the plates, spoons, forks, and bowls emerged from the rinse.

"Do you know what I'm going to be when I grow up?" she asked excitedly.

"What?" the two women queried.

"A housewife, or a horse doctor."

"Oh my!" Lizzy gasped. "Don't you think you're too little?"

"Nah," their eager helper responded with a smile. "I've seen a lot of little housewives. Grandma Hanson isn't as tall as Joey and she takes care of the whole Station."

"Well, she has a point there," the old woman nodded. "I may be little, but I'm mighty. Just ask my husband."

"Ask me what?" a voice called from the hallway.

"Grandpa Hanson," Samantha giggled, "is your wife mighty?"

"She sure is!" came the quick reply as a grinning, mischievous face appeared at the kitchen door. "She's mighty beautiful and mighty sweet. And she's as strong as an ox."

Grandma Hanson sighed. "He's so romantic. What woman doesn't want to be compared to an ox?"

Joey entered the room, his mouth jammed full of toast and peanut butter. "Good grief," he mumbled. "Everybody's talking romance around here lately. Even Wendy, if you can believe that. Whatever happened to conversations about normal stuff like horses and ranch work?"

"It's spring, my boy," Grandpa Hanson chuckled. "Don't you feel it in your bones? Don't you long for the company of some bashful, innocent young thing with blue eyes and rosy cheeks?" The old man ran over and grabbed his wife, twirling her around the room like a clumsy ballroom dancer.

"No, not really," Joey responded with an expression that clearly stated, *I think Grandpa H is finally losing it.*

"It's l'amore, the big L, huggin' and smoochin' time," the old man laughed, raising and lowering his eyebrows while gazing deeply into his wife's eyes. "I feel like a caveman on the mountain top, searching his domain for that certain someone to bop on the head and drag back to his cave."

"Easy, Bigfoot," the woman in his arms warned. "I can just see you carrying me someplace. Your back would go out, and we'd have to call an ambulance."

"Doesn't matter," Grandpa Hanson announced with a wave of his hand. "I'll sacrifice all for you my darling, my one and only, my sweetie pie."

Samantha shook her head and tossed the dishrag over her shoulder. "I think I want to be a horse doctor after all. Being a housewife is too embarrassing."

★ ★ ★

Barry Gordon stopped in midstride and stared to the west. Towering dark clouds rose in menacing heaps, hiding the blue of the sky behind a thick, angry curtain.

"Oh no!" he moaned, slapping his leg with his free hand. Just then he heard a voice call from the Station's veranda. "What time should I be ready for our picnic?"

He turned to see Debbie standing by the railing, an eager smile lighting her face. His heart skipped a beat, something it did often whenever he caught a glimpse of the lovely creature who occupied his every waking thought.

Debbie was wearing an old, faded pair of jeans and a used-to-be-white T-shirt, a far cry from her usual garb of fashionable attire hand-sewn from patterns she'd designed herself.

Laughing brown eyes sparkled beneath a pile of dark hair held in place by a yellow headband. She was everything Wrangler Barry had ever dreamed about. Surprisingly, her simple beauty often made him blush.

"Hi, Debbie," he called. "Well, I don't think we'll be going on our picnic this afternoon." He lifted his walking cane and pointed it skyward. "Rain clouds are building to the west. 'Fraid we're going to be weathered out."

"Oh!" the girl moaned, her bottom lip drooping

into a pout. "I was looking forward to it." She brightened. "Maybe we could have our picnic in the barn, or . . . or someplace else."

"Nah," Barry sighed, "it wouldn't work. Has to be the lake. That's the best place for . . ."

"For what?"

"Ah . . . for talking about stuff."

Debbie sat down on the railing. "Well, how 'bout tomorrow, or the next day?"

"I'll be in Bozeman both afternoons," came the unenthusiastic reply. "We can try for Sunday."

"Sunday it is!" Debbie declared, trying to overcome her own disappointment. "But you can still talk to me between now and then. I'll listen anytime."

Barry smiled and nodded. "I know. I just had something important to say and . . . well . . . we gotta be at Papoose Lake."

Debbie glanced at the clouds bearing down on the ranch. "Sunday for sure," she stated with firm resolve.

He nodded, waved, and continued toward the barn.

A frown shadowed Debbie's face as she watched her friend hurry over the footbridge. He leaned heavily on his cane as he went, straining to keep his feet moving as quickly as his mind wanted them to go. What was so important that they had to travel all the way to Papoose Lake to discuss it?

Suddenly, a sinking feeling gripped the young girl's heart. What if he was unhappy with their relationship? What if he'd found another girl and wanted to tell her about it at a place where no one would see her cry?

Debbie turned as sudden tears stung her eyes. What if he didn't love her anymore? That was it! She'd done something terrible and now he wanted to find someone else who wasn't always telling him to keep working on his dreams and to overcome the terrible results of the accident that had injured him so badly inside.

"Debbie?" The girl glanced up to see her father standing in the doorway. "Debbie? Are you all right?"

"I didn't mean to," she blurted as a sob shook her shoulders.

The man rushed to his daughter and encircled her in his arms. "Of course you didn't, sweetheart," he encouraged, then paused. "What didn't you mean to?"

Debbie pressed her face into his chest. "Doesn't Barry know that I love him more than anything else in the whole world and that I want him to be happy and successful at whatever he chooses to do and that I want to help him as long as he wants me to?"

The lawyer shook his head. "Of course he does."

"Which one?"

"Uh . . . all of those things you said," Mr.

Hanson encouraged. "Why, just the other night Barry said you're the best thing that ever happened to him."

"He did?"

"Yes he did. And he misses you when you're gone and enjoys being with you and thinks you're the most beautiful woman in Montana."

"He does?"

"Absolutely!"

Debbie looked into her father's eyes, then sobbed anew. "Then why does he want to break up with me?"

"He wants to break up with you?" Mr. Hanson reached down and cupped the wet chin of his daughter in his hands, lifting her gaze to his. "Did Barry say he wanted to break up with you?"

"Well, no. Not in so many words. But he told me he wants to take me to Papoose Lake to tell me something important where no one else can hear—and that makes me worried."

The lawyer pressed Debbie into his arms and glanced out across the lawn, past the footbridge, to the barn where the horses were assembling for their morning feeding. He closed his eyes tightly and held her for a long moment, feeling her close to him like when he used to rock her to sleep back in New York. She'd be frightened by a bad dream or fearful of the shadows on the wall and come running to him. They'd sit in the darkened room, waiting for the fear and the shadows to fade. The smell of her hair, her delicate breathing, the softness of her skin filled him with pride and deep feelings beyond words. Even though she was 19 years old now, the emotions he felt with her in his arms were unchanged since the first day he'd heard her cry.

"My sweet Debbie, don't be afraid," the man whispered. "Barry cares a great deal for you. He'd never do anything to cause you one moment of pain."

"Really?"

"Really. Now you go and do whatever you were planning to do today, which, considering your choice of clothing must not be too sanitary, and trust Wrangler Barry to do the right thing. OK?"

Debbie looked into her father's face. "Daddy. You're crying!"

"Am I? Well, what do you know! Must've gotten something in my eyes."

The girl hugged the man's neck. "Sure," she said. "Probably some dust or something. Better get it out."

"I will."

With that, the teenager turned and entered the Station with a lighter, happier step. Mr. Hanson walked to the railing and leaned against an upright, staring at the barn. He saw the ranch's head wrangler and Joey busily tossing hay out to the waiting animals.

"Take good care of her, Barry," he whispered.

"She's my little girl, you know."

Turning slowly, the man walked to the door and headed for his office on the second floor.

☆ ☆ ☆

Joey reined in Tar Boy and stood in the stirrups, straining to see through the downpour. Red Stone's cave loomed nearby, dark and deserted, reminding him of times past when Plenty had met him with anger and arrows, and the young girl's great-grandfather had told his visitors stories of Indian lure and tales of high adventure in the Montana mountains.

"Plenty?" Joey called, trying to be heard above the roar of the rain. "Hey, Plenty, are you in there?"

Nothing moved in the cave. Tree limbs swayed angrily in the wind, pointing their wet, leafy fingers at him accusingly as if to say, "What are you doing here? This is Red Stone's mountain."

The teenager settled back into his saddle and sighed in frustration. There was no sign of the girl from the prairie, no smoldering fire, no stored supplies, nothing. Just an empty cave and the rain.

Joey looked skyward and let the cold moisture drip down his face. Grandpa Hanson had been saying that the mountains needed a good drenching. Spring had proved to be particularly dry this year and any shower was welcome. Glancing at the ground, the boy noticed that the soil was drinking in the rain as fast as it fell. He saw no puddles, no standing water at all. It was as if the Gallatin Mountains had become a giant sponge, soaking in storms with a voracious thirst.

Tar Boy snorted and began to fidget. "Take it easy," Joey commanded, looking around for whatever was spooking his big black horse. "She's not here."

His mount snorted again, this time louder, and began backing away from the cave.

"What's the matter with you?" Joey questioned, trying to calm his steed. "She hasn't arrived yet. If she were here, we'd see som—"

A deafening roar blasted from the grotto as a huge creature emerged from the shadows and stood in the entrance, almost filling it with its presence. Tar Boy rose on hind legs and pawed the air, eyes wide with terror, screaming into the wind. His rider gripped the saddle horn, trying to remain on the animal's pitching back.

"Go!" Joey shouted. "Go, Tar Boy! Get us out of here!"

The horse didn't need a second invitation. Digging powerful hooves into the wet soil, it bolted out of the clearing, pounding the earth with fearful steps, putting as much distance as possible between him and the cave.

Joey bent low over the animal, feeling its mane whip against his face, stinging it. The boy's hands were trembling, his breath coming in short, painful heaves. In the few years he'd lived in

Montana, he'd heard about humans coming in contact with a creature some Indian tribes called Matshaw. He'd figured such tales were only fantasy. But the beast in the cave was no illusion. It was real. And it looked like it wanted him and Tar Boy for lunch.

The horse thundered down the path and finally burst onto the old logging road leading toward the valley. Joey's thoughts raced. What about the light he'd seen moving along the ridges last night? Even famed monsters like Matshaw didn't carry lanterns. If Plenty had returned to the mountain early, she might not know about the creature in her great-grandfather's cave. Or . . .

Joey brought Tar Boy to a skidding halt and spun the two of them around to face Freedom Mountain. Its summit loomed in the distance like a dark phantom. Perhaps Plenty had already come into contact with the beast. If she'd faced the monster, it was clear which one of them had survived the encounter.

The young wrangler aimed his horse at the valley and dug his heels into the animal's flanks. Tar Boy surged forward, tossing up wet debris in his wake. They had to get to the ranch right away. Plenty might be in grave danger, or she might be dead.

CHAPTER 2

Matshaw

Red Stone sat with eyes closed, listening to the gently falling rain as it brushed against the window. In the kitchen a radio softly played out a scratchy country tune, something about a man who woke up one morning to find his wife gone. It was a sad song, one that fit the mood of the dark, overcast day perfectly. But the old Indian wasn't listening. He was remembering, and remembering was always more enjoyable than listening to someone else's problems.

"I've got to go now," a woman's voice called from the back door of the cozy, simply furnished, single-wide trailer. He heard a jingling of keys and the flapping sounds of a wet umbrella being extended. "Should be back before 6:00. If you get hungry, there's some bread on the counter. Help yourself."

"OK," Red Stone called, the word heavy and unnatural. The stroke he'd suffered last summer had left much of his body paralyzed. He could speak, but just barely. His right arm worked pretty well most of the time, but tired easily. The old man spent his days watching his granddaughter and her family live their lives around him, doing their best to care for his needs.

He'd never wanted it to be like this. They had lives of their own to live. At least, before, he could go to his mountain and spend the summer on his own, a burden to no one. But in one blinding moment of pain, everything had changed.

Red Stone smiled crookedly in spite of his depressing thoughts. The one bright spot in his life, the one glowing ember that warmed his days, was his great-granddaughter Plenty Good Crops. She was also the pride of the entire Crow tribe. Her skill with bow and arrow, her ability to outrun the wind, was the talk of the reservation. Plenty had proven herself a true warrior time and time again, even though she was only 15 years old, and even though she was a girl.

The ringing of the telephone interrupted the old man's musings. He pressed a lever on the little control panel attached to the arm of his wheelchair. The motorized conveyance spun around, then headed across the room to the end table waiting beside the faded couch. Jerking to a halt, Red Stone reached down, picked up the receiver, and pressed it against his ear. "Hello?" he mumbled.

His eyes lit up when he heard the voice on the other end of the line. "Joey? That you?" He listened. "No. Plenty not here. She go to mountain. She want to go early because—" The man began to frown as he concentrated on the unseen speaker's words. "Two days ago," he said into the receiver. "My granddaughter took her to bus station. Is something wrong?"

Red Stone listened again for a long moment, then paled. The phone slipped from his grasp and fell dangling beside the table. Pressing the control lever of his chair, he whirled around and hurried across the room to the window. Beyond the rain-glazed surface of the glass he could just make out a dark gathering of mountains standing against the western horizon. He knew that beyond that range was Freedom Mountain, and the girl who gave his life meaning. Struggling to stand, he cried out in a voice choked with pleading and driven by terror. "Matshaw. *Matshaw! No!*"

★ ★ ★

Wendy burst into the den and hurried to the rows of books lining a stack of shelves. Her fingers brushed the titles of the volumes and stopped at a large, colorful spine.

Pulling the book out from the others, she ran across the room and threw herself onto the couch and began rapidly thumbing through the pages.

"Did you find it?" Joey called as he entered the den.

"Wait, wait . . . wait . . . yes, here it is!" she announced triumphantly, her index finger pressed against an article.

"How much?" Joey queried breathlessly.

Wendy mumbled as she rapidly scanned the text. She gasped. "Wow!"

"How much?" her companion repeated.

The girl blinked. "Seventeen hundred."

"Seventeen hundred pounds?" Joey breathed, his words almost inaudible.

"Yup. And 10 feet tall, head to toe."

The young wrangler sank down onto the couch beside his friend. "The creature at the cave was that big at least, maybe more."

Wendy nodded and held up the picture illustrating the encyclopedia article. "Well, this is the largest one on record so far. Yours could very well be bigger and taller and heavier. Were you scared?"

"Yes, Wendy, I was scared spitless. You would've been too. If it weren't for Tar Boy, that monster would be picking his teeth with my bones right now. I think I gave Red Stone another heart attack when I called him a minute ago. He totally freaked out."

"I don't blame him," the girl responded. "His great-granddaughter is up there with the beast."

Joey's head and shoulders shook at the thought of meeting the monster alone. "Her arrows won't help her any. And it probably can run as fast as she can."

"Not through a forest," Wendy urged. "Plenty

is agile. She can maneuver around trees and stuff better than Matshaw—at least, I hope she can."

Grandpa Hanson stuck his head through the entryway. "I've called the game warden. He said there was nothing he could do until the animal damaged something, or someone. I guess that makes sense. The nature preservation people can't go around chasing after every creature sighted in the mountains. Even the famed Matshaw has privacy rights in Montana."

"But what about Plenty?" Joey asserted. "Doesn't she have the right for some protection?"

"Protection from what?" Grandpa Hanson asked. "From a legend? A phantom beast right out of Indian folk lore?"

"No," Joey countered. "From a very real, very big grizzly bear called Matshaw who just happens to be living in Red Stone's cave on the top of Freedom Mountain."

The old man nodded. "I don't doubt that you saw him, Joey," he said. "But the officials insist they have to have something a little more urgent than one sighting to get 'em down here. They advised us to stay away from the mountain."

"But what about Plenty?" Joey repeated, anger raising his voice. "She could be in danger. We can't sit here and do nothing." The boy stood. "I'm going back. I'm going to—"

"Hold on there, young man," Grandpa Hanson said firmly, but with understanding. "I can't allow you to get yourself killed trying to save a girl who may not even need saving. We'll watch tonight. If we see the light on the mountain, we'll know she's all right. If we don't, then we'll come up with a plan of action. Deal?"

Joey stood for a long moment staring out the window. Then he turned. "Deal. You're right, Grandpa Hanson. We don't know what's going on up there. Plenty may be fine. It's just . . ."

"It's just that you care about people," the old man said softly. "That's a good thing, Joey. Caring about people is important. But you shouldn't risk yourself needlessly. Plenty's no tenderfoot. She knows those mountains. Red Stone taught her well. We'll just have to believe that she's handling the situation successfully. Besides, she knows how to get to the ranch. If she needs us, we'll hear from her."

Joey sighed. "I just hope we see the light tonight."

Wendy closed her book and returned it to the shelf. "We will," she said reassuringly. "I'll watch with you."

The young wrangler smiled weakly and left the room. Grandpa Hanson turned to Wendy and asked, "What else did that book say about the giant grizzlies?"

"It said they're most dangerous at a certain time of year."

"And when's that?"

Wendy glanced out the window. "Springtime."

33

ATTACK OF THE ANGRY LEGEND

★ ★ ★

The remainder of the afternoon slipped by slowly for Joey and the inhabitants of Shadow Creek Ranch. While all had duties to perform and much to think about, each paused often in his or her work to gaze westward, to the mountains. The knowledge that there was a young girl somewhere up there alone, perhaps unaware of the beast that lurked in the forest, caused many a shudder and sad shake of the head.

Joey's sighting of the monster at the mouth of the cave didn't necessarily mean that Plenty was in any real danger. The bear may have been only passing through, exploring the grotto out of curiosity. Bears had been moving in and out of such places for centuries.

Just before sundown the rain stopped and the sky cleared, leaving the fresh, cool scent of damp grass in the air. Suppertime came and went and night settled over Montana as all eyes began to scan the dark outlines of the mountains beyond the valley.

Wendy took up her position, as promised, in her favorite veranda chair by the railing, chin resting on hands.

Joey brought out his powerful binoculars, the ones Grandpa Hanson had given him the summer before on his seventeenth birthday.

The others on the ranch went about their

evening duties with one eye constantly searching the dark distance. Conversation was hushed, muted. If they saw even a glimmer of light on Freedom Mountain, they'd know Plenty was still alive and kicking.

Spring peepers serenaded each other along the creek, blending their voices with the chirp of crickets and the soft buzz of nocturnal insects.

As the quarter moon rose over Mount Blackmore, Mr. Hanson heard a gentle tapping on his office door. "So, who knocks in this house?" he called out, laying down his business magazine and glancing across the room.

"It's me," a voice called from the hallway. "I'd like to talk to you."

"Come in, Barry," the lawyer chuckled. "Don't get many visits here in my office from the best wrangler in Montana."

The tall young man entered the room respectfully and headed for the chair Mr. Hanson indicated. He looked around, then shook his head. "You know how to use all this stuff?" he asked, studying the computer, laser printer, and other expensive-looking pieces of equipment scattered about the neat, organized office space.

The older man laughed. "Sometimes I get the feeling that all this technology is using me. But we seem to get the job done somehow. You just gotta let it know who's boss. Kinda like horses, I hear."

Barry seated himself in a leather chair by the

window and glanced at Freedom Mountain. "Anything yet?"

"Nope. Just moon and stars. I hope everything's OK up there."

"Me too," the wrangler nodded.

The two sat in silence for a long moment, watching the night.

"So," Mr. Hanson said, "to what do I owe the honor of your visit?"

Barry cleared his throat. "I've been meaning to see you for a couple weeks now, but something always seems to come up at the last minute."

"Oh?"

"Yeah. Work and stuff, you know."

"Lot's happening here at Shadow Creek."

"That's for sure. Anyway, I wanted to ask you a serious question."

"All right. Shoot."

Wrangler Barry's brow furrowed slightly, giving him an uncharacteristicly somber profile. "How do you know, for sure, that you're in love?"

Mr. Hanson blinked, taken back by the question. "Aren't you asking the wrong guy?" he responded. "I haven't exactly been too successful in that category. You met my *ex*-wife last winter, didn't you?"

Barry nodded. "That's why you should know the answer," he pressed. "You've experienced a love that created a beautiful family, and then a love that fell apart. You gotta be some kinda expert."

The lawyer thoughtfully ran his fingers

through his thick, dark hair. Yes, it would seem that he should be able to answer almost any question on the subject. And Barry deserved a response. Mr. Hanson figured that any young man about to graduate from college should be given all the information available to help him make a decision about love, especially if that young man had designs on a certain young woman who just happened to be his daughter.

"Well," the older man said, eyebrows lifted, lips pursed, "that's a tough one." He paused. "But I'm willing to share what I've learned, if you think it would be helpful."

"Good," Barry said, leaning forward in his chair.

Mr. Hanson studied the distant mountains looming against the star-littered sky. "I think there're two kinds of love," he began. "One bubbles over with warm, fuzzy feelings, handwritten notes passed on the sly, surprise gifts to celebrate the fact that it's Tuesday, stuff like that. It's a fun, exciting love, the kind men seem to go gaga over. They fight wars, slay dragons, visit antique malls, anything to catch the attention of a member of the opposite sex."

The wrangler grinned. "I've done weird stuff like that."

"Yeah. We all have. Trying to attract girls was the only thing that got me through high school. That, and pizza, of course."

"Is there anything wrong with fun love?" Barry asked.

"No, not a thing," Mr. Hanson stated emphatically. "Keeps florists, card shops, and the people who sell stuffed animals in business. Trouble is, some people stop there. They don't let their love grow beyond that stage. When the serious times in life intrude—you know, sickness, financial difficulties, pink slips, busted dreams—when reality starts slicing away at a relationship, fun love suffers the most, sometimes even disappears."

"Is that what happened to you and Ellen?" Barry asked, then lifted his hand. "I'm really sorry about asking these personal questions, but . . . I gotta know. I gotta learn."

Mr. Hanson smiled. "It's OK, Barry. Perhaps if more guys talked about it, I mean really discussed this matter seriously, there'd be a few less couples standing before divorce lawyers arguing about who gets the gazebo. Fun love has its place, but it also comes with some serious limitations."

Barry studied his friend thoughtfully. "So, what's the second kind?"

"Well, for want of a better word, I'll call it *tough* love. This is the one that endures. Sometimes it's not any fun at all. It makes you do things you'd rather not do, such as work at a job you don't enjoy, drive a car other guys laugh at, or make payments on a kid's braces when you'd rather put down a deposit on a motorcycle. Tough love demands that you think of the other person first and yourself last.

"What happens so often is that a man and

woman get married under the influence of fun love and start their lives together filled with visions of picket fences and perfect kids. Then life, with all its problems and challenges, creeps up on them, and the emotional part of their relationship begins to fade. Without a good dose of tough love kicking in, they can't survive. They sit around listening to old romantic ballads, wondering where the magic has gone."

Barry looked down at his feet and sighed. "Doesn't make marriage sound too inviting."

"Oh, but I haven't gotten to the best part yet," Mr. Hanson urged. "Couples who've learned to love tough, who've endured hard times together, who've allowed their relationship to grow and become stronger over time, find that their compassion for each other becomes an almost breathless thing. It has power, history, hidden strengths that they can rely on no matter what happens in their lives. I've seen it in others. I've witnessed that kind of love in action."

"You mean like your mom and dad?"

"Yes. They love tough. They've endured a lot over the years, but look at 'em. They're just as crazy about each other as when they exchanged wedding vows almost 47 summers ago. They can enjoy the fun type of love because they've built in the toughness."

Barry nodded slowly. "And, you and your ex-wife didn't?"

Mr. Hanson glanced out the window. "We . . . we didn't know how. We never took the time to learn."

The younger man stared into the darkness beyond the curtains. "Forgive me for asking such personal questions," he said. "But, I . . . I want to do it right."

"Well, Barry Gordon," Mr. Hanson responded with a smile, "do I hear wedding bells in your future?"

Barry was about to answer when a voice shouted from the porch below. "There! On the left side of Freedom Mountain. I see a light!"

The two men stood and ran to the office window. "Joey's right," Barry said, his finger pressed against the glass. "There's a light 'bout halfway up. Looks like it's moving too."

Mr. Hanson slammed his fist into his palm. "Great! That means Plenty is still safe. I'm going to call Red Stone right now and give him the good news."

The man turned, then paused. "Barry, I don't have all the answers. No one does. But what I've learned, I'll be happy to share with you. Anytime."

Barry smiled. "Thanks, Mr. Hanson. That means a lot to me."

With that, the lawyer headed for the phone as Barry left the office, walking with a renewed step. Plenty was still alive, and so, it seemed, was part of a horseman's dream for the future.

Joey squinted as he pressed the binoculars

against his eyebrows. "She's moving along the upper trail. You know, the one that ends by the meadow near where Monty used to live."

"Yeah," Wendy breathed, her full attention focused on the pinprick of light floating against the dark side of Freedom Mountain. "We can see her because there aren't many tall trees on that section. They logged it 10 years ago. Nothin' up there but young pine."

"Wait a minute!" Joey gasped, causing his companion to jump. "If we can see her light, then she should be able to see ours."

"Ours?" Wendy asked. "We don't have a light."

Joey ran down the stairs and headed for the footbridge. "Don't lose sight of her," he ordered over his shoulder.

He soon returned carrying the large rechargeable flashlight he kept in the stables. "She still there?" he called.

"Yup. I think she's about to enter the wooded area by the meadow, though. You'd better hurry!"

Joey aimed his powerful beam at the distant mountain, sending a piercing shaft of light into the night like an illuminated sword. He switched the device on and off, on and off, eyes glued to the little spark of light bobbing along the mountainside. Suddenly its movement stopped.

Joey bent low over the flashlight, sighting down its long, shiny barrel. On, off, on, off. His finger pressed the switch slowly, steadily.

Then the light on the mountain responded. On, off, on, off.

"She sees it. She sees it!" the boy shouted. "She's answering."

"Well, say something to her," Wendy ordered.

"What do you mean say something? I don't know how to talk flashlight."

Wendy rolled her eyes. "It's called Morse Code, dummy. I thought all guys knew Morse Code."

"When would I ever need to learn how to communicate with a mountain?" Joey shot back. "That's what phones are for."

"I don't think Ma Bell has too many booths up there," the girl chuckled. Then she added, "Besides, even if you did know the code, Plenty probably doesn't. They've got phones on the reservation too."

The young wrangler watched the distant light blink on and off. "I just wish I could warn her. Why doesn't she come down to the ranch? I could tell her in person."

"Wait a minute," Wendy said, lifting a finger. "She has to know the bear is up there. I mean, Matshaw isn't exactly hard to spot. He leaves footprints the size of bomb craters." The girl jumped to her feet as thoughts swirled around under her tangled crop of soft blond hair. "The book says grizzlies usually hunt in the daytime and sleep at night, just like people. We see the light at night, so Plenty's up doing whatever she does while the bear is sleeping, knowing he'll be out and about during the day. Hey, she's one smart Indian."

"And," Joey interjected, warming to the line of thought his friend had started, "Plenty knows that Matshaw knows she's up there. I mean, we humans stink . . . well, to bears we do, and bears have learned that where humans are, they can usually find food nearby. So, if Plenty were to come down to Shadow Creek Ranch, and the grizzly followed her scent, she'd be putting us and the horses in danger too. She knows that, so she's staying away on purpose."

Wendy gazed at the mountain with renewed respect for the girl clicking the distant light on and off. "She's a good kid, if you don't mind being shot at or called a traitor to her people. And, she's really got guts."

Joey lowered his flashlight as the tiny glimmer faded on the mountain and disappeared among the distant trees. "Yeah, she does," he said softly. "She's probably hoping the bear will finish exploring her great-grandfather's mountain and move on downrange. Until it does, she's going to hide during the day and hunt for food and water at night. All that so we can be safe here on the ranch."

Wendy stared at him for a long moment. "You like her too, don't you?"

"Well of course I like her," the boy responded. Then seeing the sly smile on his companion's face, he added, "Now, Wendy Hanson, don't go getting any ideas in that mixed-up head of yours. Plenty is my friend, and that's all."

"Whatever you say," the girl said, lifting her hands in a defensive gesture. "But it is spring-time, and you know what Grandpa says happens during this season of the year."

Joey turned and faced the dark mountain. "She's my friend, and she's in danger. That's all I know for sure."

Wendy nodded. "I'm headin' for bed. No need for us all to stay up with Plenty. She gets to sleep in the day time. We don't. See ya."

"G'night, Miss Hanson," the boy called, not letting his gaze leave the mountain.

With one last look to the west, the girl entered the Station, leaving Joey alone at the railing.

★ ★ ★

Samantha looked up from her play and stared at the trees lining the horse pasture. She'd been building a scale model of Shadow Creek Ranch in the soft, warm soil, using rocks for buildings, sticks for fences, and stiff, green leaves to repre-sent the horses grazing not far away. The girl no-ticed that Tar Boy, Early, and the other ranch animals were also studying the green border sep-arating the meadow from the forest.

Tar Boy snorted softly, shaking his head up and down like a child bobbing for apples. Wendy's brown horse, Early, pawed at the ground, sending miniature clouds of dust drifting in the morning breeze.

It had been three days since Joey had first
signaled his friend on Freedom Mountain—three
long days of wondering and waiting. Each night,
at around 10:00, they'd see the tiny pinprick of
light moving across the face of the dark mountain. It would pause at the edge of the unseen
meadow and flash on and off, on and off. Joey
would answer with the powerful beam from his
flashlight. Then they'd watch the distant illumi-
nation fade into the shadows, leaving them with
a mixture of relief and an uneasy sense of im-
pending danger.

Samantha heard a rustling coming from the
woods, followed by a tiny cry, like the sound a
baby makes when it hiccups.

The horses began milling about nervously,
shaking their heads and snorting, backing away
from the fence line. Then they broke into a fast
run, leaving the little girl alone at the far end of
the pasture.

"Who's there?" Samantha called, feeling suddenly vulnerable. "Are you going to eat me?"

She saw a twig move and watched as the
branch of a small tree bent slowly to the ground.
Stumbling to her feet, she stood transfixed by the
movement in the underbrush.

"Do you want to play with me?" she asked. "I'm
building a ranch with horses and everything. You
can help."

The little girl could hear something breathing in the shadows.

"Are you Matshaw the bear?" she called out, her voice trembling. "Then you're stronger and taller than Joey?"

Slowly, with utmost care, the brambles at the edge of the forest began to part. Samantha's eyes opened wide when she saw a furry face sporting a long, black nose staring back at her.

"If you're Matshaw," she said, "you sure are little. Why don't you come over here and play with me. I'm not afraid because I think we can be friends. OK?"

Samantha watched as a small bear cub emerged from the forest and stood on thick hind legs, surveying her and the pasture beyond. It moved clumsily but cautiously in her direction, sniffing the air every few seconds, its moist nose wiggling with each breath.

"You're funny," the little girl giggled, "and your nose is all wet. Do you have a cold? I like your pretty brown fur. Can I pet you?"

The two creatures stood face-to-face, equal in size and curiosity. Each had never seen anything quite like the other.

The cub snorted softly. Samantha did the same. The bear shook his head from side to side. So did Samantha. Then, with no fanfare at all, the animal dropped onto the ground and rolled over on his back. Little Samantha squealed with glee and followed suit, rolling and tumbling after her newfound friend with happy abandonment. Soon the deserted end of the pasture reverberated with the growls and giggles of the bear and the girl as they frolicked in the warm sunshine and dry spring grasses.

Joey rubbed his chin thoughtfully and wrinkled his nose. He'd been sitting in his big chair in the den trying to come up with the solution to problem number 18 in his math book, but the answer didn't seem any closer now than it had 20 minutes before.

He glanced at the clock. Almost noon. Grandma Hanson would be ringing the dinner bell in just a few moments, summoning everyone to the dining room. Joey just had to finish his assignment before he ate, or he'd be working the problem in his head while everyone else was having fun at the table. The boy didn't like loose ends.

Joey looked over at Wendy who was busily writing something in her notebook, glancing occasionally at the open encyclopedia in her lap. Their home school teacher, Lizzy Pierce, was out helping Grandma Hanson put lunch on the table.

"Hey, Wendy," Joey whispered.

"Forget it."

The boy rolled his eyes. "You don't even know what I want."

"You're doing math, aren't you?"

"Yes."

"Then you probably want help with a problem."

"Well . . . yes."

"Forget it."

Joey sighed. "You're good at math. You can figure stuff out that I can't."

Wendy looked up from her work. "Are you saying I'm smarter than you?"

"Hardly."

"Then why should I help you if I'm so dumb?"

Joey gritted his teeth. "You're not dumb in math, just everything else."

The girl grinned. "What'll you give me?"

Joey thought for a moment. "Three bucks."

"Three? Only $3?" Wendy shook her head. "It's almost lunchtime. My price goes up just before a meal."

"Hey, that's not fair."

Wendy shrugged. "Supply and demand. I charge what I know you'll pay. My price is $5 and not a penny less."

"Five bucks? For help on one answer?"

"I'll also check your other work. But you'd better hurry. This is a limited time offer. I think I smell fresh bread."

Joey sighed and lifted the book. "OK. Deal. But you'd better be right. Number 18."

Wendy hurried across the room and read the question, her lips moving silently.

"Subtract the empty weight from the gross weight," she said.

Joey thought for a minute. "Eighteen hundred and nine?"

"Yup. Now subtract fuel and oil."

Joey scribbled numbers on his paper. "That leaves 1,720 pounds." He sighed. "How do you do that?"

"You're using the same book Debbie had two years ago. She figured all the answers at the bottom of the page."

"Where?" the boy gasped.

"Right there." Wendy pointed at the line of squiggles crowding the lower margin of the book.

"Those are numbers?" Joey blinked. "I thought some really bad artist was trying to draw pictures down there."

"Debbie's handwriting isn't all that great, but I can read it," Wendy stated. "See, there're the answers for problems 15 through 20." She studied the page for a moment. "You got the rest of them right. You also owe me five bucks." The girl held out her hand.

Joey sighed and pulled his leather wallet from his pocket. "Wendy Hanson, you're somethin' else, you know that?" He placed a crisp bill in her palm. "How 'bout teaching me how to figure out Debbie's handwriting so I can find the answers myself."

"I don't think so," the girl said, holding the money up to the light and studying it carefully. "I believe I'm better off financially the way things are."

The dinner bell rang out on the porch, announcing that lunch was on the table. Wendy smiled and waved at her companion before hurrying from the room, stuffing the five note into the back pocket of her jeans.

"Where's Samantha?" Lizzy asked as Joey entered the dining room.

"Beats me," the boy said, eying the bowl filled with fluffy, white mashed potatoes. He licked his lips.

"I believe she was going to play by the horses," Grandma Hanson stated, placing a boat of brown gravy at the center of the table. "Joey, why don't you run out and make sure she heard the bell?"

"OK," the teenager said. "Just don't let Wendy get hold of the potatoes until I get back and can fight for my portion."

"Very funny," Wendy remarked.

The pasture was quiet as Joey walked along one of the many horse-carved trails in the dusty ground. "Sam? Hey, Sam. Soup's on."

No answer.

"Hey, squirt. Where are you?"

Only the wind responded.

The boy studied the fence line, turning slowly as his gaze swept the meadow. "If you're out here, answer me, Sam. I'm hungry. I don't have time for a game of hide and seek. Potatoes are getting cold even as we speak. Besides, Wendy is hovering over them like a buzzard over a carcass."

A movement in the bushes by the fence caught his eye, followed by a low growl. Joey froze in place, breathing stopped.

Slowly, deliberately, he reached down and picked up a large stick and began backing away from the movement, weapon held out in front of him.

Suddenly, something cold brushed the back of his neck. He spun around, swinging wildly with the stick, hitting Tar Boy squarely across the shoulder, causing the big horse to rear up in surprise. At that same instant a form burst from the bushes and ran toward him.

Joey turned to face the attacker and stopped himself just as he was about to bring the weapon down hard on Samantha's head.

"*ROARRRRR!*" she growled playfully, hands held up like claws before her face. "I'm going to eat you up, Joey. I'm Matshaw and I'm hungry! You'd better watch out!" The girl paused. "Hey, Joey, why'd you hit Tar Boy with that stick?"

The boy dropped to his knees, gasping for breath, face pale, hands trembling. "I thought . . . I thought you were the bear."

"I *am* the bear," Samantha declared. "At least I'm his friend. We played together this morning, you know. He was nice."

"You played with Matshaw?"

"Sure. We made Shadow Creek Ranch in the

dirt, 'cept he kept stepping on the cows."

"We don't have any cows," Joey said, pressing his hand against his chest.

"I know. Matshaw kept stepping on them. Then he ate the barn."

The young wrangler sank into the grass and smiled up at his little dark-faced sister. "Then what happened?"

"We went walking in the creek and found a fish."

"And?"

"Matshaw ate the fish. He's one hungry bear."

Joey laughed. "Sounds like you had a busy morning, Sam. Think you might tear yourself away from your bear friend and come have some lunch with me? I don't think we're having fish, but Grandma Hanson has some delicious mashed potatoes and gravy on the table. You want Matshaw to come along?"

"He can't," Samantha said sadly. "He went back into the forest. Maybe he'll play with me again later. I hope so."

"Me too," Joey grinned, giving the little girl a brotherly hug. "Now let's get back to the Station before Wendy gobbles down all our food."

"Yeah. We'd better hurry!" The girl turned to face the forest. "'Bye, Matshaw," she called. "Come again soon!"

"'Bye Matshaw," Joey repeated. "See ya later."

The two headed for the Station, hand in hand, discussing bears and potatoes, and how funny

Joey had been when he thought Tar Boy and then Samantha was a big bad beast. Beyond the fence-row, deep in the forest, two sets of eyes watched them go.

CHAPTER 3

The Saddest Sad

Wendy leaned over and looked into the empty washing machine. "It did it again," she said with a frustrated groan.

"Did what again?" Debbie asked, dropping her basket of clothes on the table with a soft thud.

"This machine ate one of my favorite socks. You know, the green ones with the yellow band around the top? I'd just gotten that pair broken in nicely, then this stupid machine munches down and presto, I'm one sock short."

It was Friday, and that meant wash day. Grandpa Hanson maintained that all should be ready in the Station when the Sabbath arrived, including clothes and food. Fridays were always extra busy on Shadow Creek Ranch. "How can we enjoy God's blessed day if we're not prepared?" the old man often asked.

"Maybe it's tangled up with your other stuff," Debbie suggested, trying to be helpful.

"I looked," Wendy moaned. "Twice." She brightened. "I did find my favorite earmuffs, though. They were in the pocket of my pajamas. Sometimes I think washing machines like to play jokes on us poor humans."

The girl watched Debbie dump her white load into the machine and set the dials to warm wash, cold rinse, normal cycle. After pouring the soap into the opening, she closed the door and pressed the start button. The washer began filling.

"So, how's my little sister doin'? Keeping out of trouble?" Debbie paused and grinned. "Yeah, like that will happen."

Wendy shrugged. "I got an A on my geography test. Did you know that 90 percent of Egypt is desert? It's like this huge beach with no ocean. Of course there're lots of camels and goats wandering around, so you gotta watch where you step. Sorta like out in the pasture except there's no grass and stuff."

Debbie grinned. "I remember studying Egypt. My favorite lesson was on the pyramids."

"I was just thinkin' the other day," Wendy said, wiggling her finger knowingly, "that when people die in the desert, they can't be buried in the sand because the wind would come along and unbury them and then their family would have to find someplace else to stick them. I figured a pyramid was a great idea because the wind can't blow it away and people wouldn't have to move around a lot after they're dead. Those Egyptians were smart people, if you ask me. They got that burying thing worked out pretty good."

The washing machine started churning as Wendy finished. She pointed at the device. "That's not washing you hear."

"It's not?"

"Nope. That's chewing."

Debbie laughed. "Wendy, you're crazy."

"Not as crazy as Dad," the younger girl stated. "Have you seen him lately? It's springtime, and Ruth Cadena is in Mexico visiting her family. Father dear is like a bull elk without a doe in sight. It's pitiful."

The older girl smiled broadly. "I don't have that problem."

"Yeah," Wendy nodded. "You've got all the bull you need."

Her sister laughed again. "You still on the warpath against my sweet Barry?"

"Your sweet Barry is acting kinda weird too, or haven't you noticed?"

"He has a lot on his mind right now," Debbie responded, glancing out the window in the direction of the barn. "About to graduate from Montana State, he isn't quite sure what he's going to be doing for the rest of his life. Lots of big decisions to be made."

Wendy lifted herself up onto the dryer and studied her sister thoughtfully. "Hey, Debbie, what's it like to be in love with someone like Barry Gordon?"

The older girl smiled shyly. "It's nice, a kinda secure feeling. Someday you'll understand."

"Don't give me that *someday* garbage," Wendy said. "Tell me *now*. I just might want to fall in love too. You never know."

"You? You're only 11 years old."

"I'll be 12 next month," the girl shot back. "Twelve's old enough to know stuff. In some of the countries I've studied in my geography book, 12 is almost marrying age."

"I guess you're right," Debbie agreed as she picked up one of Wendy's freshly cleaned shirts and started folding it. "Being in love is exciting and scary at the same time. It makes you want to be with that person constantly, you know, so you can be a part of everything he does. You don't want to be left out of anything."

"You mean, like when I go to the mountains and Early wants to tag along?"

"Something like that. You think about the person a lot and want him to be happy. When he's sad, you get all depressed and try to make things better."

Wendy scratched her head and then studied her fingers. "But what if Barry asks you to *marry* him? Will you say yes?"

"He hasn't asked me, so I don't know."

"But what about his cane and all the things that hurt inside of him? What if he can't work and buy groceries?"

Debbie was silent for a long moment. "I've thought about that too and figure if I really love him, I can work while he continues to get well."

"But what if he never gets well and can't ever ride horses anymore and doesn't know how to do anything else?"

The older girl slowed her folding as a familiar fear rose in her chest. "I don't know what I'd do. He loves ranch work so much. He'd be lost without it."

Wendy sighed. "You can't live with someone who's lost, can you?"

Debbie's hands paused and hung motionless in front of her. She could hear Joey and Wrangler Barry shouting orders to a horse they were working in the pasture, a new arrival on the ranch that needed training before it could be ridden. In her mind's eye she could see Barry leaning on his cane, calling out instructions while Joey willingly did all the physical labor. The girl understood how frustrated the older wrangler felt under those circumstances.

"I'm not sure if I can live with someone like that," the girl said softly.

Wendy slipped down from the dryer and walked to her sister's side. "Oh, Debbie, I didn't mean to make you cry."

"It's OK," she said, managing a smile. "That's what love does sometimes. It makes you cry."

Wendy nodded. "I understand. Really. I've cried for people I love too. I think it's the saddest sad. But everything's going to be OK, Debbie. You'll see. Don't things just seem to work out here on Shadow Creek Ranch?"

Debbie nodded. "You're right. Things will work out for the best if I'll just be patient."

Going to the window, she placed her hand on the glass. Between her fingers she could see that Barry was moving slowly. "I just have to be patient," she repeated.

The weekend arrived, and with it an after-church visit from Pastor Webley, his wife, Virginia, and baby son, Adam. The young minister was a favorite church leader throughout the Gallatin valley with his unique approach to things spiritual. In his organization young people always had a part to play in the services, held positions of authority, and felt important even if all they did was welcome visitors. Wendy reported the man's sermons had been known to actually keep her awake, a compliment of the highest order.

The couple promised to return to the ranch sometime during the first part of the week to help the gang finish up the leftovers from Sabbath dinner. Pastor Webley gave strict orders that no one, under any circumstances, should touch the remains of the sweet potato casserole, a new recipe Lizzy had attempted with apparent success.

Monday morning dawned bright and clear.

Grandpa Hanson stumbled out onto the porch and yawned long and hard, trying to shake sleep from his body. His wife followed close behind, holding out a steaming cup of herbal tea. "Here, old man," she said, "you'd better drink every bit of this. Don't want you to catch your annual spring cold. Ever since we've moved out here, you've caught the bug the very same week the field grass needs mowing for the first time. I won't even discuss the psychological implications of that fact."

Grandpa Hanson chuckled and reached for the cup. "Did you remember to add honey?"

"Yup."

"A whole spoonful?"

"And then some."

"Good girl." He lifted the tea to his lips and took a sip. "We just may not be mowing anything for a while," he said, motioning in the direction of the pasture. "Haven't had enough rain to make things grow. I'm gettin' kinda worried. Radio says farmers in the valley are beginning to get antsy too. Without a constant wetting down, our top soil can blow away, leaving less nutrients for the spring planting. We need more rain, and lots of it."

Grandma Hanson brushed stray strands of gray hair from her husband's forehead. "Can't we irrigate?"

"Sure, as long as the ponds and rivers hold out. But with the dry spring, they're suffering too. I drove up to Papoose Lake yesterday—don't worry,

I stayed in the car. Didn't want to give any Indian legends the idea that I'd be a tasty meal—and it was down a good 10 feet. Most of the winter melt has evaporated already. It's not a pretty sight."

The woman took in a deep breath of the crisp, early-morning air. "Well, we've had dry years here before. I think we can survive one more."

"You're right. But we may end up having to be careful around the ranch with the water supply. We're not anywhere near critical, but we shouldn't be wasteful. I'll tell the gang at breakfast some things we can do to conserve until it starts raining again—you know, like take shorter showers, combine laundry loads, use dishwater to soak the flower beds, and so forth."

"Good," Grandma Hanson said with a smile. "Now, you finish your tea and I'll get breakfast started. For once in your life, I don't want you to end up flat on your back with the flu. Springtime or not, I want you healthy, wealthy, and wise."

"I guess one out of three's not bad," the old man said. "I can be healthy and wealthy later."

Grandma Hanson shook her head and walked back into the Station. "I was putting you at zero-for-three," she teased.

The old man chuckled and downed the last of the sweet liquid. He watched a gentle breeze waft across the pasture, lifting a thin layer of dust into the air and swirling it around and around with a collection of brittle leaves.

★ ★ ★

Joey hoisted his pitchfork and tossed a load of hay over the bottom half of the barn door. The other horses hadn't arrived yet, but Early was front and center, demonstrating his uncanny ability to anticipate events before they happened.

"You're a strange critter," Joey laughed, watching the small but powerful animal sniff at the freshly thrown grain. "You and Wendy are made for each other. Weird for weird."

"Look who's talking," Wendy called, rounding the corner of the barn, a newly sewn saddle blanket hanging from her arms. "You and Tar Boy are two of a kind if I ever saw it. Both of you have egos the size of Mount Blackmore."

Joey sighed. "Wendy Hanson, can't you ever say anything nice about me or my horse?"

The girl pulled open the door and stepped inside. "Yes, I can. It just takes a little more effort than I'm willing to expend right now." She tossed the blanket onto the workbench. "I promised Samantha I'd let her ride Early before home school begins. Well, actually, she said she wanted to go galloping into the mountains to hunt down Matshaw so she could send him to the nice, comfortable zoo in Bozeman."

"Bozeman doesn't have a zoo," Joey responded.

"According to Samantha, it will as soon as she builds it. Matshaw will be her prize exhibit, along

62

with her collection of bugs and that fat hamster. You're supposed to be the wrangler of all her animals, and I'm her business manager. She told Debbie that she could collect the tickets because all the boys in Bozeman will want to come to the zoo to see Debbie since she's so beautiful. I'm quoting here."

Joey tossed the last of the hay over the door and returned the pitchfork to its place in the corner. "What else is Sam planning?"

"My dad's going to be the ringmaster," Wendy announced, lifting Early's saddle down from two thick boards jutting from the wall. "I guess she's planning a zoo-circus kinda place, and Grandma Hanson will serve peach ice cream to all comers. She didn't say what Grandpa and Lizzy will be doing, but promised to E-mail me on that very soon."

Joey grinned broadly. "E-mail?"

"Yeah. She was heading for Dad's office when I left the Station."

"Well, you two be careful out there in the pasture. We're only assuming that the bear is staying in the mountains. After all, we can't be sure. Keep one eye on the forest at all times."

"Yes sir," Wendy agreed with a smart salute. "We won't have a lot of time. You know how Lizzy wants us bolted to our study chairs in the den at 8:30 sharp. If Samantha and I don't show up, send the rangers."

Joey walked to the barn door. "I've gotta get

cleaned up before school. See ya in a bit."

The girl waved without looking up as she made some adjustments to the straps dangling from the saddle. In a few minutes Samantha's smiling face appeared at the entrance to the horse barn.

"Here," she called, holding out a piece of paper. Wendy smiled. "What's this, Sam?"

"Your E-mail. Mr. Hanson sent it to you from his computer."

The older girl reached over and took the paper from her young friend. "Let's see," she said, studying the words neatly printed across the clean, white surface. "It says here, 'E-mail message to Wendy Hanson from Samantha Williams Dugan.'" Wendy paused. "Williams? Where'd that come from?"

"That's my maiden name," the little girl said proudly. "I decided to keep it when I became Joey's sister."

"Nice touch," Wendy nodded. "Very modern."

"I know," Samantha replied with a proud grin.

"OK," Wendy continued, "E-mail from you to me, and it says, 'Grandpa Hanson will clean the cages and Lizzy will feed the animals peach ice cream every day.'" Wendy looked over at the younger girl. "Are you sure my grandpa will want to clean all those cages?"

"He said he would if I paid him enough and gave him his own car," Samantha stated.

"Sounds like a good plan to me," Wendy nodded as she folded the message and slipped it into her pocket. "Now, you get ready to go out into the wilds of Montana and hunt down ol' Matshaw. He might turn out to be a little more than we can handle without some help."

Samantha laughed out loud, swaying with the effort. "Matshaw? More than we can handle? He's only as big as me!"

"Oh," Wendy said, lifting the saddle and heading for the door. "This is the *little* Matshaw."

"Of course he's little. How else are we going to rope him and tie him up with this?" Samantha walked over to the wall and pointed at a neat coil of hemp hanging from a nail. "I'll call 'em and you rope 'em. Won't take very long 'cause he's used to me already."

"Whatever you say," Wendy giggled. "Now help me saddle up Early so we can hit the pastu—I mean trail."

Soon Samantha was perched proudly on Early's back as Wendy led the animal along a dusty, well-worn path by the pasture fence. Wendy breathed deep of the fresh, morning air, reveling at the distant vistas of mountain, trees, and sky. Morning was her time of day, and she enjoyed every second of it—the earlier, the better.

"We'd better stop and get ready," Samantha said from the saddle. "I think I see Matshaw at the edge of the forest."

"OK," Wendy said, bringing her horse to a halt. "Just how are we going to make this capture?"

Samantha slid from the saddle and landed with a crunch in the dry grass. "I'll call him and you catch him with your rope."

"Oh yeah, I forgot." Wendy removed the coil from the saddle horn and played out a few feet of the loop.

"Go stand over there," Samantha instructed, pointing to a small rise in the pasture. "Matshaw always comes down that path when he plays with me."

Wendy obediently walked to the mound, twirling the lariat at her side. "Is this good?" she asked.

"More that way," Samantha called, pointing to her right.

The older girl moved a few paces to the side, facing Samantha who'd walked some distance away. "How's this?"

"Great. Now, open the rope and just let it hang there."

Wendy yawned broadly as she did as she was instructed. Hunting the big grizzly had made her suddenly sleepy. Or was it the warm sunshine caressing her face?

"Perfect!" Samantha said, clapping her hands together. "Now, I'll call Matshaw. He always comes when I ask him to."

"He sounds like a nice, obedient bear," Wendy said with a smile. She checked her watch. They still had 15 minutes before class time.

"Matshaw. Matshaw!" Samantha called, then

waited. "Come play with me. I'm here." The little girl's voice drifted over the pasture with the soft breeze.

Nothing happened. Wendy saw her companion frown slightly. "Come here, little bear. I'm ready to play with you."

They waited.

"Yo, Matshaw," Wendy called out. "My arm's getting tired."

She saw Samantha's frown turn into a broad grin. "Here he comes. Hold onto your rope tight."

"I've got it," Wendy answered, wondering what that noise was behind her.

Suddenly, something flashed by her, brushing her arm and yanking the rope out of her grasp, causing the coils to unwind through her fingers like line in a fishing pole. Without thinking, she tightened her grip and was immediately yanked forward, falling heavily to the ground. The next instant she was being pulled through the dry grass at an alarming speed.

She saw Samantha come and go, a big smile lighting the little girl's face. "You got him. You got him!" Wendy heard her shout as she sailed by.

The world was a blur of dust, rocks, and pasture weeds as Wendy struggled to make sense of what was happening to her. She tried to let go of the rope, but found her fingers intertwined tightly in the coils. "Help!" she tried to shout, but her mouth immediately filled with dirt.

Joey walked out onto the Station's veranda, summoned by the happy shouts of his adopted sister. Taking in the situation, he turned and ambled back into the house. "What's goin' on?" Mr. Hanson asked, passing him in the lobby.

"It's nothing. Just Samantha yelling at Wendy who's being pulled around the pasture by a bear."

"Oh," the lawyer said, continuing on his way. Then both froze in their tracks. "A bear!" they gasped in unison.

Almost running into each other, they raced out onto the porch. In the pasture they could see Samantha hollering and jumping, following a plume of dust being kicked up by a small brown bear with a rope tied snugly about its neck. At the other end of the line was a familiar body being dragged, torpedolike, through the grasses.

"What on earth is going on?" Mr. Hanson breathed, not knowing whether to shout or laugh.

Joey stumbled down the stairs and ran for the footbridge. "Call for help!" he shouted over his shoulder.

Mr. Hanson nodded and hurried back into the Station. At the hall phone, he paused.

"What's the commotion in the pasture?" Grandpa Hanson asked, running from the dining room.

"Who should I call to report that my daughter has lassoed a little bear?"

"A bear!" the old man gasped. "What kind of bear?"

"A fast one," Mr. Hanson answered, holding the receiver in his hands, finger poised over the numbers, unsure of what to do next.

Debbie appeared at the second-floor balcony. "Why's Joey shouting?" she asked.

"Wendy caught a bear."

"Oh." The girl shrugged and returned to her room.

Mr. Hanson slammed down the phone. "What am I doing? Wendy needs *our* help. Come on!"

The two men raced out of the Station and hurried across the lawn. They could see Joey waving his arms and shouting, telling Wendy to let go of the rope, but for some reason she refused. By now, the little brown bear was slowing, finding that pulling an 11-year-old around a pasture was pretty hard work.

Then the creature stopped and sat down, its chest heaving, nose pointed skyward in an attempt to get as much oxygen into its lungs as possible. Samantha ran up to the animal and patted it gently on the head. "Good boy," she said. "You already learned your first trick for my zoo. Good boy."

Joey knelt beside the sputtering, coughing Wendy. "You OK?" he asked, trying to catch his own breath.

"Do I look OK?" Wendy shouted. "What in the name of spruce juice happened?"

Joey pointed. "You caught a bear."

"A what?"

The young wrangler laughed. "A bear. You know, furry animal, four paws, black nose?"

"I know what a bear is!" Wendy snapped, untangling her fingers from the rope. She stumbled to her feet and walked unsteadily toward the creature sitting quietly beside Samantha. Then she paused and studied the animal thoughtfully. "Sam? Do you know this bear?"

"I already told you. We've played before. Isn't he nice? And you taught him a really neat trick. Thanks."

"Don't mention it," Wendy said, rubbing her knees and spitting grass clippings from her dusty mouth.

Grandpa Hanson frowned. "Wait a minute. This cub isn't old enough to be out on his own yet."

Joey blinked. "So?"

"That means *Mrs.* Bear must be nearby."

The four stood stock-still, listening. All at once, the ground began to tremble as a cloud of dust rose from the far end of the pasture. All eyes turned to see the ranch's herd of horses racing at breakneck speed in their direction. Behind the animals, fur shimmering in the morning sunlight, came the largest bear any of them had ever seen.

Joey stepped forward, his mouth suddenly dry. "Matshaw!" he whispered.

"Let's get out of here!" Grandpa Hanson shouted, taking Wendy by the hand. His son scooped up Samantha, and they all started running for the footbridge.

They could hear the thunder of two dozen hooves following them and the terrified screams of the animals filling the air.

Over the little bridge they raced, not bothering to pause and close the pasture gate. By the time they reached the Station stairs, the horses were splashing over Shadow Creek, sending glistening showers of water high into the air.

Struggling to the porch, Joey turned to see how close the big bear was now. In horror he found the creature was at the bottom of the stairs, heading in their direction with unrelenting speed.

The four burst through the Station entrance and quickly closed the thick wooden door behind them. At that instant the grizzly slammed into the portal, causing it to bow inward, splintering the jam as if it was made from toothpicks.

Mr. Hanson grabbed a nearby chair and thrust it against the bent door. Joey quickly added a small bookcase and steamer trunk, ordering the others to get into the dining room.

Lizzy raced out of the den, face pale with fear. "I saw you coming," she gasped. "I didn't think you'd make it."

"We haven't yet," Mr. Hanson shouted, trying to be heard over the deep, angry roar of their unexpected guest. "Make sure Debbie's in her room and then call for help. Grandma Hanson went to Bozeman with Barry this morning, so they're safe—for now."

Lizzy hurried up the stairs and pounded on Debbie's bedroom door. The girl opened it quickly. "Anything wrong?" she asked.

"There's a bear trying to get into the Station," the old woman gasped.

"That Wendy," the teenager sighed. "Why can't she take up bird-watching?"

Lizzy lifted her hand as if to explain, then shook her head. "Come. We've got to stay together. Joey wants us all in the dining room."

Debbie followed the woman down the curving stairs to the lobby where her father and Joey had piled furniture against the warped door. Outside, the bear continued its thunderous roar, splintering the portal with powerful sharp-clawed paws.

Taking a final look at the pile of furnishings resting against the door, Mr. Hanson ordered the rest of the Shadow Creek Ranch gang into the dining room where they cowered in the semidarkness, waiting for the bear to grow tired of the attack.

"Why doesn't it go away?" Joey breathed after a few moments, turning to Mr. Hanson.

"I don't know," the lawyer said, glancing over at his father.

"What if it's still there when Grandma and Wrangler Barry return?" the old man asked, facing Debbie.

"I'm kinda scared," the girl admitted, trying to smile confidently at Lizzy.

"I'm just glad we're in here where it's safe," the old woman stated, throwing Samantha a comforting wink.

"See what you started?" the little girl scolded, turning to the cub. "It's your fault."

All heads swivelled around to face the small creature crouching under the dining room table. Joey covered his eyes. "What's *he* doing in here?"

"He just followed us into the Station," Samantha said with a shrug. "I guess he was a-scared too."

"He wasn't scared," Mr. Hanson moaned. "That's his mother out there pounding the entrance to our home into wood chips. Looks like Matshaw is a 'she,' and we've got her pride and joy under our dining room table."

"What're we going to do?" Lizzy asked.

Joey thought for a moment. "The side door, you know, the one off the kitchen. Let's get Junior here out of the house, like right now, while we still have a house."

A deep roar echoed down the hallway, rattling the neat rows of china dishes stored in the glass display case.

"Samantha, can you help me take your friend back to its mama?"

The little girl smiled. "I think he'd like that. See? He looks kinda nervous. Maybe he'd rather be outside."

Joey nodded and extended his hand. The cub swatted at it, sniffed the air, then settled back into his place under the table.

"He's not going to leave," Debbie groaned. "We're doomed."

Mr. Hanson leaned forward. "Sam, what does your friend like to eat?"

"Fish and bugs."

The man turned to Lizzy. "Sorry," the woman said, "the pantry's fresh out of both."

"How 'bout a banana?" Joey interjected. "I once saw a bear eat a banana at the Bronx Zoo. Ate it peeling and all!"

"Bananas we've got," the woman stated, moving quietly to the kitchen. She returned with a bunch of the big yellow fruit in her hand. The cub sniffed the air, then ambled over to Lizzy as if to say, "Exactly what are your plans for that interesting-smelling food?"

"Good," Mr. Hanson called out, taking the bananas and holding them out for the cub to see. "Hey, little bear. You want some nice, juicy banana?" The cub knocked the fruit from the man's hand in one quick motion. "I'll take that as a yes," Mr. Hanson said.

Joey and Debbie gathered up the scattered bananas and returned them to the lawyer. "Come on now," the man encouraged, backing through the kitchen, cub following his lead. When they reached the side door, Mr. Hanson turned and opened it slowly, tossing the bananas out into the sunshine. "Go get 'em," he invited. "They're good!"

The cub sniffed the outside air, ambled through the partially opened door, waddled across the little porch, and dropped the two steps to the ground. After closing and bolting the door, Mr. Hanson and the others positioned themselves at the window over the sink and waited to see what would happen.

The scratching and pounding at the entrance stopped as the little bear sat down at the base of the telephone pole by the composter and began carefully eating the plump fruit. A dark shadow fell over him as his enormous mother approached. She smelled the little creature from head to claw, turning occasionally to stare up at the window. Mr. Hanson and the rest would lean back from the glass, then straighten again, watching, waiting, hoping the two would leave the area now that they'd been reunited.

As if satisfied that her youngster was OK, the big bear turned one last time and stared up at the window. Then, with a roar, she stood on powerful hind legs and swung her right paw, splintering the telephone pole effortlessly. The wires at the top snapped as the heavy post buckled and fell, cutting the plastic composter in half as it crashed to the ground. Then the two animals lumbered away in the direction of the footbridge.

"How are we going to explain that to the phone company?" Wendy asked, watching the torn wires sway in the breeze.

"Perhaps a better question is How are we going to call them, or anyone else for that matter?" her father responded.

Debbie moved to the window and stared out into the brightly lit landscape. "We can't phone for help," she whispered. "And as long as those creatures are out there, we can't leave the Station either."

"That about sums it up," Mr. Hanson sighed.

Samantha sank to the floor and buried her chin in her hands. "It's all my fault. How was I supposed to know that my little friend had such a big mother?"

CHAPTER 4

Love
Like the Rain

Wrangler Barry released the parking brake and pressed gently on the accelerator. The old farm truck groaned under the load of lumber and bailing wire as it eased from the curb and headed down Bozeman's West Main Street. He'd stopped by the Christian bookstore on the corner to pick up a gift for Debbie and was looking forward to giving it to her.

Traffic was light and he made good time to the mall where Grandma Hanson waited.

"I sure hope I got everything," the old woman stated as she began lifting bags of groceries from a line of shopping carts waiting by a curbside display of tall, skinny fruit trees. "I forgot my list. I hate it when I do that. Makes me buy stuff I don't need." Grandma Hanson sighed. "Oh well, it'll all get eaten eventually. Between Joey and Wendy, I could bring home rock salt and they'd insist on having it for dessert."

Barry peeked inside one of the bags. "Did you remember to get plenty of beans? I love beans."

"Yes, yes," the old woman responded, swatting the wrangler away good-naturedly. "I got pinto, green, butter, kidney, navy, and black beans. That should keep you happy for a few weeks."

"Great!" Barry said with a broad smile. "How 'bout some rice and beans tonight for supper?"

"OK, OK, just help me get this stuff loaded and we can be on our way."

Leaning on his cane, Barry used his free hand to lift some of the lighter bags out of the carts and passed them to her. He liked Grandma Hanson. Everyone did. It seemed she lived each moment of her life in an all-out attempt to make someone happy. People were understandably drawn to her.

"There, that should do it," she announced, setting the last bag beside the neat pile of fresh cut lumber almost filling the truck bed. "I see my husband has finally decided to repair the back wall of the horse barn. He also promised me some bigger raised beds for the vegetable garden."

"They're in there too," Barry chuckled, latching the wooden gate guarding the cargo area. "Lumber yard had a sale on two-by-tens. Bought a bunch. You'll have enough beds to fill a dormitory." He laughed at his own joke.

Grandma Hanson lifted herself up into the cab and buckled in tightly. "Of course, if we don't get any more rain, we'll just be growing dust devils in the garden."

Barry joined her and fastened his own seat belt before turning the key. "Maybe we should get a message to Plenty to perform a rain dance or something."

"I wouldn't be at all surprised at what that girl is capable of making happen," the old woman chuckled. "Right now she seems to be successfully sharing a mountain with a grizzly bear. No simple accomplishment for a teenager, Indian or otherwise."

The truck swung out onto the highway with a grind of gears. Grandma Hanson looked about the cab with obvious disdain. "I've been after that husband of mine to buy us a new farm chariot for years," she sighed. "He keeps saying, 'As long as the old one runs, we don't need a new one.'" She turned to Barry. "You have my permission to have another accident."

The wrangler grinned. "No, thank you. One's enough to last me a lifetime. But I could be a little less careful about missing the bigger potholes. Maybe we can bust an axle or something like that."

"Fine," Grandma Hanson nodded as the shuttering vehicle lurched along the highway. "And if anyone asks, we didn't have this conversation."

The two rode in silence for a few miles, watching the approaching mountain range rise higher and higher before them.

"Grandma Hanson?" Barry shifted gears as the

truck slowed on a hill.

"Yes?"

"What's a woman look for in a man?"

She thought for a moment. "Good credit."

Barry chuckled. "Other than that."

"Well, I don't know about what other women are hunting for, but I can tell you what would be high on my list."

"And that's?"

"Oh . . . sincerity, honesty, commitment to the relationship."

Barry frowned. "Yeah, I know about those. Everybody wants that kind of person, even for a friend. I'm talking husband and wife here."

Grandma Hanson studied him for a long moment. She saw a handsome, strong man who'd been beaten down by a terrible event in his life. Also she recognized in his eyes a desperate need to be of value to someone—valued to a person who just happened to be near and dear to her as well.

"Barry," she said, "I think I understand what you're trying to say. So if you'll allow an old woman a moment of reminiscing, I'd like to tell you a story, something few people have heard."

"I'd be honored."

"Well, many, many years ago, when Grandpa Hanson and I were in college together back East, I used to sit and listen to him tell me how he was going to change the world. He said he was going to be the best lawyer in all of New York State, make truckfuls of money, and open a chain of law firms from Maine to California and back. It certainly impressed me. I was young and believed that this man could make any dream come true.

"Then, that very semester, his father passed away unexpectedly, leaving the family farm and his mom alone to face an uncertain future. He came to me with the sad news and announced that he was leaving school to run things back home. 'But what about your chain of law firms, the money, being the best lawyer in New York State?' I asked, openly disappointed at this new turn of events.

"The man looked at me and said, 'All those things are still inside me, but it looks like I'll be taking a different road to the future. I sure would appreciate it if you'd come along.'"

Wrangler Barry smiled. "And you said yes?"

The woman shook her head. "I said no, Barry. I wanted to marry a rich lawyer, not a simple farmer."

"So what happened?"

Grandma Hanson watched the dry fields float by outside the window, lost in the pain of remembering. "We rode the bus to the train station together. As he boarded, he looked back at me with such hurt in his eyes. 'I can only give you what I am,' he said. 'Isn't that enough?'

"I turned and walked away, thinking I'd made the right choice. But as the weeks and months dragged by, I began to realize that I missed him very, very much. All that time I thought it was his big plans and the promise of a happy, successful life together that had been the main attraction. But I found I missed the little things about him most: his voice speaking my name, the way he'd stop and listen to a bird singing in a field, his always boisterous laugh, even his silly jokes no one got but him. Little by little I realized that I was in love with the person, not his plans and dreams. I was attracted by the heart of the man, and that heart was breaking because of me."

Grandma Hanson lifted her hand. "Well, when I came to my senses, I got on the very next train that I could find heading for upstate New York. After I arrived at the town near his farm, I called his number from a phone booth. When he answered, I simply said, 'Forgive me?'"

The woman closed her eyes as the memory rose in her throat. Turning to Barry, she said softly, "He did."

Barry nodded. "What about the chain of law firms?"

"That didn't matter anymore," Grandma Hanson responded. "Nothing did. I just wanted us to be together to face whatever the future brought our way. So, to answer your question about what a woman looks for in a man, I'd have to say that, if the lady is serious about her feelings, it's an attitude of caring that beats out bank accounts and credit cards every time. It's not money and business success that pulls you through the years. It's love, plain and simple. Without love, everything else is meaningless."

Barry downshifted in preparation for turning off the main road onto the gravel lane leading to Shadow Creek Ranch. "And does a woman always know when a guy is really, truly in love with her?" he asked.

"You mean like Debbie?" The man reddened. "Yes, like that."

"She knows," Grandma Hanson said with a smile. "She's known it for a long time, just like you've known that she's in love with you."

Barry thought for a moment, then grinned broadly. "Yeah. You're right. I shouldn't be afraid, should I?"

"Never," Grandma Hanson responded. "Never be afraid of love."

The old farm truck rattled and shook as it continued along the winding road, heading into the mountains. Barry pressed harder on the accelerator, causing the motor to whine at a higher pitch. He must get back to the ranch, for now he knew he couldn't wait any longer. There was something he just had to ask Debbie Hanson.

☆ ☆ ☆

Debbie was sitting in her dad's office when she heard the approaching vehicle. Glancing through one of the broad windows fronting the Station, she saw the farm truck trailing dust up the driveway. Barry was driving, with Grandma sitting beside him in the cab.

The girl hurried out onto the high deck, reaching the railing just as the truck skidded to a halt at the base of the stairs and the driver's side door popped open. The wrangler stumbled from the cab and glanced up in her direction.

"Debbie!"

"Barry, you'd better—"

"Debbie, I've got to ask you something."

"OK. But first you and Grandm—"

"It's very important and can't wait another minute."

"Barry, listen!"

"I've put this off far too long as it is. But now I know how I feel about you an—"

A low rumbling roar echoed from the direction of the footbridge. Barry's mouth froze in midword as his eyes opened wide.

"Get back into the truck!" Debbie whispered loudly, trying not to attract the attention of the creature standing ankle-deep in Shadow Creek, surveying the Station.

Barry nodded nervously and slowly reentered the cab. He closed the door quietly, face pale. "What is it?" Grandma Hanson asked.

"I'm not sure," he said quietly. "But Debbie looks scared to death." He leaned forward and glanced up at the high deck. Debbie's father and

Joey had joined her and they all seemed to be staring at a spot just behind the truck.

As Barry leaned back in his seat, a huge face appeared beside him just beyond the closed window. Grandma Hanson screamed as a giant paw shattered the glass and tore the top half of the steering wheel away. The wrangler jammed the truck into reverse and stomped down on the pedal, jerking the vehicle backward. The creature withdrew its arm and stumbled hard, almost falling under the front tire.

Barry spun the wheel in a desperate attempt to keep from ramming into the bank that slanted up to the road curving by the Station. As the vehicle turned, he caught a glimpse of the bear running at full speed in their direction. Jamming the gear into first, he raced forward, barely missing the creature as the truck careened past the front porch and roared around the corner of the Station, engine groaning with the effort. The side porch slid into view and he immediately adjusted the partially mutilated steering wheel, putting him and Grandma Hanson in a direct collision course with the wooden structure. With a splintering crash, they smashed into the tiny deck and jolted to a halt beside the kitchen door.

Lizzy's face appeared behind the screen, eyes wide with terror. "Rip it open!" Barry commanded, leaning over and unbuckling Grandma Hanson's seat belt and quickly rolling down her window.

Lizzy tore into the screen with her fingers, pulling the thin mesh away with desperate jabs of her hands. Joey appeared and quickly finished the job. The wrangler had positioned the truck so that the passenger door was pressed up against the kitchen entrance.

Suddenly the vehicle shook violently as the grizzly slammed into the driver's side, teeth bared, throat bellowing a piercing, bone-chilling roar of rage. Eager hands grabbed Grandma Hanson's arms and shoulders, lifting her bodily out of the cab and onto the kitchen floor. Seeing that one of its prizes was getting away, the bear shrieked in frustration, doubling its efforts to get to the one remaining person left in the cab.

Barry slid as far away from the driver's side as he could, thrusting his cane into the face of the creature who was now trying to squeeze itself into the truck. Its mammoth head and one arm was all it could manage.

Mr. Hanson and Joey reached out and gripped the wrangler's thin, leather jacket and began lifting, straining against the weight. They groaned, teeth clenched, trying to keep their hold on their defenseless friend.

Barry could hear Debbie screaming out his name as he kicked at the creature, attempting to distract it long enough to get safely out of the cab. He knew he had to stay away from the animal's mouth. Grizzlies could snap a leg in two with one bite.

The bear's sharp claws dug into Barry's left leg in a last-ditch effort to keep him from being snatched out of reach. The wrangler cried out in pain as Mr. Hanson and Joey jerked him free from the cab and pulled him sprawling onto the kitchen floor. Joey slammed the door shut. Blood flowed freely from the wounded leg as Debbie dropped breathlessly to his side.

"Barry!" she screamed.

The young man tried to smile and hold up his hand. "There's something I gotta ask you," he moaned.

"Yes, Barry, anything," she said, wrapping her fingers around his wrist.

Barry's eyes rolled back in his head as the room whirled about him. "Debbie Hanson, will you . . . will you . . ."

He grew limp as his hand slipped to the floor.

"Barry!" the girl cried. "Barry, no!" She glanced over at her father who was hurriedly wrapping dish towels around the wounded leg.

"He's not dead, honey," the older man said. "I think he's fainted because of loss of blood. If we can get it stopped, he'll be OK. Joey, run up and get some bed sheets and blankets. We've got to keep him out of shock. Mom, boil water so we can make sterile bandages." Turning to his oldest daughter, he said quietly. "Barry will be fine, honey. But he needs you to stay right beside him so when he wakes up, he'll see you looking down at him. OK?"

Debbie nodded, her trembling face covered with tears and dusty sweat. Leaning low, she whispered into her friend's ear, "Barry, I'm here. I'll always be here. I'll never leave you. Never."

Outside, the animal roared out its frustration over losing yet another battle with the strange inhabitants of the big Station.

As evening settled over the ranch, the gang gathered in the dining room to discuss the situation. Barry was resting comfortably under a soft pile of blankets on the mattress that had been placed across the table. Mr. Hanson and his father had monitored their friend every few minutes, watching for any discoloration above the wound and for the first sign of fever, either of which could indicate the deadly onslaught of infection. So far, only the area below the knee showed the frightful effects of the attack.

They'd been able to stop the flow of blood and now could only wait for him to regain consciousness.

Debbie sat by his side, stroking his face with her fingers. Sometimes, she'd lean forward and press her cheek against his, whispering words no one could hear.

"What are we going to do?" Lizzy asked, placing a cup of steaming tea on the table beside Mr.

Hanson. "We can't call, we can't leave, and Barry sure could use the services of a qualified physician."

Mr. Hanson shook his head. "I don't know. We can only hope that the bear and her cub will leave on their own. It's too dangerous to try to take Barry out of the Station. Even if we could get him to my minivan or the pickup, they're parked behind the house by the garden and there's this big ol' truck blocking their escape route." He paused. "One thing's for sure, we've got to have someone watching the driveway at all times. If the Dawsons or Pastor Webley and his wife try to visit us, they'll be in terrible danger. We saw what the bear did to Barry and my mother. And they were in a large farm truck with a big, heavy cab. I don't want to even imagine what our furry friend would do to a Toyota."

Grandma Hanson shifted her position on her chair and rubbed her neck and shoulders. "That was not a pleasant experience," she reported.

Joey stood and walked to the window. "We could shoot him."

"No!" Debbie asserted, her eyes not leaving the face of her injured friend. "The bear was only trying to defend the cub."

"Sweetheart," Mr. Hanson said, "grizzlies have been known to attack without provocation."

"Not this one," his daughter stated flatly. "Don't you remember what was happening when she rushed the house for the first time? We had her baby with a rope tied around its neck. And we even brought it into the Station with us, although we didn't mean to. She believes we're a very real danger to her cub and is determined to protect him at all costs, even if she has to sacrifice her own life." Debbie turned. "She's a mother, and that's what mothers do."

Grandpa Hanson nodded. "The girl's right. I don't think that creature will be satisfied until we're no longer a threat."

"Oh great," Joey sighed. "We've got an overprotective she-bear hunting fish by the footbridge, a wrangler with a torn up leg, and our horses are scattered to the four winds. What else can happen?"

A gentle knock sounded at the front door. Mr. Hanson looked up sharply. "What on earth?"

Wendy blinked. "I didn't know bears could knock."

Joey ran out into the hallway and raced to one of the den windows. "It's Pastor Webley and his wife," he reported, his face grim. "And they've got their baby."

Mr. Hanson and his father immediately began tearing away the pile of furnishings separating them from the door. "Hurry!" Lizzy screamed. "Hurry!"

Pastor Webley's head tilted slightly when he heard the grinding and pounding on the other side of the strangely bent door. Suddenly it scraped open. He smiled and was about to say hello when firm hands grabbed him and his wife and pulled them quickly into the Station. The door crunched closed behind them as people threw furniture back into position. The man's smile faded, replaced by a look of surprise and deep concern.

"What's going on?" he asked.

Lizzy guided them toward the dining room. "We're under attack," she said.

"By what?"

The minister's wife gasped when she saw the form lying on the table. Handing the baby to her husband, she rushed across the room. "What happened here?" she asked, squeezing in beside Debbie.

"A bear got hold of his leg," the girl stated. "Tore him up pretty bad."

The woman lifted the blankets and peered under the bandages. She grimaced. "We've got infection."

"How do you know?" Mr. Hanson asked, walking into the room.

"I just know. I was a medic in the Army, remember?"

"Oh, that's right!" the man responded, a relieved smile creasing his face. "Bet you didn't have too many bear attacks to deal with."

Mrs. Webley began pulling away the wrappings. "No, just regular stuff like automatic fire and land mines. It's amazing what soldiers can do to themselves even in peace time. I've been continuing my training in the reserves. Looks like I'm going to be glad I did." Mr. Hanson joined her at the table. "See?" She pointed at some thin, red streaks under the skin running past the wrangler's knee advancing toward his thigh. "If this gets any worse, we're in trouble. I don't have any medical supplies with me, but I did learn a few tricks of the trade in field work." Turning to Grandma Hanson, she asked, "Do you have any onions?"

"Onions? Sure. Out in the pantry."

"Good. I'll need as many as you can get. Also some charcoal from the fireplace. We've gotta clean out the wound again and kill any germs on the skin surrounding the lacerations. An onion and charcoal poultice should do the trick. If it worked for Montana pioneers, it should work for us. Also, keep a cool, wet rag on Barry's face. He's in trauma shock. We've got to keep him as calm and comfortable as possible. You guys've done a great job so far, now let's see if we can get him conscious again." Glancing at Debbie, the woman added, "OK?"

Debbie smiled gratefully. "OK," she said.

Soon the new dressings were in place and a rag rested on the wrangler's forehead. Debbie hummed softly, her head resting next to his as she sat leaning against the table. Grandma Hanson and Lizzy had prepared a simple meal for the people gathered in the dining room, but no one felt much like eating. Even Samantha had refused a small piece of peach pie, a first in the little girl's history. She spent most of the evening staring at

Barry, then out the window into the darkness.

As conversation eased into silence, she slipped from the room and sat down at the base of the stairs out in the lobby. Joey saw her leave and followed.

"Hey, Sam. Whatcha doin'?" he asked, joining her on the landing.

"Thinkin'."

"What about?"

"About that I'm a really bad person."

"You? Why?"

The little girl sighed a trembling sigh. "I made Wrangler Barry get hurt because I played with the little bear."

"No, it's not your fault."

"Yes it is. I made the mama bear a-scared of us. She thinks we were going to hurt her baby and came and knocked on our door really hard. Then she hurt Barry. I didn't mean to make it happen. I didn't." Samantha buried her face in her hands and fell into Joey's arms.

"No one blames you," the boy replied. "You were just playing. You didn't know that that baby cub had the mother of all mothers hiding out in the forest." He reached down and lifted her face in his palm. "And you didn't hurt the cub, did you?"

"No."

"So, if that mama bear thinks we wanted to do her baby any harm, then she was wrong. Isn't that right?"

"Yes. I guess so."

"So, it's not your fault. That mama bear just doesn't understand that we love her cub too, and would never do anything to harm it."

Samantha nodded slowly. "Will Wrangler Barry be mad at me when he wakes up?"

"No! He understands about grizzly bears and stuff like that. Barry'll just be glad that you're OK and that the bear didn't eat you up like I'm going to do right now!" Joey reached out and grabbed his adopted sister and tickled her tummy, roaring softly. The girl squealed and laughed, fighting off the friendly attack. Then she quieted and leaned her head against his strong arm and was still for a long moment. "Joey?"

"Yes."

"Did my mommy take care of me like the bear takes care of her cub?"

The boy nodded and stroked the girl's soft, curly hair. "She sure did. When things got so bad for her in the city, she left you right where I could find you so that I could take care of you from then on. Your mommy loved you. And now I love you and will protect you from anything and everything that tries to hurt you."

"Good," Samantha said.

The two sat side by side, listening to the night sounds drifting in through the partially destroyed front door. They were thinking about the past, about East Village and how they'd fought to survive the streets before Mr. Hanson, Wendy, and

Debbie had entered their lives. After a few minutes had slipped by, Samantha yawned sleepily. "I think that every baby bear needs a mother bear, don't you?"

"Absolutely," Joey responded.

Samantha snuggled against her brother's chest and closed her eyes. "Goodnight, mama bear," she whispered.

"Goodnight, baby bear," the boy responded quietly.

☆ ☆ ☆

As the moon rose majestically over the distant mountains, Joey took his place at the railing of the upstairs porch. It was time for the light to appear again, as it had night after night since he'd first seen it. He held his big flashlight at the ready, freshly recharged batteries standing by to send the piercing beam toward Freedom Mountain.

Wendy walked up beside him and stood for a long moment studying the dark vista beyond their small valley. "I wonder if she knows Matshaw is down here with us."

Joey shrugged. "I don't know. She may think it's still in the cave and that everything is going along as usual."

"Maybe there are two bears."

"No way. That's the same creature I saw on the mountain. You don't forget something like that. Trust me. She's the one and only Matshaw—at least, the only one in this part of the Gallatins." The boy glanced at his watch, switching on the illuminated face for a second or two to make sure he got the time right. "She's late. I hope she's all right."

"It's not Plenty I'm worrying about right now," Wendy sighed. "Ol' Barry's not doin' so good. Mrs. Webley says his fever's going up slowly." She studied the dimly lit horse pasture, straining to catch a glimpse of the bear and her cub. "Maybe we should try putting Barry in the Webley's car and getting him to a hospital where he belongs."

"Too risky," Joey responded. "The bear could be anywhere, behind the barn, under the footbridge, in the cottonwood grove. You saw how fast she can move. We're just lucky the creature was off doing something else when the pastor and his family arrived."

Wendy shuddered. "I don't want to even think about what would've happened to little Adam if Matshaw had attacked."

The two gazed eastward without speaking for a few moments. "I don't think she's going to show tonight," he said, a touch of concern in his voice. "She's never been this late."

The girl glanced at her companion. "Joey, tell me something."

"OK."

"How come people in love do such strange things?"

Joey chuckled. "Like what?"

"Well, take Debbie. When she first met Barry, he was this macho horse tamer with lots of energy and strength who could do just about anything. Then the poor guy gets racked up bad in an accident, loses his dream about running his own ranch, doesn't know how he's going to make a living, and then a stupid bear chews on his leg for good measure. He's down there in the dining room fighting for his life without any way for us to get him to a hospital. Yet through all this, Debbie has fallen deeper and deeper in love with him. She's even more nuts about the guy now than she was two years ago after they first met. Can you explain that to me?"

Joey shook his head. "Grandpa Hanson once told me that the two greatest mysteries in this world are love and weather. He said the only sure way to predict that it's going to rain is to stand out in a field and wait for a cloud to dump on you. Then you can say, 'Yup, it's going to rain.' Grandpa H said love is sorta like that 'cept a lot of folk see the cloud and think they're in love. They don't wait for the rain to know for sure."

Wendy frowned. "What's he mean by that?"

"I'm not exactly sure," Joey chuckled. "Maybe he's saying that true love changes things, you know, like the rain? A good soaking shower makes things grow, gives life to plants and animals, fills the streams and ponds, turns everything green again. Without rain, stuff would die."

Wendy nodded slowly. "I think I understand. Grandpa was saying that without love, we'd die too. So, all this mushy stuff, all this huggin' and smoochin' and sitting up all night with Barry and feeling sick in your stomach when someone you like is hurting, is just love, pouring down on us like rain."

"I guess," Joey agreed. "And with all the divorce and running around people are doing, they sure are screwin' up a good thing."

"Like my mom?"

The boy turned. "I didn't mean—"

"That's OK. I know what she did, and what she is. It seems my mother wanted lots of clouds, but she wouldn't let it rain."

Wendy moved away from the railing and walked back to the sliding glass door leading into her father's office. "Grandpa's pretty smart," she said.

"Yeah, he is."

The girl nodded, then entered the Station. Joey took one last look to the east. Freedom Mountain remained dark, its face sullen in the moonlight. Plenty hadn't shown. Why?

He glanced toward the meadow where the shadows lay dark and heavy on the dry grasses. Nothing moved. The only sound disturbing the stillness were the chirps of the spring peepers and the soft splash of Shadow Creek as it trickled past the footbridge and disappeared into the night.

CHAPTER 5

Truck Lunch

Wendy awoke suddenly and lay in the stillness, wondering what had disturbed her.

No dog had barked. As a matter of fact, since the grizzly had taken up residence somewhere in the immediate area, all of the ranch animals, including Samantha's furry friend Pueblo, had vanished into the surrounding woodlands like shadows chased by the sun. Grandpa Hanson's valley spread had become deathly still, devoid of all the usual noises reverberating around a working horse ranch.

Perhaps someone had called her name. Wendy listened. No, only the soft breathing of her young roommate disturbed the predawn silence.

Rising, the girl pressed her feet into a pair of well-worn slippers and wrapped her favorite robe about her shoulders. Tiptoeing across the room, she pushed open the door and stepped out into the hallway. Nothing stirred in the Station.

The tiny light at the end of the hall seemed bright to her eyes as she shuffled past the kitchen door and paused at the entrance to the dining room. Barry lay still in the shadows, cocooned in warm blankets to ward off the night chill. Debbie sat in a chair at his side, sleeping, one hand holding his. Her other arm lay across the man's chest, fingers resting on his cheek to catch the slightest movement.

Wendy leaned against the doorjamb and stared at the scene for a long moment. What was this strange emotion called love over which everyone seemed to be so insanely passionate? She knew how to care for people and for animals—knew how to be concerned about them, protect them. Why, no girl on earth knew how to take better care of a horse than she did.

And, didn't she love her dad, her grandparents, and even Debbie, although how to love Debbie was getting more and more confusing as the months slipped by? It used to be easier because Debbie was . . . just . . . Debbie. Now, everything was changing. Wendy felt that she wasn't as important to her sister as before. Ever since Wrangler Barry had entered the picture, she'd been forced to share her sibling with the handsome man who, at one time, could ride horses better than anyone she'd ever seen. This same man seemed to work overtime in an all-out attempt to get her to be his friend. Well, he did save Early last fall while she was down in the cave nose to nose with Monty. That counted for something. He couldn't be all bad. But why did he have to take Debbie away from her? And why was her sister accepting the attack on their relationship so willingly?

Wendy's brow furrowed. It was all because of this *love* thing, the silly condition to which even her father had fallen victim. And Joey? That loser got all tongue-tied whenever any pretty girl crossed his path. It was sickening. If she was supposed to fall in love someday like everybody said, well, so be it. But she wasn't going to go down without a fight.

The girl glanced over at Mrs. Webley who was lying on a pile of blankets with only her nose showing above the folds. Now there was a woman to be admired. She played the organ at church as if she was performing at Carnegie Hall, knew how to patch up injured legs, and jumped out of airplanes the first Sunday of every month with all her Army Reserve friends. Now *that* was cool.

Of course, Mrs. Webley had been bitten by the love bug too. Wendy had noticed the respect in the woman's eyes whenever she looked at her husband, how she listened to every word of his sermons on Sabbath, and how she proudly showed off Adam, their little son, to anyone and everyone willing to meet him.

Love. It was like a disease, spreading from person to person without regard to race, creed, or financial stability. Whoever could come up with an antidote for the condition would make a fortune.

The other human inhabitants of the ranch were scattered about the dining room and foyer, resting on cots or balancing on hastily assembled mattresses, breathing softly as dreams drifted in the darkness.

Climbing the curving staircase, Wendy shuffled quietly into her father's office on the second floor and ambled out onto the upper deck. A yellow moon hung motionless in the sky, casting silver shadows over lawn and meadow. Nothing stirred. Even Shadow Creek seemed to be sleeping, its regular song now soft and muffled as it slowly meandered past the pasture, under the footbridge, and slipped by the Station before disappearing.

The girl pulled the robe up tightly around her shoulders. It was cold, not like the winter, but like the spring when the sun warms the earth though the air still carries a chill.

She knew Early, Tar Boy, and the other horses were out there, somewhere, keeping a safe distance between themselves and the bear. They'd come back after the danger had passed. But she missed them nonetheless, especially Early. Never had she cared for something so fiercely, with such devotion. Maybe that was love. Maybe not. All she knew for sure was that her horse was important to her. Without him nearby, she felt just a little lost.

Becoming suddenly sleepy again, Wendy

yawned. She reentered the Station and slid the door closed behind her. Moving across the room, she lowered herself into her father's big office chair. It smelled good, a mixture of leather and aftershave. Pulling her feet up under her, she closed her eyes and soon fell into a deep, dreamless sleep.

☆ ☆ ☆

Just as morning was beginning to blush on the eastern horizon, Barry opened his eyes. At first, he wasn't exactly sure where he was. The ceiling looked familiar, but, somehow, it didn't quite belong in a room where he was supposed to sleep.

He blinked a couple times, then noticed someone sitting by his side in the half-light of dawn, face hidden behind a small pillow. The hair was dark and shiny. Long strands flowed over his arm and nestled themselves by his chin. That was Debbie's hair. He was certain. How beautiful it was so close to him, so soft and touchable.

But something else was very strange. Her hair smelled like onions.

Barry tried to speak. He wanted to say, "Hey, Debbie, you really need to change your shampoo." A sputtering cough came out instead.

Debbie's head shot up, eyes trying to focus through the haze of disturbed slumber. "Barry? Barry?" she whispered.

The wrangler cleared his throat. "What . . . where am I?"

Her expression turned from concern to joy. "You're in the dining room, and I'm right here beside you."

"What happened?"

"The bear got your leg and you lost a lot of blood. You kinda fainted, but Dad and Mrs. Webley are trying to fix you up."

"Which leg?" the man asked.

Debbie smiled. "Not your cane one."

"Thank goodness." He paused. "Oh yeah. I remember being attacked, but that's about all. Why does everything smell like onions?"

"Mrs. Webley put a poultice on your wounds. It's supposed to help control infection."

"I'm not surprised," Barry said, stopping to clear his throat again. "No self-respecting germ would stick around with that strong an odor." Sluggishly he propped himself up on one elbow and surveyed his neatly wrapped leg. "What else she got in there?"

"Charcoal, from the fireplace. Supposed to draw out poisons. She learned all this stuff in the Army. How're you feeling?"

"Like a bear got me."

Debbie grinned. "Well, I've got you now, so just relax and I'll take good care of you."

"You . . . you sat with me all night?"

"Of course, silly. I didn't want you flirting with all the cute nurses in this ward."

"I kinda like the one on this shift. She has long

dark hair and smells like a salad. What'd you say her name was?"

"Hanson. Debbie Hanson. And she's kinda fond of you too. But don't let that get around or she might lose her job."

"It'll be our secret," he said with a wink. "You wouldn't happen to have any water in this dinin—, I mean wing, would you?"

"This medical institution comes complete with running water and a barn," Debbie announced proudly. "I'll see if the kitchen staff can rustle you up a sip or two."

As the girl left the room, Barry called over at the mound in the corner. "Mrs. Webley? Is that you?"

"Yes?" came the muffled reply from under the blankets.

"Can I talk with you for a minute?"

A smiling face appeared from under the coverings. "I see you've decided to rejoin the living. How do you feel?"

Barry frowned. "My leg. It hurts pretty bad. I didn't want to say anything with Debbie here. You know how she worries."

"Oh, I know," Mrs. Webley said, shuffling to the table. "I keep telling my nurses not to fall in love with their patients, but do they listen?"

The wrangler grinned painfully. "Maybe you'd better check your work before she gets back."

The woman pushed aside the blankets and examined the area under the bandages. "Got some

105

swelling . . . and the unmistakable smell of infection, probably near the bone."

"Yeah. I noticed that too. You can always tell when a horse's hoof is ailing. Smells like cake. Am I in any danger?"

"Maybe. I'd like to see this swelling come down a bit and a little more natural color return to the affected area. Reminds me of an artillery sergeant I worked on 'bout a couple years ago during training exercises in Colorado. Caught some shrapnel in his arm. One of his unit's mortar shells fell short and vaporized his Hummer."

"You're not going to start telling war stories, are you?"

Mrs. Webley grinned. "Oh, maybe another time. They can wait until everyone's up. I like a big audience. As for your leg, I've seen worse. But this could develop into an ugly situation. I've used up all the onions and charcoal in the house. May have to chance a run to the car so I can bring back a real doctor from Bozeman."

"I don't think that's a very good idea," Barry said softly. "The next person who tangles with that creature out there might not get off as lucky as I did."

Debbie returned with a glass of water, stepping lightly around the sleeping forms scattered across the floor. "Hey, everybody," she announced with a voice filled with renewed energy and optimism. "Our head wrangler is awake and lucid.

Well, at least he's awake."

Pastor Webley stirred and stretched as Joey shuffled into the room from the hallway. "Hey, Barry," Joey said sleepily. "How's the leg?"

"Picture a log in a switched-on garbage disposal. Sorta like that."

Joey shuddered. "Ew. I needed that lovely image in my brain before breakfast."

Mr. Hanson entered the room and smiled at his daughter. She reached over and gave her father's hand a squeeze. "I was here, Daddy," she whispered. "I was right here."

"Good girl," the man said. Turning to Barry, he added, "She wanted to be the very first person you saw when you woke up."

Barry shook his head. "Sorry to disappoint you, Debbie, but you weren't exactly the first. I kinda surfaced a few hours ago, before it was light, and noticed someone silently snooping around my leg."

Mrs. Webley blinked. "Wait a minute. This is the first time I examined you since going to bed last night."

"Oh, it wasn't you," the wrangler smiled. "It was Plenty. Where is she, anyway?"

"Plenty!" Joey gasped. "She was here in this room?"

"Of course. Didn't you . . ." Barry looked at the astonished faces by the table. "Didn't you know? She put some package or something by the kitchen door as she left. I was like really, really out of it. Couldn't even say hello to her. She just looked at me, then left. Didn't make a sound."

Mrs. Webley hurried across the room and paused at the passageway into the kitchen. There, on the floor, beside the tall wooden and glass hutch, was a plastic bag. She picked it up and peeked inside. Slowly a broad smile lightened her face. "It's clay," she announced.

"Clay?" Mr. Hanson repeated. "Why would Plenty leave a bag of clay in our dining room?"

Mrs. Webley shook her head as her grin widened. "Anyone who has studied natural or field medicine will know exactly why." She held the bag up for all to see. "Fresh clay, when mixed with warm water, has the amazing ability to draw out toxins from a wound and fight infection. Barry, your Indian friend may have just saved your leg."

Joey's mouth dropped open. "Plenty was here? Here in the Station?"

"It seems so," Mrs. Webley said. "Looks like we've got a friend on the outside who knows what's happening to us. Makes you wonder what else the girl has planned."

Joey moved to the window and stared out across the pasture. A thin veil of mist hung motionless in the brightening air. "Yeah," he said quietly. "Makes you wonder."

By midmorning the mysterious properties of

the clay had begun to work their magic on Wrangler Barry's leg. His fever, which had been hovering around the century mark, slowly began to drop, aided by a nourishing breakfast of warm vegetable soup and a couple glasses of grape juice which, according to Mrs. Webley, would help build his blood back up, whatever that meant.

As promised, Debbie stayed by his side, even as they moved him to a more comfortable spot in the den. The curtains hanging beside the large windows were drawn tightly. "Don't want our friend Matshaw to see us all comfy-cozy in here," Grandpa Hanson reported. "She might decide to join our happy bunch. All we need is a vindictive mama bear roaming around the inside of the Station looking for someone to chew on."

"How do you feel?" Debbie asked when the two of them were alone in the dark confines of the heavily shaded room.

"About the same as 10 minutes ago," the wrangler responded with a grin.

"Oh, did I ask you that before?"

"A few times." He reached for her hand. "I'm going to be fine, Debbie. Really."

The girl held back a sob that rose suddenly in her throat. "When . . . when I saw you lose consciousness, I got so scared. I thought maybe you'd never wake up again and—"

"I'm going to be fine," the man repeated, brushing his fingers across Debbie's cheek. "Besides, I couldn't leave now because . . . because there's something I gotta ask you."

"What?"

Barry cleared his throat. "You see, I know I don't have a lot to offer, being all banged up like I am, first by the accident, and now this. But I can't seem to be satisfied with life unless you're nearby where I can hear your voice and watch you smile. You're in my every thought and my every dream."

Debbie gripped his hand and pressed it against her face as tears trickled down her cheek, moistening his fingers.

"I can't imagine a future without you in it," he continued. "I know you could do better than me, a lot better. But no one could love you more than I do." He closed his eyes and let out a frustrated sigh. "Oh, I'm not doing this very good. This was supposed to happen up at Papoose Lake surrounded by chirping birds while we were sitting on the soft grasses by the water, not entombed here in a dark den with a mad bear guarding the exits."

"You're doing fine, Barry," Debbie said, smiling through her tears. "Don't stop. Please don't stop."

"OK. Here goes. As I was saying, I just gotta have you in my life, so, Debbie Hanson, will you—"

CRASH!

The girl jumped as a shattering, explosive sound ripped through the Station.

"What was that?" Joey called from the upstairs balcony.

110

"Sounded like it came from the kitchen," Mr. Hanson stated as he rushed out of his office and ran down the curving staircase.

Grandpa Hanson burst from his bedroom and hurried down the hall. "Where's my wife and Lizzy?"

"We're in here with the Webleys," the women called from the dining room. The group hurried to the kitchen and peered out the big window above the sink.

CRASH, BANG, CRACK!

"It's the bear," Joey whispered. "She's tearing the back end of the truck apart."

"My groceries!" Grandma Hanson breathed. "There's a week's worth of supplies in there."

"Not anymore," her son announced, shaking his head. "Looks like Big Matshaw and the little Matshawette will dine in style today, complete with appetizers and dessert."

Outside, beyond the safety of the window, the huge bear dug into the neat row of grocery bags in the rear of the truck, tossing aside long lengths of lumber and other building material that got in her way. She ripped up the wooden support frames forming the bed and then shattered the window glass separating the cab from the storage area. Wordlessly, they watched as the mammoth creature tore away the metal skin of the vehicle as it searched for every morsel of food that might be hidden out of sight.

Her cub joined her, nibbling first on a split open package of frozen spinach, then lifting a bottle of orange juice and letting the yellow liquid splash down its arm and soak its face. What had been an old farm truck was, in the course of 15 minutes, turned into a twisted pile of metal, debris, and broken boards.

Grandma Hanson turned to face her husband. The man smiled weakly. "OK. Now we can get a new truck."

The woman nodded and walked out of the room.

Debbie stood in the den entryway, waiting for word from the kitchen. "What happened, Grandma?" she asked the old woman when she strolled into the foyer.

"Matshaw just ate our truck," came the happy announcement.

Debbie grinned. "How's Grandpa taking it?"

"Right in the wallet."

The girl hurried back into the den. "Looks like we're going to get a new truck here on Shadow Creek Ranch," she stated, taking her place beside Barry. "The bear just had our old one for lunch."

Barry grinned broadly. "What a shame."

"This is getting serious," Joey declared as he entered the den, followed by the others. "Now Matshaw knows there's food at the Station, she may decide to stay all summer. What're we going to do?"

Grandpa Hanson seated himself by the cur-

tained window. "You're right, Joey. The bear figures she's got it made. Food, water, shelter, and
we're no threat as long as we stay put in here."

Wendy chuckled. "Even giant grizzlies know a
good thing when they see it."

Little Samantha ambled into the room carrying
a piece of paper in one hand and a collection of wildflowers in the other. "I got an E-mail for the bear,"
she announced. "I sent it over Mr. Hanson's computer." She held it up in front of her, then turned
the paper so she could read the handwritten squiggles spread across its white surface. "It says, 'Dear
Mrs. Bear. Please go away and stop scaring us.
Here are some pretty flowers as a going away present. Signed. Samantha Williams Dugan.'"

"Williams?" Joey blinked.

Wendy lifted her hand. "I'll explain later."

"So, let's go give it to the bear," Samantha
urged, looking up at her brother.

The boy sighed and took the girl by the hand.
"Hey, it can't hurt. Come on, Sam, we'll send your
E-mail airmail directly to the bear from the upper
deck. Maybe Matshaw will check it out after she
finishes chewing on Grandpa Hanson's truck—
you know, the way Grandpa Hanson reads maga-
zines after supper."

"I loved that truck," the old man moaned. "She
had many more miles left in her."

"Yeah, it's a real pity," his wife declared. "I'm
going to miss the way it shook up your insides as

you drove down the road."

"And the way it backfired so thoughtfully in heavy traffic," added Wrangler Barry.

"And how," chimed in Mr. Hanson, "on a cold winter day it chose not to disturb the early-morning stillness with anything so noisy as starting."

"And the way it always left a puddle of oil on the lawn wherever you guys parked it," Wendy interjected, shaking her head sadly.

"All right, all right!" Grandpa Hanson moaned, lifting his hands in surrender. "So, it may have had a few . . . how shall I say . . . quirks."

"Quirks? It was a pile of junk!" his wife stated flatly. "Matshaw was kind enough to put it out of its misery. For that I'll be eternally grateful."

Joey and Samantha approached the railing wrapped around the outer edge of the upper deck and surveyed the ranch. A dry, warm wind stirred the trees, lifting occasional dust devils from the pasture and twirling them for a few seconds before tiring of the dance. Joey folded his sister's message into a paper airplane and sent it sailing out over the lawn. Samantha tossed her wildflower bouquet and watched it fall, tumbling through the air, finally landing with a soft *pat* on the grass.

A trail of broken bottles and food wrappings led from the side of the house to the footbridge, indicating that the creatures had tired of their destruction and elected to carry off a few supplies for later, just in case the hunger bug bit.

"What a mess!" Samantha breathed. "Grandma Hanson is going to be mad at Matshaw. Wendy and I have to keep our room neat or she says to us, 'Girls, you're people, not pigs. Clean up this room or I'll start feeding you corn husks and table scraps.' That makes Wendy and me laugh, and we straighten up our messes fast."

Joey chuckled. "I'm glad Grandma Hanson doesn't visit my summer room in the horse barn very often or I'd have a sudden change in my diet."

The two were turning to leave when a soft *swish* followed by a loud *thud* split the air. Joey looked up to see an arrow jutting from one of the porch's support beams a few feet from his head.

He spun around and studied the pasture and barn area. Nothing moved. There was no sign of life beyond the lawn.

"Look, Joey," Samantha said, pointing, "someone sent you an E-mail on that arrow."

The boy noticed a small piece of paper wrapped tightly around the vibrating shaft. Reaching up, he wiggled the arrow free from the beam and quickly unfastened the note. In neat, carefully formed letters, someone had written, "Stay inside the Station. Don't come out for anything. I'm working on a plan. If Wrangler Barry is better, raise your right hand and hold it above your head."

Joey lifted his arm and waved it back and forth, searching the meadow and mountains. He could see no indication that another human being was anywhere near the ranch.

"Who are you waving at?" Samantha asked.

"The one person who can save our skins," the boy responded. "Come, Sam, we've got to show this to the others. I don't know what Plenty's big plan is, but I hope it works."

Brother and sister hurried from the deck and headed for the downstairs den, message firmly in hand. The boy felt a twinge of concern press against his heart. Plenty was their only hope. From now on, it would be an Indian girl against a dangerous legend. One would win, the other would lose. The way things stood right now, the coming battle could go either way.

CHAPTER 6

The Greatest Gift

As evening settled over the ranch, activity in the Station began to lessen. Hours earlier Grandpa Hanson had announced, "Just because a giant bear is holding us captive doesn't mean work must come to a halt. Let's everyone get busy doing something useful." Even the Webleys willingly put their hand to the task of helping clean up the kitchen and dining room.

Samantha kept little Adam entertained with her tales of traveling to Canada and hunting elephants in the jungle. When Lizzy pointed out that Canada had no jungles, the little girl reluctantly agreed and decided she'd really been on safari in the swamps of Alaska instead.

All afternoon Mr. Hanson stayed at his computer, writing and editing court briefs for his law partners in New York City. The documents were safely stored on the computer's hard drive, waiting for the day when they'd be launched over the ranch's repaired phone lines to modems and fax machines waiting many miles away.

Joey and Wendy spent their usual hours in the den, studying their lessons. Barry was gracious enough to allow classes to take place in his "ward" as he now called the cozy room with the darkened windows and neat rows of bookcases. He even invited Wendy to read aloud from her geography book. The girl had happily obliged, adding her own comments to the text she presented, lifting Barry's spirits and giving him the opportunity to forget the pain in his leg for a few minutes at a time.

Grandma Hanson and Lizzy stayed in the kitchen and dining room areas, preparing food and entertaining their guests. Virginia Webley was thrilled when Grandma Hanson offered to teach her the recipe for her famed potato casserole. Her husband took a few minutes each hour to play with Adam and Samantha, grateful for a break in his usual hectic schedule of church work, counseling, and hospital visits.

When Samantha wasn't hunting wild boar in Antarctica, she was writing and delivering E-mail messages to anyone and everyone, outlining her proposed Bozeman zoo and circus.

Debbie remained by Barry's side, doing her best to keep him comfortable. Since their earlier interrupted conversation, they'd not had a moment alone. The girl thought she had a pretty good idea of what her friend was trying to ask her, but she couldn't be sure. She didn't want to jump to any wrong conclusions. That could prove to be embarrassing.

But in the back of everyone's mind was the constant question, *What was Plenty's plan, and would she survive her coming encounter with the legendary Matshaw?* All anyone could do was wait, and hope for the best.

Now it was evening, and conversations slowly eased into peaceful silence. Like a big machine spinning down, the Station grew quieter and more serene, allowing the outside stillness to wrap its shadowy arms about it, lulling all inside toward a gentle rest.

One by one the inhabitants of Shadow Creek Ranch began to find their sleeping spots, tossing tired "good-nights" to the others. Before retiring, Joey walked out onto the Station's upper deck and studied the distant form of Freedom Mountain. The moon was fuller than it had been during the last few evenings, casting a silvery glow across the land, illuminating the trees and meadows with a soft light.

Plenty hadn't signaled at her usual hour, causing the boy to conclude that she must be working on her plan of action, whatever it happened to be.

He dropped a thin mattress on the deck and spread his thick sleeping bag over it. When and if Plenty got down to business, he wanted to be there to witness every detail. His Indian friend

119

enjoyed a deep understanding of nature and possessed an uncanny ability to blend into it like a shadow. Red Stone had been her mentor. She'd learned her lessons well. Now she'd have to put all of her skills to the ultimate test. Lives were at stake, including hers.

A movement by the sliding glass door caught his eye. "Hey, Pastor Webley," the boy called out warmly. "You headin' for bed too?"

"Yeah," the man nodded. "Just came up to get some fresh air and talk with my Friend." He pointed skyward.

"You mean God?"

"Yup. We talk often, especially at the beginning and end of every day. Makes me feel better inside."

Pastor Webley stood by the railing and drew in deep lungfuls of the cold night air. "It's so beautiful out here on Shadow Creek Ranch," he sighed. "So peaceful. Hard to believe we're being held hostage by an angry bear."

"Doesn't seem like it fits the surroundings, huh?" Joey responded.

The man was silent for a moment. "Kinda like this ol' world. It contains so much beauty, but we can't fully enjoy it because of—not a bear—but a lion. It's holding us hostage just as surely as Matshaw." Pastor Webley lifted his hand and waved his finger as if preaching to a great throng. "'Be sober, be vigilant because your adversary the devil, as a roaring lion, walketh about, seeking whom he may devour.'" The man shivered. "I'm not all that fond of bears or lions. Anything that considers me a snack isn't exactly high on my invite-home-for-dinner list."

Joey chuckled. "You're just like Grandpa Hanson. Everything reminds him of something he read in the Bible."

"He's a good man," Pastor Webley responded. "I've learned a lot from him. Grandpa Hanson's a true friend."

The boy sighed and shook his head. "Right now he's on a love kick. You know, springtime, romance, huggin' and smoochin', junk like that."

"Junk?" the pastor gasped, smiling broadly. "Why, my boy, love is the greatest gift God ever gave to us pathetic human beings. I put it right up there with breathing and ice hockey. Wonderful thing love. It causes us to do stuff we'd never do without it. Good things. Makes me all goose-pimply just thinking about how much power there is in a person who loves other people." He turned to the boy. "Grandpa Hanson's springtime kind of love is part of it. You ever experienced that type of emotion?"

Joey blinked. "Me? Nah. I don't think so. Not like with all this flowers and candy weirdness my boss is rantin' and ravin' about. Although it does sound kinda fun."

"It'll happen," the minister said firmly. "Knock you right out of your saddle. I think God gets a big kick out of us falling in springtime love, seeing how He created it and all."

Joey frowned. "So, if this love is such a wonderful thing, how come so many people get their hearts broken?"

"The lion!" Pastor Webley said, waving his hand. "It's the lion! He gets you feeling all proudful and selfish, you know, doing stuff you shouldn't, such as thinking your relationship is a mistake and that you'd be better off with some other wife or husband." The man clutched his chest in mock anguish. "Poor me. I'm such a fool for committing myself to this woman. Why, just look at all the other fish in the pond. I'd be better off with her, or her, or her. My marriage is a big mistake. She's not fulfilling my needs. Oh, woe is me!"

Joey laughed at his antics, enjoying the man's eagerness to get his point across. "So, this lion, he makes people fall out of love?"

"You bet. Does it all the time. But there is a defense."

"What?"

Pastor Webley pointed toward the mountains. "The God who created the beauty. The God who created love. Like your friend Plenty, He's got a plan. A very effective one. He's promised to help us fight the enemy of love. We've just gotta study His ideals and guidelines for survival."

"In the Bible?" Joey asked.

The man grinned. "For a guy from East Village, you're pretty smart."

122

The young wrangler nodded. "Hey, as long as God's plan doesn't include a lot of math, I can handle it."

"Don't like math, huh? Well, God's brand of love comes with only one equation. Some might consider it rather radical, you know, sorta biblical new math. Here it is. 'Therefore shall a man leave his father and mother, and shall cleave unto his wife: and they shall be one flesh.' That's in Genesis."

"Wait a minute," Joey said, raising his hand. "That sounds like one plus one equals one."

"And you said you weren't good at math! That's right, Joey. One flesh. Not two. One. Romantic love, as God intended, combines a man and a woman into a single power that the lion, Satan, can't tear apart. Neat, huh?"

"Yeah," Joey said softly. "Makes all this springtime love business not so scary, if you do it God's way."

"Correct, my friend," Pastor Webley said with a yawn. He stretched and breathed deeply one more time. "Now, I've got to get down to my lovely wife and make sure she's safe and happy for the night. After all, she's part of me. Right?"

"Right."

The man walked to the doorway, then paused. "When the big one hits you, Joey, think of it as God tapping you on the shoulder with an invitation to something very beautiful. You might have to practice for a few years, you know, kinda testing the waters, finding the person who best suits your personality and stuff, but it'll be worth the wait. Trust me. Love's the greatest gift of all, whether you give it to a friend, a neighbor, or a life partner."

Joey nodded and watched the man enter the dark building and disappear into the shadows. The greatest gift of all. Wow. That's the kind of love he wanted to enjoy.

The young wrangler slipped into his sleeping bag, folded his arm under his head, closed his eyes, and drifted slowly into slumber, serenaded by the spring peepers hiding along Shadow Creek and the gentle moan of the wind.

Joey awoke with a start, his nose wrinkling immediately as a certain smell set off silent alarms in his mind. Anyone who's ever been given the task of caring for horses becomes keenly aware of situations that would jeopardize their safety. The odor filling his nostrils at this predawn hour triggered just such an alarm.

The teenager sat up and sniffed the air, eyes narrowed. It was faint, but definitely there. Glancing to the west, Joey's heart stopped midbeat as a sight so unreal, so fantastic, drove all sleep from his body like a cold wind robs a person of warmth.

Freedom Mountain was on fire. Silent flames moved in slow motion, drifting up from the darkness like serpents creeping among unseen trees.

124

There was no sound, just an eerie glow, and the unmistakable odor of burning grass and wood. Beyond the mountain, dawn's approach outlined the horizon with a faint, thin thread of light.

The boy leapt to his feet and rushed into the quiet Station. Hurrying down the stairs, he ran to the den and made his way to Barry's side. Debbie looked up sleepily at his approach.

"What's the matter, Joey?" she said, seeing the concern in his eyes.

The boy shook Barry. "Wake up, wake up," he urged.

"What . . . what's going on?"

"Barry. There's a fire. A big one."

The wrangler rose on one elbow. "Where?"

"Freedom Mountain. It looks like the whole west face is burning."

Barry rubbed sleep from his eyes. "Show it to me."

The teenager ran to the window and pulled back the heavy curtain. Debbie gasped when she saw the burning mountain standing torch-like against the dark skies.

"Which way is the wind blowing?" Barry asked.

Joey thought for a moment. "I could smell the fire," he said.

The wrangler nodded. "Wind's from the east." He paused. "It must be Plenty's work. We haven't had any lightning in the area, and there are no roads up there, campsites either. But, why would she set her mountain on fire? It's too far away to scare the bear."

"Wait a minute," Joey breathed. "The fire may be too far away, but . . ."

"The smoke!" Debbie asserted. "The smoke will ride the winds into our valley. No animal likes the smell of smoke. Makes them nervous."

Barry shook his head. "That might be it. Is Plenty trying to smoke the bear and her cub away from the ranch?"

"Maybe . . ." Joey frowned as he stared at the bizarre sight beyond the window. "But forest animals smell smoke all the time. Grandpa Hanson told me that small-scale fires are common in the western states. Storms, careless campers, jerks who toss cigarette butts from their cars—they all can light up a stand of trees in no time. A legend like Matshaw would be used to smelling smoke."

"Well, why else would Plenty want to set the place on fire?" Debbie asked.

"I don't know," Barry responded thoughtfully. "Look, we'd better get everyone else up. I don't know what our Indian friend has in mind, but we should be prepared for anything."

Joey turned. "I think I'll start with Wendy," he said with a grin. "I've always wanted to wake *her* up for a change. Debbie, you get the folks in the dining room, OK?"

Debbie nodded. "Take it easy on my sister. She's just a child, you know."

"Yeah, like a mountain lion is just a kitty cat. This is going to be fun!"

Barry smiled. "If I could walk, I'd want to see this."

Debbie pushed him back against his pillow. "You guys are just awful."

Silently Joey slipped down the long hallway to Wendy's room. Squeaking open the door, he gazed into the dark chamber. Samantha lay in her small cot by the window, eyes closed in slumber. The boy edged past the desk and paused by Wendy's bed, hovering over it like a vulture circling a fresh kill. He lifted his hands, formed his fingers into claws, and prepared to strike.

"Hey, Joey," a voice called from behind him, causing the teenager to jump sideways and slam into the dresser. He fell over the waste can and sprawled across the floor, sending a miniature volcano of crumpled papers and assorted discarded items into the air. They floated back to earth, partially covering his prone figure collapsed over the scatter rug.

"What're you doing up so early?" Wendy asked, standing at her closet, fully dressed, slipping her favorite jacket over her shoulders. "I was about to come wake you up. Do I smell smoke?"

Joey pressed his hands against his chest, trying to keep his pounding heart from exiting through his ribs. "Yes, you smell smoke," he gasped. "Plenty's barbecuing Freedom Mountain."

"Why?"

"How am I supposed to know? She didn't arrow-mail me about it, OK?"

"OK. You don't have to get so hyper. I just asked a simple question."

The young wrangler pushed himself to a sitting position. "Don't you ever sleep?"

"Of course I sleep. But I'm a morning person. Remember?"

"This is not morning!" the boy countered. "This is . . . is . . . late night, it's predawn. Human beings aren't supposed to be up yet."

"Well," Wendy nodded, "that explains why you're sneaking around the Station. I've never been convinced that you're human."

Joey dropped his hands and let them lie limply in his lap. "I give up. Just go get your father and Grandpa Hanson. I'll bring Sam." He paused. "Someday, I'm going to look back on these years and laugh."

Wendy smiled. "They already make me laugh. You gotta loosen up, Mr. Dugan. You're far too tense."

With that she skipped from the room, leaving Joey sitting in the middle of the floor surrounded by the scattered contents of the waste can.

☆ ☆ ☆

Morning arrived with its usual majesty beyond the mountains, but for the inhabitants of Shadow

Creek Ranch the dawning day was accompanied by the increasing presence of smoke in their valley. The odor of fire grew steadily stronger as visibility began to diminish. First, the distant mountains to the east vanished behind a veil of smoke. Then the cottonwoods disappeared, followed by the pasture. Now the world seemed like a collection of dark forms, moving in and out of waves of exhaust generated by the glowing western face of the mountain.

"Make sure all the windows are closed," Grandma Hanson directed. "Don't want to fill the Station with that odor."

"Are we going to burn up?" Samantha asked for the hundredth time.

"No, Sam," Joey stated, placing wet towels around the partially destroyed front door. "The fire is too far away right now."

"But is it going to come down here and make our barn burn up?"

"I don't think so, Sam," the boy said. "Besides, when the forestry department gets their act together, they'll be arriving with lots of trucks and airplanes to put water on the fire." He paused. "Hey. Maybe that's what Plenty had in mind. To bring people through Shadow Creek Ranch to fight the blaze." Then he shook his head. "Nah. It's easier to get to Freedom Mountain from the east. The firefighters will use the logging roads running around the base of Blackmore."

"Will my zoo animals get hurt?" Samantha asked. "They're in the barn and can't get out."

"No, they'll be fine. We won't let anything bad happen to them. They're safe in their jars. We gave them lots of leaves to eat and a nice bowl of water just the other day, remember?"

The little girl nodded. "How 'bout Pueblo and the horses? Will they run away from the fire?"

"Oh, yes. I'm sure they'll stay where it's safe. Now, you'd better go help Wendy. She and Dizzy are making some sticky buns. They may need someone to taste-test them, you know, to make sure they're up to their usual deliciousness."

"Sticky buns? I love sticky buns almost as much as I love peach ice cream." The girl turned and ran through the foyer.

Joey inspected his work and sniffed the air. He could smell the fire, but the odor wasn't nearly as strong as when he stood out on the upper deck. Walking into the den, he picked up his binoculars and headed for the window. Pulling back the curtain, he looked out across the hazy yard. "Still can't see anything. Haven't been able to for hours," he told Barry. In the distance came the muffled sound of a helicopter. "Sounds like the state forestry people are on the job."

"The radio reported the burn about 15 minutes ago," Grandpa Hanson stated, entering the room. "They're calling it a localized flare-up. Said they should have it contained by midafternoon. I hope Plenty can get done whatever she had in mind by then or she'll have to come up with another plan. Why don't we head to Tyler's office for a better look?"

A deep roar echoed through the thick curtains. "Sounds like Matshaw's not too comfortable with the fire and smoke either," the old man stated. "She's gettin' nervous. Been grumbling a lot for the last hour. Are all the doors and windows secured? We wouldn't want her and her cub deciding the Station would serve nicely as a new den."

"Everything's as tight as a drum," Joey announced. "This is no longer a way station. It's a fort."

Barry strained to get up. "Take me with you. I'm tired of just lying around. Makes me feel helpless."

"Are you sure?" Debbie asked. "Mrs. Webley says you shouldn't be too active right now. Might reopen those cuts in your leg."

"I'll take it easy. I just . . . don't feel comfortable in the den. I don't know why."

"Well, OK," she sighed. "Come on, you guys. Let's carry ol' nervous man out into the foyer. Then we can—"

SMASH! CRASH! The large window by the bookcases exploded inward as a heart-stopping roar tore through the stillness. Joey's hand shot to his face as shards of broken glass pelted him with the force of sprayed water. Where the window had been now stood a huge bear, jaws opened wide in an evil grin, curved incisors dripping with saliva.

"Get me out of here!" Barry screamed as Debbie grabbed his arm and pulled him from the mattress, dragging him across the floor. Grandpa Hanson took hold of Barry's shirt and rolled him through the door, pushing Joey in front of them.

The creature bellowed out another angry roar, fanning the air with mammoth paws.

"Get back!" Grandpa Hanson called to the Webleys and Lizzy as they ran from the dining room. Mr. Hanson raced down the stairs and took hold of Joey who was still fighting to see, shoving him through the door. The others followed close behind, dragging Wrangler Barry as if he were a sack of coal. The man cried out in pain as his leg slammed against the doorframe.

"Where's Sam?" Joey called, his eyes blinking painfully, blood staining his forehead and left cheek.

"Isn't she with you?" Grandma Hanson shouted, trying to be heard over the creature's rage.

"No. I sent her to the kitchen."

"Joey!" A little girl's call sent cold chills down the teenager's back. The voice came from somewhere in the Station.

"Sam. Stay where you are!"

"Joey, I'm afraid!"

The teenager tried to break free from Mr. Hanson's grasp. "Where are you? Sam! Where are you?"

"I'm upstairs. I wanted to send you an E-mail. Now the bear is coming inside and I'm a-scared."

Grandpa Hanson rushed to the doorway. He could see the huge animal rummaging through the den, smashing chairs and tables as it hunted for the voices it was hearing echoing through the Station. Up above, at the balcony railing, Samantha stood alone, hands shaking, face contorted with fear. "Go into Mr. Hanson's office and close the door!" the old man shouted. "Do it *now*, Samantha!"

The girl began to cry. "Will Matshaw kill me?"

"Not if you hide," Lizzy yelled. "Please, Sam. Do what Grandpa Hanson said."

The creature lumbered out into the foyer. Samantha screamed when the mammoth animal turned and stared up at her, teeth bared, eyes flashing with an anger she'd never seen before.

"Go away!" the little girl cried. "Go away, Matshaw!"

The grizzly roared out a response and headed for the curving staircase. Joey broke loose from Mr. Hanson's grasp and raced out of the dining room, straight at the bear. "Hey!" he screamed, waving his arms and throwing anything he could find along the way. "Hey. Come get me instead!"

Matshaw turned and faced him, taken back by the sudden charge. Joey skidded to a stop, brushing blood from his eyes. "You want to eat me? Do you? Well, come on! I'm not afraid of you!"

The creature lifted its head and shook the air

with another unearthly bellow.

"Well, maybe a little," the boy said, his voice and hands trembling.

Matshaw started toward Joey, towering above him, jaws soaked with the white foam of rage. Slowly, one step at a time, the teenager backed out of the foyer and into the hallway. He reached down and took hold of a broken chair leg and held it out in front of him, waving it from side to side. The bear, focusing on the strange creature who would dare disturb his attack on the child, followed.

The two passed the dining room entrance and continued along the dark hallway, facing each other, each determined to win the battle they both knew was coming.

"Joey!" Mr. Hanson called, his summons lost in the overpowering sound of the bear's roar. Then he turned to his father. "There's no escape down there," he whispered. "Joey's backing himself into a dead end."

"Mr. H, Grandpa Hanson," they heard the boy call, "get everyone upstairs. I've got the animal's attention. Hurry. Go *now!*"

Joey saw Mr. Hanson and Wendy creep out into the hallway, followed by the Webleys.

"Come on!" the teenager shouted at the grizzly, waving the chair leg, trying to cover up any sound that might escape from the other end of the hall. "You want me, don't you?" he shouted at the creature. "That's right. You keep looking at me. Don't

134

you turn around or I'll crack your skull."

The beast tilted its mammoth head slightly. Never before had any human stood up to it like this. They'd always run away. It wasn't exactly sure how to handle one who didn't.

Debbie and Grandpa Hanson appeared, helping Wrangler Barry hobble painfully, silently, out of the dining room to the base of the stairs.

"Hey, Barry," Joey called, trying to control his intense fear. "If anything happens to me—"

The wrangler paused and glanced down the hallway. He could see his young friend pressed up against the wall, bear slowly approaching.

Debbie pulled on Barry's sleeve as tears flowed down her cheeks. Grandpa Hanson's hands trembled as he helped the injured man up the stairs. He knew none of them could do anything for the boy. Joey had chosen to focus the bear's attack on himself, and the plan was working. To help him in any way would put everyone else in extreme danger.

"I love you guys," Joey called after them, his voice breaking. "I know what that means because you taught me good. You made me really, really happy, and I'm glad I came to Montana."

Matshaw lifted a giant paw and poised it above her head, ready to smash it down with enough force to silence the creature waving the weapon in her face. Joey closed his eyes. "I love you, Sam!" he shouted.

From someplace outside, a tiny cry carried in

the smoky air. It was like a baby's whimper. The giant grizzly froze, suddenly silent.

The sound repeated itself, this time with more urgency.

The creature whirled around and lumbered down the hallway, crashing through the foyer and into the den. Without slowing, it smashed through the partially demolished window and burst out onto the porch. With a mighty scream of rage, it stumbled down the stairs and raced out across the lawn.

The chair leg slipped from Joey's hand and rattled to the floor. Barely able to walk, he staggered to the shattered window in the den and stood staring out toward the horse pasture. A wind rustled the leaves, parting the smoke like a knife, revealing a young girl wearing tattered blue jeans and a hand-sewn leather jacket standing at the far end of the meadow, holding one end of a rope. The other end was tied securely around the neck of a bear cub. At her feet lay a wooden bow and collection of arrows.

Matshaw raced along the fence and then burst through its timbers, her roar echoing across the valley.

"No," Joey whispered. "Plenty, *no!*"

On and on lumbered the bear, straight toward the defenseless Indian girl and the crying cub.

As the distance between the grizzly and the visitor narrowed, Joey gripped the broken window frame. He was about to see his friend die.

Rearing up on her hind legs, the creature strode the final 100 feet, ready to rip to shreds the being holding her baby captive.

Then, silently, in the blink of an eye, the bear disappeared. It simply sank into the ground, leaving Plenty and the cub alone in the pasture.

Joey's breath rushed from his lungs in a trembling gasp. Had he seen right? Was he crazy? Had the Indian girl just worked some sort of ancient magic right before his eyes?

"Joey?"

Mr. Hanson's voice carried from the upstairs balcony.

"I'm OK," the boy responded. "The bear is gone."

Footsteps shook the foyer as the man and his family raced down the curving staircase and rushed into the demolished den. Joey turned to face them. "She's gone."

Mr. Hanson tried to speak, but could get no words out. He hurried to the window and wrapped the teenager in his arms, holding him tightly as his shoulders heaved in muffled sobs.

Debbie and Wendy joined their father, adding their arms to the embrace. Grandpa Hanson leaned against an overturned chair. "Joey. You . . . you were going to die for us."

Pastor Webley walked over and placed a hand on the teenager's shoulder. "Son," he said softly, "you've just given us all the greatest gift a person can give. Heaven is proud of you today. Thank you."

Joey nodded. "I had some help," he said quietly, pointing toward the horse pasture. Everyone gathered at the shattered window where they saw clouds of smoke drifting randomly across the valley. At the far end of the meadow stood a bear cub. Alone.

The boy's breath caught in his throat. "She was there!"

"Who?"

"She was standing beside the cub!"

"Who was?" Mr. Hanson asked.

Joey broke free and stumbled through the torn opening. "Stay there," he called over his shoulder as he raced down the stairs and hurried across the lawn. Quickly he covered the distance between the Station and where the little cub stood looking lost and forlorn.

From deep in the earth came an angry roar. Joey stopped, then edged forward, stepping lightly over the dry, dusty ground.

A large, gaping pit surrounded by cut branches appeared at his feet. At the bottom stood Matshaw, clawing the soil, screaming in rage. The cub stood peering down into the freshly-dug trap with an expression on its furry face that said, "Hey, Mom, whatcha doin' in that hole in the ground?"

A coiled rope lay nearby. At its center, embedded in the soil, rose an arrow. Joey noticed a note tied securely around its carefully crafted shaft.

He knelt and untied the message. Opening it,

he read: "Joey. Sorry it took so long, but I had to work at night, without making any noise. Call the state forestry people. They can tranquilize the bear and move her far away from Shadow Creek Ranch. Yeah, even White men can be useful—sometimes."

Joey smiled to himself as he continued reading. "I'm going back to Pryor to care for Red Stone. He worries about me, you know. Sorry 'bout burning the mountain, but I had to hide the pit from the bear while I finished it. I'll come back someday. And Joey, whenever you remember the fire on Freedom Mountain, think of me. Your friend, Plenty."

The boy folded the note and slipped it into his pocket. In the distance he could hear the drone of airplanes heading in the direction of Red Stone's towering former home. He knew they'd have the fire contained soon and that everyone would wonder what had caused the flames to suddenly appear.

Through breaks in the smoke, he could see the mountain glowing red on the horizon. The danger had passed. Everything would be all right now, thanks to his mysterious friend who, like her great-grandfather, had brought peace to the valley he'd come to love.

"Thanks, Plenty," Joey whispered, "and I'll remember you, always." Then he began walking back to the Station, a smile spreading across his face. They had work to do—horses to track down, walls and windows to repair, and a zoo to build for Samantha. Yup. There was much to be done on Shadow Creek Ranch. And he was alive to do it all!

CHAPTER 7

Wind and Rain

"Where are we going?" Debbie asked as Wrangler Barry gently pulled her across the porch.

"You'll see."

"Is this a date?"

"Sorta."

"Am I dressed correctly?"

The horseman rolled his eyes and laughed. "Yes, Debbie. You're *always* dressed correctly."

"Are we going in the car?"

"Nope."

"Walking?"

"Nope."

The girl's brow furrowed. "Space shuttle?"

"I don't think so."

The bright early summer sun hung warm and inviting over the ranch, bringing life to all living creatures below. It'd been exactly a month since the bear attack, and things had quickly settled back to normal on Shadow Creek Ranch.

Wrangler Barry had been taken to the doctor in Bozeman who'd announced him not too much worse the wear, thanks to the quick action of Mrs. Webley and her concoctions of ancient remedies. The young man still wore a large bandage on his leg which, according to Debbie, was so he could continue to receive sympathetic glances from his friends and relations.

Everyone had quickly made repairs to the Station, hiding the evidences of the grizzly bear's fury under carefully cut timbers and fresh coats of paint.

A note from the Montana State Forestry Department brought the good news that the enormous grizzly and her cub were now happily roaming the Bob Marshall Wilderness in the northwestern portion of the state and should never bother another human being again. "I think maybe we should take our camping trips in Yellowstone for the next few years," Grandpa Hanson suggested. Everyone agreed.

In the flurry of activity following their close encounter of the dangerous kind, everyone on Shadow Creek had stayed quite busy, preparing the spread for the summer and for the new crop of city teens scheduled to arrive later in the season.

When Ruth Cadena returned from Mexico, Wendy and Samantha filled her in on every detail of their adventure. By now Matshaw had grown to well over 15 feet high and weighed at least as much as a fully loaded boxcar. The woman sat enthralled with each telling, urging the storytellers on as evening crickets chirped and the wind carried faint reminders of the fire.

Before long, the only visible sign of the ordeal was a large, dark stain of ash and destruction spread across the western face of Freedom Mountain. Even the pit had been filled in so as not to "catch Samantha by mistake"—a suggestion Lizzy had made as soon as the forestry people had trucked the bear out of the valley.

Tar Boy, Early, and the other horses had returned, mostly on their own. They seemed content to munch on field grasses and forget the terrible creature that had scattered them across the meadows and mountains.

As Debbie and Barry approached the barn, the girl noticed that Joey had hitched up the ranch's most handsome horse to the wagon. In the back of the carriage waited a food-filled basket covered with a soft, colorful blanket. "Our picnic!" Debbie gasped. "Are we really, finally going to go?"

"You bet your cross-stitch," her companion said firmly. "Nothing, absolutely nothing, is going to stop us this time."

Joey grinned from ear to ear as he helped the two take their places on the high seat. "Have fun," he said. "Watch out for stray grizzlies."

Barry shook his head. "I don't care if we meet

a whole herd of 'em. We're going to Papoose Lake or die trying."

Debbie sighed. "He's my hero," she said. Glancing down at Joey, she added, "Why, I believe that if we met a dragon on the road, Barry'd get out his trusty lance and slay that critter with one swift stab."

"You got that right, Genevieve," Barry laughed. "Now get up, animal. Take us to Camelot—I mean Papoose Lake—and make it snappy!"

The horse lunged forward, pulling the buggy and its occupants away from the barn, over the footbridge, and down the long driveway. Joey watched them go, laughing at Barry's antics as he swung the whip over his head as if he was doing battle with an unseen creature. He could hear Debbie's lilting laughter drifting in the warm breezes.

The road led into the mountains, carrying the happy couple higher and higher, lifting them above the valley and into a world filled with pine trees, granite outcroppings, and song birds. Butterflies flitted with shimmering wings among the summer grasses while wildflowers added splashes of color along the way. Old, weathered crows watched the travelers pass by under their lofty perches and called down raspy greetings.

Debbie felt almost light-headed, not because of the altitude, but because of the man seated beside her, his hands gripping the reins as he expertly guided the carriage along the trail. All of her young life she'd wondered what it would be like when she found the person who would whisk her heart away. The first time she'd seen the strong, handsome horseman, she'd known he was the one, although she had no idea how to tell him so.

The girl smiled, remembering how silly she'd acted during those first months, how she'd tried valiantly to get his attention, even accidentally dunking him in Shadow Creek because of her eagerness.

Then there were those horrible days buried with him under the heavy Montana snows in his crushed truck, watching his life fade while being helpless to do anything about it. The physical therapy sessions that followed, the anger and frustration of discovering that dreams can be as beautiful and as fragile as the mist, had served to bring them closer together in some areas, yet push them further apart in others. They'd endured so much. But each incident, each challenge had only nurtured the desperate need they felt in their hearts to give themselves to each other, although how they could accomplish that wasn't exactly clear sometimes.

Now Barry was a college graduate, and the future stood before him like a blank canvas. To most men, it would be a challenge eagerly accepted, but the man with whom she'd fallen in love had no idea how to begin the painting that would become the rest of his life.

The girl sighed. All that didn't matter to her this fine day as the carriage continued its climb up the mountain road. She was with Barry. Everything else was unimportant.

"You're so quiet," she heard him comment. "Whatcha thinkin'?"

Debbie smiled. "Oh, happy thoughts."

"Good," Barry responded. "Don't lose them."

The girl glanced at him. "Oh, I won't. Not as long as you're with me."

He grinned. "Don't lose that thought, either," he ordered.

The mountain track led through a meadow circled by swaying spruce trees and filled with golden grasses. Then it reentered the forest, only to emerge a quarter mile later at the edge of a blue sparkling lake set like a gemstone at the base of a hill. Wrangler Barry reined in the horse, and the two travelers sat gazing out over the shimmering expanse of water, lost in its beauty and solitude.

"Grandpa brought me up here after our first winter on the ranch," the girl breathed. "He talked about spring, and how sometimes hearts need to be reborn. I'll never forget that day here by Papoose Lake. This place will always be important to me."

Barry nodded. "I've only been by twice before, and it just seems to get more beautiful each time I see it." He turned. "Sorta like you."

She grinned. "I'll bet you say that to all the girls."

"Nope. Just you."

Barry clucked at the horse and guided it along the edge of the lake to a small, grassy rise sprinkled with flowers and a few fallen logs. "How's this?" he asked. "Should make a nice spot for our picnic."

"Perfect," Debbie responded with a satisfied sigh. "I'm curious to see what Grandma packed for our lunch."

"Grandma? She didn't make our picnic. I did. All by myself, too."

"*You* fixed the food?"

"Certainly. I know how to do stuff like that." Barry eased himself down from the high bench and retrieved his walking cane. "You like beans?" he asked.

"Ah . . . sure."

"Good."

Debbie jumped onto the soft grasses and headed for the rear of the buggy. "So, what kinda beans did you prepare?"

"You'll see."

The girl chuckled. "D'you . . . ah . . . bring anything else?"

"Of course," the man snickered as he picked up the heavy basket and plopped it down at his feet. "I've got milk, a loaf of Grandma Hanson's bread, a can of olives, and a box of oatmeal cookies that I had to rescue from Samantha's grubby little fingers."

Debbie blinked. "Beans, olives, milk, and bread? Sounds . . . yummy."

147

"And cookies," Barry added. "Don't forget the cookies."

The two spread the blanket over a level spot and placed the basket in the middle. Barry led the horse to a nearby area of fresh grass and removed its harness so it could graze. "And ignore those clouds up there," he called, pointing with his cane. "They're just passing through. The weatherman promised blue skies until tomorrow evening."

The girl glanced up at a collection of dark vapors rising over the western peaks. "Maybe we should eat a little faster than usual," she responded.

"No way," Barry countered. "It's not going to rain. Trust me."

A distant rumble of thunder echoed among the mountaintops. "Ignore that too," he ordered, lowering himself onto the blanket. "They're just practicing for tomorrow night." He opened the basket and peered inside. "What shall we begin with?"

Debbie pursed her lips. "How 'bout the olives?"

"Good choice," Barry responded, grabbing a can opener and fastening it to the container. "I'm hungry as a bear—" He grimaced. "Bad choice of words. Nothin' like a ride into the mountains to turn on the ol' appetite."

After joining hands and offering a short prayer, thanking God for the lake and the food, they consumed the olives, plucking them one at a time from the can and enjoying their salty taste.

"Not bad," Debbie encouraged. "My compliments to the chef."

"Want some bread?" Barry asked.

"Sure." The girl paused. "Ah . . . Barry, what did you have in mind to put *on* the bread?"

The wrangler frowned, then moaned. "I knew I forgot something. Oh well, Grandma Hanson's wheat bread is so good you don't *have* to put anything on it at all, right?"

Debbie nodded. "I agree. Why mess up a good thing with butter, jam, or some other silly stuff like that?"

"It'd only cover up the natural baked-in flavor," Barry added, trying to sound like a television announcer.

"My feelings exactly."

The man broke a chunk from the loaf and handed it to her. "Enjoy!" he said with an eager smile.

Debbie took the wad of bread and held it up in front of her. "A work of culinary art if I ever saw one," she announced.

"Grandma Hanson's bread should be hung in a museum," the wrangler remarked. "Right up there with Whistler's Mother and that Lisa chick."

"You mean the Mona Lisa?"

"Yeah, her."

The two chewed for a few minutes, listening to the song of a bird and the cry of a distant hawk.

"You know," Barry said between bites, moving

the words around his mouthful of food, "this would be a great place for a house. Put the barn over there by that stand of aspen, fence in that section over there for the horses, and set the house right here on this spot." A splash of rain hit the basket with a soft thud. "I can even see a little dock out in the water with a gazebo on it. Wouldn't that be great?"

Another drop splatted against Debbie's hand. "Yes, it would," she said with a firm nod. "There could be a flower garden around that tree and, perhaps, another one over there by the bank."

Several more raindrops thudded against the blanket and crackled through the grasses as an ominous rumble rose to the west. The sunlight suddenly dimmed, casting Papoose Lake into shadows.

"Of course, there'd have to be a tack house, you know, for the horses," the wrangler added, "and a greenhouse in which to grow seedlings."

"Absolutely," she stated, eyeing the approaching clouds.

"Ignore them," Barry ordered.

Debbie quickly glanced back at him. "Sorry."

The raindrops increased in number and intensity as Barry fished about in the basket. "And now for the main course," he said, lifting a serving bowl and holding it out for Debbie to examine. The girl smiled and lifted the lid. "Is this a Gordon family recipe?" she asked.

Barry shook his head. "Nah. I think it's a Bush's family recipe. But they're my favorite beans. I hope you're really hungry 'cause I heated up a bunch."

"I see that," Debbie nodded. "They'll go nicely with . . . with"—she peeked inside the basket—"with the oatmeal cookies."

By now the rain was falling in earnest, splashing against the plates as he laid them out on the damp blanket. Barry happily worked on, piling a heaping mound of the brown mixture of beans and sauce on each plate. Adding a spoon to the concoction, he handed Debbie her meal, complete with a soggy napkin. "Dig in," he invited, "while they're still warm."

The girl swatted a wet strand of hair from her forehead and took the offering. "They smell wonderful!" she said, dipping her utensil into the pile and lifting a portion to her lips.

A sudden cold wind rushed down from the mountain and swept across the lake, turning the placid surface into a dark, boiling mass. One of the blanket corners lifted and shook as if fearful of the approaching storm.

"You know, Debbie," Barry said, trying to be heard above the moaning wind and splashing raindrops, "we've known each other for a long time." The girl's shoulders trembled slightly from the chill in the air. ". . . and I think we're about as compatible as two people can be. Don't you?"

Debbie nodded, moisture dripping off the end of her chin as her wet hair fluttered in the gusts.

"In the time we've been together, I've grown quite fond of you," he continued. "I mean, really fond of you."

The plate lifted from her hands and drifted away. She remained right where she was, palms held out above her knees. A crack of thunder shook the hillside as a bolt of lightning arched across the sky and disappeared behind the mountain. Barry gripped his plate tightly, fighting the increasing press of rain and wind. His face was drenched and rivulets of water poured from the rim of his leather hat.

"So, I was thinking that maybe we should do something about our relationship. You know, make it a little more permanent?"

Debbie nodded, her teeth beginning to chatter as cold rain soaked through her jeans and hand-sewn blouse and settled against her skin. "OK," she mumbled, finding that her mouth didn't work quite right.

"So," her companion said, placing his plate on the blanket where it immediately rose and tumbled away in the blowing wind, "here's what I've been trying to ask you for the last month." He removed his hat and pressed it against his chest, exposing his brown, wavy hair to the elements. Strands of it began to stick to his collar. "Debbie Hanson?"

The girl nodded.

"Debbie Hanson, will you—"

ZAP! CRASH! Thunder roared just overhead,

shaking the ground with its percussive fury as the clouds threw heavy sheets of rain against the lake and the two defenseless people seated at its shore. Barry closed his eyes and ground his teeth together. Then he stumbled to his feet.

"I give up!" he shouted as angry tears stung his eyes. "*I just give up!*" He moved away from the blanket, leaning on his cane as he limped along. "Why won't You let me alone?" he demanded, gazing skyward, addressing the tempest. "Why? I'm just trying to live my life, that's all. I'm just trying to be a good person and not cause anyone grief. But You hurt me. You keep hurting me! You've taken my legs and my body; You've stolen my dreams and my future. Why God, *why are You doing this?*"

Debbie rushed to his side and took hold of his arm. "Barry!" she shouted, trying to be heard above the raging winds. "It's not God! It's just a storm!"

"Storms can't choose," he yelled, spinning around, his face twisted in anguish. "They can't decide to hurt one person and not another. But God can. He can decide that I'm not good enough, or hard-working enough, or valuable enough. He can hurt me. And He has. The accident? The bear? I was the one who took the fury. I'm always the one who pays the price. And for what? What have I done that's so terrible? Why am I being punished?"

"No!" Debbie screamed. "That's not the way God is. He's kind and loving. He helps people. I learned that at the ranch. I learned by getting to know the kids that come there. They've been hurt, too, Barry. They've been scarred. That wasn't God causing the pain. But it was God who touched them while they were here and made them believe in themselves again. He gave them hope. That's what you need to do, Barry. You need to believe in yourself. And God can help. I can help."

The gale screamed about them as lightning flickered, the ground trembling with each thunderclap. Papoose Lake had transformed from a placid, peaceful body of water into a churning, angry sea.

Barry stood on the shore, facing the wind, feeling the powerful deluge slam against his body. Slowly, as sobs shook his frame, he turned to face her. "I need help," he pleaded, his voice almost lost in the tempest. "I need *you*."

The girl gripped the man tightly in her arms. "I need you too," she said, pressing her cheek against his. "Grandpa said we weren't meant to live life alone. That's why God made Eve." She cupped his face in her hands, and gazed into his eyes. "And that's why God made me."

Barry looked at the girl, drinking in her words. Could it be that God wasn't a God of hurt, but rather a God of healing? Could it be that here, in his arms, was heaven's response to the pain he'd been forced to endure, and to the pain he'd have to face in the years to come?

"Debbie," he whispered. "Will you marry me?"

The girl smiled through the driving rain and howling wind. "In a heartbeat," she said.

Papoose Lake trembled under nature's fury as the two people on the shore held each other tightly, lost in the kind of love that offered the only real shelter from the angry tempests of life. As the storm raged, the mountains of Montana accepted the gale as they had for centuries, letting the winds blow and the rain fall, absorbing the sky's fury without protest or fear.

All along the Gallatin range the scene was the same—boiling clouds, shouting thunder, sheets of wind-driven rain. But under it all, the rocks, trees, and soil remained as they had since time began. The storm would pass, leaving behind a land refreshed and shaped by the angry gale.

So it would be with the couple on the shore of Papoose Lake. And so it would be with the men and women, boys and girls, who traveled from their past to the Gallatin Mountains of Montana and found new hope at a place called Shadow Creek Ranch.

Stranger in the Shadows

Charles Mills

Dedication

To Dorinda,
the center of my world

Contents

CHAPTER 1

Land Beyond the Lights

The dark form drifted along the midnight alley like a phantom. Cold rain fell steadily, creating glassy pools on the rough pavement, hiding torn newspapers and discarded beer cans amid shimmering reflections of neon signs and streetlamps.

Pausing at a corner, the pedestrian looked first one way then the other, searching not for traffic but for other occupants of the deserted section of the city. Seeing no one, the figure slipped quickly across the intersection, hurried to a passageway halfway down the block, and dropped from view, following a crumbling flight of steps to a door hidden below street level.

The shadow in the stairwell fumbled with the lock. A faint click, and the door opened and then closed, leaving the alley empty except for the driving rain and the night. Above the entrance, a faded sign swung on rusted chains, announcing to anyone interested that they were about to enter a portion of a building belonging to the city of Washington, D.C. In letters etched in faded and peeling paint the placard boldly proclaimed: Police Department, Section 31, MORGUE.

The darkened subterranean room consisted of bare block walls and stainless steel examining tables. A rectangular window resting above the outside entrance allowed a dim, colorless light to invade the stillness, illuminating with a slow pulsating glare the scrubbed floor tiles and metal-topped trash cans. If it hadn't been for the marquee across the street, the chamber would have been in total blackness.

The visitor walked slowly across the room and stopped at a table supporting a cloth-draped body. A wet hand reached out and tugged at the covering, revealing the lifeless face of a young man whose beard, cheeks, and hair were still soaked from the storm.

"You had to stay, didn't you?" the stranger said, his words barely above a whisper. "You had to prove somethin', like you was tough. Like you was a man." The voice broke slightly. "Well, now you're dead. So, whad'ya prove? Nothin'. Except that you can die like everybody else."

Pulling the stark white sheet down a little farther, the speaker saw a tiny hole surrounded by a patch of dried blood on the shirt just above the left breast.

Light pulsing from the window brushed across

the visitor's face, revealing angry tears. "Why didn't you run?" he cried out, his words louder than before. "You could'a got away with us. You could'a made it back to the neighborhood, back to the warehouse. You saw the gun. I mean, that jerk was wavin' it around like it were a flag! Knives is one thing. You have to be up close, you know, hand-to-hand stuff. Everybody's got a fightin' chance. Isn't that what you's always teachin' me? But a gun can chase you down. It can kill you from a distance. You knew that. You knew you shouldn't mess with a banger who's got a gun!"

The visitor flipped the covering back over the motionless form on the table, hiding it from view. "So, what am I 'sposed to do now, Karl? Huh? What am I 'sposed to do?" He turned and walked across the dark room. "You're my friend, my *best* friend. We're a team, you and me. We're the best there is in this part of the city. Some people said we even look the same, 'cept I can't grow no beard like you." He paused, then continued, addressing the draped body on the table. "You take good care of me, like a big brother. You know? You teach me stuff. You teach me not to let nobody kick me around."

A muted conversation echoed from the hallway beyond the closed door over by the big sink. The boy stiffened, listening as the voices faded away.

"Captain Harrison said we'd end up down here if we didn't get our stuff together," the young man continued. "Remember? He kept saying, 'Hey

Karl, hey Jared, you two are gonna end up checkin' into my morgue if you don't stop facin' down bangers on your street.' Remember he said that? I guess he's pretty smart—for a cop. He figured out stuff pretty good, 'cause here you are. Now you're dead, and I ain't got nobody. Yeah. He figured it out good."

Jared closed his eyes and released a long, painful sigh as he brushed errant strands of brown hair from his face. The faded Redskins baseball cap he wore shadowed his flushed cheeks and deep-blue eyes. A thin, worn jacket hung from his shoulders, doing little to keep the chill from invading his slender, well-proportioned body.

He'd seen dead people before. Guys got hit a lot on the streets. Every night he'd hear the guns, sometimes close by, sometimes far in the distance. The sirens would arrive quickly because cops would park their patrol cars at the outskirts of the neighborhood in the evening, knowing from experience that someone was bound to be shot, or cut, or bashed before their shift ended. They knew they'd find a body or two lying by a curb or sprawled across the floor of a dirty apartment bedroom. That was life in the land beyond the lights, where the beautiful city with its monuments and government buildings ended and the streets grew dark and dangerous as the sun sank beyond the Potomac.

To the world, Washington, D.C., represented freedom's power and the hope of democracy. But it was a different type of power that ruled the midnight alleys in this capital city.

Tonight was no different than the others save for one fact. Jared had watched his best friend fall dead.

The teenager slumped onto a metal chair and watched the reflected light from the bar marquee across the street pulsate over the floor tiles. He lifted his hand and brushed the cap from his head, letting it drop to his lap.

He wasn't sure how he felt. Angry? Yes. Sad? He didn't totally understand sad, because he'd never known joy. He figured that if he had ever felt joy, even just once, he'd know for sure what sad was. The streets had only sadness. It was almost normal, like breathing, and sighing—and dying.

Leaning forward slightly, the young man studied the still, draped form resting on the table across the room. After a long moment, he spoke. "I'm gonna leave." The announcement came as if the dead body had been waiting for a response to a previously asked question. "I'm gonna go away, far away," Jared continued. "There ain't nothin' here in the neighborhood. You was all I had. Now there ain't nothin'."

The boy stood and walked slowly to the table, trying to find justification for his sudden statement. "You always said, 'What's mine is yours.' Remember? So I'm gonna take some stuff—from you and from the warehouse. It's my stuff now."

13

He pulled on the cover and let its soft, white folds billow at the dead boy's knees. "I'll need the keys," he said. "And I'll take the money from behind the bricks. Should be enough."

Jared slipped his hand into the jeans pocket of his friend and retrieved a small set of keys tied together with a string. Then he explored the back pockets until he found a thin wallet.

Suddenly, he heard voices in the hallway—voices that grew steadily louder.

Quickly he jammed the keys and wallet into his jacket pocket, pulling the sheet back over the prone form before stumbling through the dim light to the door. For a second he turned to look back toward the body. "I'm gonna miss you, Karl," he whispered. "You was my best friend."

He left just as the door across the room burst open, flooding the dim chamber with brilliant light. Racing along the rain-swept street, he rounded a corner and vanished.

Captain Joseph Harrison, a stocky Black man with friendly eyes and close-cropped hair, dropped a pile of forms on the desk by the metal cabinet. His companion, a man wearing a white smock, flicked on the overhead lights and jammed his fingers into tight-fitting plastic gloves as he crossed the room. Stopping by the body, he pulled back the covering and bent low to study the still face. "How old did you say he was?" he asked.

"Eighteen. Nineteen," the officer sighed, rummaging for a pencil. "Brought him in an hour ago. Gang-related. Guess someone didn't like his brand of deodorant."

"Any family?" The medical examiner saw the policeman shake his head. "It's amazing what a little hole can do to a big body," he mumbled, fingering the puncture wound. "Don't see any other signs of struggle. Fingernails are clean, relatively speaking. No bruises or abrasions visible. We'll do a complete workup as soon as my overpaid but thankfully incredibly lazy assistant gets back with the van. I mean, how long can it take to get pizza?"

Captain Harrison grinned. "Death make you hungry?"

"Yeah. Weird, huh?" The coroner chuckled. "So what's with this guy? Did you know him?"

The officer nodded. "Name's Karl. Karl Castanza. I watched him grow up on the streets. He was a nice enough person. Even tried to help people, taking in strays, you know, runaways with no place to go. He'd get 'em food, tell 'em to read books and not skip school. 'Course he also worked both sides of the law, and that's why he kept showing up here at the station handcuffed to one of my men. But we could never prove he did anything outstandingly bad, so we always let him go. Either he was really, really smart or we were really, really dumb."

"You were dumb," a voice called from the hallway. A second later outstretched hands holding a large pizza box entered the room followed by a

plump, middle-aged woman wearing a rain jacket.
The aroma of hot tomato and cheese blended with
the faint odor of formaldehyde. "They didn't have
any olives left," the newcomer announced, dropping the warm box onto an empty examining
table. "I mean, what's pizza without olives?"

"A *good* pizza," the coroner said without looking up. "I hate olives. And what took you so long?"

"Why, Dr. Milton, sounds like you missed me."
The woman blinked her eyes, trying to look seduc-
tive. "I was gone only a few minutes." She turned
to face the captain. "He just can't live without me."

Harrison grinned. "You know, he *did* have that
lonely, frustrated, lost-little-kitty look. As a matter of fact, he even mentioned that he felt you'd
been gone far too long."

"See?" the woman declared, pointing at the police officer while looking at her boss. "Even our
precinct captain can sense how much you love me."

Dr. Milton rolled his eyes. "Just get me a piece
of pizza, Ashly. We can talk about my love life, or
lack thereof, later."

Captain Harrison shook his head and chuckled.
Ashly Peters had been trying to attract the attention of her coroner boss ever since she had transferred to Washington, D.C., eight years before. He
was being as stubborn as she was determined.

Glancing past the pile of papers, he noticed
something peculiar on the floor. "Hey, Doc," he
said, "have you or Ashly used the side-street en-

trance during the past hour or so?"

Dr. Milton gently rolled Karl's body to one side and peered at the blood staining the back of his shirt. "Nope. We've been using the precinct entrance."

The officer rose and walked across the room, following a trail of wet footprints embossed on the black-and-white tiles. "Looks like we may have had a visitor."

Ashly glanced up from the pizza. "Someone musta stumbled in here by mistake, although I'm sure we keep that door locked. Whoever made the wrong turn had quite a shock when he or she realized where they were."

"He," the captain said thoughtfully. "Those are hiking boots, probably a size 11." Harrison stopped and turned. "Check his pockets."

"Whose?" the doctor asked.

"His," Harrison said, pointing at the body on the table. "Check to see if his wallet is missing."

Dr. Milton stuffed his hand into each of the four pockets of the victim's jeans. "Nothing," he said.

Captain Harrison frowned. "Karl always kept a wallet and set of keys on him. I've seen them enough times when he'd come in and we'd search him for drugs or drug paraphernalia."

"Maybe they were lifted at the scene, perhaps by the shooter," Dr. Milton offered.

"No. My men got there within 60 seconds of the gun going off. Witnesses say everybody vanished even before our friend hit the pavement. He just lay out there in the middle of the street alone 'til we got there."

Ashly tilted her head slightly. "So why would someone come all the way to police headquarters to pick the pocket of a dead guy?"

Harrison walked slowly to the door. "Not just someone. A very specific someone who is also very good at picking locks."

"Who?" Dr. Milton asked.

The police officer opened the door and climbed through the downpour to the top of the steps. The darkened street was empty, void of all life. Only the pulsating light of the bar marquee broke the midnight calm. Harrison glanced toward the corner and studied the shadows lining the buildings across the street.

Suddenly, realizing how wet he was getting, he turned, then stopped, staring at an alleyway beyond the intersection. A sad sigh escaped his lips as he watched the rain splash on the sidewalk. "Jared," he said, knowing no one heard. "Jared, I'm so sorry."

With that he descended the steps and reentered the building. He had reports to fill out, schedules to check, and a shift to complete. Understaffed and underbudgeted big city police departments didn't have time to deal with the broken hearts of young boys who'd lost best friends. However, he'd try to stop by the warehouse on his own time. He knew Karl's young companion would be hurting.

Jared pulled the blanket up to his chin and stared at the rafters arching high overhead. He could hear the rough, crackling breathing of others in the big room, sounds to which he'd become accustomed long ago when he first joined "the gang."

A tired smile twitched at the corners of his mouth. The gang. What a joke! Unlike the traditional collections of egos roaming the streets, the gang of which he was a member consisted of the strangest ragtag collection of human beings he'd ever seen—old homeless men, poverty-stricken ex-factory workers, a few handicapped souls in wheelchairs, and even a college graduate who'd found himself on the guilty side of the law. They all lived at the warehouse, an abandoned building within a stone's throw of the Capitol.

Each day they'd head out onto the streets, panhandling the commuters around Union Station, begging on the steps of the Library of Congress, even asking hurried senators and political bigwigs for handouts beside the various government offices sprinkled about their section of the city.

Karl had served as their unofficial leader, offering rousing pep talks on cold, rainy days, encouraging each to "allow the good citizens of Washington, D.C., to be kind to you because it makes them feel noble." He was the one who taught them to be on the lookout for the various news crews buzzing about in search of a story. Members of Congress loved to be photographed acting gracious and tenderhearted to homeless people even if their kindness lasted only as long as the cameras were taping. Such an encounter was always good for a few bucks and the possibility of getting seen on national television. Of course, since there wasn't a TV at the warehouse, no one could be sure if their timid wave ended up on screen or in the network editor's outtake basket.

But Jared had other thoughts rushing around in his mind as he lay beneath the faded blanket listening to the rain brush against the high metal roof and broken windows of the large structure. He was leaving at first light. Unconsciously, his fingers pressed against the set of keys hiding in his pocket. He knew something the others didn't know. Karl had had one secret possession, a "Dream Seeker" as he called it, safely tucked away in another building nearby. No one else knew about it. Just he and Karl. It had been their secret.

A few weeks before, the two of them had taken their mystery machine out of hiding and raced through the dark streets, reveling in the delicious sensations of speed and power. But such excursions had been few because gasoline cost money, and money also bought food at the concession stands at the train station as well as "preowned" clothes at the Salvation Army by the harbor.

Dream Seeker was a luxury item they could seldom enjoy.

Karl had patiently taught Jared how to drive it, but there hadn't been much time for practice. "Someday we'll leave the city," the older boy had promised after a late-night ride. "Just you and me. We'll go to a place I know about, a magic spot far, far away. There you won't have to be afraid, and you'll see such amazing things, stuff you've never laid eyes on before."

To a 15-year-old those words held skin-tingling mystery and excitement. The very thought of heading out on a journey was enough to get him through a day filled with hunger and a night punctuated by gunshots and shouting.

Now Karl was gone, and he wasn't coming back. It was time to leave, and Jared knew it. Often his friend had said, "These streets have a way of eating young boys alive, of stealing their souls and their innocence." Karl had been his protector, his mentor, his friend. But tonight, in the blinding flash of a gun, death had snatched all that away.

Before the city awoke, before the other members of his group would miss him, before early-morning rush hour clogged the streets and interstates, he'd be gone, heading west to a destination he could only imagine.

Time and time again, Karl had promised that joy was out there beyond the city lights, where mountains touched the sky and the valleys breathed pure, unpolluted air. Yes, he'd go before the sun caught him, and he knew he'd never look back.

🐾 🐾 🐾

Captain Harrison parked his pickup by the curb and surveyed the street thoughtfully. The warehouse loomed about a half block away, its neglected exterior faded and worn by seasons and time. The late-afternoon sun did nothing to enhance its appearance. Even though it had been washed clean by the storm the night before, it still looked old and neglected.

In some parts of the city wearing a police uniform marked you as an outstanding citizen worthy of respect and honor. But here, in the long shadow cast by the distant Capitol building, it simply marked you as a target. That's why Harrison had come dressed in jogging clothes and sneakers. His sweatshirt proclaimed in bright, bold letters: "Washington, D.C., a Capital City." Underneath in smaller print it asserted, "Be glad. We could be all be living in Los Angeles where they have crime, racial tension, unemployment, and *EARTHQUAKES!*"

The street was deserted except for an occasional taxicab hurrying by, its driver obviously happy to be watching this part of the city grow smaller in his rearview mirror.

22

A crumpled newspaper rolled slowly along the sidewalk, driven by warm, moist breezes drifting in from the Chesapeake Bay. Such was the autumn weather in the nation's capital—cold nights, warm days. Sometimes that trend would reverse itself unexpectedly, leaving commuters shivering as they hurried between workplaces and their trains and car pools.

Harrison locked the door of his small truck and dropped the keys into his pocket. He'd been to the warehouse a few times looking for suspects or "perps," as police lingo referred to perpetrators. They'd never found anything, but he'd learned of the odd collection of souls hiding behind its walls. He understood how they operated and how far they ventured throughout his city. And he also knew that this particular group of individuals were more interested in surviving than breaking the law, although it was common for some to do one to accomplish the other.

Striding quickly to the front entrance, he looked back at his pickup, hoping that in his absence it would remain all in one piece without sacrificing its innards to some chop shop or quick-fingered entrepreneur who could readily trade car parts for drugs.

Satisfied that the vehicle would be safe for a few minutes, he entered the dark confines of the structure.

"Anybody here?" he called out, knowing that

his shout would clear the area of those who'd rather not be seen. They weren't the people he was interested in at the moment. Harrison wanted information. That was all. He wanted to know where Jared was.

"Who's asking?" a deep male voice called from the far end of the expansive building.

"Captain Harrison. District police."

He heard a broken chuckle. "Why don't you just say, 'Hey, somebody shoot me'?" the unseen speaker declared.

Harrison grinned. "Yeah, like you guys can aim. I'm looking for someone."

"Aren't we all?" another voice said from a different section of the huge, high-ceiling room.

"I'm looking for a young boy. Name's Jared. He was a friend of Karl's."

A long silence. "We was all friends of Karl's," someone else said. "And we're going to nail the jerk that wasted him."

"I'm sure you are," the police captain stated, searching the shadows for a face. "Just don't do it on my beat. Take your war up past Florida Avenue. They've got better ambulances."

A rough, coughing chuckle echoed in the stillness. "Whadda ya want with young Jared?"

"Nothin'. Just wanna talk to him. I'm sure he's takin' last night pretty hard."

After another moment of silence, Harrison saw a lone figure walk from the shadows and stand backlit by the stream of light tilting down from a high window to his left. "He's strong. He'll get over it," the man stated without emotion.

The policeman nodded. "Sometimes a guy needs a little help."

The shadowy figure moved slightly. "Whadda ya gonna do, adopt him?"

Harrison smiled. "Already got a son. Just wanted to see if Jared's OK."

The figure moved closer, allowing front-angled light to fall on his face. Harrison saw an old man, skin lined by years of neglect, staring back at him. "Jared's special. He ain't like the others."

"I know," the officer said softly. "He's been protected. But now that protection's gone. The boy may need help."

By now the old man stood a dozen feet from the visitor. Shocks of snow-white hair jutted from a torn winter cap. "He gone," he said. "Left early this morning."

"Gone? Gone where?"

"Away. Took his bedding, his jacket, his bag, and left."

The policeman frowned. "He's on the street?"

"Sorta."

"Whadda ya mean, sorta?"

The old man moved even closer. "Can I trust you?"

"I'm a cop!"

"That don't mean nothin' 'round here. Can I trust you?"

Harrison nodded. "Yeah. You can trust me. I'm no saint, but I care about people, especially young teens stuck on the streets keeping company with the likes of you."

A smile cracked the scowl on the old man's face. "You said your name is Harrison, right?"

"Yes. I'm Captain Joseph Harrison."

"I heard Karl talk about you, about how you was OK for a cop, about how you could never get anything on him, but he figured you'd hand him a fair shake if you had."

The policeman nodded. "Karl was one of our smarter felons."

"Yeah. He was. He was smart, but not smart enough to run from a gun."

"Is that really the way it was?"

The old man's smile broadened. "Say, you are kinda smart for a cop, Captain Joseph Harrison. You know Karl wouldn't face down a gunman on the street. That'd be suicide."

"So?"

"So, you wanna know what really happened?"

The officer tilted his head slightly. "Is this off the record or on?"

He saw the smile fade. "They was after Jared. The bullet was meant for him. Karl put himself between the gang and his friend, and they shot him down cold, just like that." The man attempted to snap his fingers. "Karl sacrificed himself for the young boy, and Jared don't even know it."

26

A distant siren wailed and warbled for a moment. The two men stood facing each other in the dusty expanse of the warehouse. Finally, Captain Harrison spoke. "Do you know who pulled the trigger?"

The old man pointed to the window and to the city beyond. "Take your pick."

Harrison realized there was a lot of truth behind the old man's words. People died on big city streets for a lot of reasons. Poverty, desperation, lost dreams, the agony of waking up to face another day of neglect and rejection—all these factors helped hold the gun steady as the finger pressed the trigger. He knew his men might find the owner of the bullet, but they could never capture the devil that gave it flight.

The police officer shook his head. "So whadda ya mean by he's on the street, *sorta?*"

The old man grinned. "He got himself a Dream Seeker."

"A what?"

"It's supposed to be a secret, but I knew. Karl told me. He says to me, 'If anything ever happens, I got a way to get Jared out of the city.' And he showed it to me. Nice machine. All shiny. Lots of chrome. Real powerful—"

"What are you talking about, old man?" Harrison interrupted, a touch of impatience in his voice. "Are you telling me that Jared, a 15-year-old juvenile, has a car?"

"A car? No. No! Something better. Something faster." The speaker lifted his arms out in front of him and rolled his right fist up and down. "He's got a Dream Seeker, and you can't catch him. Varoom, VAROOM!" The old man roared out the sound of an engine from deep in his throat. "VAROOM!"

Other unseen voices joined his, echoing the sound of powerful exhaust throughout the building, the noise growing in intensity and volume. "VAROOM! VAROOM!"

Captain Harrison stood in the middle of the abandoned warehouse surrounded by the deafening roar coming from a dozen men's throats, shouting out the sound of escape, the sound of longing, the sound of the mysterious Dream Seeker.

♪ ♪ ♪

VAAA—ROOOOM! A metallic streak of yellow and silver roared along a West Virginia back road, causing the leaves and bushes along the asphalt to flutter and bend violently forward, then return to their normal position facing the sun.

The rider leaned low over the handlebars, sensing the powerful vibration between his legs, marveling in the sensation of speed he'd experienced several times before when he and Karl had raced along darkened city streets.

His right wrist twitched, causing the machine to raise the tone of its whine slightly, propelling him forward at an even greater clip.

The world was a blur. Only the road stayed in focus while broken lines of white flicked by underneath in rapid succession.

Jared felt the warmth of the engine mixing with the cool, mountain air blasting past him in a constant, jacket-grabbing stream. Sounds were muffled, thanks to the tight-fitting helmet encasing his head and jaw. A clear, plastic visor covered his eyes.

He'd dreamed it would be like this, fast and free, with new sights waiting at every bend. But he'd never imagined just how alive he'd feel, hugging the sleek, shiny motorcycle, admiring the four pitch-tuned exhaust pipes extending from the broad engine and sweeping back, two to a side, past his footholds in the direction of the rear wheel where each tilted upward slightly, shouting their angry roar into the slipstream.

Was this it? Was this happiness? It felt so deliciously good, so heart-stoppingly fantastic, so sensual all at the same time. He was free—he was away from the city. At last he was safe.

Cresting a hill, he noticed a broad, empty parking area beside the road. "Grand Lookout" a small sign announced.

Gearing down exactly the way Karl had taught him, he slowed the machine and followed the arrows to the rest area. With a squeak, the motorcycle came to a complete stop, and Jared reached over and turned the key. The roar disappeared, leaving only a ringing, a wonderful, restful ringing in his ears. He sat for a long moment, feeling the silent machine under him as it supported his weight, holding him comfortably aloft, save for his left toes that rested gently on the graveled ground.

Transferring his weight to his right foot, he kicked the stand down and leaned the bike back to the left before swinging himself off. Walking slowly, he headed toward the stone fence separating him from the breathtaking vista of mountain range after mountain range stretching far to the west. The sun hung low over the horizon, waiting for night to summon it into darkness.

Turning, he gazed back at the motorcycle. Karl had stated that it was a Honda CB750, assembled many years ago in a factory in Japan. But Jared knew better. It truly was a Dream Seeker, a magic carpet of escape, a savior for young boys desperate to leave the city.

Reaching into his back pocket, he pulled out a worn and tattered brochure. The document had been safely stored with the motorcycle in Karl's secret hiding place. It told of a ranch far to the west where teens could find safety and acceptance. His friend had spoken of it with longing in his voice. "They got horses," he'd said. "They got mountains. They got trees and rivers. See?" He'd hold the brochure up for his companion to study. It had photographs of teens racing along meadows and climbing mountain paths. The faces were all smiling, all joyous, all satisfied. This was where he was going—where the Dream Seeker would take him.

Jared watched the last rays of the sun sink below the horizon. He stood motionless for a long moment, helmet tucked under his arm, drinking in the sight. Then it hit him. He was feeling happiness. For the first time ever he felt joy.

But, just as suddenly as those new feelings entered his mind, he felt terribly alone. Karl was dead. His best friend in all the world would not be making the journey with him.

In the half-light of dusk, alone on the mountaintop, the boy sank to his knees, clutching the brochure. Evening shadows lengthened about him as he wept, his young heart breaking. Now he knew sadness. He really knew it because, for the first time he'd experienced a moment of true joy.

Nearby, the Dream Seeker sat waiting, its engine clicking and snapping as it cooled in the night air. A small canvas duffle bag, containing his only earthly possessions, sat tied securely to the luggage rack. Inside were other brochures boasting of the beauty of a faraway horse ranch in Montana. In big, bold letters, each invited, "Leave the past behind. Find a new direction at Shadow Creek Ranch."

Night swallowed up the machine and the rider, drawing a silent curtain about the boy, hiding his sorrow in darkness.

CHAPTER 2

Escape-proof

Captain Harrison rubbed his chin thoughtfully, feeling rough stubble scratch against his fingers. He frowned. Forgot to shave again. His wife was constantly nagging him to take the time to plug in his electric razor and relieve his face of its daily growth, an activity and piece of advice he ignored all too frequently.

A knock on his office door brought his thoughts back to the day's work. "Here's the autopsy report on the Castanza stiff," Ashly called with a smile. "Dr. Milton said to tell you that he has no doubt as to cause of death."

"And?" Harrison encouraged.

The woman dropped a folder onto a stack of papers. "The victim was shot."

"You know," the captain said with a sigh, "that's why you people in the morgue make the big bucks. You can see right through the suspicious and get directly to the obvious."

Ashly grinned. "We do our best. Probably a .38. No powder burns, so the gunman wasn't trying to be up close and personal. Our boy was dead when he hit the ground. Didn't find any drugs on or in him. Don't even think he smoked. Alcohol levels were OK. If he weren't dead, he could drive." The speaker paused. "Doesn't exactly fit the profile of your typical street bum."

"I'm discovering he was a very special street bum," the officer stated, glancing at the report. "Took the bullet for a young friend."

Ashly frowned. "I thought there was no honor among thieves."

"The street is full of surprises." Harrison sighed. "Thanks for the report and tell Dr. Milton to send the body on for disposal. Karl didn't have any family that I know of. I've done a computer search and made a few phone calls. As far as society is concerned, Karl Castanza simply never existed."

"OK," Ashly agreed, turning to leave. She paused at the door. "Captain, are you all right?"

The policeman glanced up from the report. "Yeah. I'm fine. Just tired. Too many late nights and soggy pizzas."

The middle-aged woman nodded. "I know what you mean. We all could use a good vacation. How 'bout it? Let's just close up shop and go to the mall."

"Sounds like a plan," Harrison declared. "But first, go out and convince everyone in Washington to play nice. Then we're outta here."

The woman groaned. "Yeah. Like that's going to happen. Well, there's no reason why you shouldn't take a few days off. If you don't mind me saying so, you look like someone me and Doc should be examining, not working with." She smiled. "You might wanna shave, too."

He grinned. "You must've been talking to my wife, both about the shaving and the vacation part. I'll be OK. Thanks for your concern."

Nodding, she left, closing the door behind her.

That evening Captain Harrison quit work early and drove through the crowded streets to his modest home in a subdivision just outside of Silver Spring, Maryland, north of the District. He liked the cracked sidewalks and thick, gnarled trees lining the avenues, their heavy branches echoing the late-day laughter of children.

Many years before, the real estate agent who'd sold him the property had labeled his particular section of town as "mature." Harrison knew that really meant "old." But it didn't matter. He loved the peaceful feel of the place even though his, and all the other houses facing the streets, had seen more prosperous days. Besides, mature also meant cheap. Police captains working for the city didn't need to spend much of their day searching for tax shelters or studying the *Wall Street Journal.*

"Luella? I'm home." Harrison slipped off his windbreaker and hung it by the door. "Thought I'd kick off early." He unfastened his holster and jammed his gun into the wall safe over the bookcase. "Is Perry back yet?"

A smiling face adorned with a set of soft brown eyes framed by dark curls appeared in the doorway leading into the kitchen. "Hey, handsome," the woman called, wiping her hands on her apron. "They said you'd already left when I phoned a few minutes ago. Are you sick? You don't usually come home so early."

The policeman swept the woman into his arms and danced her around the room. "I've come to take you away from all this, to carry you off on my noble steed to my secret castle in the sky."

"Terrific," the woman stated, eyeing her husband thoughtfully. "But can we stop by the grocery store on the way? I need some toilet paper and a can of beans."

Harrison grinned. "Beans and toilet paper. You're fixing Mexican tonight, right?"

Luella rolled her eyes and pulled away from her husband's embrace. "No, silly. I made me and Perry a bowl of soup and some sandwiches for supper which you're welcome to share as soon as he gets home. The beans are for tomorrow."

"But what about my castle?" the man asked, feigning frustration. "When can I take you away from it all?"

The woman thought for a moment. "Thursday. After band practice."

"Fair enough," the policeman chuckled. "Gives me something to look forward to. Perry will be surprised to see me, won't he? I mean, I'm not usually here when he gets home from school."

Just then the front door burst open and a tall, lanky teenager entered, dribbling a basketball as he walked. "Ma? I'm ho—" He stopped in his tracks, allowing the ball to bounce unaccompanied across the room. "Hey, what are you doing here?"

"This is where I live. I'm your dad. Surely you've seen pictures."

The teen shrugged. "What's for supper, Ma? I'm starved." He brushed past the man and headed for the kitchen, retrieving the ball along the way.

Captain Harrison watched him go. This was the way it had been for some time now. He and Perry seemed to be living in different worlds, moons of different planets, their paths crossing less and less frequently.

"Hey," the man called, trying to sound cheerful. "How 'bout us going out to eat? You know, Taco Bell? Something like that?"

Perry turned. "I don't have time, Dad. Gotta get to the gym for practice before the game."

"Gotta big game tonight?"

"Sorta."

"Hey, I'll come and cheer you on. I've been

36

practicing the wave." Harrison lifted his arms and let them drop again. "See? It kinda works better with more people."

"Yeah. Great, Dad. You can come if you want. Whatever."

Harrison stood in the entryway in silence, remembering times when his presence brought shouts of joy and little chubby arms around his neck. Try as he might, he couldn't even remember the last time he'd hugged his son.

"I just want to be there for you—you know, dear old dad cheering from the stands. Didn't I hear you say you were going to be playing the eastern division state champions? Don't want to miss that one."

Perry adjusted his baseball cap and cleared his throat impatiently. "That was last month, Dad. We beat 'em 97-94."

The man's smile faded. "Oh. I see. Well, good for you. Guess I musta had an emergency down at the precinct."

"Yeah," Perry stated coldly, "like you always do. Gotta keep the citizens safe."

"Yes, that's right. It's my job."

"Well, don't let me get in the way of you doing your job. Why don't you call the office right now? There's probably somebody killing somebody even as we speak. Maybe even two homicides if you're lucky."

"Hold on there, young man," Harrison warned.

"People getting killed is no laughing matter."

Perry lifted his hand. "Hey, I'm not laughing. I don't do that anymore. Don't have anyone around to show me how."

With that, the teen picked up the ball and headed back through the entryway and out the door.

"Sweetie, how 'bout supper?" he heard his mother call.

"I ain't hungry." The slamming door punctuated his departure.

An uneasy stillness settled over the house. "What's with him?" Harrison asked, his voice strained with frustration. "What'd I say?"

"Nothing," Luella stated quietly. "We just haven't seen a whole lot of you for the past year—ever since your promotion."

"I can't help that. There's lots to do. People in the District keep messin' with each other. Somebody's gotta track down the bad guys and keep them from doing any more damage. It's my job to run the department. I happen to think what I do is important."

"And you do your work very well," Luella responded reassuringly. "But—"

"But what?"

"But you might try to spend a little more time with Perry. He feels kinda left out."

Harrison lifted his hands, palms up. "I keep a roof over his head, don't I? And he's not exactly starving!"

"No, his stomach's doing quite well. He eats like any healthy 14-year-old. But it's his heart that could stand a little attention. He misses his daddy. He misses the times you used to spend together."

The captain lowered his gaze and studied the designs in the carpet. "I do the best I can," he said.

"I know you do, honey. Perhaps you could do even better. Maybe you could find a few minutes each day to spend with him—just him. He's growing up and has questions only a father could answer. He's—"

RING! The urgent call of the phone interrupted the woman's words. Captain Harrison sighed and raised a finger. "Don't go away," he said, "I want to hear what you have to say."

The woman smiled. "I'll be here when you're finished."

RING! The policeman hurried to the phone resting on the end table at the far side of the little living room. He picked up the receiver as he settled himself on the couch. "Harrison here," he announced.

"Captain? This is Rodney. Hope I'm not disturbing anything."

"No, it's OK. What's up?"

"I mean, I know you knocked off early to be with your wife for supper and I—"

"It's all right, Rodney. Just tell me why you called."

"Well, Captain, something kinda weird has

happened, and I thought you might want to know about it."

"OK."

"I mean, you're not going to believe this."

"Rodney, just tell me what's goin' on."

He heard his coworker shuffling papers. "Well, we got a call from a constable in Ohio. You know that dead guy we brought in two days ago?"

"Which one?"

"Ah . . . Karl somebody."

"Karl Castanza?"

"Yeah, him. Well, we just got a call from a small-town police station in Ohio. Seems they picked him up for speeding."

"They picked up Karl Castanza for speeding?"

"Yup. That's pretty amazing, seeing he's dead and all."

Captain Harrison sat forward in his chair. "What else did they say? And why did they call us?"

"Well, Sheriff North—that's the officer who phoned—said they found a note in Karl's wallet that read, 'In case of trouble or accident, call Captain Joseph Harrison in Washington, D.C.' Our number was written below the message. So North phoned and wants to know what to do."

"What else did he say?"

"He said that Karl was doing 65 in a 45 zone earlier this afternoon. When his deputy gave chase, our guy gave 'em a run for his money. The officer pursued him clean out of town. He would'a gotten away 'cept our guy's motorcycle ran outta gas."

Harrison picked up an envelope resting by the phone and extracted a pen from his shirt pocket. "Give me the Ohio number, and I'll talk to this Sheriff North."

He wrote the information out carefully as Rodney dictated. When he finished, the policeman on the line asked, "Hey, Captain, how can a dead guy get busted in Ohio?"

"I'll explain later. And listen, don't talk about this with the guys at the station, OK? I'll take care of it. Thanks, Rodney."

"Sure thing, Captain. Have a nice relaxing evening with your wife."

As the phone went dead, Harrison released a long sigh. That poor officer in Ohio didn't know what he was up against. He thought he had a freshly shaven speeder named Karl Castanza in custody when, in reality, he was making his ID based on documents found in a dead man's wallet and the word of a fast-talking youngster named Jared. North also didn't know he was trying to detain a streetwise teenager who'd found his way out of more lockups than he cared to remember. Jared wasn't about to stay in Ohio one minute longer than he had to.

But where was he going? Most vagrants headed south in the fall, toward warmer climates. This lad was heading northwest, into cold country. What could possibly be on his mind?

With a plaintive glance at his wife, he placed the phone on his lap and began dialing. Luella smiled knowingly, shook her head, and headed back into the kitchen.

.Å. .Å. .Å.

Sheriff North heard the phone ringing while he was in the ticket booth searching for a box of staples. His office, the pride of Stoneman, Ohio, occupied the old train station, a structure revered throughout the county as the building that once had a freight train run, literally, through it.

It had happened more than 100 years ago, but people still talked of the night when a fully loaded express, headed for the stockyards of Chicago, jumped the tracks and plowed through the loading ramp and waiting room. Since it was an express, and it happened at 2:00 in the morning, no one was in the building except the sleeping station manager, who woke up to find a collection of somewhat dazed beef cattle milling about his place of employment.

Years later, after the trains stopped running along the tracks fronting the rebuilt loading dock, the building had served as a warehouse, then a library, a restaurant, and finally headquarters of the Stoneman Police Department. Other than the fact that it had been the scene of the great cattle crash of 1884, the station boasted another first for the town. It had a jail. And in the jail sat a frustrated young man whose name everyone thought was Karl.

"Andy, can you get that?" Sheriff North called.

No answer. Just the ringing of the phone.

"Andy, are you deaf? Answer it!"

Nothing.

"He ain't here," Jared called, his arms jutting between the bars of his little cell. "Went out for burritos."

"Whadda ya mean burritos? Who ordered food?"

"I did. Got hungry."

Sheriff North, a short, stocky man in his early 60s with leathery skin, white hair, and riding boots, strode across the room shaking his head. "You're not supposed to tell my deputy what to do. You're being detained."

"Well," Jared responded, "being detained is making me hungry."

North rolled his eyes and picked up the receiver. "Stoneman Police Department," he said authoritatively.

Jared saw the man nod, then turn in his direction. "Yeah, he's here. Got him locked up. He broke all kinds of laws rushin' through my town like a bat outta hades. But I was just wondering why he had your number in his wallet."

The man nodded again. "Oh, I see. He's from your precinct and you know him. Well, looks like he'll be staying with us for a few weeks. You can come and get him then, if you like."

Sheriff North frowned, then smiled. "Why, yes, it is a strong, modern jail. Designed it myself. Why do you ask?"

The man lifted his chin slightly. "Yes, we pride ourselves in taking very good care of our offenders. We keep 'em safe and sound here in Stoneman. Haven't lost a detainee yet. We'll certainly take good care of young Karl for you."

Officer North paused. "What's that? You want to talk to him? Sure. Let me get the phone over to him."

The constable pulled out a wad of cord from behind the desk and played it out as he crossed the room until he stood by the cell. "A Captain Joseph Harrison in Washington, D.C., wants to talk to you," he said, passing the receiver through the bars while holding the phone snugly in his own hands. "Make it quick. This is long distance."

The prisoner nodded. "Sure thing, Sheriff. Thanks." He lifted the handset to his ear. "Hello?"

"Jared, what are you doing?" The voice on the line sounded tired.

"Well, hello, Captain Harrison. It's good to hear from you."

"What are you up to, Jared? Where are you going?"

"Yes. I'm fine. They're treatin' me just fine. Deputy's out getting burritos. I love burritos."

"Jared, listen to me. I know why they think

44

you're Karl. You took his wallet and his keys that night in the morgue. But you're not making it any better for yourself running away like this. You don't even have a driver's license, at least one that really belongs to you."

"Yes, I did have to explain that I shaved off my beard, but Sheriff North said the eyes were the same. He's pretty sharp."

The officer holding the phone smiled and nodded.

"Jared," Harrison continued, "there are social services programs right here in D.C. that can help you. You didn't have to leave the city."

Jared grinned broadly. "Well, thank ya, Captain Harrison. You be sure to tell all those nice folk on the third floor that I'm doin' just fine on my own."

"You're in jail!"

The teenager wagged his head. "Now, Captain, I got a roof over my head and lots of food to eat. I just may stick around for a few days. Or maybe not."

Sheriff North frowned slightly.

"'Course, that depends on the kind heart of my arresting officer. Mr. North may insist that I hold up here for a while." Jared smiled at the policeman standing on the other side of the bars. "I know one thing, I won't be drivin' my motorcycle through any more towns so fast. No sir, I done learned my lesson there."

"Listen here, Jared," the voice on the line pressed. "You're shovelin' it pretty deep right now.

That small-town constable may buy your innocence act, but I know better. You're out of your element, young man. You don't know how to survive in a civilized world. Ohio isn't the streets. There are nice people out there whom you can hurt. And there are not so nice people out there who can give you a ton of grief. Karl put my number in his wallet for a reason. He knew you'd do exactly what you're doing if anything happened to him. As a matter of fact—"

"No! You listen to me, Harrison," the boy countered, his young face taunt with sudden tension. "Karl understood about holier-than-thou police departments and how helpful city social programs can be. He knew about foster homes and juvenile detention centers and all those turn-a-perp-into-a-model-citizen projects. That's why he give me the Dream Seeker. And that's why I'm not going to stop 'til I'm where I'm going. You can try to catch me. You can try to run me down, but I'm faster'n you, Captain. I'm faster 'cause I got nothin' to lose."

"Jared. There's something you need to know about Karl. He—"

"He's dead. That's all I know. He stood up to that loser with the gun and got himself shot dead. End of story. Well, I ain't gonna die on some greasy street in no city. I ain't. This is my only chance, and I'm gonna take it."

"*Jared!*"

"Goodby, Captain. It's been a real joy talkin' to you."

The prisoner passed the receiver back through the bars and slammed it down on its cradle. "We're finished," he said coldly. "I ain't got nothin' more to say."

Sheriff North studied the young face staring back at him. "What're you runnin' from, boy?" he asked.

Jared lowered his gaze. "A lot of stuff," he said. "But mostly the streets. I'm runnin' from the streets." He kicked at the base of the bars. "I can't let 'em catch me. Never again."

🥾 🥾 🥾

Captain Harrison sat for a long moment, hands lying limp in his lap. He'd recognized the hurt in Jared's voice. Had heard it before, many, many times in the shouts and anger of young people caught in street crimes throughout the city. The sound was always the same, filled with sorrow and hopelessness, despair and rage.

But the overriding emotion always seemed to be guilt. Poverty and the street made you do things you normally wouldn't do. It turned your thoughts inward until survival became the motivating force in your life. Soon, your very existence became a question of him or me, my needs or his, my life or the life of someone else. All decisions revolved around the need to survive. Emotions such as compassion, tenderness, unselfishness, and forgiveness became buried deep within the soul where they ultimately died from mental suffocation.

Was that happening to Jared? Or was there still hope?

"Is everything OK?" Luella stood nearby, a cup of hot chocolate from the kitchen warming her hands.

Harrison glanced up, then shook his head. "No, honey, it's not. I've got a teenage runaway halfway to who knows where looking for who knows what!"

"Honey," the woman said, seating herself beside her husband. "Don't forget that you've got a problem right here at home—with Perry. He's kinda running away too. You need to help him as well."

The policeman nodded slowly. "I know. Seems I've got myself two young men who are hurting, huh?"

Luella smiled. "Yes. You do."

"OK. Then I'm going to do something about this situation."

"Which one?"

The man stood and faced his wife. "Both. I'm going to do something about both of 'em."

"How?"

"I don't know. But the answer's not here in the city."

"Where is it?"

The man narrowed his eyes. "When I took the promotion, the outgoing captain told me of a place he knew about, out in Wyoming or something, where there was this ranch for troubled kids. He said he was always passing out brochures and stuff, trying to get sponsors for juveniles in the neighborhood. I got a feeling that Jared's heading that direction. That's why he wasn't driving south, but northwest. Ohio is between here and there. As a matter of fact, I remember seeing a folder on this place in the files at work. Yeah. The old captain showed it to me. Montana. It's in Montana!"

"Wait a minute," Luella interrupted. "I thought I heard you say something about the young man being in jail. Can't you just let him serve his time there, then have him sent back here?"

Harrison grinned. "This is Jared we're talkin' about. He uses jails like we use motels. Believe me, he can check out anytime he wants. Besides, he's not guilty of any crime I know about here in the District that would merit us having him shipped back at taxpayers' expense."

"So what are you going to do?"

The policemen walked to the door. "I'm going to go back to the office, find those files, make a few phone calls, and start my vacation."

"What?"

"Yup. I'm headin' west."

"But . . . but, what about Perry?"

The man grinned. "He's going with me."

Luella gasped. "You're taking our son with you to chase down a runaway?"

"Hey, some fathers drag their kids to Disney World. I bring mine along to track down felons. Besides, Jared isn't dangerous. He's just a confused boy trying to deal with the death of his friend and his past life on the streets. You know I'd never put Perry in any danger."

"Are you sure about this?" the woman pressed.

"I'm sure. I've got to do something or I'll lose both boys. And that would be a terrible crime."

Luella walked over to her husband and slipped her arms around his chest. "I love you, Joe," she said softly. "I'll trust that you're doing what you think is best. Just bring you and Perry back home to me in one piece, OK?"

"OK," the man said tenderly. "And maybe, in the process, I can find a home for Jared in this world too."

The captain placed a gentle kiss on Luella's lips, then slipped into his windbreaker, wrapped his gun holster about his waist, and headed out into the cool evening air.

🐾 🐾 🐾

Jared shivered as the frigid predawn air rushed past him. Even though he felt extremely cold, he was smiling. In his mind's eye he could imagine a certain Ohio sheriff arriving at work to find that his modern, carefully designed, and completely escape-proof jail cell now held a new occupant. His deputy.

The late night maneuver had gone off without a hitch. First, he'd asked the dozing assistant lawman for a glass of water. A few minutes later he'd requested another. Then a third. The deputy had finally decided to make life a little easier for himself by bringing the amazingly thirsty prisoner a large pitcher filled to the brim with fresh water from the outside spigot. Since the container wouldn't fit through the narrow spaces between the bars, he'd opened the cell door. Jared, who'd used this ruse once before with a degree of success, happily grabbed the gift from the officer's grasp only to knock the pitcher out of his hands. A gallon of cold water had splashed against the constable, causing a moment of temporary blindness and breathless confusion. That's all Jared needed. By the time the deputy could see clearly again, he found himself to be the soul occupant of Sheriff North's jail cell.

Jared had unhurriedly retrieved his wallet and keys from the station desk while apologizing profusely to the drenched lawman, spent a few minutes in the back room looking for the keys to the fenced-in impoundment area behind the station, strolled out to where his motorcycle was parked, siphoned a tankful of gas from the department's cruiser, and after leaving enough money to pay for the fuel on the front seat of the car, had made his escape, slowly driving along darkened streets, keeping the sound of the Honda just above a low rumble. Once outside of town, he'd twisted the throttle and lunged into the night, leaving a wet and embarrassed constable to await the wrath of his confident boss the next morning.

Not long after the sun had risen to warm the earth, a phone rang in a modest home on the outskirts of Silver Spring, Maryland, and a sleepy police captain answered.

Luella awoke with a yawn as she heard her husband speaking into the receiver.

"He what? When? Oh my! Your deputy? Oh dear. Is the man OK? Good!"

The woman hoisted herself up on one elbow and laid her chin on her husband's shoulder, listening to the one-sided conversation.

"No. No, listen Sheriff North. We're going to track him down ourselves. Besides, I'm sure he's out of Ohio by now, probably halfway to Chicago. Yes. I'm taking on this case myself. No, he's not wanted here in Washington, but I've got a personal interest in this young man. He . . . he needs help. I think I do know where he's going. Montana. Yes, the one with the big mountains. I have reason to believe that's where he's heading. Of course, if I catch him, I'll bring him right back to Ohio so he can finish serving his sentence in your jurisdiction. That's only fair. Yes, sir, I know this is the first time anyone has ever escaped from your jail. It's still a record you can be proud of. And please tell your deputy that the people of Washington, D.C., apologize for the discomfort he had to endure at the hands of one of our juveniles. We're certainly sorry for what happened and hope he stops sneezing soon. That's right, you'll hear from me when I've made the capture. What's that?" Luella saw a smile spread across her husband's face. "Oh, yes, sir, we'll be careful with him. He won't get hurt. You're right, he's a nice young man in his own way. So you'll be hearing from me, OK? Good. Talk to you later, Sheriff North. Goodbye."

Harrison hung up the phone and sank back onto his pillow. "Jared checked out even earlier than I thought he would. That boy must want to get to Montana pretty bad."

"So, will you be leaving today?" the woman asked.

"No, but tomorrow for sure. I've got to work out some things back at the office before I go. You haven't said anything to Perry have you?"

"No. I'll let you break the good news."

"He's not going to like the idea very much, is he?"

"Probably not."

The man sighed. "Funny how, when a guy gets aimed in one direction, it's kinda hard to stop him."

"Oh, really?" Luella responded. "I wouldn't know about that. All the men in my life are so stable and predictable."

Harrison grinned. "Yeah. We are."

The woman chuckled, then rested her head on the man's chest. "What if he doesn't want to get caught?"

"Jared? Oh he'll—"

"No. Not Jared. Perry. What if this doesn't

work? What if it drives the two of you further apart? What will you do then?"

The officer lay still for a long moment. "I don't know," he said softly. "I just don't know."

Outside the bedroom window the morning sun rose higher, warming the leaves and the buildings, lighting the city for another day. Soon commuters would fill the streets, each in his or her own way running to or from what they believed to be their destiny. For some, the journey would bring happiness. For others, disappointment waited at the end of the road.

CHAPTER 3

Shadows

Jared sat sucking on a long, flexible straw, enjoying the sweet taste of chocolate on his tongue. Compared to the fast-food restaurants back in D.C., where it seemed you had to stand in line to do anything, the little eatery had the atmosphere of an empty baseball stadium with just a few customers enjoying a quick meal. No, it wasn't Washington. This wasn't even *near* Washington. He was in Bozeman, Montana, glad that his journey was coming to an end. After four days of riding and as many nights of shivering under increasingly frigid skies, Jared was happy to be anywhere that didn't boast a mile marker.

The little orange pup tent he'd purchased back in Virginia at the beginning of his journey had done a fair job of keeping out rain. But the cool winds and frost-tinged air that increased steadily as he moved north had ignored the space-age material of his shelter and settled somewhere unreachable in his bones. It usually took half a day for the sun to warm him enough so he felt more like a human being and less like an ice cube.

The seemingly endless flatlands that greeted him in Ohio had finally lost their hold on the earth's surface just beyond Billings. Jared saw the mountains coming, rising up from the prairie like proud sentinels, shutting out the sky with their lofty peaks and spiny pine forests. The mountain ranges seemed like magic curtains to the boy, drawing themselves back at his passing, presenting sweeping vistas and heart-stopping grandeur at almost every turn.

From his perch on the speeding motorcycle, he'd caught glimpses of strange curved-horn wildlife roaming the valleys and cliffs, giant birds circling overhead, mammoth beasts wearing what looked like shag carpets on their backs. Groundhogs regarded his passing without even a twitch of their tail. They just followed him with their eyes.

In the pass separating Livingston from Bozeman he'd seen an incredibly long train straining to reach the summit. Every sight was awe-inspiring, every view more wondrous than the one before. If he hadn't been so tired of traveling, he'd have wished that the road would go on and on and on forever. But the signs on the interstate announcing that the next two exits would land him right in downtown Bozeman itself were certainly a welcome sight.

Relief and regret mingled as he leaned into the wind and guided the powerful vehicle off the superhighway and soon found himself driving along Main Street.

Now he sat by the window of the little restaurant, gazing at the mountains to the east and north. Everywhere he looked, he could see vivid reminders that he wasn't on the prairies anymore.

As soon as Jared hit town he asked a few questions. The man at the filling station by the interstate had heard of Shadow Creek Ranch, but wasn't quite sure where it was located. The woman behind the counter at the antique shop across from the tire store said she knew of the ranch but suggested that he visit the co-op a few blocks away. "Most of the ranchers in the area do business there," she'd stated. "They probably can give you good directions."

A man in dusty coveralls and slightly torn flannel shirt had greeted him with a toothless grin. "Shadow Creek? Sure, I know 'em. Come in here all the time. Usually on Thursdays." He'd paused. "Hey, that's today. Why don't ya stick around? Old man Hanson usually shows up about 1:30. That's just an hour from now. If you'd like something to eat, there's a fast-food restaurant down the street. 'Course, food there tastes just like the junk they serve in California or Florida. Might not be the most nutritious fare, but it'll fill you up. You can get a bite to eat and then come back. Shall I tell Mr. Hanson that you're looking for him?"

"Ah, no!" Jared had responded quickly. "I'll just find the restaurant and come back a little later. See ya."

The boy put his burrito down and glanced at his watch. Quarter past 1:00. Almost time.

He noticed a battered flatbed truck pull into the restaurant parking lot. While he watched, an old man and young girl slipped down from the cab and headed toward the front door. They seemed to be in a lively conversation about something. Jared figured the younger of the two was probably about 12. A short crop of blond hair stuck out from under her western hat and her rosy cheeks moved as she talked. She wore riding boots, a pair of worn blue jeans, and a leather jacket covering an *I Love NY* T-shirt.

Her companion, a man in his late 60s, looked at home in his worn coveralls and straw hat. Both seemed enthusiastic about something. And both looked tanned and healthy, as if they lived or worked out-of-doors.

As they entered the building, Jared heard the old man speaking. "Honey, I'm sure Debbie will be happy that you're so willing to help out, but I really don't think she'll be any too thrilled with the idea of having Early in the ceremony. She's planning a wedding, not a rodeo."

"That's just it," the girl insisted, "she's having

a wedding on a ranch. A *ranch!* Ranches have horses, so there should be horses in the wedding."

The two put their discussion on hold long enough to order four bean burritos and a side of Mexican rice. The girl poured herself a glass of ice water and scooped up a supply of hot sauce packets from the condiments bar.

"What exactly do you have in mind?" the man asked as he retrieved a small pile of napkins. "Do you want Early to pull a wagon or something?"

"Pull a wagon? My horse? No way. I think he should stand up with the bride—you know, with the other bridesmaids. Tar Boy could stand up with Barry. It would be so neat! I'll bet no one has done *that* in a wedding before."

"I think you're probably right," the old man said with a chuckle. "Instead of a best man, we could have a best horse."

"Exactly," the girl enthused. "Then they'll know they got married Montana-style. The idea is brilliant."

After picking up their order, they made their way to a table by the window, not far from where Jared sat. The boy frowned. That youngster in the leather jacket looked familiar, as if he'd seen her before. Or was it just her picture? Wait a minute. Yes! Her picture. She was one of the smiling faces in the brochure.

Jared turned quickly and studied the battered truck parked across the lot. It was covered with mud and dirt, but he could just make out some letters printed on the door. Squinting, he studied their random outline carefully. Sure enough, with a little imagination he could just make out the words, *Shadow Creek Ranch, Bozeman, Montana.* He glanced back at the couple. They were the very people he'd been asking about. As luck would have it, they enjoyed Mexican food too.

"So if Debbie doesn't want Early to stand up with her, what can he do?"

The man Jared now realized must be the ranch owner leaned forward in his chair. "How 'bout if, when your dad walks Debbie up the aisle and Pastor Webley says, 'Who gives this woman to be joined with this man?' Tyler can say, 'I and these horses do'?"

The girl puckered her lips slightly. "I don't know," she said between chews. "Early is really hoping to take a more active role in the ceremony. He and that glue factory of Joey's are feeling a little left out."

Her companion sat for a moment savoring the spicy taste of his meal. "How 'bout if we had them as greeters? They could stand out on the lawn welcoming everyone to the ceremony."

The girl nodded. "Keep talking."

The old man stopped chewing. "I've got it. Early and Tar Boy can be in charge of the guest book. Of course, you'll need to be out there as well, showing people where to sign and stuff, but this way the horses are actually on the program. We can list their names in the printed order of service and everything. It will say, 'Guest book: Early, Tar Boy, and Wendy Hanson.' It's perfect!"

The youngster nodded. "I think you're on to something here, Grandpa. Now if we can just convince my airheaded sister of our plan, we'll be home free."

"You just leave that to me," he advised. "I'm sure she'll see the value of having such fine livestock in her ceremony. Why, she should be proud that those two stallions even want to attend. Most horses could care less about who marries whom."

Wendy edged closer to him. "You're the best, Grandpa," she said with a smile. "Sometimes we even think alike."

Jared saw the old man frown, and then nod. "I guess we do. They say great minds run in the same vein."

"That's right," the girl stated. "Take your new old truck, for instance. I, like you, miss the old truck and am extremely upset that that stupid bear ate it." Jared blinked as his throat seized in mid-swallow. "This truck just doesn't have the same soul. It doesn't even *start* as often."

The old man lifted his hand. "Let's keep that little piece of information to ourselves, OK?" he said. "Your grandmother is still mad at me for not buying new. Why, new trucks don't have any soul at all. They just sit there looking shiny and perfect.

61

Who wants that? Give me a vehicle with a little character, a flaw here and there. I can relate to a truck like that. And you're absolutely right, nothing will ever take the place of my old one. Nothing."

The two sat in silence for a moment as if remembering a long-lost friend. Then they quickly finished their meal and gathered up their plates, napkins, and cups. "Just one more stop at the feed store," the old man said as they walked out the door, "and we'll be headin' home."

"I just know Debbie's going to like our guest-book idea," Jared heard Wendy say. "Imagine. She wanted a ceremony with no horses at all. What kinda wedding is that?"

The door swung shut and the teenager watched the two retrace their steps to the truck. At one point the girl noticed the shiny motorcycle resting nearby and ran over to have a look. The old man followed, and they stood admiring its clean lines and sleek profile. He saw the rancher study the license plate and then glance back at the restaurant. Jared turned his head and pretended to take another sip from his glass.

The ranch owner placed his hand on the young girl's shoulder, and they ambled over to the old ranch vehicle. After buckling themselves in and blowing a puff of blue smoke out the tailpipe, they drove away.

Jared hurried to the door and ran to the Honda. This was going to be a piece of cake. From here on out it was simply a matter of keeping the old truck in sight. He knew it would eventually lead him out of town and directly to his destination. But he had to be careful. Shadow Creek Ranch might be a welcome destination for troubled teens, but they usually showed up only when invited and after making proper arrangements. He didn't know how those people would react to having someone appear unexpectedly on their doorstep. For the moment at least, he'd play it safe and learn a little more about this strange family who were, apparently, planning a wedding that included horses manning the guest book.

With a smile Jared shook his helmeted head as he pressed the starter button by the throttle grip, bringing the engine to life. And he thought *city* people were weird.

.𝕃 .𝕃 .𝕃

It was late afternoon by the time the truck pulled up to a big hotel-like structure hidden in a cozy valley formed by folds of the Gallatin National Forest. Jared, who'd been following the vehicle since it left Bozeman, guided his motorcycle off the gravel road and studied the distant scene, hands shading his eyes from the western sun. He noticed that the large dwelling rested beside a sparkling stream running the length of the valley. A small footbridge arched over the waters, and a well-used pathway led to a fenced-in pasture where horses grazed contentedly on warm autumn grasses. A shed and barn guarded one end of the enclosure while a stand of trees stood watch over the other.

He'd been careful to stay far behind the truck while on the highway. For the last five miles he'd followed its dust trail. Jared knew the occupants of the vehicle had no idea anyone was following them.

As he crouched behind the bushes by the road, he could see other people moving about the ranch, seemingly busy at work. A boy, about his age, maybe older, went in and out of the barn, carrying newly arrived supplies over the footbridge. He saw an older woman make her way to the truck, gather up several bags of groceries from the back, stand for a moment looking at the vehicle, then walk away shaking her head.

Edging closer, making sure no one detected him, Jared positioned himself on a hillside to the north of the big building. A younger man appeared on the upstairs balcony and waved at the girl he knew to be Wendy. She returned the greeting and motioned toward the pasture and shouted something about going to see Early. Then she raced across the footbridge and hurried through the open gate, almost toppling the boy burdened with a load of feed sacks.

The ranch seemed to buzz with activity—people running here and there, carrying things, talking to each other, laughing, or sometimes just gazing out over the expanse of mountains to the east and south. It was so peaceful even amid the tumult of activity. The air smelled fresh and pure. The sky hung blue and unpolluted overhead, like a newly painted canvas punctuated with cotton candy clouds and a brilliant sun.

Even the trees seemed to appreciate their surroundings, standing straight and tall as if proud to be a part of the valley.

Out onto the porch ambled a young woman with dark flowing hair and slender build. Jared's breath caught in his throat. She was beautiful—more beautiful than any girl he'd ever seen. "This must be Debbie," he said to himself, "the one who's getting married."

Sure enough, a man walking with a cane came up beside her and slipped his free hand about her waist. They spoke softly to each other while the late-afternoon sun outlined them both with a ring of yellow light, reminding Jared of a couple standing under a trellis atop a wedding cake in a bakery window. Even from this distance, it was plain to see that the two people were deeply in love.

The old man he'd observed at the restaurant climbed the steps and stood by the couple. All three gazed out across the valley. Suddenly the girl turned and spoke one word Jared recognized. "Horses?"

The boy stifled a giggle. The old man apparently had told Debbie of Wendy's plan for the wedding. By appearances, it didn't look as if she were accepting the concept with any degree of joy. The girl spoke the word again. "Horses?"

Jared saw Debbie's male companions discuss the idea between themselves. Then they presented their case to the girl once again, this time with much arm waving and encouraging gestures. It seemed Wendy had found not one but two advocates for her plan.

At long last, the girl nodded, but seemed to have some conditions for her agreement. After hearing her out, both men also nodded and left, leaving the bride-to-be standing alone on the porch. Before reentering the building, she glanced out across the pasture where Wendy was leading a handsome brown animal along a winding path toward the barn. Jared saw Debbie shake her head and say the word one more time. "Horses?" Then she turned and shuffled back into the building.

The boy studied the sun as it continued its journey toward the western mountain tops. It would be night soon, and if the recent past served as any indication, he'd have to find a spot somewhat sheltered from the cold to set up camp. He had food and several changes of clothes left in his bag, so he could stake out the ranch for at least another three or four days.

The last thing he wanted was to be sent back to Washington, D.C. Of course, he did have the little matter of Ohio to contend with. In that state he was a wanted man, a fugitive from justice, a jailbreaker.

Jared looked around. No, this was too close. They'd see his campfire. Besides, he was probably on Shadow Creek Ranch property.

Then he remembered a dirt road turnoff several miles back, between the ranch and the highway. Yes. He'd follow that road deep into the woods and find a spot where he could set up his tent.

Camping out was nothing new to the boy. He'd been doing it all his life. Of course, in the city he usually found shelter under a bridge or in abandoned warehouses. But the Montana countryside had no bridges or warehouses here. Just trees and mountains and rocks.

Jared hurried back to his hidden motorcycle, then walked it the first half mile away from the ranch. When he knew that no one would hear it, he brought the engine to life and sped away. Tonight, the woods would be his home. Tomorrow, he'd discover more about the people who lived on Shadow Creek Ranch.

"This is kidnapping." Perry sat, arms crossed, staring out at the city lights as they flashed past his passenger-side window.

"I'm not kidnapping you," his father laughed. "You're my son, my own flesh and blood. We're just going on a little vacation. I thought we'd get a four-

or five-hour jump on our trip before turning in."

"What about school?" the boy countered. "If you take me away, I'll flunk out for sure. You wouldn't want me to do that, would you?"

"We'll be gone only a couple weeks," the driver responded with a chuckle. "Besides, I talked with your homeroom teacher. She gave me some assignments for you to complete while we're on the road, so you won't get behind. She even said that me taking you to Montana is a great idea. Of course, I didn't say *why* we were making the trip. Your teacher mentioned that she wished more fathers would spend quality time with their kids."

"Quality time?" Perry chuckled. "This isn't quality time. This is kidnapping."

Captain Harrison eased into the traffic crawling along Interstate 495, the heavily traveled beltway around Washington, D.C. "Look, Perry. We've been through this before. I just want to spend some time with you, that's all. At home we're both so busy, our lives are jam-packed with school and work. We never see each other. Now we can. For two whole weeks—14 wonderful days!"

"Yeah, but it's not really a vacation 'cause you're huntin' down that stupid runaway. What kinda jerk would drive to Montana? He must be a real loser. Man, I'd head for California or Miami if I had a motorcycle."

"You would? Why?"

The boy shook his head. "Well, for one thing,

it's warm. And you're not gonna get buried in a blizzard or eaten by a wolf or somethin'. Another thing, you can't make any money in Montana. How many people have you heard about that make money in Montana?"

Captain Harrison shrugged. "None?"

"Exactly. Rich people, or people who want to be rich, head straight for Los Angeles or Miami. That's where the big bucks are."

"So you want to be rich?"

"Of course. Doesn't everyone?"

Harrison carefully switched lanes. "Not me. I don't want to be rich. I just want to make a good living, bring home the groceries, and pay the mortgage every month."

"Yeah, well, then you'll never make it big," Perry said with a sigh, as if he'd considered his father's financial situation before. "If you ain't gotta dream, you'll stay just where you are for the rest of your life."

Harrison studied his son's face. "Is that what you dream about? Making money?"

"Sure. I'm gonna to be loaded, you know, live in a big house. Drive a Lexus. You won't find me workin' at some useless job in a run-down police station—" He stopped suddenly. "I mean . . ."

"I know what you mean," his father stated. "You're not going to be like me, right?"

"No. I didn't say that."

"You didn't have to," Captain Harrison asserted. "And . . . I guess I can't blame you."

Perry lifted his hand. "You're a good cop, Dad. Really."

The man gazed out at the bumper-to-bumper line of cars. "I don't know. I might be an OK police officer, but I'm not doin' all that great in the dad department. I mean, look at this. The only way I can get my son to go on a vacation with me is to kidnap him."

Perry didn't respond. He just sat watching the traffic as it snaked along the beltway. Truth is, he didn't think too much of his father's work. After all, it snatched him away day after day, keeping him in the city for long hours. When he needed him, he was always gone. Weekends, evenings, even some holidays the story was always the same. Mom never complained. She'd always say, "What your father is doing is important." Yeah, sure. That was the one excuse that kept eating at his young mind. Whatever was occupying so much of his father's time in the city must be more important to him than his own son. Perry hated that thought, but it kept returning over and over again. It had gotten to the place where even seeing a policeman on the street made him cringe. The bad guys got more attention than the good sons who stayed at home.

Now there came out of the blue this Jared jerk who could make his father drive for days and days to some godforsaken state in the middle of nowhere when *he* couldn't even get the man to show up for a basketball game. *Let one street bum run off, and dear ol' Dad is hot on his trail like a coonhound baying through the woods.*

Vacation? Who was he trying to kid? This was police business—*official* business. It was nothing but the same old story, except this time he'd had to come along and get his nose rubbed in the very activity that kept his father a stranger to him.

Dad was right. He didn't want to be like him. No way! He'd find his happiness in big expensive houses and a cream-colored Lexus. Then he wouldn't have to worry about those idiots on the streets who stole guys' dads along with jewelry and VCRs. When he grew up, things would be different. Life would be different.

The little pickup truck followed the line of cars onto the I-270 spur heading toward Frederick, Maryland. His father insisted that he go along on this joyride to nowhere, but he didn't have to like it. In a couple weeks they'd be back in Washington and he could surround himself once again with things that really mattered—basketball, friends, and dreams.

♫ ♫ ♫

Jared sat bolt upright, eyes wide with terror. They were coming. He could hear them in the hallway.

Hide! Hide in the closet!

Voices. Angry voices. They were saying something about his dad, about how he cheated them. His father's voice was thin, almost breathless as he tried to explain something.

Bang! Bang! The sound shook him with each percussive jolt.

Shouts. Running feet. A door slamming. Silence.

Wait. Don't go out. Stay in the closet. Don't make a sound. They'll hear you. They'll hear you!

Jared's hands trembled as he gripped the tent pole for support. *What's that? What's that noise? It's . . . soft, like breathing.*

The grimace contorting the boy's face began to relax. *It's pretty, the sound.* Soft like his mother's voice used to be. She'd sing to him—would hold him and rock him back and forth, back and forth in the chair that squeaked.

See? There's her face. She's smiling and brushing her hand against his cheek. *Listen to her singing. It's so soft, like the wind in the trees. Like the voice of the wind sighing in the branches overhead.*

Jared released his death grip on the pole and sank back onto his sleeping bag, body drenched with sweat, causing him to shiver in the cold night air. The wind. It had been only the wind.

He pulled the sleeping bag over his head and pressed the material against his face until the pressure hurt. The dream had come again. Or was it a dream? It seemed so real, almost like a memory.

Jared's shoulder's shook as tension gave way to tears. He felt so lonely, so lost. No one wanted him. No one cared about him. For a while, Karl had been his friend. But now he had no one to protect him. He had to run, to hide, to keep in the shadows like some fearsome beast afraid to show his face to the world because they'd catch him and put him in a little room with metal bars. It had happened before, many times. But he'd always run. He'd find a way to escape because they really didn't want him. They just needed someplace for him to be.

If people he met at gas stations, stores, and on horse ranches knew the truth, if they understood who he really was, they'd turn away. "You're just a street bum," they'd say. "A loser like all the others polluting our cities and town. You belong where I can't see you. Now, go way. Stay away. You're not wanted on my street, in my city, on my road."

But he wasn't a loser. He knew that. He was Jared, a boy who had no one to love. Just down the road was a beautiful home filled with people who cared about each other, but he couldn't join them. No. They'd send him back—they'd tell him, "This ranch is for young people who don't run and hide. You can be only a stranger here, a stranger in the shadows. Haven't you seen the pictures? Haven't you seen the smiles? Can you smile? No. You don't know how to smile so you must stay away or we'll be afraid of you."

The boy closed his eyes tightly. "I ain't a bad person," he sobbed into the sleeping bag held tightly against his face. "I wanna learn how to smile like those faces in the pictures. Please, somebody teach me. Somebody hold me and rock me back and forth, back and forth. I won't cry. I won't make a sound. Oh, please! I don't want to be a stranger no more."

The tiny tent hiding in the big woods fluttered with the passing of the wind. High overhead, far above the trees, the stars regarded the scene without emotion. They simply hung in space waiting for dawn's arrival like passengers at some cosmic train station.

Jared's sobs grew fainter and fainter as sleep recaptured him, pulling him into the stillness, shutting him away from the reality of the present and the terrifying images that haunted his past and his dreams.

A few miles down the road an old man stood on the front porch of a stately way station staring out into the darkness. He listened to the wind moaning through the trees and watched the stars drift slowly across the heavens.

His lips moved, forming words to a familiar prayer. Then he turned and reentered the building, leaving the night to the shadows, and the strangers who lived among them.

CHAPTER 4

The Loft

Jared settled himself as comfortably as he could among the bales of hay, making sure he was well hidden.

At dawn he'd driven along the gravel road to the spot where he could safely hide his motorcycle in the bushes. Then he'd scrambled down the embankment just as the unseen sun began to touch the eastern sky with the blush of a new day. Following the creek, he'd quickly skirted the big way station and stumbled through the dew-dampened grasses to the horse barn.

As he passed the house, a dog had begun barking, but he'd heard a young female voice call out, "Quiet, Pueblo! It's against the law to bark before the sun comes up." That seemed to do the trick, because the commotion ceased immediately.

Now he had snugly tucked himself into a small corner of the barn, up among the hay bales where he could watch everything that went on below and where, hopefully, no one would see him. He'd noticed a lot of activity in and around this structure the day before, so he figured this would be the perfect place to learn more about the people who inhabited the ranch.

Satisfied that all was well, he reached into his jacket pocket and withdrew his breakfast—an apple and a piece of peppermint candy. He also had a stick of gum in there, but decided to keep it for later. His other pocket contained lunch—five carrot sticks and an extra burrito he'd purchased the day before at the restaurant. As far as he was concerned, he was all set. Of course, there was one problem. His lofty perch didn't come with a bathroom. He figured he could slip into the bushes behind the barn if nature summoned him with any degree of urgency. There'd be no need to worry about any strange odors. The place smelled exactly like what it was . . . a barn.

He could hear horses milling about in their stalls and could see others out in the pasture standing like statues in the cold morning mist. The view from the loft out through the open window was tranquil—like paintings he'd seen on art store walls and in books during those rare occasions when he'd actually shown up for classes at the local public school. "You gotta get educated," Karl had told him many times. But it was hard to learn something when your stomach was empty. Besides, survival on the streets was a full-time job. Learning to read would have to wait for another time, another place.

On some days the homeless group he lived with ate like kings. On others, they had to spend many hours on the streets panhandling enough money to buy even a small meal. The cash reserve tucked away in Karl's secret hiding place where he'd kept the motorcycle had allowed the teenager the luxury of eating twice a day since leaving the city. Food, gas, and some much-needed camping supplies had drained that fund considerably. Jared figured he could eat for one more week and fill the motorcycle's gas tank one last time. Then he'd have to switch over to plan B. He hoped that wouldn't be necessary.

The sound of footsteps interrupted his thoughts. The boy lowered himself behind a bale of hay and waited, half-eaten apple in his hand.

"Early? Come here, boy." It was Wendy, the girl he'd seen at the restaurant. She entered the barn and shuffled over to one of the large covered containers by the door. Lifting the lid, she thrust her gloved fingers into a pile of what looked like brown seeds. Retrieving two handfuls, the girl closed the lid with her elbow and walked back to the door.

A small, brown horse galloped up to the entrance and happily munched down on the feed held out to him.

"You're in," she said, watching the animal chew.

"Both you and Tar Boy. Worked it out last night. We all can stand on the lawn and welcome everyone to the wedding. I'm supposed to tell people to sign some book with a stupid big pen with a feather stuck in it and hand out printed programs. Yeah, like they need a program to know what's going on. Debbie will say 'I do,' Barry will say 'I do too,' and they'll be married. How complicated is that?"

Early gobbled another mouthful of the feed piled in Wendy's cupped hands. "I don't know what the big deal is," the girl continued. "I mean, why even have a ceremony? They can get Pastor Webley to marry them without all the fuss. I asked Dad and he said to be properly married in Montana, all you have to do is go down to the Law and Justice Center on South 19th Street in Bozeman, get picture IDs made, have Debbie tested for rubella—that's some kinda gross and disgusting disease—and then she and Barry would fork over about $40 each. Some bozo would say a few words, they'd all sign a paper, and, bingo, end of story. Now, doesn't that sound like a whole lot less hassle to you?"

Early snorted, spraying feed all over Wendy's legs. The girl didn't even seem to notice. "My feelings exactly," she said.

More footsteps from somewhere nearby. "There you are," a male voice called warmly. "I thought I might find you out here."

"Hi, Grandpa," the girl said as the old man ambled up beside her. They stood looking out over the dimly lit pasture, drinking in its quiet beauty.

"We'll have a killer frost any morning now," the man declared. "Yup. Any morning. I can feel it in my bones."

Wendy brushed off the last of the feed from her hands and settled herself with a sigh in the entrance to the barn. "Grandpa, why do people have to get married?"

The old man lowered himself to the girl's side. "Love, I guess. When a man and a woman love each other, they get married."

"Yeah, but, why? Why can't they just be good friends forever. I mean, take for instance, Debbie and Barry. They go around like idiots hugging and kissing each other until I about barf. They give each other love notes and wink across the table and sit by the window with their heads together. They're always sighing and laughing at the dumbest things."

"They're in love," Grandpa Hanson said.

"So, why can't they be in love and not get married? Then Debbie can stay in her room down the hall from mine and Barry can live out here in the barn in the summer with Joey and everything can be the same as it is."

The old man smiled. "That would be all right for us, but Debbie and Barry want to be together all the time, to be part of everything the other person does. They want to *belong* to each other."

"Well," the girl said, "Early *belongs* to me, but you don't see us asking Pastor Webley to marry us."

Grandpa Hanson chuckled. "No, I don't, although the way you care about that horse, I wouldn't be a bit surprised at the request. You see, being friends is one thing. But Debbie and Barry want to be more than friends. They want to be what the Bible calls 'one flesh.' They want to join their lives on all levels—spiritual, emotional, and physical. I guess you could say that Barry wants to know what Debbie looks like the moment she wakes up in the morning."

"Hey," Wendy sniffed, *"I've* seen that. He's in for a shock."

The old man stifled a giggle. "What I'm trying to say is Debbie and Barry want to share their nights together too, to enjoy being man and woman."

Wendy gasped. "You mean, they want to have *sex?*"

"Yes."

The girl lifted a finger. "Does Dad know about this?"

"I'm sure he does."

"You mean, marriage is just so you can *sleep* together?"

Grandpa Hanson leaned back against the door frame. "They want to do more than that. Debbie and Barry want to *live* together, to spend their lives as committed partners, two people who've promised God and humanity that they will love and care for each other come what may. It's a very

80

beautiful thing. God invented marriage in Eden when He made Adam and Eve. They were earth's very first married couple, and God Himself performed the ceremony."

Wendy tilted her head slightly. "So this marriage stuff is God's idea?"

"Yup. He created it so a man and woman could feel secure in each other's lives, knowing that they've promised to weather the storms of life together. God even says He'll help them keep their promise if they'll let Him."

"How?"

"Oh, He gives them loving thoughts, provides strength to forgive, power to overcome temptations, stuff like that."

Wendy thought for a long moment. "Is that why my mom left my dad?"

"What do you mean?"

"She didn't let God help her stay in love?"

Grandpa Hanson nodded slowly. "I think that's a pretty good description of part of what happened."

"So," the girl continued, "Debbie and Barry are doing what God wants them to do by getting married?"

"Yup."

Wendy nodded. "I guess that makes pretty good sense, except the sex part. That's still a little weird to me. But if Barry wants to start his day seeing what Debbie looks like when she wakes up, then I guess it's his funeral."

"I guess," the old man agreed.

After a long silence, the girl turned to her companion. "Grandpa?"

"Yes?"

"Do *I* have to get married someday?"

"Only if you want to . . . if you find the right guy."

Wendy gazed out across the pasture. "What will he be like?"

"I don't know. Tall, dark, handsome. That seems to be the standard nowadays."

The girl nodded. "Sorta like Early?"

Grandpa Hanson chuckled. "OK. But with a few less legs. And I don't think you'd want a guy with such a big nose. I mean, imagine if he caught a cold."

"*Gross!*" Wendy squealed.

"And I don't think you'd want your man eating hay in bed."

"No. No!" the girl giggled.

"And you might want someone a little neater in the personal hygiene area."

"All right. *All right!* I get the picture!"

Wendy and her Grandfather laughed and laughed, holding each other for support. Even Jared couldn't help but join in their mirth, burying his giggles in his hands.

After a few moments the two people seated at the barn entrance calmed down and grew silent. Wendy turned to her companion, her face serious once again. "Grandpa, just one more question. Will Debbie still be my sister after she marries

Wrangler Barry? Will she still love me?"

The old man slipped his arm around the girl's shoulders. "Honey, I can guarantee you that Debbie will love you as much as a sister can love a sister, maybe even more."

"I don't know," the girl stated. "She doesn't pay all that much attention to me lately. Now she's always talking about the wedding and how she and Barry are going to build a house up by some lake somewhere someday. I don't feel like I'm very important to her anymore."

Grandpa Hanson gently brushed blond strands of hair from the girl's face. "Well, maybe you should talk to her about how you feel. Maybe you need to remind her that you're still around and sure could use a little attention."

"You think so?"

"Absolutely. As a matter of fact, you could even ask if there was anything you could do to help her prepare for the big day. But you might want to leave horses out of the deal. We've already convinced her to have Early and Tar Boy manning the guest book. That might be all the ranch-type stuff she'll tolerate."

The girl sighed again. "OK. I'll see what I can do. I did have this idea for having Pueblo help Samantha with the flowers when she throws them down the isle, but I'll keep that to myself."

"Good," the old man stated while stumbling to his feet. "You can save up all your great wedding plans for *your* wedding day."

"Grandpa, I'm only 12!"

"Hey, Debbie was 12, and she grew up faster than a sunflower stalk in the spring. You'll be a young lady before you know it, and heaven help the boys in Bozeman."

"Grandpa!"

The two hurried away, throwing punches at each other and laughing, filling the quiet pasture with their joy.

Jared settled himself in the hay and took a bite of his now slightly brown apple. Grandpa Hanson seemed like a nice man, full of wisdom and good advice. A bit like Karl had been. It was plain to see that Wendy loved him dearly.

But who was this God he was talking about, the One who came up with the whole marriage thing? Was He really real? And could He actually help two people stay in love with each other?

The boy shook his head. Maybe it was something that the old man made up so Wendy would feel better. But if it was true, that would be neat. Imagine a God who helped people stay in love.

Jared sat chewing the sweet fruit, watching the sun rise above the distant mountains. Shadow Creek Ranch was full of surprises. He wondered what would happen next.

.ᴸ .ᴸ .ᴸ

Perry threw his suitcase into the back of the

pickup and glanced over at his father who was coming from the motel office where he'd paid the bill and returned the room key. "Are we almost there?" he asked, a hint of a smile on his face.

Captain Harrison grinned. "What are you, 7? That's what you were always asking when we drove down to see your great-grandmother in North Carolina. Remember?"

"She made the best butter-bean stew," the boy stated, hopping into the right front seat. "And spice cake. I miss 'em. I miss Great-grandma."

"I know," the boy's father said, buckling his seat belt and slipping the key into the ignition. "She was one-of-a-kind. Loved to tell stories about the slave days, when her great-grandfather got snatched out of Africa. She ever tell you the one about the mule in the tree?"

"'Bout 500 times," the boy laughed. "It was her favorite."

"*You* were her favorite," the man said. "She thought the sun rose and set over you." He steered the pickup out of the motel parking lot and headed for the interstate on-ramp. "'You be shar ta tell dat Perry boy dat I'ze thinkin' on him today,' she'd say on the phone. 'You be tellin' him to makes sometin' of hisself. You hear? You be tellin' him ta study hard and don't sass nobody causin' if he do, I'll be comin' up dare to Washington, Dee Cee, and box his ears good, and I doesn't even mind if da president seez me do it.'"

Perry was silent for a minute. "Dad? Did Great-grandma want you to be a policeman?"

The man nodded. "She just wanted me to help people. When I was growin' up, she'd sit me down every once in a while and tell me, 'Now you listen heah, boy; da'is two kindsa folk in dis world—doze dat hep people, and doze dat don't. You be one a dem dat do.' I'd raise my hand and solemnly swear to her that I promised I'd always try to be one of *dem dat do*. I guess being a police officer is part of that.

"Funny, when I'm out chasin' a bad guy, runnin' down a dark alley, climbin' the stairs in some junked-out apartment building, I can almost hear her talking to me, giving me encouragement. She loved people and wanted everyone to live peaceable without violence and pain. Great-grandma had a great sensitivity to the needs of others. I'm proud that some of her blood flows in my veins, and flows in yours too. 'We'ze come from slaves,' she'd say, 'but now de only one we'ze gotta ansa to iz ouwselves.'"

Perry watched the flat Ohio countryside drift by. "I miss her," he repeated. "She was my friend."

The little pickup truck continued on its journey to the west, closing the gap between itself and the runaway with each passing minute.

♩ ♩ ♩

During the morning three more Shadow Creek

Ranch inhabitants visited the barn. First came a powerfully built teenager, the one Jared had noticed working in and around the structure the day before. The boy went about his business with practiced precision, grooming the horses with a big brush, cleaning the stalls and filling them with fresh straw, then doing some repair work on a collection of leather straps lying across the workbench.

A huge black horse seemed to be his favorite. The teen spent an extra amount of time with the animal, talking to it, watching it eat, even asking it questions. "Must be Tar Boy," Jared said to himself, "Wendy's so-called glue factory. That creature would make a lot of glue!"

A short time after the horseman wandered out across the pasture, a little dark-skinned girl stumbled into the barn carrying a jar of bugs. Her companion, a dog she called Pueblo, stood barking up at the loft where Jared was hiding all the time he and the girl were there. The hound's companion told him to stop making such a fuss. "Haven't you ever smelled a rat before?" she asked. That comment made Jared a trifle uneasy.

Then came the man with the cane. He hobbled in and lowered himself wearily onto a wooden bench by one of the stalls. The young horseman returned, leading a sleek tan-colored animal by its harness. They clamored into the barn work area amid the clattering of hooves and steady stream of soft-spoken commands. "It's healin' up pretty good, Barry," the teenager announced. "See?"

The two bent low and studied the hind leg of the animal, poking around and gently rubbing an area just below the horse's knee.

"That stuff's amazing," Barry breathed. "Ol' Red Stone said it would work, and it does."

"What's it called?" asked his companion.

"Aloe. Aloe vera to be exact. It's juice from a plant. The Indian said his people have been using aloe to heal skin problems for generations. Guess it works on people *and* animals. Skin is skin, I suppose. So, Joey, the next time you catch your hind leg on barbed wire, you just glob some of this aloe on the wound and, voila, you'll be as good as new. 'Course you can't jump any fences for a while."

The younger boy chuckled. "I'll remember that when I'm out galloping around the pasture or pulling the wagon."

Barry laughed, then hobbled over to the table. Joey watched him carefully. "Bad today?"

"Yeah," the older horseman responded, reaching down and massaging his thigh. "Sometimes it's just a dull ache. Other times it's a royal pain."

"It's better'n being dead," Joey declared.

"Well, you're right there."

"And besides, if you were dead, you wouldn't be getting hitched up to Miss Debbie Hanson in a few days. That should put a little fire in your walk."

Barry grinned. "It does. She's certainly worth living for."

The two went about their work for a few minutes, then Joey asked, "So, are you scared?"

Barry looked up from the feed bin. "Of what?"

"Of gettin' hitched—you know, married, the ol' ball and chain act, taking the plunge, giving up the simple things in life, like . . . freedom and manhood?"

The older cowboy laughed. "Is that what I'm doing?"

"Sure. Marriage changes guys from strong, I-can-do-anything types to groveling Is-it-OK-honey geeks."

Barry laughed louder. "Oh, my! I didn't know. Tell me more."

Joey leaned forward, as if what he was about to say could offend a casual hearer. "I knew this guy back in East Village. Real tough character, know wha. I mean? Anyway, he falls in love with this female-type from Jersey and they get married. Flowers, cake, preacher, the whole nine yards. Then she moves in with him and the first thing you know they got curtains on the windows. *Curtains! Green ones!*

"I come over one night and say, 'Hey, Mike'— that was his name, Mike. Anyway, I say, 'Hey, Mike, how 'bout you and I going down to check out the docks?' Well, this big, tough street-wise guy looks at me and says, 'Sure, just let me ask the wife.' I mean, *excuse me!* Since when does a fellah have to ask a woman if he can go down to the docks?

"She says OK and we head for the river, you

89

know, to hang out and stuff, and he's checking his watch like every three minutes. So I say, 'Mike, you got an appointment or something?' He laughs and says, 'Nah, I just don't want to stay out too late. Nancy,' that's his wife, 'Nancy doesn't like to be alone at night. She gets scared.' Well, I'm thinkin' this is New York. You're supposed to be scared at night. Anyway, we head on back to the Village and it's like 11:00. I mean, the streets are just getting interesting. Mike says, 'Hey, gotta go. See ya.' Isn't that pathetic?"

Barry, who'd been politely listening to the story, nodded. "Do you know what your problem is?" he said with a smile.

Joey lifted his hand. "Hey, I ain't got a problem."

"Yes, you do," the horseman countered. "Problem with you, Joey, is that you've never been in love with a girl."

"Me? In love?"

"Yup. You see, it's not marriage that changes you. It's love. It makes you something you've never been before."

"No kidding?"

"And," Barry continued, "I know it's true because I've seen love change you in other ways."

"Me? Like how?"

"I've seen you become less focused on yourself and more interested in other things like . . . these horses, this ranch, the people who live here, and especially our guests. You've learned to treat folk with respect. Now, be honest. Are you the same Joey Dugan who roamed the streets of East Village a few years back?"

The boy thought for a moment. "Well, not exactly."

"There you see? And what made the difference?"

Joey turned and gazed out across the pasture. "I guess I became a little different when Mr. H and everybody let me be part of the family. They didn't treat me like a street bum. Everybody here treated me like a regular person."

"That's love, Joey," Barry said softly. "They loved you. Still do. Even Wendy loves you in her own way."

Joey grinned. "Her affection gets a little painful sometimes."

"But don't you see? Love makes things better. If you were to ask your watch-checking friend if he was more content roaming the streets with you or sitting across the room from his wife listening to a Yankee double-hitter on the radio, I'll just bet you he'd take the game over the docks any day."

Joey nodded. "You're probably right."

Barry tapped his cane on the floorboards. "I love Debbie," he said, "and I want to be changed by her. I want to become what she needs because I know she accepts me, bum leg and all. Don't ever underestimate the power of love. When you find it, hang on for dear life. There's nothing better anywhere in the world. Nothing. Not the street, not the docks, not anything."

As Barry hobbled to the barn entrance he leaned heavily on his cane. "Hey, Joey, I gotta go. I think I heard Debbie calling."

"I didn't hear noth—" The boy paused, then grinned broadly. "Yeah. I did hear her call. You'd better hurry."

Smiling, Barry started for the footbridge. Joey watched him go then returned to the workbench and attacked the leather straps once again. Jared saw him pause, look out over the pasture, then shake his head. "Me? In love?" the teenager mused. Then he chuckled softly. "I don't think so."

Captain Harrison hung up the pay phone and stood watching the traffic buzz by the filling station. He frowned as an uneasy feeling crept over him, a feeling he'd experienced before many times. But today it was especially disturbing. He may have been wrong about this whole trip, about taking his son to Montana. Worse yet, he may have been wrong about Jared.

"What's the matter, Dad?" Perry asked, ambling up beside the man, a bottle of orange juice in his outstretched hand.

The policeman took it and shook its contents absentmindedly, still studying the traffic.

"What's wrong?" his son asked again.

Captain Harrison turned as if seeing the boy for the first time. "Oh. Hey, thanks for the juice."

"Dad. You're acting kinda weird. Who was that on the phone? Is Mom OK?"

"Oh, yeah. Mom's fine. She says hello and that you're supposed to write to her every day."

"Write to her? We call each evening. Why does she want me to write to her?"

"OK. Whatever. Did they have orange juice?"

Perry blinked. "Dad. What's that in your hand?"

The man glanced at the bottle held between his fingers. "Oh. I guess they did."

The boy tilted his head. "Earth to Harrison. Earth to Harrison," he said, as if speaking into a microphone. "Come in, Harrison."

His father sighed. "I also just got through talking to my assistant back in D.C. He said Sheriff North called earlier. Seems we have a problem."

"Yeah? Like what?"

The police officer frowned, as if not believing what he was saying. "North said that when he checked his safe today, there was some money missing."

"How much?"

"'Bout $500."

"Wow!"

"But that's not my biggest concern. He said that something else was taken from the station."

"What?"

"A gun. A very powerful handgun. He said he

93

kept it and some ammo with the money in the safe."

"So? They got a quick-fingered burglar who was a little low on cash and needed some firepower. They'll catch him."

The officer shook his head. "You don't understand. The money and weapon were there the night they brought in Jared, and no one has opened the safe since the boy escaped."

Perry blinked. "You mean—"

"Yeah. They think our runaway made off with the money and the gun, which means dear ol' Jared is not only driving without a license, he may be guilty of robbery and possession of a deadly weapon. If all that's true, our boy is in deep, deep trouble. And worse, the people around him may be in very grave danger. Jared has lost someone dear to him, he's running from the law, and has nothing to come home to. His emotions may be screwed up. Who knows what he's capable of doing."

The teenager frowned. "I thought you said you knew this guy."

"I do. Well, I know the Jared who followed Karl around like a shadow. But it looks like I don't know the Jared who's in Montana even as we speak staking out a dream, a dream he may very well turn into a nightmare for someone, including himself. The boy may be unstable, and an unstable person who happens to also have a gun isn't something to take lightly."

Perry lifted his hands. "So, what're we going to do?"

"Well, for starters, I'm going to ship you back to D.C. on the next airplane I can find."

The teenager gasped. "Hey. Wait a minute. I don't want to go back. Besides, we've come this far. We're doin' the ol' dad-son thing, you know, gettin' to know each other. I think it's cool."

Harrison nodded. "It is cool. But being shot at isn't. I'm not about to put you in any kind of danger."

"Dad, you don't even know if Jared took the stuff."

"But what if he did? You could get hurt, or even killed."

The boy stepped forward. "Come on. I'll be OK. I mean, we live in Washington, D.C. I walk the streets all the time, and tons of people are packing guns. How safe is that?"

Harrison didn't respond.

"Besides, I've got one of the finest cops in the East protecting me." The boy glanced at his watch. "Look. We can get a few more hours in tonight, then hit the road early tomorrow morning. We can be in Montana before you know it. You can collar this jerk, I can look at the mountains, and then we're outta there. Piece of cake."

The man hesitated.

"Come on, Dad. Whadda ya say? Montana can't be anymore dangerous than our neighborhood in Silver Spring after dark."

"Well, you gotta promise to stay out of this," the man asserted. "I don't want you anywhere near Jared, do you understand?"

Perry lifted his hand. "I'm not even there. Scout's honor," he promised.

The man grinned. "You never were a Scout."

"Oh . . . well, then, I swear on my ancestor's slave bones. I promise."

Captain Harrison shook his head. "I'd forgotten just how persuasive you can be."

"Mom says I should be a lawyer," the boy stated. "That's OK. Lawyers are rich, right?"

The two walked to the car and got in. For each of them, the emotions of the trip had changed. Perry was beginning to enjoy having his father all to himself. It reminded him of how it used to be, before the promotion, before the late-night shifts and missed basketball games.

But for Captain Harrison, the journey had taken on a new urgency. If he got the Bozeman authorities involved, they could frighten Jared, perhaps causing him to become violent, or even scare him clean out of the state. Who knows where he'd go then.

For now the boy was where he could find him. The police officer just hoped he could get there before something terrible happened out on that peaceful ranch filled with innocent people. He knew he'd have one chance to bring the runaway to justice. One chance. If he failed, lives could be at stake.

CHAPTER 5

Somebody

Saturday morning dawned bright and cold. During the night the breeze had changed from crisp to numbing. Jared burrowed deeper and deeper into his sleeping bag, like a bear seeking out the hidden recesses of its underground cave.

Instead of slipping through the woods to the ranch as he had the day before, the boy waited with many other creatures of the forest for the brilliant, glowing orb to the east to warm the earth, chasing the cold away, loosening night's frosty grip on the land.

Jared ate breakfast encased in the tent, listening to the sounds of nature unseen beyond his protective enclosure. He heard a bird land nearby and scold loudly before flying away. A mouse or mole scratched at the entrance as if asking permission to come in. What he guessed was a deer walked gingerly past the tent before snorting a sudden warning and bolting through the underbrush.

The boy sighed. There was something peaceful about an early-morning forest, even a cold one. Back in the city it was usually a distant siren or car horn that drove sleep away. Often he'd hear someone being sick in the next room or suddenly awaken to a torrent of angry shouts. Here, nature spoke gently in a voice filled with feeling and energy. In the forest, morning crept reverently into your dreams like an invited guest and lifted you up with friendly, nonthreatening arms.

Jared took his time this morning, drinking in the sounds and aromas of the woodlands, basking in the serenity of his little campsite, allowing the sun to warm his body and his soul. The city seemed so far away, with its pain and memories. Here, among the towering pine, he felt secure.

The boy paused as he started to straighten up the confines of his plastic sanctuary. What would it be like to live here? What would it be like to awaken every day to the sounds of birds, wildlife, and the wind?

Just as quickly as the thought entered his mind, anger shoved it aside. No. It wasn't possible. Such a place was reserved for good people, teenagers who kept the law of the land, who did all the right things for all the right reasons. They deserved to be here. He didn't. After all, wasn't he on the run? Wasn't he an outcast? Didn't he have to hide, even now, from others?

Jared leaned his head against the tent pole

supporting the dome of his little orange world. Such a place as this could never be his. He was a street bum who could experience forest and meadows only from hiding places in barn lofts or from behind bushes beside the road. He wasn't good enough for Montana. He wasn't good enough for the mountains. He wasn't good enough for Shadow Creek Ranch.

Suddenly, Jared felt intensely lonely. His hands went limp in his lap as he listened to the forest beyond the confines of his tent. A familiar longing rose in his chest, filling him with deep regret. He didn't fit in. Wherever he was, whatever he was doing, he couldn't seem to make the world accept him the way he was.

Glancing down at his duffle bag, he saw the corner of the brochure jutting out from under a wad of dirty underwear. Picking up the colorful paper, he sat looking at the pictures—photographs of young people riding horses, swimming in mountain streams, climbing trees, racing along meadow roads in bouncing, jolting wagons pulled by powerful animals with Joey holding the reins. Everyone was smiling, their faces tanned and flushed with excitement. Oh, how he wanted to be in the picture! How he longed to experience their joy! Instead, here he was, hiding in the forest, afraid to reveal himself to others for fear of what they'd say or do. A worthless piece of humanity—that's all he'd ever be.

The brochure slipped from his fingers and fluttered to the tent floor where it lay among the remnants of his breakfast. Karl's reserves were vanishing. Soon Jared would be forced to begin living a life that would keep him on the run forever.

The teenager allowed his body to relax completely. He felt tired, sleepy. As the rising sun continued to caress the earth Jared slept alone in his little tent, surrounded by the forest, hidden from view by trees and the past.

⊾ ⊾ ⊾

Perry yawned broadly, covering his mouth with his fingers.

"Didn't you sleep well last night?" his dad asked, checking the rearview mirror for traffic before changing lanes.

"Sleep? With you across the room sounding like a wild animal park?"

The man grimaced. "I snored, huh?"

"Snored? I wouldn't call what you did *snoring*. It was more like your throat and your nose were locked in mortal combat with each other. How does Mom put up with it?"

Captain Harrison shrugged. "I guess she's gotten used to my strange noises. Some nights are worse than others—at least that's what she says. Sorry."

Perry sighed. "That's OK. Actually, I finally figured out a way to get to sleep, although it took me half the night."

"Oh yeah? How?"

"Well, I just pretend that we've left the television on and an old Tarzan movie is playing. Then, when I hear some new animal sounding like it's being attacked, I try to picture it in my mind. First thing you know, I'm dreaming about visiting a zoo. Works great."

The policeman chuckled. "You might want to share that with your mother in your next letter."

"Don't have to," the boy stated. "Already told her on the phone this morning while you were in the shower. She said she's tried it. Worked for a while. Then she started dreaming that she *lived* in a zoo. Now she just buries her head under her pillow or throws things at you."

"That explains it!" Captain Harrison gasped.

"Explains what?"

"Why I sometimes wake up with my side of the bed piled high with kitchen appliances."

Perry snickered, then burst out laughing. "And why it's hard to find the toaster some mornings, right?"

"Yeah, and why the can opener has a piece of my pajamas jammed in it."

The two sat giggling, trying to outdo each other. Harrison grinned broadly. This was the way it used to be—he and Perry laughing together, being silly, making jokes out of anything and everything.

He glanced over at his son. Perry's eyes were bright, filled with happiness. His face shown with a peace his father hadn't seen for many, many months. He wished he could bottle up this moment and pass it on to other dads who'd allowed work and career responsibilities to crowd out their relationships with their children.

However, he was a cop. And he couldn't stop being a cop. He'd just have to find more ways to be a father again while keeping his obligations to those in authority over him, and especially to the citizens of Washington, D.C., who depended on him for protection. It was a tall order, one he knew he had to obey.

"So," the man said after the giggles had died down. "Tell me about school. How are your classes?"

"Dad," Perry countered, "we're on vacation, remember? I don't wanna talk about school. Too depressing. Besides, you've got me doing homework every night before we go to bed, so let's discuss more interesting stuff like . . . basketball, OK?"

"OK. No more talking about school. We'll chat about anything *but* school."

"Good."

The man thought for a moment. "So, how's your education comin' along?"

"*Dad!*"

Harrison laughed. "I'm sorry, Perry. I'm really interested. I mean, I've been so busy I don't even know what grade you're in. What are you, third, fourth?"

Perry rolled his eyes and sighed. "Dad, you're

not funny. You know very well that I'm in ninth! And I'm doing so-so in math and science, got a B in history, a B in French, and an A in P.E., although I almost got a B because I missed two games because of the flu."

"You got a B in French?"

"Si, senor."

The policeman nodded. "I can see why. That's Spanish."

"It is?"

"Oui."

Perry grinned. "We what?"

"We'ze goin' to Montana."

The boy nodded. "Yes, we is."

Father and son burst out laughing again as their little pickup continued along the interstate. A passing sign announced Minneapolis 60 miles ahead. They were well over halfway to their destination. Evening would find them in North Dakota. Tomorrow, Montana!

Something was weird. The big way station stood deserted. Jared could hear no voices echoing across the broad lawn. He saw no activity out by the barn. Even the horses remained at the far end of the pasture, as if they understood that no one would greet them if they galloped to the gate.

"Where is everybody?" Jared asked himself as

he hung back behind the row of trees lining the creek west of the house and barn.

He saw the big farm truck resting by the kitchen entrance, and a car sat in the shade of the cottonwoods behind the building.

Wait, there'd been a third vehicle the day before, a red minivan parked out front. It was gone and, apparently, had taken everyone with it.

Jared wrinkled his nose slightly. Shopping? Perhaps. It was the weekend. Or maybe they had gone on a picnic or off to visit a neighbor. Hard to tell.

The teenager strolled across the empty lawn and slowly climbed the steps leading up to the porch. The boards creaked under his feet. At the top, he turned and glanced back at the valley. The view was breathtaking with towering mountains blotting out the distant horizon and massive groups of trees standing tall and proud everywhere he looked. No wonder he saw so many of the ranch inhabitants pause on the porch and gaze eastward. They were drawing inspiration from the panorama just as he was.

Jared listened for a long time, ears straining for any sound from within. Nothing. The ranch was silent except for the soft breath of the breeze and the far-off cry of a hawk.

He tried the front door. Locked. Reaching into his pocket, he withdrew a crooked piece of metal and inserted it into the knob. Click. The door opened at his gentle pull just as so many other doors had back in the city.

He'd have to be careful. The little red minivan could return at any moment. Jared wanted to be long gone before it pulled up to the base of the steps.

Not sure what he was looking for in the big way station, he knew he wasn't there to rob anyone. He wasn't there to fill a duffle bag with other people's treasures. Not this time. Instead he wanted to discover what made the people at the ranch so contented, so interested in each other. Maybe he'd find it here, amid the trappings of their lives.

Woof! Woof! Jared jumped at the deep-throated warning of an animal approaching from a dark hallway. He saw a mangy dog burst into the foyer, teeth bared, eyes focused on his legs.

"Hey, Pueblo, shut up!" Jared shouted.

The dog skidded to a halt. What was this? The stranger knew his name? Was he supposed to know this guy?

Pueblo sniffed the air, edged closer, and sniffed again. Oh, yes. He'd smelled that odor before, early yesterday morning and then again in the barn. None of the human beings who lived on the ranch had seemed overly concerned with the new aroma wafting about their living and working quarters, so the stranger must be OK.

The dog barked one more time, just to remind the visitor who was boss, then slunk back to his spot somewhere at the end of the hall.

Jared watched him go, then released the

breath he'd been holding in his lungs. "Good dog," he called, his voice a little shaky.

For the first time, the boy focused on the contents of the big lobby. He saw twin stairs curving up from the floor to a banistered balcony overhead. A large den and fireplace fronted the building, filled with comfortable-looking chairs and bookcases lined with colorful volumes.

Strangely, scattered about the place in random confusion were piles of white lacy ribbons, a curving arbor fashioned from painted wood, a padded bench, a table brimming with opened and not-yet opened gifts, another table burdened with a large glass punch bowl and rows of matching cups. Folding chairs leaned against each other along the walls, and assorted items he'd never seen before rested on unopened boxes and end tables.

Then he understood. They weren't bad housekeepers—they were getting ready for a big party, a wedding for Debbie and the man with the cane. That's what all this stuff was about. And it looked like the happy event would take place right here on Shadow Creek Ranch.

In the den he discovered envelopes and invitations, shiny shoes, colorful clothes hanging from makeshift racks, more gifts, several cardboard boxes filled with cloth, and a powerful cassette player with speakers.

A small wooden podium waited by the window. On it was a guest book, opened to the first page.

Across the top was printed in carefully formed letters "Wedding Guests of Debra Hanson and Barry Gordon." Below that line Jared saw a date and time printed carefully in colored ink. The boy glanced at his watch, checked the number indicating which day of the month it was, then gasped. The wedding was scheduled for tomorrow afternoon at 3:00.

Suddenly he heard the rumble of an approaching automobile. He ran to the window just as a red minivan passed by the house on the hillside road leading down the valley to the cutoff where the long driveway intersected it.

Jared hurried around all the waiting paraphernalia to the dining room and continued through to the kitchen. At the door, he paused and glanced over his shoulder. So this was what it took to be happy—a home filled with things that brought happiness. Isn't that what Grandpa Hanson had said out in the barn, that God wanted everyone to love someone else? Weddings celebrated the love of one person for another. These people understood that, and had filled their home with all kinds of things to make the celebration joyous.

The boy unlocked the back door and slipped outside. Then he jumped from the deck and scrambled to the protection of the bushes and trees lining the creek.

What was it like to love, and be loved? Jared wondered. Karl had said that love was nice if you could find it. On the streets there wasn't much to be found. Few cared about each other at all. Everyone was too busy just surviving another day.

It seemed so different out here on the ranch. But why should it be? Surely these people had problems too. They must have doubts and uncertainties. He assumed that they had to work hard to earn their keep, just like city dwellers. Jared knew that Joey spent hours in the barn cleaning, repairing, looking after the horses. The old man was never still as he kept the ranch running smoothly, gathering supplies, checking out the livestock, caring for the property. The women in and around the big house always had something in their hands as they rushed here and there. Everyone was involved in their own acts of survival.

The boy ran along the stream, thoughts rushing through his head in mild confusion. While it was true that, other than himself, not many criminals were sneaking about the place, he understood that nature could be harmful as well as beautiful. He was sure that the inhabitants of Shadow Creek Ranch had faced challenges from the very mountains, streams, and skies that inspired them day after day. The boy had seen and heard reports of forest fires, floods, earthquakes, and blizzards. So why was this valley peaceful when city streets had such sickening amounts of violence?

Jared shook his head. He didn't know the answer—he just knew he couldn't seem to figure out how to make the jump from one world to the other.

The teenager ran until he had placed a great distance between himself and the Station. He'd seen inside a place where love lived, and it looked bright and happy even in its confusion. If only he was good enough to be a part of all that. If only they would accept him into their circle. But they wouldn't. He knew it. They wouldn't because he wasn't smart enough or well-mannered enough or sophisticated enough to be a part of their world.

Bitter tears stung his eyes as he slowed his pace and walked along the stream. In the few short years that he'd lived, he'd experienced love only once, but he had been so young then. All that lingered from those misty days were scattered fragments of memories. Even they mingled with darker images. What had happened? Why had his world come crashing down around him?

Jared paused by the bank and lowered himself onto a rock. Sometimes he'd dream of a house with little rooms and brightly painted walls. As he slept he'd hear voices, soft and gentle, calling him by name.

He'd told Karl about the dreams, about the warm feelings they generated somewhere deep in his soul. His friend would always say, "Now don't go dwellin' on such junk. You'd better concentrate on reality, where your next meal is coming from. You leave dreams out of your life or they'll catch up to you and make you crazy." Jared didn't understand, but he figured Karl was older and wiser and knew more about life than he did.

However, the dreams and the feelings they produced wouldn't go away. They'd return from time to time, like strangers in the shadows, enticing him, calling to him.

Sometimes the dreams would turn dark and haunting. He'd wake up screaming. What did they mean? What was the night trying to tell him? How could he feel so warm and safe one moment, then have his heart stop in mid-beat as terror flooded his thoughts? It didn't make sense. Nothing made sense.

Jared stumbled to his feet as his stomach growled. He was hungry. Food waited for him in the tent back in the forest. Perhaps he'd feel better after he ate and spent some time in his little orange sanctuary.

The boy climbed the embankment and walked to where his motorcycle waited. He'd head back to the Station later that day, perhaps after the sun had set, allowing him to get close to the building. For some reason he felt drawn to the big dwelling in the valley, attracted to it by its strength and energy. While he was on ranch property, his fears seemed further away.

Jared slipped his helmet over his ears and adjusted the chin strap. He'd hurry back to the tent before any forest creatures figured out how to open his duffle bag and help themselves to his food supply.

With a twist of his wrist, he was gone.

.л .л .л

The lights of Bismarck, North Dakota, shimmered in the distance. Traffic on Interstate 94 was light and sped quickly across the flat prairie land as Captain Harrison guided his pickup truck along the highway. Perry snoozed against the passenger-side window, oblivious to the fact that they'd traveled almost 100 miles since he'd fallen asleep.

Harrison squeezed his eyelids together in a repeated grimace, trying to bring a little more clarity into his vision. It had been a long day, but the bright glow ahead signaled that they'd soon be checking into a motel and enjoying the sensation of *not* moving for a few hours.

"Hey, Perry?" the man called softly.

The boy smacked his lips.

"Perry, wake up."

He heard the teenager draw in a deep breath, then expel it.

"Earth to Perry. Earth to Perry. Come in, Perry."

His son lifted his hand then let it drop. "Perry's not here. He's in Jamaica."

"Jamaica? What's he doing in Jamaica?"

"Lying on a beach watching girls."

Harrison blinked again. "Girls? Are you the same son who said he thought female-type people were a pain?"

The boy yawned broadly. "That was two years

111

ago, Dad. Now I think they're just fine, especially the ones in Jamaica."

The police captain chuckled. "I don't think I want to know what you were dreaming about."

"Her name was Philomena," Perry stated. "We were about to stroll along a deserted beach, hand in hand, with the waves washing over our toes."

"Philomena? The girl in your dream had a name?"

The passenger nodded. "Well, actually, Philomena sits in front of me in math class. She thinks I'm a dork. But, hey, it's my dream." Perry glanced out the window. "Where are we?"

"Bismarck. We'll find a motel and then get an early start tomorrow."

The teenager turned to his father. "Wait a minute. You woke me up to help you find someplace for me to go to sleep?"

"Life is just full of contradictions, isn't it?" the man declared. "Remember, we're on a budget, so don't try to talk me into anything with a pool."

The boy sighed. "Your idea of acceptable lodging is a place that's still standing when we drive away the next morning."

Harrison chuckled. "Why pay exorbitant prices when all you're going to do is sleep?"

The little pickup truck followed an exit ramp to a parallel street lined with motels and fast-food restaurants.

"Dad?"

"Yeah."

"What makes a guy like Jared become a criminal?"

The officer thought for a moment. "I've been in the cops and robbers business for almost 20 years, and the closest answer I've come up with is hopelessness. People, young and old, break the law because they don't have any confidence in themselves. They've lost hope."

"You mean, they get discouraged?"

"It's more than that. Law-abiding people get discouraged every day, but you don't see them holding up liquor stores or stealing company secrets from their bosses. They figure, 'Hey, I can work something out. I can lift myself back on my feet.' So they get busy and make something of themselves.

"Now, criminals on the other hand, I mean men and women who can't seem to break out of the mold they've cast themselves in, feel hopeless all the time. They don't see any way out. Thinking that the world is rejecting them, they turn to a life of crime as a way of surviving. 'Since no one else is gonna watch out for me,' they tell themselves, 'I'll just take care of myself, no matter if what I do is lawful or not.' Such people have little respect for the law. They feel they have no value."

Perry thought for a moment. "That's sad."

"Yes, it is," his father agreed. "Unfortunately, we all pay for their insecurities. We all become victims of their anger and hopelessness."

The boy pointed. "Hey, how 'bout that one?"

Harrison glanced at the motel on the corner. "Nope. Has a tennis court."

"We're not sleeping on the tennis court."

"Yeah, but we'd be helping to pay for it because they'll charge more for their rooms. Keep looking."

Perry sighed, then said, "So how do you give someone like Jared hope, or some self-confidence?"

"I don't know," the man admitted. "I usually deal with older felons. Sometimes they listen to reason. Sometimes they don't." Harrison turned to his son. "Where do you get your self-worth?"

The boy was silent for a minute. He watched a couple more motels slip by as he pondered his father's question. When he spoke, he seemed to carefully select his words. "I guess I like myself because Mom keeps saying how I'm so smart and handsome and junk like that. This Jared guy doesn't have anyone to tell him stuff—you know, to make him feel good. He's all alone."

"You're right," the man stated. "He's very much alone and doesn't know who he is or how he fits into society. That's a dangerous condition for a young person."

"Why?"

"Sometimes an individual who doesn't fit in tries to force himself on others and make them accept him. He or she can become violent in the process. That's my greatest fear in Jared's case. The boy's like a wound-up spring full of emotional tension and pent-up frustration. Twang! He could go off at any moment. I just hope we get to him before that happens."

"How 'bout that one?" Perry asked, pointing out the window. "That motel looks like a dump, has no pool, probably's been condemned by the state of North Dakota, and is held together by duck tape and kite string."

Harrison smiled and spun the wheel. "Perfect," he enthused. "And the No Vacancy sign isn't lit yet either!"

"I wonder why," Perry said as the truck pulled up to a modest, clean row of rooms. He watched his father slip from the front seat and head for the office. OK, so it didn't look like a dump, but it wasn't anything near like the fancy places in and around Silver Spring. Policemen were such tightwads, working their tails off for a small salary. What fools!

The boy glanced toward the western sky where the last hint of day was fading away. Out there, beyond the horizon was a boy, lost in a world of his own making, alone among the mountains. For the first time since the journey began, Perry felt a tinge of sympathy for the runaway.

Tomorrow the two young people would meet face-to-face. Tomorrow they'd discover just how tightly wound Jared's emotions had become.

🥾 🥾 🥾

Jared wrapped his jacket about his chest and tried to make himself comfortable in the thick bushes by the house. He'd been here for almost an hour, waiting for someone to wander out for a breath of fresh air.

This was a bad idea, he said to himself. *It's too cold out here for anyone to lounge about on the porch. They're all inside sitting in the den enjoying the fire.*

He could see movement beyond the window curtains, shadows that rose and fell amid the yellow light filtering out onto the deck. From his vantage point halfway up the hill by the Station, he could see clearly the smooth, wooden surface of the porch and smell the hot breath of the chimney as, inside, a fire crackled in the hearth.

All at once, the front door creaked open and a long shadow fell across the floor. Then it closed again, leaving a dark figure standing in the moonlight. Jared recognized Debbie, the girl with flowing dark hair and smooth skin. She stood with a shawl wrapped about her shoulders, gazing silently across the pasture to the mountains beyond.

He heard her sigh. Was it a happy sound or a sad one? Jared wasn't sure.

The girl slowly crossed to the railing and sat against it, her face still turned to the valley. He could just make out her eyes and the gentle curve of her nose and cheeks, caressed by the silver light of the moon. Her hair shown like waves he'd seen on the Potomac as it skirted the city.

Such beauty. Such gentleness in a face. There was no hardness in her expression, no anger as so often seen on the streets of Washington.

"Debbie?" A voice called from the entrance as the door opened a crack.

"I'm out here, Daddy," the girl replied.

Jared saw a man walk from the light into the shadows. "Are you OK, sweetheart?"

Debbie nodded. "I'm fine. Just had to get away for a moment. Lot of commotion in there."

"I know," the man agreed. "Everyone's so excited about the wedding tomorrow."

"Me too," the girl said with a smile. "I've been counting the days."

Man and daughter stared out across the valley for a long moment. Jared saw Debbie slip her arm around her father's waist. "I love Barry," she said. "I love him so much."

"I know," the man said with a smile. "Although it's hard to tell with all that sighing and giggling that goes on whenever you two are together. And the hand-holding and snuggling? What's *that* all about?"

Debbie laughed. "I guess we don't exactly hide our feelings for each other, huh?"

"Not exactly. But I think it's wonderful. My little girl is getting married." He paused, then repeated the phrase as if saying it for the first time. "My little girl is getting married."

Debbie grinned. "Now, Dad, we've been

through this before. I'll *still* be your little girl. I'll *still* come to you with some of my problems. I'll *still* buy you ties for Christmas—"

"And you'll still ask me for money?" the man interrupted. "It just wouldn't be the same without that."

His daughter lifted her chin slightly. "Oh, I think between me and Barry, we'll make ends meet, sorta. I've got my part-time job at the mall, and he's been doing some consulting work on the side, teaching ranchers how to judge horseflesh. Or, maybe he'll be a teacher at the university. They've offered him a position in the Agricultural Department as a lab technician. Said they'd cover the costs of his getting an advanced degree. Wouldn't that be great?"

"Professor Gordon," her father said solemnly. "Sounds good. I know he'll be a success at whatever he tries to do."

The two were silent for a moment. "Daddy?" Debbie asked. "Do you think I know how to be a good wife? I mean, I want to be the best partner for Barry. He's the kindest, most wonderful man in the world, and I want to live up to his expectations."

The older man shook his head. "Listen, honey, Barry doesn't have expectations when it comes to you. That's what makes him so kind and wonderful. He loves you. He loves whatever you are or whatever you will become. You've known him for several years now. Have you ever seen him try to make someone something that they're not? No, he's not going to be making demands on you. He's going to accept you just the way you are. If anything changes—if you change—it will happen because you're *responding* to his love, not trying to earn it."

Debbie nodded slowly. "I just can't believe this is happening. I'm getting married. Me. Married. Mrs. Debbie Hanson Gordon. Has a nice ring, huh?"

"I like it! It'll be an honor tomorrow to officially welcome Barry into our family. He's been an important part of our lives since we moved out to the ranch. Now he's becoming our own flesh and blood. It'll be a pleasure to call him my son-in-law."

She snuggled close to her father. "Oh, Daddy. I'm so happy. Is it OK that I'm so happy?"

"I wouldn't have it any other way," the man declared. "Now, soon-to-be Debra Hanson Gordon, you get in there and finish preparing for your big day. I think I saw Wendy eyeing the arbor. She's probably trying to figure out where to hang a few horseshoes."

The girl laughed. "I wouldn't be surprised. Guess I'd better go in and protect what's left of my ceremony. I've already got two horses greeting the guests."

"I love you, sweetheart," the man said softly. "I'm proud of how you and Barry have shown us all how beautiful and pure love can be."

After planting a gentle kiss on her father's cheek, Debbie walked back into the Station, leaving the man standing alone by the railing.

Jared saw him gaze out across the moonlit pasture. A single tear slipped from the man's eye and left a silver trail on his upturned face. "Oh, God," he heard him say softly, "be with my baby girl tomorrow. Bless her new home. And thank You for letting me be her daddy."

With that, the man turned and reentered the building.

Jared sat on the hillside, hidden behind the bushes, lost in thought. Who was this God that everyone here seemed to know? Why was He so important?

A familiar longing flooded his musings. He felt lonely, cut off, abandoned. Everyone seemed to have someone else. Everyone seemed to be happy. Everyone but him.

Suddenly, a deep anger began building inside the boy, a rage that surfaced every so often, especially in times of great disappointment or loneliness. When it came, it almost blinded him with frustration and resentment. Why should he be the outcast? Why should others live in joy while he ran the streets, hiding from the law, living like a fugitive? It wasn't fair. It just wasn't fair!

He hadn't asked to be born—hadn't asked for the kind of life he lived. It had been dropped into his arms like a dirty, smelly garment. "Here, wear this!" society had told him. "Wear this and stay out of my way!"

Jared scrambled up the hill and began walking down the road, away from the ranch. Faster and faster he walked, then began running. "I'm worthless," he told himself between gritted teeth. "I'm no good to anyone. No one loves me. No one cares if I live or die. No one talks to this God about me."

Stumbling through the night like an out-of-control animal, he crashed through bushes and stumbled over rocks, blinded by angry tears.

He hated life. He hated people. He hated all those perfect people living on that stupid ranch. He deserved better. He deserved to be happy. Why should they have all the joy in life?

The boy skidded to a stop and sat down heavily on a rock to rest, his breath short painful heaves, fists clenched at his side, nails digging into flesh. Jared's eyes narrowed as he groaned out his frustration, his cry blending with the gentle sounds of nature. It wasn't fair. It just wasn't fair.

All at once he looked up, jaw set tightly. He'd show them. He'd show them all. Tomorrow would be that stupid wedding with all those stupid people running around loving each other. No, he wasn't invited. But he'd come anyway. They had no right to reject him. No right! And he wouldn't show up alone. No sir! He had a friend to bring with him, a friend that was powerful and spoke a language that everyone understood and respected.

That's right. Tomorrow he and his friend would roar down the road and turn at the driveway leading back to the Station. He'd make himself at home on the ranch, walking around in plain view, eating cake and cookies, drinking punch from those little glass cups, checking out the gifts on the long table with the white cloth draped over it. If anyone tried to stop him, well, he'd ask his friend to do his talking for him.

Jared stood and walked over to where his motorcycle waited in the bushes. Swinging his leg over the saddle, he inserted the key into the ignition. Pressing the start button he brought the vehicle to life. The time for dream seeking was over. Tomorrow would be his day, the day he stood up for himself and told the world that he *was* somebody. And everyone would listen.

With a throaty roar, the Honda and rider sped away, leaving the valley to the night, and to the excited inhabitants of Shadow Creek Ranch.

CHAPTER 6

Mountaintop

Captain Harrison laid the phone back on its cradle and sighed. It was Sunday morning—early. Very early. Shuffling to the window, he drew back the curtain a few inches and gazed out at the parking lot. Rows of cars sat in the predawn darkness, waiting to whisk their drivers and passengers to destinations unknown.

The officer glanced back at the sleeping form of his son who lay sprawled on his bed, blankets rolled in a heap at his feet. Ever since the boy had turned 4, he'd thrown off his covers, preferring to spend nights unburdened with excess layers of fabric. A semiclean T-shirt and pair of boxer shorts seemed all that he needed to satisfy him, even when snows framed the windows.

Harrison moved through the dim light and seated himself at the end of his own bed, lost in thought. How could he have separated himself from the boy? How could he have made anything—*anything*—more important than their relationship? Perry was his son, flesh of his flesh, bone of his bones! The very idea that he'd missed the all-important state finals basketball game filled the man with deep remorse.

His son wasn't a star player. No one chanted his name during a game. But he was a valuable guard on the high school squad, a guy on whom his fellow teammates could depend. To think he'd let him play in such a big meet without hearing his dad cheering from the sidelines caused a lump to form in the man's throat.

"I'm sorry," he whispered to his sleeping son. "I'm sorry, Perry."

The boy stirred, then blinked open his eyes. "Wha—? What did you say, Dad?"

Harrison smiled. "I said we gotta get up."

"Is it morning?" the boy asked, yawning, stretching his arms out in front of him.

"Almost."

"Almost?"

The policeman chuckled as he rose and headed for the suitcase propped open atop the dresser. "Well, in parts of New England it's morning. Come on, up and at 'em or we'll be late."

"Late to what?"

"You'll see."

Perry sighed. "Dad. You're not making any sense."

The man grinned. "Just get your skinny self into the bathroom and wash your face. Train's leaving in 15 minutes."

Perry gasped. "What about breakfast?"

"We'll get something down the road. Now, are you going to get up, or do you want me to carry you like I did when you were small?"

"Yeah," the boy chuckled, "I can see that happening. You'd hurt yourself."

"I would not," Harrison countered. "Why, I'm as strong as the day you were born!"

"In your dreams," Perry laughed.

Suddenly, he found himself being lifted out of bed in the arms of a grinning, straining man. "See," his father moaned, weaving drunkenly under the load, "I can still toss you around like a rag doll."

Perry looked at his dad, then at the bed below. "So why aren't we going anywhere?"

Harrison grimaced. "Because . . . I think I hurt myself." With a muffled plop, the boy landed on the sheets, a giant grin spread across his face. "Dad, I think I weigh a few more pounds than when I was 5."

"Yeah," the officer agreed, rubbing the small of his back. "Must be all those beans your mother fixes."

Perry rolled his eyes then bounded out of bed and hurried to the bathroom. "So," he called over the gurgle of running water, "are you going to tell me why we're getting up in the middle of the night?"

"Nope."

The boy splashed cold water on his face and

shivered slightly. "Is this Jared guy makin' a run for it?"

"Hope not."

"You just want to surprise me, right?"

"Right."

"OK. Sure hope it's worth all this trouble."

Captain Harrison walked to the window and gazed to the west. The sky was still dark. "I hope so, too," he said.

🔱 🔱 🔱

RRRRING! A phone resonated in the bedroom of a modest home in Silver Spring, Maryland. Outside, the sun was just beginning to peek above the horizon, sending soft, golden rays of light through the colorful leaves crowning the trees that shadowed the streets and cracked sidewalks.

Mrs. Harrison reached out, expecting her fingers to brush against her sleeping husband.

RRRRING! She searched the pillow resting beside her, then lifted her head. Oh, yes, her husband wasn't there. Hadn't been for days.

RRRRING!

The woman's hand moved to the phone perched on the nightstand beside the bed, bumped the receiver off the hook, and sent it tumbling to the floor.

Groggily, Mrs. Harrison pulled herself to the side of the mattress and began reeling in the cord like a fisherman hauls up a net. She placed the handset to her ear, frowned, then turned it end for end. "Hello?" she said, half coughing out the word.

"Mrs. Harrison?" The female voice on the line sounded far too cheerful for such an early-morning hour.

"Yes?"

"Hi, this is Ashly Peters. I work the night shift at the morgue in your husband's precinct."

"Yes?"

"Do you know how to contact Captain Harrison?"

"Ah, I've got the number of his motel in North Dakota."

"Good. Great! I need to talk to him."

Mrs. Harrison cleared her throat. "Is there a problem?"

"Well, not exactly. I've got some information he should know about before he finds that Jared fellow—you know, the runaway? Has he told you about him?"

"Yes."

"And, I wouldn't be bothering him with it except I just discovered a new file on the boy. It's different than the one your husband keeps at the precinct—you know, concerning his criminal activities. You see, I'm heading out of town with Dr. Milton for a coroner's convention in Florida, so I really need to talk to your husband before I go."

Mrs. Harrison tried to blink sleep from her eyes as she sat up in bed. "Ashly, I speak with my husband every morning before he sets out on the road. He'll be calling me in about an hour or so. If you'd like, I'll relay your message. That way you can get an early start on your trip, and we won't have to wake Joe up. They're in an earlier time zone. Would that work all right?"

A pause on the line. "Well, I guess," she agreed. "That is, if you don't mind. Got a pencil and some paper?"

Mrs. Harrison sleepily rummaged around in the nightstand drawer and withdrew a pen and small pad. "Yeah. I'm all set. What do you want me to tell him?"

She heard Ashly shuffle some papers. "I found this information mixed in with another set of records in Dr. Milton's office. He asked me to clean out his file cabinet, something that hasn't been done since Kennedy was in the White House. Seems our runaway's got some problems other than the fact that he's a runaway."

"What do you mean?"

"Well, according to this report, the boy experienced a series of . . . how do they put this . . . psychologically significant traumatic occurrences in his past. That means he's mentally screwed up. First event took place when he was 2½ years old. His father got into some kinda trouble with a drug ring here in the District. The police report, which was included with the coroner's write-up, says that a Dan and Merril Everett were confronted in their downtown apartment by two thugs who demanded payment of a large sum of money. When the couple couldn't deliver, the visitors pulled out handguns and shot them both dead on the spot."

Mrs. Harrison cringed. "Good heavens!"

"Yeah," Ashly agreed. "With friends like that, huh? Anyway, seems there was an eyewitness to the double murder, a little boy whom police found cowering in a closet. The report says the kid was as white as a cloud, shaking from head to foot. It took 'em an hour to talk him out. He was a mess."

"And?"

"Kid's name was Jared."

"*Our* Jared?"

"'Fraid so. Report said the boy went totally bonkers, would scream for days on end, wouldn't eat, threw up whatever food was forced down him. Can't say as I blame him, poor little guy. Social Services finally shipped him off to a foster home but, apparently, that didn't work out any too good either. Police arrested the foster parents for child molestation. Jared got bumped around like a bag of dirty laundry until he simply disappeared from the system about a year ago. Write-up says he ran away from his assigned facility. Your husband will know that's about the time he started showing up at the precinct on the shirttails of Karl Castanza, the young man who was killed before Jared left."

Mrs. Harrison felt an uneasiness in the pit of her stomach. "Is there anything else I should tell my husband?"

"Yeah. According to the file, Jared Everett has

a history of violent behavior and should be handled with extreme caution. He experiences mood swings and has been suicidal on more than one occasion. I thought Captain Harrison should be aware of these facts before he confronts the runaway. Hunting down a criminal always carries a degree of risk. If that criminal has a history of deviant psychotic behavior, it makes the job a little more spicy, if you know what I mean."

Mrs. Harrison pressed the receiver against her ear, trying to steady her trembling hands. "Yes, I understand."

"I would've told you sooner, but I just discovered this information moments ago. Jared's psychiatric history was jammed in with the coroner's report on his parents' death. Some clerk, who hopefully no longer works for the city, got a little confused. It should've been added to the current criminal activities file in your husband's office. Sorry 'bout that."

"Thank you, Ashly," Mrs. Harrison breathed, finding it hard to speak. "I'll contact my husband right now. He's got to know about this."

"Kinda figured as much," the caller agreed. "Tell Joe I'll be in the office for a few more minutes if he wants additional information, then I'm heading for National Airport and the sunny beaches of Miami. Sorry to wake you."

"That's OK, Ashly. Thanks."

Mrs. Harrison hung up the phone and reached

for the slip of paper resting by the lamp. She hurriedly dialed the number written across it. When a sleepy voice answered, she requested, "Room 23, please."

The lines crackled and snapped as the call was being routed, then Mrs. Harrison heard the electronic chortle of a distant phone being rung. She held the receiver against her ear and waited anxiously.

In a Bismarck, North Dakota, motel room a telephone rang, its jarring voice shattering the predawn stillness. The suitcase on the dresser was gone. The lights had been turned off. The parking space in front of the unit stood empty. The little pickup truck and its two inhabitants were miles away, speeding west, drawing closer and closer to the Montana border.

♨ ♨ ♨

Jared heard the steady, gravely crunch of passing cars in the distance, signaling that the procession of invited guests was beginning to make their way toward Shadow Creek Ranch.

The sun hung high overhead, bathing the trees and rocks in pure, clean light. It was a beautiful day, a little cool, but perfect for an outdoor celebration.

The boy sat on a fallen log, listening. Everything was ready. He had carefully packed the duffle bag with food and clothing, rolled his sleeping gear up tightly, folded the tent, and cleaned the campsite and buried every piece of garbage. Jared wanted absolutely no trace of his presence to remain behind after he was gone.

Then he had firmly strapped his possessions to the Honda that now waited in the shade of a tall pine.

The teenager's anger had grown through the night, keeping sleep at bay. Now, as he lingered some distance from the road, he found himself kicking at an embedded stone at his feet.

After dislodging the rock, he stood and began pacing back and forth between the motorcycle and the log, mumbling under his breath. What he was saying didn't matter to him. The words made no sense. He just felt filled with energy, an almost uncontrollable compulsion to move about, like an animal in a cage.

Every once in a while he'd stop and glance down the forest path toward the road. "I'm coming," he'd say. "I'm coming." Then he'd begin stiffly pacing again, back and forth, mumbling.

Finally it was time. He didn't know why, didn't know what prompted the decision. Jared just knew it was time for him to leave the shadows of the forest and present himself on the ranch, in full view of everyone there.

He pressed a hand against the small of his back. A thick bulge met his groping fingers. Yes. He was ready.

Mounting the Honda, he jammed his head into

the helmet, turned the key, and pressed the start button while twisting the throttle. *Rrrrummph!* The engine barked to life. *Rrrrummph, RRRRUMMPH!* The bike responded quickly to his commands with its deep-throated growl. Jared loved the sound. It reflected perfectly the anger boiling deep inside him.

Lifting his left foot, he depressed the gear lever while squeezing the clutch with his fingers. The vehicle lurched forward slightly as the transmission engaged the drive chain. They had no right to keep happiness all to themselves. They had no right to exclude him from their lives.

As the roar built to a whine, Jared released the clutch and felt the powerful motorcycle lunge from the clearing. He lifted his feet from the forest floor and sped away, leaving the campsite empty.

"I'm coming," he repeated, his whisper lost in the shriek of the engine.

Joining the gravel road, he fell in behind a station wagon filled with well-dressed visitors. *Follow 'em,* Jared told himself. *Stay behind this car. No need to hurry.* When *I get there ain't as important as that I get there.*

A laughing child in the vehicle turned and waved at him. Jared didn't respond. He kept looking ahead, eyes locked on the road, ignoring everything else.

As the motorcycle and automobile passed above the Station, the teenager saw that the usually quiet, uncluttered horse ranch had become a scene of chaotic activity. From the elevated road he could see people and cars lining the driveway. Tables ringing the front lawn proudly showed off festive decorations as white ribbons and bows fluttered from every fence post. Brightly colored flower arrangements peeked from every nook and cranny.

White-painted stones formed a pathway from the Station steps, across the lawn, and through a gently curving arbor that guarded an area where dozens of folding chairs sat facing the footbridge.

The little structure itself had been transformed into a flower-encased monument, reminding Jared of some of the floats he'd seen in holiday parades. At the base of the bridge a soft, white carpet lay across the grass, and a little podium rose amid silver candlesticks and leafy plant stands.

At the head of the driveway, beyond which no cars could pass, stood two horses, their coats brushed to a high sheen, hooves polished black, soft tails and manes reflecting the warm sunlight. Wendy stood in front of them, guarding a small stand with an open book resting on top. She held a feathered pen out to the arriving guests, looking a bit uncomfortable in a pink-and-white dress with puffy sleeves.

Jared chuckled in his helmet in spite of his anger. Wendy didn't seem to be the type for frilly dresses with puffy sleeves. It was clear that festive occasions didn't suit her all that well.

However, he wasn't here to be festive. He was here to show the world that he was somebody, that they couldn't shut him out or keep him from the happiness that he deserved.

By now the car and motorcycle had reached the cutoff. Each turned and started back toward the Station. Jared slowed his vehicle and slipped it into an empty space not far from the road.

Once the bike was securely leaning on its stand, the boy laid the helmet on the seat and unzipped his jacket. With a final check of the lump pressing against the small of his back, he squared his shoulders, lifted his chin, and began walking up the driveway toward the ranch.

Like everyone else, the first person he met was Wendy, flanked by two horses. The girl looked at him, surveyed his jeans, T-shirt, and jacket, and offered a hesitant smile. "Welcome," she said, holding out the feathered pen and sounding a little like a recording. "Are you a friend of the bride's or friend of the groom's?"

Jared frowned. "Why do you wanna know that?"

The girl's smile faltered, then returned. "Well, if you're a friend of the bride's, I'm supposed to tell you to sit over there in those chairs to the left of that flowery wooden thing. But if you're a friend of the groom's, you're supposed to sit in those chairs to the right."

Jared lifted his chin slightly. "I ain't nobody's friend."

Wendy blinked, then cleared her throat. "Then

. . . I guess you can sit anywhere you want."

"What if I don't wanna sit at all?"

The girl stiffened and studied the visitor for a moment. "Then you can stand in the creek," she said coldly.

Jared moved closer, eyes narrowed. "What's *that* supposed to mean?" he asked.

"Nothing," Wendy responded without flinching. "I'm just telling you where to go."

"Hello there." Jared heard a voice behind him. Turning, he looked into the kind eyes of the old man who owned the Station and the land surrounding it. "Welcome to Shadow Creek Ranch," the gentleman said, adjusting his tie. He, too, looked a little uncomfortable in his own special garb—a three-piece suit. "I don't think I've had the pleasure of meeting you. My name is Mr. Hanson—Grandpa Hanson to most folk. What's your name and where are you from?"

Jared backed away a bit. "I . . . my name's Karl. I ain't from around here."

"Oh. Are you a friend of Barry's?"

The boy shook his head and frowned. "Hey, what's with all these stupid questions?"

Wendy leaned forward as if to tell her grandfather a secret. "Karl doesn't have any friends," she whispered. "Said so himself."

Grandpa Hanson smiled. "Everyone's got at least one."

"I don't," Jared stated, looking around nervously. "All my friends is dead, so just leave me alone. I ain't here to celebrate no wedding."

"Oh? Then why are you here?" the old man asked quietly.

The boy hesitated. "Just leave me alone. I ain't gotta answer your stupid questions. And you can't tell me to leave. You hear me? Just let me be."

Grandpa Hanson lifted his hand in warning, his smile fading just a little. "Listen, son, this is a wedding celebration. My granddaughter is getting married to my ranch foreman. You're welcome to enjoy the day with us, but I don't want any trouble."

"Hey, I can do whatever I want," Jared countered as the anger boiling inside him began to rise even higher. "This is a free country. I got just as much right to a good time as anybody." He thrust a finger in front of the old man's face. "I seen you guys goin' around actin' so high and mighty. I seen you talkin' 'bout God and love and junk like that. Well, that ain't the way it is outside this valley. So get real. It ain't like that at all."

Wendy moved closer to her grandfather, pen still in her hand. "Why is he saying these things?" she asked, genuine fear in her tone. The old man motioned for her to remain quiet.

"Besides," the visitor continued, "there ain't no God. There ain't no love. It's all just a bunch of lies."

"That's not true," the old man said quietly.

"Yeah? Well, where was your God when I

137

needed Him? Huh? Where was all this love garbage when I got shoved around like a stinkin' bag of horse manure? Answer me that!"

Grandpa Hanson lifted his hand again. "Jared, listen—"

"No, *you* listen. I ain't . . ." The boy stopped as his breath caught in his throat. "Wh'd you call me?"

"I called you by your name. Jared."

Wendy glanced up at her grandfather. "No, Grandpa," she whispered. "His name is Karl."

The teenager stood staring at the old man. "What's goin on here?" he breathed.

"You tell me, Jared. What *is* going on here?"

"How do you know who I am?"

Grandpa Hanson looked the boy in the eyes. "That's not important. What *is* important is why you're here and what you intend to do."

Unconsciously, the teenager's hand moved behind his back, his fingers searching for the thick, heavy burden jammed under his belt.

"Why don't we just go someplace where we can talk?" the man invited quietly.

"Grandpa," Wendy asked, looking first at her grandfather then at the visitor, "do you know this guy?"

"I know enough about him to realize he needs a friend."

Jared licked his lips as the old man continued to hold his gaze. He glanced about nervously. No one else was aware of the conversation taking place at the guest book table. However, other visitors were approaching, wanting to sign the register before joining the festivities.

"I . . . I gotta go," the boy stated, taking a step backward.

"Go where?" Grandpa Hanson asked. "Where do you have to go, Jared?"

A movement caught the boy's eye. Looking past the old man, he saw a little pickup truck slipping by a cottonwood tree. Behind it followed another vehicle, this one adorned with the logo and colors of the Montana State Police.

Jared glanced back at Grandpa Hanson, his face suddenly lined with rage. "You're just like all the rest of 'em," he growled. "You don't care 'bout me. You just want me off your land and out of sight so you can have your stupid wedding."

Grandpa Hanson, seeing the approaching vehicles, turned and spoke in a voice filled with feeling, "I do care, Jared. I care very much."

The boy gritted his teeth and locked the old man's eyes in an icy stare. "I needed you. I needed this ranch. Now I ain't got nobody."

The boy spun around and ran along the driveway.

Perry felt his dad bring the truck to a skidding halt and watched him leap from the cab, but not in time to catch a fleeing boy who sped by. The runner skirted the swerving police cruiser and raced on down the driveway.

"Get out!" Captain Harrison shouted to his son.

Before the boy could grab the handle, his door flew open and an old man wearing a formal suit jumped into the cab, wedging him back into the seat. "Hurry!" the unexpected passenger shouted. "He'll get away if we don't hurry."

Harrison hesitated, watching the teenager mount the distant motorcycle.

"Come on! Please!" the old man pleaded. "I know the roads. I know the places he might go."

The officer slipped back behind the wheel, pressing Perry even farther into the seat. He spun the truck around, sending wedding guests scurrying for cover. They roared past the police cruiser as it, too, executed a quick U-turn in the driveway before falling in behind the pickup.

Within seconds, Harrison was trailing the fleeing motorcycle as it fishtailed out of the trees and raced toward the cutoff, swerving recklessly around arriving cars and visiting ranch vehicles.

At the intersection Jared swung to the right and headed up the valley toward the distant mountains. "Yes!" the old man shouted. "He's heading into the hills, away from the ranch and the main highway. There are only abandoned logging roads up there. If we can keep him in view until he comes to a dead end, we've got him."

The speaker turned. "By the way, I'm Mr. Hanson. You must be Captain Harrison."

"Yeah," the driver responded, gripping the

steering wheel tightly as they plowed through a sharp turn. "Nice to finally meet you face-to-face. We've been talking on the phone for days now. And this is my son, Perry. He's not supposed to be in on this chase, and that's why he's going to promise to stay in the cab no matter what happens, right?"

The boy, wedged between the two large adults in the tiny cab, barely able to see out, nodded. "Sure," he gasped.

Jared leaned heavily into a corner, feeling the rear tire skid slightly. His wrist made quick, skillful adjustments on the throttle, controlling the power driving him forward at an alarming speed.

The boy's body shook violently as the motorcycle slammed into ruts and boulders scattered randomly along the mountain road. The Honda's engine howled, blending with the sharp, angry roar of the wind as it blasted past his helmet. He didn't know where he was going. Nor did he know where he'd been. He just knew he had to keep racing up this mountain, away from the ranch, away from the police car, away from Captain Harrison.

It had been a trick—a dirty, rotten trick! They'd known about him all along. Harrison and Hanson had been in contact with each other from the start, although the old man must not have revealed his presence to anyone else on the ranch.

Now the very men he thought would understand his longing to escape the city and find refuge in a land where teenagers smiled and laughed and

141

slept peacefully under the stars—they were chasing him up an old logging road. The boy gritted his teeth in an effort to keep them from slamming together as the motorcycle jolted over the rough road. It was useless. He had nothing left to dream about. Nothing. Why go on? Why try anymore?

Captain Harrison gripped the wheel as he felt his truck skid outward before bouncing off the turn's thick, raised bank. The vehicle lurched forward as the bike up ahead raced on. His foot pressed the accelerator as the little pickup jolted onto a short straightaway.

"This is a city truck, not an off-road vehicle," he shouted above the metallic blare of the engine.

Grandpa Hanson braced himself for another sharp curve and felt his body being thrown against the door frame as the vehicle skidded sideways. "You're doing fine," he encouraged. "Looks like Jared is taking the Blackmore road. It ends on a plateau overlooking a long valley. When he gets there, he'll have no place to go."

The old man glanced at Perry, who remained wedged between him and his father. "You OK, young man?"

The teenager blinked. "Sure," he gasped.

Jared saw the road level out, then begin to climb again. He squeezed his knees together and tightened his hold on the handlebars. What was the use? If Shadow Creek Ranch had no place for him, there'd be no place for him anywhere. Life would be jail cells and cold, friendless streets. No, that wasn't life. That was death, only you were still breathing. Karl was the lucky one. He didn't have to worry about where his next meal was coming from, wouldn't have to hide anymore. He was free. He was safe.

Suddenly, the motorcycle burst from the forest road and sped across an open meadow high atop a flat plateau. In the distance rose more mountains, some with a dusting of snow covering their summits. The air rushing by was cold and clean.

Jared studied the far end of the expanse. He could see nothing beyond the meadow. It simply ended, falling away into empty space.

The pickup blasted out of the forest and sped across the open area, keeping the bike in view. Harrison's eyebrows rose slightly. "Hey! He's not stopping!"

Grandpa Hanson leaned forward. "Oh, dear Lord. No!"

Jared felt the bike accelerate, carrying him closer and closer to the edge. Yes. This was the best way out. He could be like Karl, asleep forever, never to know fear or guilt or sadness again. It would be so simple. He'd sail off the edge, drift for a moment or two, and then it would be over in a bone-crushing instant.

He thought of the woman who lived in his dreams, of her face smiling down at him, of her voice singing softly in his ears. "Mommy," he whispered as he shot forward, closing the distance between himself and the precipice. "Mommy. Hold me! Hold me now!"

In the tumult of his thoughts, amid the agony of his loneliness, he heard something afar off, like a distant call. The sound pierced his soul, his sadness, his anger. What was it? Who could be summoning him at his final moment?

The edge of the cliff raced toward him. He could see the valley stretching out to the mountains beyond. There was peace down there. It was the answer to all his longings.

But what was that noise, that piercing shout from behind? Was someone trying to tell him something? Was someone trying to call him back from the valley, back from the final sleep he deserved? He hesitated, his right hand releasing its white-knuckled grip on the throttle. The bike slowed slightly. Why was someone calling? Didn't they just want to hurt him, keep him hidden from view, away from the icy gaze of society?

Wait. What if they didn't? What if they were calling out in love, the same love the woman in his dreams offered so freely as she held him, rocking him back and forth during those long-ago nights that lived only in memory? Should he try just once more? Should he give whoever was calling him a final chance to fill the deep void in his heart?

Grandpa Hanson saw the bike turn suddenly, then begin to slow. After a long, sweeping turn at the edge of the cliff, it came to a complete stop.

Captain Harrison skidded the truck to a halt some distance away and saw the police cruiser come to rest beside them. As the boy straddling the motorcycle turned and looked back in their direction, the old man in the passenger seat lifted his hand from the steering wheel, letting the horn fall silent.

The two stepped out of the cab and stood by the vehicle. The cruiser doors burst open as the two officers jumped out, guns drawn and leveled at the distant form at the edge of the clearing.

"Jared!" Captain Harrison called, the word echoing across the high meadow. "Jared, it's time to stop running. Put the gun on the ground and walk away from it. Do you hear me, Jared? Do it now!"

The boy slipped off his helmet and shook his head. "It's all I got left, Captain. It's all I got."

"That's not true," the officer responded, his hands raised nonthreateningly by his sides. "You've got a future same as everyone else. But you're not going to enjoy much of it if you don't lose the weapon and let me take you back to Ohio." Harrison's voice softened. "You need help, Jared. You're messed up inside. You've been through stuff that's hurt you bad. Now you're getting even deeper in trouble with the law. It's gotta stop, and this is as good a place as any, don't you think?"

"Whadda ya mean, messed up inside?" the boy countered. "What are you talkin' about?"

145

"Jared. When I checked in at state police head-quarters in Bozeman, they told me my wife had called with some information I wasn't aware of. Got the whole story from my office back in the District. I know about what happened to your folks. I know about the foster homes and the abuse."

The teenager looked away, then back at the officer. "So what?" he shouted. "That ain't why you hunted me down. You just wanna throw me in jail for disturbing your friends in the District and for rippin' off that sheriff in Stoneman. That's your job. You're a cop."

"Yes, Jared. I am a police officer. And I did come after you because you broke the law. But that's not the only reason, especially after talking with my wife and hearing the complete file on you. Son, I came after you because you also broke my heart. You don't have to live like this anymore. There's good in you, Jared, but it's hidden under years of pain. Karl knew it. He understood."

"You leave him outta this!" the teenager warned angrily. "Karl's dead. That's all there is to it."

"No," the man responded. "There's more. You don't know *why* he died."

Jared laughed. "He died 'cause he was dumb enough to face down a banger with a gun. He deserves what he got—"

"But," Harrison interrupted, "the shooter wasn't after *him.*"

Jared stiffened. "What do you mean?"

146

The policeman moved a little closer. "You know a guy named Preston?"

"Preston?" Jared chuckled. "He's a royal jerk. We hate each other's guts."

"I'm sure you do."

"So?"

"So *he* was the shooter. He was the guy on the street that night waving the gun around. Don't you remember?"

"No!" the boy called. "It was somebody else. Karl said so and told me to run back to the warehouse. That's when I heard the shots."

Captain Harrison edged forward a few more paces. "You're wrong. It was Preston in the alley, and he was out to get *you*. Karl saw him first and stepped in the way. He took the bullet that was meant for you. Do you understand? Jared, he died for you. Karl died for you."

Jared stood unmoving as the meadow grasses fluttered at his feet.

"Karl saw more in you than anyone else," the police officer pressed. "He believed that you had a future, that you could make something of yourself. So he took the bullet just so you could live another day and maybe, just maybe, get away from the streets. I couldn't let you run forever without knowing what he did that night. He loved you, Jared. Believing in you, he wanted to give you a fighting chance in life."

Harrison saw the boy's body slump forward as

sounds of anguish filtered across the open meadow. "Just give me the gun," he called, "and let me take you back. Spend your time in Ohio. Spend your time in D.C. Then begin living a life Karl could be proud of. OK, Jared? I want to be proud of you too."

Grandpa Hanson slowly walked up beside the police officer, then continued past a few steps. "Jared," he called, "I want you to come back to Shadow Creek Ranch when this is all over, after you've made things right with the law. I want you to meet everybody, ride horses through the hills, walk the mountain paths, visit these meadows. That's why you came to Montana, isn't it? That's what you really wanted. Right?"

He saw the sobbing boy nod slowly. "It's here for you, Jared. The ranch, the horses, the valley— they'll all be waiting. Promise you'll come back. OK? I'll ask Wendy and Joey and some of the others to write to you, send you pictures and stories about what happens here. That's why there is a Shadow Creek Ranch—to give you and others who've experienced pain a place to come when you need to escape, not from the law, but from yourself, from your past. Give us a chance to be your friends. You're always welcome here. Always. Whadda ya say, Jared?"

The boy slowly slipped off the motorcycle and reached behind his back. The two policemen standing behind the cruiser held their guns steady, sights centered on the boy's chest.

Jared brought his hand forward, letting the gun dangle harmlessly from his fingers. Captain Harrison ran over and accepted the weapon. Then the boy unzipped the duffle bag and retrieved a wad of money, handing it silently to the officer.

"Thanks, Jared," the man said softly. "I'm so sorry for what happened to you, about Karl, about everything. I just wanted you to know that. But you've broken the law and I've gotta take you back. Do you understand?"

The boy nodded, then lifted his gaze to Grandpa Hanson, who stood a short distance away. "Will you wait for me?" he asked, his voice trembling.

"We'll be right here," the old man responded, fighting back tears. "We'll always be waiting for you, Jared."

The two police officers hurried over and guided Jared back to their car. Perry saw them place him in the back seat, then hop into the front and start the engine. As the cruiser turned to drive away, Jared glanced over at him. Perry smiled. The prisoner returned his quiet greeting with a wave of his hand. Then they were gone.

The boy helped his father and the old man load the motorcycle onto the back of the pickup, securing it snugly with ropes. Then they left the meadow and drove down the mountain, following the winding logging road toward the valley floor.

"Dad?" Perry asked as they maneuvered slowly

around the ruts and fallen branches. "What's going to happen to Jared?"

Captain Harrison smiled. "Oh, he'll do his time in Ohio, then we've got some unfinished business in the District to clear up. We'll find a safe foster home for him and I'll recommend he undergo intensive psychiatric evaluation and treatment to help him deal with his past. After that, it's up to Jared." The man paused. "But I think he'll do just fine. He knows someone gave up his life so he could have a second chance. That's got to make a difference in a person."

"It does," Grandpa Hanson stated.

Perry glanced over at the passenger pressed in beside him. "Did someone die for you?"

"Yes," the old man said softly. "A long, long time ago."

As the little pickup truck continued down the mountain road, a wedding party waited patiently by the big Station. Some distance away, a police cruiser headed for the paved road. Inside, a teenager gazed out the window at the passing scenes. He knew that here on Shadow Creek Ranch he'd never feel unwelcome again. Instead, he was now an invited guest, someday free to roam the mountains without fear or guilt, free to laugh and shout out his newfound joys just like the people in the pictures.

Jared gently placed his hand on the window glass as if touching the trees with his fingers. "I'm gonna come back," he whispered. "Wait for me. I'm gonna come back."

A random wind rippled the leaves as if in response. Then the stately aspens and tall pines regained their composure, standing erect, proudly guarding the valley where love lives, where young men and women find hope for tomorrow and are strangers no more.

Planet of Joy

Charles Mills

Dedication

To Dorinda,
The joy of my life,
the wings of my dreams.
I love you.

Contents

One Wedding and a Duck

Wendy Hanson tried to decide if anything in the world could possibly be more uncomfortable. She pulled on it, yanked on it, tried her best to ignore it, squirmed around in it, and finally decided that, even though there was a yardful of people staring at her, she was going to get out of it once and for all.

Walking stiff-legged and determined, she stumbled up the broad steps of the Station and burst through the front door just as her sister exited the den.

"Wendy? Where do you think you're going?" the older girl asked, as if she already knew the answer.

Wendy paused at the base of the curving staircase and turned to face her sibling, trying to look pleasant. "Well, hello, Debbie," she said sweetly. "Hey, nice wedding dress. You look like an angel. Gotta go."

"Gotta go?" Debbie asked, edging in her direction. "Go where?"

"To my room."

"To do what?"

Wendy frowned. "To spray paint a car."

The older girl eyed her 12-year-old sister suspiciously. "You wouldn't be thinking of changing your clothes, would you?"

"Who me? Change out of this? Why, I like this noisy, scratchy, cuts-off-my-circulation, makes-me-look-like-a-pumpkin dress. Whatever would cause you to think that I wanted to do such a totally insane thing?"

Debbie gathered the billowing folds of her wedding dress with one arm while trying to follow her sister up to the second floor. "You can't change now. The ceremony is about to begin. Grandpa just got back, and Samantha says Pastor Webley is beginning to clear his throat."

"I don't care," Wendy shot back over her shoulder. "I feel like an apple dumpling in this stupid dress. I'm going to put my jeans and sweatshirt on before I explode." She paused at her bedroom door. "I'm going to put on my riding boots too. So *live* with it!"

Debbie grabbed her sister's arm with her free hand. "Please, Wendy. Do I ever ask you to do anything for me?"

"Every minute of every day."

The older girl nodded. "Yes, but have I ever asked you to wear a dress before?"

"No. And now I know why."

The older girl groaned in frustration. "Wendy Hanson, you just can't change now. You'll spoil my wedding. What will people think if they see you standing by the guest book or sitting on the front row looking like . . . like . . . Lewis and Clark?"

"*They* can live with it, too!"

As the girls stumbled into the room, Wendy already had her dress down around her ankles and was reaching for the pair of soiled and faded blue jeans draped over the end of her bed.

"Wait . . . wait!" Debbie pleaded, trying to come up with some sort of enticement to stop the half-undressed girl from transforming herself from sister of the bride to wilderness explorer. "If you do this for me, I'll never ask another favor from you for the rest of your life."

"Never?" Wendy said, leg paused in midair, pants positioned below the heel.

"Never. I may want you to do something so bad it makes my teeth itch, but I won't ask. I'll just do it myself."

The younger girl turned. "Does that include washing dishes and cleaning your bathroom that smells like a perfume factory?"

"Yes."

"Does that include taking messages for you from your boring business friends in Bozeman who call you all the time wanting you to do stuff out at the mall and I can never find you 'cause you're out dancing around in the pasture with Barry Gordon?"

"That too."

Wendy thought for a minute. "Do you . . . do you promise to go riding with me every once in a while even though Barry wants you to do something with him?"

A gentle smile began to soften Debbie's worried face. "Yes, if that would make you happy."

"And do you promise to talk to me like in the past when I needed to know about girl stuff and Dad got all embarrassed?"

"Yes."

Relaxing, Wendy lowered herself onto the bed. "And do you promise that you will forever and ever and ever be . . . my sister even though you're getting married and moving up to Papoose Lake where Barry is building you a house with a porch on it?"

Debbie sat down beside her. "I will always be your sister, and you are always welcome to come up to my house and sit on my porch and we can talk about anything you want."

"Including boys?"

The older girl blinked. "Boys? You want to know about boys?"

Wendy shrugged. "Hey, you never know. I'm becoming a young lady—at least that's what Dad says—and young ladies sometimes have to do crazy things like go out on dates with boys, although I don't see what the great attraction is."

Her sister nodded. "Yes. We can talk about boys, or anything else." She paused. "So will you wear the dress just a little longer, at least until after the ceremony? Then you can put on whatever you want for the reception."

"Can I wear my ranch hat?"

"If that will make you more comfortable."

With a sigh Wendy reached for the pink and white folds of cloth billowing about her ankles. "When I get married," she said, "everyone can wear whatever they want, *including* jeans and sweatshirts. They can even wear a bathing suit if they choose to."

"Fair enough," Debbie said, helping the younger girl readjust the waistband and smooth the twisted sleeves. Running gentle fingers through her sister's short, blond hair, she added, "There, you look beautiful—even in this dress."

Wendy nodded shyly. "And . . . you look beautiful too, Debbie. Even in this . . . this long white thing."

The older girl smiled. "Thanks, sister."

Leaning over, Wendy hugged the bride. "You're welcome . . . sister. Now, let's go out and do this thing before I get scratched to death and you have to call the paramedics."

Hand in hand the two left the bedroom and made their way down the long staircase and across the foyer. From outside, soft guitar and organ music drifted in the cool autumn air. Across the lawn, by the footbridge, Pastor Webley stood next to Barry Gordon, still clearing his throat.

Seven-year-old Samantha sat on a folding chair near the front of the gathering with Lizzy Pierce on one side and Grandma and Grandpa Hanson on the other. Behind them in neat rows ranged the other wedding guests, each with smiles lighting their faces, expectantly waiting for the bride to appear on the broad front porch of the Station situated behind them, beyond the smooth, carefully clipped lawn. Heads turned while whispers mingled with the sweet scent of the roses lining the center aisle separating the friends of the bride from the friends of the groom.

"I see Wendy," Samantha announced, pointing at the young girl who quickly descended the steps and walked, somewhat awkwardly, over to where Mrs. Webley, the minister's wife, sat pumping the pedals and tapping the keys of an old organ. The girl in the pink and white dress leaned close to the musician and whispered something in her ear. The music stopped. The guitarist put down his instrument, and the organist joined her fingers in front of her and cracked her knuckles with a resounding *snap*. Then, after pumping furiously to build up pressure in the old organ, she lowered her hands until they hovered just over the keys. Finally, with a determined flourish, she pounced on the keyboard, sending the familiar chords of the wedding march out across the gathering and over the horse pasture beyond the footbridge.

All eyes turned to stare back at the Station, while Barry Gordon suddenly found it hard to swallow. There, standing at the top of the broad steps, white gown glowing brightly in the early afternoon sun, stood Debbie, a thin, wispy veil covering the soft flush of her face. A train of lacy fabric cascaded past the dark folds of her perfectly arranged hair, slipped by her shoulders, and flowed to the floor before forming silken waves that washed out behind her. Across the crown of the veil was a row of delicate wildflowers, and in her hands she held a bouquet of yellow daisies.

So impressive was her image at the top of the stairs that everyone's breath caught in their throats, sending an absolute silence out over the lawn. Even Mrs. Webley's fingers froze in midchord, her eyes unable to tear themselves away from the young woman waiting at the top of the stairs.

Lizzy Pierce leaned down and spoke softly into Samantha's ear. "That's your cue, sweetheart," she said.

Samantha nodded, then glanced at the basket nestled in her lap. "Oh yes. *Oh yes!*" the little dark-skinned girl breathed, stumbling to her feet. Still staring at the beautiful bride at the top of the distant steps, she made her way to the end of the long carpeted aisle and stopped at her assigned post, waiting for her signal to start spreading rose petals down the aisle between the two groups of guests.

Mrs. Webley, suddenly realizing that the music had stopped, attacked the keys with an even greater sense of determination, sending the soaring chords out across the gathering once again. Dressed in a dark suit and tie, Mr. Hanson appeared next to his daughter, and Debbie slipped her hand around the curve of his arm. Slowly, carefully, they descended the steps and made their way toward the seated assembly. As they crossed the lawn, young ranchhand Joey Dugan and much-loved neighbor Merrilee Dawson took up positions behind Samantha and, following the little girl's lead, walked along the rose-bordered aisle until they arrived at the base of the footbridge. Once there, they stood beside the minister and groom, waiting for the bride to make her way toward them.

Barry found unexpected tears welling up in his eyes. How he loved Debbie! And to think that she would love him enough to agree to be his wife was more than he could comprehend. It was here by the footbridge that he had discovered for the first time that he was in love with her.

He remembered the day she'd shyly tried to catch his attention and they'd both ended up falling into the very cold and very wet waters of Shadow Creek. It was here above the moon-sparkled waves that they'd first spoken intimate whispers of commitment and affection to each other. And now, it was here that they'd join their lives forever with the blessing of God and approval of family and friends. Theirs had been a courtship of mutual growth and restrained passion. It had been a relationship built on the dreams of the future, not on the desires of the present. Each knew that he or she could trust the other, come what may, to remain faithful and true to promises they'd be sharing that day.

As the grand chords of the old pump organ filled the valley, Barry Gordon knew that he'd found the girl of his dreams and that he would love her until the day he died.

Debbie stepped forward, supported by the arm of her father. She smiled, holding back tears of her own. It was her day, her time, her moment. And it was perfect.

Tugging gently on the reins, Wendy slowed her horse to a walk, allowing the warm sun to soak into their faces as they clippety-clopped along the mountaintop trail. It was midday in late October. The wedding and its scratchy, uncomfortable dress were only fading memories now, replaced by new challenges, new problems to endure, the latest of which weighed heavily on the young girl's mind.

"Let's stop and rest for a minute," Wendy suggested, guiding her horse Early toward a fallen log lying at the edge of a high meadow. The animal snorted softly as if to say, "Rest? *You* need rest? Just who's been climbing these mountains all morning, anyway?"

The girl slipped from the saddle and landed with a muffled plop on the short, dry grass that just a few weeks before had been thick with summer growth. Repeated nights of heavy frost had turned the meadow carpet into straw. Early ambled a short distance away in search of something to munch on while his young rider settled with a sigh on the log.

"Now what am I supposed to do?" he heard her say. "Everything's changing and I can't stop it." He saw her kick at a piece of rotting bark. "Just when life's going pretty good, along comes something that messes it all up. Man, being 12 is the pits!"

Early sampled some still-green growth hiding behind a large boulder and decided to let Wendy work out without his assistance whatever problem was making her so grumpy. After all, he'd been working hard, carrying her halfway around Montana since they'd left the Station after breakfast. He deserved a little peace and quiet . . . and a snack. She'd just have to figure things out by herself.

Wendy watched a hawk glide effortlessly in the clear blue sky overhead. How often she'd wished she could fly on powerful wings, rising high above the earth with its pain and troubles like a bird riding mountain thermals. But she was a person, not a hawk. She was also a 12-year-old sixth grader who lived on a beautiful ranch with a loving family and had her very own horse to ride. But even all of those blessings weren't enough to keep problems from plaguing her, spoiling her fun, making her work harder at happiness than she thought necessary.

The latest attack on her contentment had come just yesterday, at breakfast, when her father raised his hand, indicating that he had an important announcement to make.

"We got a phone call from New York last night," he said after everyone had either stopped talking or stuffed enough oatmeal into their mouths to make speech difficult. "Seems Lizzy's sister is ailing and needs someone to care for her right away. I've arranged for Mrs. Pierce to fly back on Sunday. We hope this will be only a temporary situation, but illnesses like these can be tricky. In any case, we'll miss our good friend and home school teacher very much."

All eyes had turned to the end of the table where Lizzy Pierce sat looking anything but pleased with the latest turn of events. "I'll miss you all so much," she said softly. "But Sissy needs me, and I'm the only one left in the family who can care for her. She lives alone out on Long Island, and if I don't go, she'll suffer more than she needs to."

"We understand," Mr. Hanson stated, deep sym-

15

pathy filling his voice. "You just go and do what you need to do, and we'll muddle on without you until you get back. Don't you worry about us, OK?"

Lizzy nodded, then glanced at Wendy. "I . . . I won't be able to be your teacher this year for home school, and your father and I have decided that perhaps you should attend the local public school until I get back. Joey's busy with his freshman studies at Bozeman State three days a week, and Grandma Hanson has volunteered to help Samantha with her courses. But you, Wendy dear, would need someone to keep you motivated. School work isn't exactly your favorite activity, right?"

Wendy grinned. "I'd rather hike in the mountains, if that's what you mean."

"Exactly," Lizzy responded with a smile. "So we figured you could use a firm hand to keep you on track educationally."

Joey leaned forward. "That's a nice way of saying that without someone to ride your case, you'd flunk everything but recess."

Lizzy shook her head. "You see, Wendy, school is supposed to teach you more than facts, figures, and history dates. Whether you attend classes at a public facility or do your lessons in the Station den beside the hearth, you're learning self-discipline, keeping schedules, meeting challenges, and seeing projects through to the end. That's what life is all about, especially when you get older."

Samantha waved her hand. "If Lizzy isn't here

16

and Grandma Hanson is my teacher, do I still have to learn how to add three numbers?"

"Yes," the old woman beside her said lovingly, adding a hug to her response. "And multiply and divide and subtract them, too."

The little girl sighed and looked up at her adopted grandmother. "If I have to do too many problems like that, I'll get as sick as Lizzy's sister."

Wendy frowned. "I don't want to go to public school." Then she brightened. "Tell you what, I'll study harder here at home. Honest. I'll read every assignment and look up stuff on the Internet and even finish that report on . . . on . . ."

"South America?" Lizzy prompted.

"Yeah, South America. I'll even get it in on time. When's it due—tomorrow, Friday?"

"Two weeks ago," the woman sighed, with a knowing grin.

Wendy blinked. "Well, what about that science experiment where I'm supposed to grow a seed in a jar with only water and no dirt?"

"*That's* due tomorrow."

The girl glanced about the table in sudden desperation. "Anybody here have any fast-growing seeds on you?"

Lizzy shook her head. "You're a very smart girl, Wendy," she said with pride. "It makes you able to do anything you want without even breaking a sweat. But it's just that you need someone to keep you in those books, someone to make sure you complete your assignments. Grandma Hanson says that with me gone, housework will take up too much of her time. Samantha will be all she can handle. I'm sorry, Wendy. We don't have any other choice."

"Any other choice," the girl repeated as the hawk disappeared behind a distant mountain. "Great. Now I've got to go to school with a bunch of morons who'll probably hate me and call me things like Pyrite Head." She fingered the unruly golden strands of hair sticking out from under her favorite ranch hat. "And I'll have to wear clean clothes and everything. Every day! Man, life is the *pits!*"

The hawk reappeared and floated down through the valley that spread toward the east. Mount Blackmore rose stately and proud beyond, its snow-covered 10,000-foot summit crowning the boundaries of the Gallatin National Forest. Wendy had attended public school for several years back in New York City. Not having liked it then, she knew beyond a shadow of a doubt she wouldn't like it now.

It wasn't that she hated learning—it was just that she liked to learn at her own pace, on her own schedule. During the past three years Lizzy had accepted her rather unorthodox study habits and worked around them. Wendy did get everything done—eventually. But the girl knew that public school with its stricter schedules and more exact rules would blow her learning style clean out of the water. Home school suited her perfectly. Going to class with a roomful of other students didn't. And, most troublesome of all, she'd be out of reach of her beloved mountains every single school day.

"Hey, Early," she called, rising on tired legs. "Come on. Let's get back to the Station. I'm getting kinda hungry myself, and this meadow grass doesn't look all that appealing." The little stallion obediently sauntered over to his master and stood patiently as she lifted herself up and settled comfortably in the saddle. "We'll have to save our rides for the weekend," she announced, as if breaking a bit of horrible news to the horse trotting below her. "But don't worry, they can take the girl out of the mountains, but they can't take the mountains out of the girl. If I have to attend school like all the other lemmings in the world, they'll just have to learn that this rodent is a force to be reckoned with." She paused. "Wait, that didn't come out quite right."

Horse and rider galloped away, catching the cool breezes off the high meadow. With a growing feeling of uncertainty, Wendy headed for the valley far below where the grand Station stood by a sparkling creek, and where 12-year-old girls had to learn that, even in Montana, life didn't always unfold to their liking. Still, she figured that if she could survive being knocked off a mountain by a stray lightning bolt, getting snowbound in a house with no heat, or being swallowed by the earth it-

19

self, she could withstand attending public school for a while. What were a bunch of kids compared to the force of Mother Nature herself?

"Wendy?" a male voice called from the other side of the closed bedroom door. "Wendy, are you awake?"

"No," the girl moaned.

"Well, you'd better get awake. Grandma Hanson's got pancakes on the stove, and your dad sent me up here to find out if you're still alive."

"Go away."

"I'm supposed to take you to Gallatin Gateway this morning. It's your first day at your new school, remember? Are you nervous?"

"Why are you talking to me?"

"Besides, you get to ride in my new old truck, if it will start, although it should 'cause Grandpa Hanson put a new battery in it yesterday. That vehicle sure makes the girls' heads turn at the university."

Wendy pulled the covers up over her ears. "They're trying to figure out what idiot would buy something that looks like the Montana Air National Guard used it for bombing practice."

The teenager opened the door and stuck his head into the room, a smile lighting his sun-tanned face. "It just needs a little paint."

"Paint? Listen, Mr. Dugan, I don't mean to be

the bearer of bad news, but paint doesn't stick too good to rust."

Joey laughed. "You're just jealous that I've got a vehicle and all you've got is a scrawny horse."

Wendy sat up straight. "Scrawny? Early isn't scrawny. You must mean Tar Boy, that ugly collection of skin, bones, and hair you call a horse. Now, *that's* scrawny!"

"Tar Boy can outrun, outjump, outclimb, and outpull any horse on the ranch, and you know it."

"In your dreams."

"Dreams nothin'! Why, Tar Boy is the best horse in southern Montana. Even Wrangler Barry says so."

Wendy shook her head and frowned at him. "Barry has about as much horse sense as he does girl sense. I mean, look who he married!"

"Guys, guys, guys," another male voice called from the hallway. "It's too early in the morning to listen to you two get on each other's cases." Mr. Hanson's frowning face appeared at the door. "Wendy, get up! Joey, go . . . go do whatever you do out in the barn so you can help get little Miss Congeniality here and your overconfident self to your respective places of higher education on time. OK?"

"Good morning, Daddy," Wendy said, her words stretched by a wide yawn.

"Yes, sir, Mr. H," Joey called, turning to leave. "I was just trying to get her up. Now you can have the pleasure." He paused and placed an understanding hand on the man's shoulder. "Good luck."

Mr. Hanson chuckled. "I've been doing it longer than you have and know what you mean. Thanks for the encouragement."

As Joey trotted away, the lawyer entered his daughter's bedroom and sat down at the foot of her bed. "How're you doin', sweetheart? Usually you're up long before this, wandering the halls like the ghost of Christmas past. As a matter of fact, you're usually up before the roosters crow in *Ohio.*" He smiled down at his daughter. "Are you ready for your new adventure?"

"Isn't that what Caesar said to the Christians right before he dropped them off at the Coliseum?"

"No. He told them that the lions had invited them over for dinner."

"*Yuck!*" Wendy winced.

Mr. Hanson smoothed the hair streaking her forehead. "It won't be all that bad. You'll see."

Wendy sighed. "I don't like crowds of people anymore," she said. "I like being alone, up in the mountains with Early, exploring the old logging roads every afternoon. Now, three days a week, I have to take my life in my hands and ride with Joey Dugan, and the other two days I've got to sit in a big yellow school bus with a bunch of noisy strangers."

"The logging roads will still be there on the weekends," Mr. Hanson encouraged, "and Early's not going anywhere either. It's just for a few months or a little longer. You'll do fine."

Wendy edged close to her father and settled herself in the circle of his arms. "But what if they don't like me? What if they think I'm weird?"

"You *are* weird," Mr. Hanson stated.

The girl grinned. "Yeah, well, I don't like anyone reminding me of that fact."

The man held his daughter close. "If anybody bothers you, you just tell me about it. I'll personally go over to that school and sue those little monsters for everything they own. They won't have disposable income until they're 50!"

Wendy batted her eyes. "Why, Mr. Hanson, you'd do that for little ol' me?"

"Absolutely. Now, as your lawyer it is my duty to inform you that breakfast is being served and that if you don't get out of this bed in the next three seconds, I'll get Samantha in here with Pueblo the dog, and they'll start your day in their own special way."

"I'm up, *I'm up!*" the girl giggled, jumping out of bed. "Just keep that dog and his overactive spit glands away from me."

Mr. Hanson laughed. "Deal," he said, walking to the door. He paused for a moment and studied the pajama-clad form of his daughter. "I love you, Wendy," he said softly. "And I know that the Lewis and Clark Elementary School will be a terrific place for you to learn. Says so in the brochure."

Wendy narrowed her eyes. "I'm sending a jar of

vitamins to Lizzy's sister so she'll get better *fast*—just in case."

With that she grabbed her cleanest pair of blue jeans, pulled her favorite red sweatshirt down from a closet hook, and headed for the bathroom door. Before turning to leave, Mr. Hanson noticed something unusual in the now empty room. Wendy's riding boots, the pair she wore most, had been shined. A Station first.

Joey shifted and released the clutch, causing the vehicle to slow slightly as it rounded a curve. Wendy studied the somewhat mismatched dials and engine instruments fronting the cab of the little foreign truck and shook her head in disbelief. "And you paid how much for this pile of junk?"

Joey grinned proudly. "$500."

The girl ran her fingers along the top of the dashboard, inspecting a long gash. "Boy, they saw *you* coming."

"Hey," the driver said, "this is a great truck. Engine works—most of the time. It's got good tires, and the brakes are only a year old. Grandpa Hanson showed me how to adjust them myself. Besides, Wrangler Barry taught me how to drive, remember? He said my skills behind the wheel were—how did he put it?—beyond description."

Wendy chuckled. "And I suppose you took that as a compliment?"

Joey frowned. "Well, yeah. Wasn't it?"

The girl smiled. "Sure, Joey. You're a natural."

The truck slammed into a deep rut and bounced out again. Joey glanced at his passenger and cleared his throat. "I'll bet you didn't think I saw that one, huh? Well, I just wanted to show you how strong this ol' vehicle is." He patted the steering wheel lovingly. "Built like a tank."

"Rides like one too," Wendy moaned, rubbing the small of her back. "And to think I get to sit in this . . . this Spam can with wheels twice a day, three days a week."

"Hey," Joey responded with a frown, "you can get out and walk if you want."

Wendy shook her head. "Nah. I'd get to school way too early. Besides—*watch out!*"

Joey swerved as what looked like some type of animal appeared out of nowhere and flashed by the front of the truck. The two occupants heard a sharp *thump,* then the vehicle skidded to a dusty stop.

"You hit it. *You hit it!*" Wendy wailed.

Joey's hands began to tremble. "Yeah. I think I did. But I didn't mean to. Honest. I didn't see whatever it was until it was too late. Oh, what have I done? What have I done?"

The girl, seeing how truly shaken he was, softened a little. "It's OK, Joey. You couldn't stop in time. It was an accident."

"But I may have killed some animal with my

truck. I wasn't going fast or anything. It just shot by and I hit it."

"Really, Joey, it's OK. Maybe the animal isn't hurt bad. Maybe it just got up and ran away."

The boy slowly opened the door and looked back in the direction they'd just come. At first he couldn't see anything because of the dust. Then as the air began to clear, he noticed a small mound of feathers lying in the gravel by the road 15 to 20 feet behind them. The feathers didn't move and no sound disturbed the valley silence.

The door creaked and snapped as Joey opened it wider and stepped out of the truck. "I think it's a goose or a duck," he whispered, as if the fallen fowl were asleep and he didn't want to wake it. "Do you see it, Wendy? Do you see what I did?"

Wendy unfastened her seatbelt, slipped from the truck cab, and joined him at the rear of the vehicle. Both stood staring at the bird, afraid to think of what they'd see if they moved any closer.

"You didn't mean to," Wendy whispered. "Really, Joey. It was an accident."

Suddenly the mound of feathers shifted slightly, then became still again. "Hey," Joey breathed, "I think it moved. Didn't it move?"

Wendy shook her head. "Yeah. There, it did it again. I think it's still alive."

The two edged forward, pressed against each other for support, moving as one toward the pile of broken feathers by the side of the road. As they neared the bird they heard a faint *quack*. Then a *quack, quack.*

Joey pointed. "Dead animals don't quack, do they?"

"No," Wendy stated. "They just lie still and don't say anything."

Quack.

The boy studied the creature for a long moment. "It's alive."

"I think you're right," his companion agreed.

"Maybe we should take it someplace, you know, like to a vet."

Wendy slowly knelt beside the stricken bird and ran her hand over the rumpled feathers, some of which jutted at odd angles from the body. "I don't think any bones are broken," she said. "And there's no blood." She leaned forward and examined the creature more thoroughly, being careful not to cause any more pain. "It's a duck, a male mallard duck. See the green head and gray rump feathers? These guys fly over the Station all the time, especially in the fall. This one's kinda late. He must've been left behind when the rest of the flock headed south. Maybe he's old and can't fly all day like the others."

Joey joined her. "Will he be OK? I mean, is he going to die?"

The girl shook her head. "I don't think so. Red Stone taught me and Plenty a lot about animals and how they're strong and can live through stuff,

27

even getting creamed by a really ugly truck."

Joey frowned. "My truck's not ugly. It has character. That's what Grandpa Hanson says."

Wendy chuckled. "This from a man who thinks primer is a fashion accessory."

"So?" the boy pressed, "will the duck be OK?"

Wendy reached down and gently lifted the bird into her arms. The animal's eyes blinked open and he stared at the young girl for a long moment, as if trying to size her up. Was she a danger to him? Or would she help him? The little duck must've decided on the latter because it slowly, painfully tucked its brown beak under a collection of dirt-stained and somewhat frayed wing feathers and went quickly to sleep.

"Yes," Wendy nodded, stumbling to her feet, duck held securely against her chest. "He'll be fine, although he's pretty badly bruised. Maybe he's got some cracked ribs and stuff. It'll be a while before he can fly again, or even walk for that matter, but our friend will live if he gets lots of care and someone brings him food to eat. Out here in the wild, the mountain lions would put him out of his misery fast."

"Should we head back to the Station?" Joey asked.

"No," Wendy sighed, glancing at her watch. "I'm going to be late to school as it is now. We've gotta go on." The two started for the truck. "I'll watch over Feathers for the rest of the day. Then

28

we'll find a nice quiet place for him at the Station when we get home this afternoon."

Joey slipped into the driver's seat and twisted the key in the ignition. "Let me get this straight," he said. "You're going to show up at a new school filled with people you don't know while carrying a duck in your arms?"

Wendy groaned. "It's gonna look kinda strange, isn't it?"

The driver shook his head. "They'll crucify you, Wendy. They'll laugh you right out of class. Wouldn't you rather that we drop the little guy off somewhere?"

The girl smoothed the soft down covering the sleeping bird's back. "We hit 'im. We should take care of 'im. Just don't be late picking me up this afternoon. I don't wanna stand around after school for very long—if you know what I mean."

Joey guided his rattling, vibrating truck over the rutted road and glanced over at his two passengers. "I'll be there right at 3:00," he said. Then he added, "You're somethin' else, Wendy. Do you know that? You're one of a kind."

"Why, Mr. Dugan, I appreciate the compliment."

The driver blinked. "Compliment? You took that as a compliment?"

With a smile Wendy continued stroking the creature resting comfortably in her lap. The day was going to be one of a kind as well. She closed her eyes. Just how would she face a new school filled with curious eyes while holding a sleeping duck in her arms?

The old truck turned right onto State Highway 191 and headed north. Gallatin Gateway was but a few miles ahead. Whatever the day held in store, she'd just have to face it, duck and all.

CHAPTER 2

Birds of
a Feather

Joey's truck clattered away from the curb, leaving Wendy standing in front of a large brick building with tall glass windows and a row of thick pillars guarding the entrance. From her shoulders hung a backpack filled with pencils, notebooks, and a pocket calculator. In her arms she held a duck.

The structure reminded her of pictures she'd seen of elegant Southern plantations except, in this case, it had no long porches or wispy webs of Spanish moss hanging from the almost leafless trees nearby. A sidewalk curved gracefully from where she stood to a set of wide steps fronting enormous green doors. Above the entrance, in glowing yellow letters, were carved the words, "LEWIS AND CLARK ELEMENTARY SCHOOL —Teaching Tomorrow's Great Explorers Today."

"Oh great," the girl groaned to herself, looking around at the empty front lawn and silent playground off to her right. "Everyone's inside just waiting to make my day more miserable than it already is."

She glanced down at the mallard held tightly in her arms. "Are you ready for this?" she asked.

The duck wiggled its head and snorted softly as if to say, "Thirty minutes ago I got hit by a really ugly truck. I've got enough to worry about."

Drawing in a deep breath, Wendy walked up the sidewalk, climbed the steps, and pushed open one of the doors. The hallway was empty. From places unseen echoed the sounds of education as future explorers learned whatever their teachers and the state of Montana had decided was needed to prepare them for the wildernesses of life.

Wendy noticed a sign hanging above a nearby door: "Registrar." "This is where we go," she whispered. The duck didn't respond. Like all wild animals trying to heal themselves, it had fallen asleep again.

The girl opened the door and approached a woman sitting stiff and businesslike at a metal desk, typing furiously on an old, rattling typewriter. Her dark brown hair had been cropped close to her head, making her ears stick out like miniature wings. "I'll be right with you," she said without looking up.

With a few more pounding entries, she whipped the paper from the machine and held it at arm's length, examining the results of her labor through thick, silver-rimmed glasses. "You can keep your computers and fancy printers," she proclaimed to no one in particular. "Just give me a good ol' IBM Selectric and a clean piece of 20-pound and I can create correspondence anyone would be proud of." She quickly folded the letter and jammed it into an envelope. Lifting a preprinted form from her drawer, she dropped it expertly into the typewriter, twisted it into position, and called out, "Name?"

Wendy blinked. "Ah, Wendy. Wendy Hanson."

"Oh, yes," the woman said, still not allowing her eyes to move from the machine, her fingers tapping like pistons in an engine. "You're from Shadow Creek Ranch. Your father was in here last week. Age?"

The girl cleared her throat. "Twelve. Twelve and a half. My birthday's in June."

"Everyone's in a hurry to grow up," the woman said, continuing to type. "Any special diet or scheduled medicines?"

Wendy frowned. "I'm a vegetarian, if that's what you mean."

"No animal products." The registrar spoke the words as she typed them. "Any allergies?"

"I think homework gives me a rash."

The woman didn't flinch. "No reported allergies," she typed-spoke. "Money?"

The girl smiled. "Sure, I'll take some."

The registrar's fingers paused for a split second. "I meant, do you have money on you to pay meal or lab fees, but I take it you don't. I'm glad you find our school admissions form humorous. You can laugh your way clear through the sixth grade if you like." She lifted the paper from the typewriter and expertly thrust it into an open file drawer at her knee. Then she rose and hurried across the room, calling over her shoulder. "You're in room 1-F. Teacher's Miss Elrod. And you're late. First class has already begun. Welcome to Lewis and Clark."

Wendy watched the woman busy herself at a tall file cabinet. "Thanks," she said.

The registrar responded with a melodious, "You're laaa-ate."

"Yeah. 1-F. I'm outta here. See ya."

She saw the woman wave without turning, then dig into some papers, mumbling something about how her work was never done and completely unappreciated.

Back in the hallway, Wendy studied the room numbers and letters screwed tightly into the doors. 1-C, 1-D, 1-F. "Here we are," she said, trying to sound hopeful. "I wonder what Miss Elrod is like."

The door burst open, startling her as a boy her age exited the classroom. He glanced at Wendy and the duck. "Weird," he said, then hurried down the hall toward a door emblazoned with the silhouette figure of a man.

"Is someone out there?" Wendy heard a woman's

voice call. Stepping through the doorway, she found herself standing at the front of a large room filled with students, all staring at her in complete and utter silence. The teacher stood by the blackboard, hand poised in midword, fingers dusted white with chalk. "May I help you?" she asked.

Wendy shifted her position. "Ah, yes ma'am. My name is Wendy Hanson, and I'm supposed to be your student." The girl suddenly discovered that all the saliva in her mouth had vanished, leaving her tongue feeling as if it was lying on a bed of desert sand.

Miss Elrod's eyes narrowed slightly, giving her otherwise friendly face a somewhat tense look. "My dear, are you aware that you're holding a duck in your arms?"

"Yes, ma'am," Wendy breathed, her knees trembling. "You see, Joey—that's the guy who takes care of the horses on the ranch—hit him with his truck, and I'm trying to make him well again. We couldn't just leave him by the road, and we were late already, so I decided I'd bring him to school with me . . . if that's OK. He won't bother anyone."

Just then the duck raised its head and let out a loud *QUACK!*

The room erupted into laughter as Wendy's face glowed crimson. Miss Elrod immediately called for silence and walked over to where her new pupil stood. Her movements were graceful and professional, an easy match to her carefully ironed dress and polished shoes. Every strand of her auburn hair was in place, held tightly by a set of small matching combs. "Will you be bringing wild animals to school every day?" she asked.

"No, ma'am. Only those that Joey hits with his truck."

Laughter burst throughout the room again. This time Miss Elrod's rosy lips quivered slightly in a suppressed grin. "That will be fine. Now take your place in that empty seat over by the window, and we'll find a nice, comfortable box in which to place your feathered friend for the day." She paused. "Does he have a name?"

"Well," Wendy said, edging to her spot by the large expanse of glass, "Joey and I kinda call him Feathers 'cause he's got a lot of 'em."

Miss Elrod nodded. "Well, put Feathers in that box over there by the bookcase and cover him with something so he can rest. We'll talk about this more later, OK?"

"OK," Wendy whispered. She'd never been so embarrassed in all her life. Her world during the past few years had been cozy dens and wide-open spaces high atop endless mountain ranges. Now, here she was, jammed into a classroom with dozens her age who must be thinking that she was the weirdest individual ever to walk the earth.

Eyes followed her every movement. Giggles hissed through fingers held tightly against mouths as she lowered the injured duck into an empty box and covered it with an open newspaper. Then she took her seat and folded her hands in front of her, not looking to the left or to the right. Her greatest desire at that moment was for the ground to open up below her and allow her to fall into its inky darkness.

"Welcome, Wendy," Miss Elrod said with a genuine, but cautious smile. "We're studying geography during our first session this morning. Your textbook is under your seat. Please open to page 69."

As Wendy bent to retrieve the assigned book, she heard someone behind her quack softly. Then a student across the room did the same, followed by several other renditions of what the young mimics believed was a reasonable imitation of duck talk. The girl closed her eyes. Yup. This was about what she'd expected her day to be like. Glancing at the big clock above the blackboard, she took note that she'd been at the Lewis and Clark school for exactly 18 minutes. Only six hours and 42 minutes to go.

"We're studying South America," Miss Elrod announced for the new student's benefit. "Can anyone list five of its countries?"

Sighing, Wendy shook her head. South America was proving to be an extremely persistent continent in her life.

The noon hour provided some welcome relief to

the day's strangeness. Wendy gathered her lunch at the cafeteria line and hurried out into the cool late autumn air, selecting a spot at the far end of the playground to enjoy her food. At her feet was the box containing the somewhat more lively duck.

"You're lucky," Wendy said between bites of her lettuce and tomato sandwich. A steaming bowl of cream of celery soup sat on the bench beside her. "You don't have to go to school. All you need to do is fly south to some deserted beach and tan your feathers all winter." She paused. "Of course, you've got to dodge hunters' bullets, keep an eye open for hungry hawks, stay out of reach of snapping turtles while swimming in ponds, and fly above truck level, especially over roads. H'mmm. I guess we both have our problems."

The duck's head tilted slightly as he watched the girl with the short blond hair take a bite out of her sandwich. Wendy noticed the careful scrutiny she was receiving from her web-footed friend and grinned broadly. "You're hungry, aren't you? That's great. That means you're not hurt too bad inside. Red Stone, my old Indian friend who used to spend his summers up on Freedom Mountain, taught me and his granddaughter Plenty that if an animal or person is hungry after an injury, that's a good sign. Healing takes energy. Energy comes from food. So . . ." Wendy pulled out a fat chunk of lettuce and dangled it in front of the duck. "How would you like a piece of—"

In an instant the big green leaf vanished.

"Wow!" Wendy breathed. "You *are* hungry." She extracted another portion from her bulging sandwich. Feathers downed that offering too, his beak smacking in jubilant ecstasy. "This is good. This is very good," she said, watching her small companion eagerly take the food she offered. "You'll be well and flyin' south in no time."

"I like your duck," a voice said. Wendy glanced up to see a girl standing some distance away, as if too shy to approach any farther.

"Well, at least he likes lettuce," she said. "'Cept I'm about to run out."

"Here," the stranger called, lifting her tray of food. "He can have some of mine."

Wendy watched her visitor walk slowly, almost methodically, toward her. The girl's faded jacket and much-worn pants hung from her bony arms and legs like flags without a wind. Her face appeared etched with frown lines, and dark shadows hung under her slightly puffy eyes. Her hair was thin and wayward. "I'm really not hungry. Feathers can have as much as he likes."

With a smile Wendy made room for the girl on the bench. "Are you sure?" she asked.

"Oh yes. I don't eat much. I've been kinda sick, and food doesn't taste too good sometimes." The stranger held out a slice of apple in the duck's direction. "My name's Emily, and I sit near the back of Miss Elrod's class. Boy, you musta been embarrassed this morning, new kid in school, comin' in late, Feathers."

Wendy grinned. "I've had better days."

"Well, I for one think that what you're doing is very nice, taking care of this little guy and all. It's not fun to hurt. Believe me." She offered another morsel to the duck. "Some days I feel like a truck smacked into me too."

Frowning slightly, Wendy asked, "What's the matter with you?"

Emily shook her head. "Oh, I got something wrong inside. Been kinda ailing since the day I was born. Doctors just shake their heads. I mean, I'm not gonna drop over dead anytime soon, at least I hope not. But I can't run around and stuff. Just gotta walk slowly."

"Do you have cancer or something like that?"

Chuckling, Emily said, "Strange as it may seem, I'd be better off if I did. They can do a lot of stuff with cancer nowadays. No, picked up something new recently that nobody is supposed to have anymore."

Wendy watched Feathers gobble down a chunk of bread. "So, what is it?"

The other girl stumbled slowly to her feet, her eyes not leaving the duck. "Ever heard of TB?"

Wendy gasped. "Tuberculosis? You have tuberculosis?"

"Bingo."

"I thought they—"

40

"Yeah," Emily interrupted, "everyone thought they'd gotten rid of that nasty little disease years and years ago. 'Cept the TB bacteria changed themselves enough so the vaccinations don't work anymore for some people. I've got a modern version of an old killer. Lucky me."

As if to clear her thoughts, Wendy shook her head. "So, what do you—"

"Listen, I've gotta go do some studying," the girl said, pointing toward the school building. "Here, you and Feathers can finish my lunch for me." She paused and studied the bird resting comfortably in the box. "Hey, Wendy, thanks for taking such good care of him. It's not fun to hurt. It's not fun at all."

With that she ambled away, her walk slow and steady, her feet shuffling slightly as she moved past the kick-ball game that filled the playground with excited laughter. No one paid any attention to her as she passed by. Everyone was too intent on the game, on the runners, on the score.

Wendy sat in silence for a long moment watching a girl lost in a crowd, surrounded by activity and laughter. And all that girl could do was shuffle slowly past without anyone noticing her, without being a part of the world in which she moved.

With a sigh, Wendy tossed the last remnants of her lunch in Feather's direction. The bird sniffed at it, then turned his head.

41

School buses vied for position as long lines of children clamored to board. Shouts echoed across the parking lot while diesel fumes tainted the air and crossing guards waved traffic along the roads and driveways fronting the building.

Wendy stood at the far end of the sidewalk, getting madder and madder at Joey Dugan, who hadn't made his appearance yet. Occasionally a group of girls would stroll by, glance at the duck hiding in the box at her feet, giggle to themselves, then hurry away, whispering and pointing over their shoulders.

The school day had finally ended—almost. Now all she had to do was make her escape. Except that Joey hadn't kept his promise of picking her up at exactly 3:00. *Typical male,* she thought with a frustrated shake of her head.

Beep. Beep.

A car squeaked to a halt in front of her, and a smiling face peered from the driver's side. "You look kinda lost," a voice called above the din of departing buses and chatter of students.

Wendy blinked. "Why does Joey Dugan look so much like Ruth Cadena today?" she asked.

"Because Joey Dugan asked me to pick you up," came the pleasant reply. "He had to stay late to finish an unexpected lab assignment. Hope you don't mind."

Opening the back door, Wendy gently lowered the duck box onto the seat. Then she opened the front door and jumped in. "I wouldn't care if he sent the space shuttle to pick me up. Just get me outta here! Take me back to the ranch where I can count everyone around me on two hands without using my toes."

Ms. Cadena chuckled as she guided the automobile away from the curb. "Bad first day, huh?"

"Ever heard of the Gulf War?"

"Yeah," the woman said.

"It was like that," Wendy stated, "except the only bombs that got dropped on me were dirty looks. Of course showing up for class with a duck in your arms isn't going to win you any bonus points in the popularity contest. Everyone thinks I'm a real freak. One guy called me Noah and asked me where I'd parked the ark."

The woman winced. "Ouch. I see what you mean."

Wendy stared out the window, watching the last remnants of Gallatin Gateway flash by. "Well, not everyone was a pain," she confessed. "There was this one girl. Kinda nice, but sorta strange too." Wendy turned to the driver. "Did you know that it's possible to get TB again?"

Ruth Cadena nodded. "Oh, you met Emily Wells. Yeah. She contracted the disease about a year ago."

"You know about her?"

"Sure," the woman chuckled, "it's my job. After all, I am a social worker, remember? *And* western director of Project Youth Revival? *And* enthusiastic supporter of Shadow Creek Ranch for three years?"

"And *very special* friend of my dad for those same three years, right?"

Ms. Cadena nodded shyly. "You noticed, huh?"

Wendy grinned, then grew pensive. "So what's with this Emily person? She seems so sad."

"Well, she doesn't exactly have a lot in her life to make her happy. Her folks are struggling financially. Hospital bills have devastated them, to say nothing of watching their only child suffer from a disease that no one is supposed to get. But they seem to be surviving somehow. She has to get X-rays of her chest every month or so and repeated skin tests. Her case is proving to be tricky because today's TB strains seem to be resistant to traditional treatments and medications. From what the doctor told me, her lungs are very damaged."

"Will she get better?"

"Eventually, yes—to a point. But how fast that happens no one knows. I guess it depends on how strong her body is and how hard it can fight to heal itself. For now, all she can do is make the best of a very dangerous situation."

For a long moment Wendy was silent. "I guess I'm kinda lucky, aren't I?"

"We all are."

The car sped along State Highway 191, heading

south toward the towering mountains that rose up ahead like a granite curtain. Wendy watched the bare fields and tree-lined roads flash by. That morning she'd rescued an injured duck who couldn't fly. Now she was wondering what she could do to help a sixth grader who couldn't run.

Seven-year-old Samantha jumped from her perch on the porch and ran to greet Ms. Cadena's car as it rumbled down the long driveway leading to the Station. The girl's face shone with the excitement reserved only for greeting family members whom she hadn't seen for at least five minutes. "I got an A on my spelling test," she called through the open window while holding up a piece of paper with the grade written in bold red ink near the top. "I even spelled 'hotel.' Can you spell 'hotel,' Wendy?"

Wendy grinned broadly as the car moved slowly toward the parking spot under a tall cottonwood. "Hey, that's great, Sam. Good for you! No, I don't think I could spell such a hard word."

Samantha glanced in at the back seat. "What's in the box?" she asked, her breath a little labored from all the excitement and running around.

Wendy jumped out as soon as the car stopped. "It's a duck."

"A duck?" the younger girl gasped. "Did you buy it in Bozeman?"

"No, we hit it in the Gallatin National Forest. Joey's truck and our little friend here were trying to occupy the same spot at the same time. The duck lost."

"Is he dead?"

"No. He's alive and hungry. Poor fella's kinda banged up, so he can't walk or fly yet. But he'll get better, I hope."

Retrieving the box from the back seat, Wendy let Samantha peek inside. "Hello, Duck," Samantha said.

"His name is Feathers."

"Oh, hello, Feathers." The little girl grinned. "I like that name."

The three started walking toward the Station steps. "So," Ms. Cadena said, "are you going to help Wendy take care of the newest member of the ranch?"

"Sure," Samantha stated firmly. "I can even teach it how to spell 'hotel.'"

Tyler Hanson appeared at the second-story balcony as the trio entered the large foyer below. "Hey," he called. "Where's Joey?"

"He had to stay late at the university," Ms. Cadena answered, waving up at the man. "So I picked up our schoolgirl and brought her home."

Wendy glanced up at her father. "I know how disappointed you are," she said. "We'll try not to let it happen again."

The man descended the steps and took Ruth in

his arms. "Oh, I think I'll get over it," he said, gazing into her eyes. "Hi, Beautiful," he whispered.

Glancing at Samantha, Wendy said, "Why do I get the impression that we just became invisible?"

The younger girl giggled. "I think they like each other . . . a lot."

Ms. Cadena blushed. "Tyler, aren't you going to say hello to your daughter?"

"Daughter?" the man frowned. "I have a daughter?"

Wendy rolled her eyes. "It's like Debbie and Barry all over again."

Mr. Hanson scooped up the girl with his arms and lifted her off the floor. "Wendy! My sweet Wendy! Oh, yes, I remember you. Likes to ride a horse named Early, gets up before air, and never, ever gets into any kinda trouble no matter how hard she tries." He paused. "When did you get so big?"

Staring at her father nose to nose, Wendy giggled, "Maybe you should put me down before you hurt yourself."

He lowered her back onto the polished wood floorboards. "They grow up too fast," he said, almost to himself. "Much too fast."

"Well," Wendy stated, bending down and picking up her box, "while you contemplate the years as they roll by, I've got to get Feathers something to eat and a comfortable place to sleep here in the Station."

"Feathers? What's a Feathers?" Mr. Hanson asked.

Ms. Cadena smiled and took his arm in hers. "I'll explain everything if you'll join me for a short walk down by Shadow Creek."

Wendy watched the two adults amble out of the Station hand in hand and head for the distant footbridge. She sighed. Romance still puzzled her, but, for some unexplainable reason, it seemed a little less disgusting lately. Maybe her dad was right. Perhaps she was growing up.

A loud *quack, quack* from the box brought her thoughts back to the present. Love could wait. Now she had a hungry duck to feed. She and Samantha headed for the kitchen where the clank of pots and pans meant Grandma was beginning to fix supper. Sometimes the mysteries of life just had to make way for the reality of hungry waterfowl.

Evening shadows threaded their way among the cottonwoods and pines at the far end of the pasture. The air turned from chilly to cold, sending forest creatures deep into dens and the human inhabitants of Shadow Creek Ranch to their favorite spots before the roaring fire in a den of their own.

Joey yawned broadly and stretched his long legs as Samantha dozed by his knees. Grandpa Hanson turned the pages of a ranching magazine while his wife munched on kernels of popcorn left over from supper.

Wendy busied herself with newly assigned homework, allowing the warmth of the fireplace to wash over her like billowy waves from a hot sea. She glanced up to see Mr. Hanson and Ms. Cadena enter the den both laughing over some shared secret. They found a spot together on the long couch by the bookcase and settled in for an evening of relaxation. The lawyer surveyed the high-ceilinged room with satisfaction. "Isn't this great?" he said. "Just like a Grandma Moses painting, although she usually didn't include a duck in her images."

Feathers, who was resting among the folds of a fluffy towel in his box, looked up as if to say, "Well, maybe Grandma Moses didn't recognize the true potential of including mallards in her masterpieces."

Ms. Cadena sighed. "I miss Debbie and Barry. I hope they're having a good time in Mexico while our favorite wrangler checks out those horses. He's got a good eye for livestock, that's for sure. Any animals he selects will make a wonderful addition to the Shadow Creek herd."

Grandpa Hanson grinned. "I told them to think of the trip as an extended honeymoon. Debbie thought that perhaps looking at horses all day long might not be the most romantic activity for newlyweds, but, hey, they're in Mexico, and I'm paying all expenses. She promised she'd do her best to keep Wrangler Barry from getting lost in his work."

Wendy tapped her pencil on her paper. "How do you spell 'Argentina'?"

Samantha's eyes popped open. "H-o-t-e-l," she said.

"That's *hotel*," the girl by the fireplace chuckled.

"Yeah, I know," Samantha said proudly. "If you ever need to know how to spell it, just ask me."

"I think it's A-r-g-e-n-t-i-n-a," Grandma Hanson called.

"Thanks," Wendy said. "I'm supposed to write a report on it and figured I probably should spell it correctly." She was silent for a moment. "Do you think people get tuberculosis in Argentina?"

Mr. Hanson blinked. "What?"

"Tuberculosis. You know, TB. There's this girl at school named Emily who has it. She looks pretty bad. I wish I could help her."

Ms. Cadena leaned forward. "You can," she said softly.

Wendy glanced over at her. "How?"

"By being her friend. By not laughing at her. By understanding her limitations."

The girl thought for a minute. "I may as well. After today my classmates aren't exactly standing in line to get to know me. They all think I'm from Mars. Guess I don't blame 'em."

The woman held Wendy's gaze with hers. "You told me that one person doesn't think you're from Mars. She even shared her lunch with the very focus of everyone's laughter. You see, Wendy, you don't have to earn someone's friendship by being a certain way or acting like everyone else.

50

Friendship comes through acceptance, and I think someone accepted you today, duck and all."

The girl nodded slowly, then sighed. "I'm getting confused by all this. I'm in a strange school with strange people. I don't know *how* to act or what to think anymore."

Ruth Cadena rose and walked across the room to settle beside Wendy. "I don't blame you," she said. "But that doesn't change the fact that a young girl needs you to be her friend. This ranch exists to help people, young people with problems. You're part of this ranch. That means that even in strange schools with strangers, you have a work to do, a promise to keep. So why don't you think of Emily as a guest here on Shadow Creek, as someone with a real problem. No, her parents haven't deserted her. Nor is she in any trouble with the law, but she's still hurting inside. She needs what you've learned to give while living on this ranch." The woman paused. "What do you say, Wendy? Will you take on the responsibility of helping her?"

Wendy's eyes narrowed slightly. "You knew about Emily all along, didn't you? When you found out that Lizzy was going back to New York for a while, you told Dad to send me to Lewis and Clark, didn't you?"

Ms. Cadena smiled. "Hey, it's my job, remember?"

The girl shook her head, a cautious grin lifting the corners of her mouth. "How did you know we'd meet, that she'd talk to me?"

"Because I know Emily and she's a great kid." Glancing at the box by the fireplace, the woman added, "Sometimes birds of a feather like to gather together. You needed a friend. She needed a friend. Mission accomplished."

The girl frowned. "Mission *not* accomplished. She was friendly all right, sorta. But she still stayed off by herself most of the day. Besides, she was more interested in the duck than me."

"Maybe she identified with the bird. Both she and it are hurting, both are stuck dealing with a lot of pain. And both feel out of place, as if they don't fit in."

"Yeah," Wendy agreed. "That makes sense, I guess. But I can't take the duck with me every day just so she can have someone to be miserable with."

Ms. Cadena stared at her for a long moment. "Why not?"

Wendy's eyes widened. "Wait a minute. Wait just a big, huge Montana minute, here. You're not saying that I should take Feathers to school with me again? It was a disaster! Everybody laughed at me and made quacking sounds behind my back. You can't be serious!"

Ms. Cadena smiled gently. "You're the first person Emily has talked to since the school year began. She probably feels comfortable with you because of how you treat that injured animal. And she feels safe in your presence because she knows you know how to care for something *or someone* in pain."

Wendy closed her eyes and let out a long moan. "Man oh man. Helping people can sure be embarrassing sometimes."

Ruth nodded. "So what do you say, Wendy Hanson? Wanna give it a try? After all, you live on Shadow Creek Ranch. Being helpful is in the water out here. You can't stop yourself."

Peering into the box, Wendy studied the now sleeping mallard, his head tucked securely under one somewhat disheveled wing. "Miss Elrod will have a cat."

"You leave Esther Elrod to me," the woman said softly.

Wendy sighed, then nodded. "Oh, OK. I guess I don't have anything to lose except my sanity and every hope I ever had for a normal dating life."

Mr. Hanson's head jerked up from his reading. "Dating life?" he gasped. "Did you say *dating* life?"

His daughter grinned. "Did I?"

Ms. Cadena reached over and hugged her young friend. "You won't be sorry," she said. "Really, Wendy, you won't be sorry."

Outside, the cold winds of late autumn moaned among the bare branches of the trees surrounding the Station. Inside, snuggled safely in the den, the inhabitants of Shadow Creek Ranch rested from their busy day. But one of those feeling the warmth of the fire couldn't relax completely. Because of her belief in what the ranch stood for, she was going to return to her new school and try her best to touch the life of someone who was hurting. Wendy stared at the flickering fire for a long time, then returned to her studies, an uncomfortable fear growing deep inside her. Would she be strong enough to accomplish her goal? After all, she was just a human being. And as unbelievable as it may seem, she just might be forced to spend sixth grade in the company of a duck.

CHAPTER 3

The Bully

Since waving goodbye to Grandpa Hanson and climbing aboard the big yellow school bus where the road to Shadow Creek Ranch met Highway 191, Wendy had sat silently contemplating her fate. All around her were the whispers, giggles, and barnyard sounds she'd come to expect.

Her first challenge that morning had been to convince the bus driver that the box held tightly in her arms contained a school project, which it did—kinda. But it was the thought of facing the strange woman she'd met the day before when she first entered the school building that got Wendy really nervous. Somehow she and Ms. Cadena would have to persuade the registrar that Feathers needed to attend classes as much as she did.

When she arrived at the school she found the hallways crowded with noisy young people. Wendy made her way to the office, still clinging to the cardboard container with its injured occupant.

Closing the door behind her, she stood waiting to face the challenge.

"May I help you?" a hurried voice called from behind the file cabinets across the room.

"Yes, ma'am," Wendy responded. "I need to make arrangements for another . . . ah . . . class-mate . . . sorta."

"Certainly," came the quick reply as the woman crossed the room and seated herself before the archaic piece of office equipment. As before, the registrar never looked in Wendy's direction, so intent was she on her work. She adjusted her glasses, then poised her fingers above the keys. "Name?" she asked.

"Feathers," Wendy responded with a nod.

The woman typed quickly. "Last name?"

Wendy blinked. "Ah . . . Mallard?"

"Mallard," the woman repeated as she pounded the word onto the paper. "Sounds foreign. Grade?"

Wendy thought for a moment. "First. Yeah, definitely first."

"That would make him . . . it is a him, isn't it?"

"Yes."

"That would make him about 6 years old, right?"

The girl shrugged. "Sounds good to me."

"OK," the typist announced, ripping the paper out of the typewriter and holding it at arm's length while fishing in her desk drawer with her free hand. "Just take this form to the child's guardian, have him or her fill in all but the shaded portions, and sign at the bottom. Place the completed form in this envelope, seal it, and return it to me. Is the student here today?"

Glancing at the box, Wendy answered, "Yes, ma'am."

For the first time, the registrar looked in Wendy's direction. "Then have him go directly to Mrs. Emerald's room—that's 1-A—and tell her the enrollment process has begun. Has Feathers attended kindergarten?"

"Probably not."

"Then I won't be needing to update previous records." The woman nodded, then hurried back to her filing cabinets to continue searching for whatever was hiding behind them. "Make sure all blanks are filled in and tell young Mr. Mallard welcome to Lewis and Clark. Will that be all?"

"Yes, ma'am."

"By the way," the registrar called, "have you seen a set of keys? There's five on a ring with a little tag that says, 'Have a nice day.'"

"No, ma'am. I haven't seen them."

She heard the registrar sigh. "Have a nice day," the woman called.

With a nod Wendy left the room, carrying the box in front of her.

As she was beginning to make her way to her locker, weaving through running classmates, she heard a familiar male chuckle. "Well, if it isn't Noah and her duck. Do I say hello or just quack?"

Ignoring the speaker, she kept walking along the crowded hallway.

"What's the matter, duck got your tongue?"

The girl tightened her grip on the box. Dad had told her that, in a new school, she'd find some individuals who seemed to take pleasure in teasing people. One of those freaks of nature just had latched onto her.

"Tell you what," the boy called, "I'll trade you three chickens and a pig for that critter. I'm getting kinda hungry for duck soup."

"Leave her alone!" Wendy heard someone respond in a raspy tone. She frowned. Where had she heard that voice before?

"Well, well, if it isn't Breathless in Montana."

"Just leave her alone," the unseen girl repeated. "She's doing a good thing, taking care of that duck." The words sounded labored and strained.

"Mind your own business," the boy warned.

Wendy slowed slightly.

"You woulda probably just left that duck by the side of the road, wouldn't you?" the other girl stated. "You woulda let it die there or get eaten by some wild animal. That's what you woulda done."

"Back off!" the boy shouted, anger driving his words. "What's it to you, anyway? You're no better than that stupid duck."

Suddenly silence filled the hallway. Only the girl's raspy breathing and the distant roar of departing school buses broke the stillness. Without saying a word, Wendy placed the box gently on the floor, turned, and walked through the motionless crowd to where the boy was standing. He was just a little taller than she, slightly overweight with short curly hair and thin slits for eyes. Emily Wells stood off to one side, face buried in her hands, her sobs choked and labored.

Wendy stuck her nose within an inch of the boy's. "My name is Wendy, not Noah. And, no, I don't want to trade my duck. Also, I'd appreciate it if you'd be a little nicer to my friend Emily. Do we understand each other?"

The boy stood his ground. "Why don't you go back to your ranch and stay there with all the other animals?"

"I will," Wendy said, "this afternoon. Until then, I've got to go to class. So do you. If you stay out of my way, and I stay out of your way, everything will be fine."

"What's with you?" he sneered. "I was just teasing."

Nodding, Wendy said, "Making fun of me is OK. Making fun of my duck is fine, too. We don't mind. We can take it. But you were just mean to someone who can't defend herself. And that makes me angry."

The boy chuckled, still standing nose to nose with her. "You don't scare me," he said.

Wendy smiled. "I should."

The class bell clanged loudly, piercing the heavy tension like a sharp knife. Young people scurried away, glancing over their shoulders at the two sixth graders facing each other. Finally, Wendy turned and walked to where she'd placed the box. Picking it up, she glanced around. The hallway was emptying fast. Emily had disappeared.

The morning passed as if in slow motion. Each tick of the large clock above the blackboard seemed to last an hour. Wendy tried to concentrate on what Miss Elrod was saying, but she kept glancing at the empty seat near the back, the spot Emily had occupied the day before. What had happened to her? Where had she gone after the confrontation in the hallway?

Nearby sat the boy whose name Wendy learned was Garwin Huffinger, a title the girl decided would turn any normal person into a jerk. He would stare at her from time to time, his expression as if bullets were shooting from his eyes and cutting her down where she sat.

Finally, noon arrived and with it an opportunity to search for the missing girl. The first place Wendy explored was the logical choice—the infirmary at the far end of the main hall.

"Yes, Emily Wells was here earlier today," the pretty young nurse behind the desk said, placing her half-eaten sandwich on a napkin and taking a tiny swig of milk from the pint container next to her apple. "Poor girl. She has these attacks. Can't breathe. Her doctor has me put her on pure oxygen for a few minutes. Seems to help." The woman pointed at a tall metal cylinder propped against a corner of the room. A thin, blue, plastic mask dangled from it by lengths of clear tubing. "She rested for a while here on the examining table, then seemed to be all right." The woman shook her head. "What a way to live. Poor girl."

After eying the device for a long moment, Wendy turned to the nurse. "Do you know where she is now?"

"In class, I guess."

Wendy shook her head. "I didn't see her all morning. Maybe she went home or something."

The nurse frowned. "No, I would've had to sign her out if that was the case." She brightened. "Emily has to be somewhere on the school grounds. Why not check the ball field or bus parking area? If you don't find her, stop by again and I'll get security on her trail. She'll show up. It's a big school, but not that big."

With a nod, Wendy said, "OK. Thanks."

As she walked down the hallway, she paused at Miss Elrod's homeroom door to check on Feathers. There, kneeling by the box, surrounded by the emptiness of an abandoned classroom, sat Emily talking quietly to the mallard, stroking its feathers while resting her head on the bookcase next to her.

Wendy entered silently and stood by the

blackboard, watching. *What must it be like to have to fight for breath sometimes? What must it be like to know that certain parts of your body, important parts like the lungs, have been damaged and can't function fully like normal people's? How do you live with that? How is it possible to survive not being able to stand up for yourself because it takes too much energy, too much breath?*

"I missed you this morning," Wendy said softly. "I kept watching for you, but you never came to class."

The other girl didn't look up. She just kept stroking the sleeping bird. "I . . . I had to do something."

"Yeah, I know. I just talked to the nurse."

The girl frowned. "Now you know all my deep dark secrets. You can laugh if you want to."

"I'd never laugh about something like that," Wendy said firmly. "Your notebook, the one with the sunglasses on it? That I'd laugh about. Or maybe your desk. What's with all those drawings of flowers on the front? Now, *that's* funny."

The soft wrinkles of a grin creased Emily's pale face. "So I'm no artist."

"Artist? My horse can draw better flowers."

The grin broadened. "Don't make me laugh too much, Wendy. Takes a lot of air to laugh."

Wendy felt a lump rise in her throat. Emily didn't even have enough breath to laugh? "Sorry.

62

I'll keep my jokes on the tee-hee, not the ha-ha level. Deal?"

"Deal," Emily said with a smile, then paused. "How's Feathers doin' today?"

Walking across the room, Wendy sat down at her desk. "He's OK. Ate more breakfast than I did. But I think he's hungry again."

Emily glanced up at her. "Well, go get him some lettuce or something. He's already gobbled down most of my lunch."

Wendy nodded. "OK. You keep him company and I'll see what the cafeteria has that might interest a hungry waterfowl. Maybe they've got a fresh shipment of grubs and spiders. I understand that ducks love grubs and spiders. Would you like some too?"

Slowly Emily lifted her hand. "Take it easy. That's pretty close to a ha-ha joke if you ask me."

"Sorry. I'll just get some boring lettuce and bread. Totally unfunny food. Might even make you cry if you let 'em. Would that be better?"

Emily shook her head. "You're *crazy*, Wendy."

"I've heard that comment from people who are supposed to love me," the girl called over her shoulder. "So you're in good company. I'll be right back, OK?"

"Me and Feathers will be waiting for you," came the gentle reply.

After stopping by the infirmary to let the nurse know that she had found the missing student, Wendy hurried to the cafeteria and gathered what she and her duck might like to eat. Then she returned.

While the bird enjoyed crisp leaves of lettuce and milk-soaked pieces of bread, Wendy attacked her vegetable plate and side of rice. Both girl and bird seemed pleased with her choices.

"Tell me about your ranch," Emily invited after a few minutes. "Is it pretty?"

"Sure," Wendy answered between chews. "It's like a lot of other mountain ranches in Montana, only more beautiful. At least I think so."

"Does it have lots of trees and flowers on it?"

Wendy paused. "Yeah. And a stream that runs right by the house and lots of pastures and meadows and stuff. It's your normal amazing, wonderful, ranch."

Emily hesitated. "And birds? Does it have lots of birds there too?"

For a long moment Wendy studied her new friend. "You've never been on a horse ranch, have you?"

"No."

"You've never been outside of Bozeman, either. Right?" A shake of the head. "Why?"

Holding a lettuce leaf for Feathers to examine, Emily said, "My folks, they kinda don't have a car anymore. When we did, my dad only had enough gas in it to go to work and back. Now, when we want to go shopping, we take the bus or a neighbor lets us ride to the store with him. I've seen the mountains in the distance. They look so peaceful, so beautiful. And I've seen the big birds sailing high in the sky, going around and around, just floating without even flapping their wings. I know they must live in the mountains 'cause I've never seen any of them land in the city. Flying looks like fun. You can go anywhere you want and just ride the air. It'd be nice to be a bird, don't you think, Wendy?"

Wendy felt a lump lodge in her throat. "Yeah. It would."

"And here's poor Feathers. He can't even fly, so he has to eat lettuce from the fingers of people he doesn't even know. But he's doing OK, see? He's not scared or anything. Although he can't fly, he's doing OK, right Wendy?"

The other girl nodded. "Listen, Emily, I've got an idea, but I can't talk to you about it right now. I've gotta check with my grandpa and stuff. But until I do, will you promise me something?"

"Sure."

"I don't want you to stick up for me like you did this morning. Creeps like Garwin can be trouble. I mean *big* trouble. Just keep out of his way. Do you promise?"

Emily glanced at her. "I didn't like what he was saying to you."

"I know," Wendy smiled at her, "and I really, *really* appreciate what you did. But I've met a lot of people like Garwin. He's just a hot air balloon, all puffed up and full of gas." Her friend grinned at her description. "So let me deal with him, OK? He can't hurt me. But he can hurt you. My dad calls me a bulldozer, and I guess sometimes I act like one." Wendy pointed at Garwin's unoccupied desk. "It's just not fair when someone like him dumps on someone like you."

"Because I'm sick?" the other girl asked coldly, her smile fading.

"No," Wendy said softly, "because you're Emily Wells who isn't *anything* like a bulldozer."

The girl frowned. "Are you saying you want to be my bodyguard or something?"

"No, I just want to be your friend."

Emily sat for a moment, contemplating what Wendy had just said. All of it was new to her. Never in her young life had someone come out and said they wanted to be her friend. Even before she had contracted tuberculosis, she'd been a sickly child, shy and reserved, the one who sat by herself in a crowded room, the student who never raised her hand in class.

"Why?" she asked. "Why do you want to be my friend?"

Wendy studied the thin, gaunt lines etched across her companion's face. "Well, I'm a girl with a duck. And you're the first student who talked to me without making an animal sound or saying I was weird. I figure it's you or no one."

Chuckling, Emily let her expression relax into

a grin. "OK. Fair enough. We can be friends."

"Great. Now, since we're officially long-lost buddies, I need for you to help me take care of ol' Feathers here and also come to my rescue on the South America assignment. I've never set foot in the place, yet I hate it with all my heart."

Emily laughed. "I like South America! It's got mountains and rivers and jungles and parrots. Who doesn't love a parrot?"

"I think I'll just concentrate on this particular bird for a while," Wendy said, frowning and motioning toward the box, "although, I must say, if Joey was driving in South America he'd probably run into a parrot too. He seems to be very good at hitting flying wildlife with his truck."

With the sounds of recess drifting through the tall glass windows, the two girls settled in beside the box and opened their textbooks to read the next day's geography assignment. For now, short-haired bullies and long metal oxygen tanks would have to wait.

Traffic was particularly heavy as Grandpa Hanson guided the ranch pickup truck through the maze of back streets and headed for the farm co-op at the east end of Bozeman. Wendy sat on the passenger side of the cab, watching the houses and garages slip by, feeling relaxed and happy. It was Friday afternoon, and Friday afternoons meant three things. First, school was closed for the next two days. Even if she showed up at the front door of Lewis and Clark there'd be no one to let her in, a thought she found thoroughly refreshing. Second, she and Grandpa Hanson were paying their weekly visit to the feed and supply store, an activity she savored with the same intensity that one girl she happened to know experienced when visiting the fashion apparel departments of upscale Manhattan retailers.

Last, but certainly not least, was the fact that on Fridays Grandpa always took her to Charlie's, an ice-cream shop located across the street from the Baxter Hotel. No school, musty-smelling sacks of high-grade oats, and a big dish of Rocky Road— what more could life possibly offer?

"Grandpa?"

"Yes?"

The girl thought for a minute. "Is it OK for us to be happy when someone we know is sad?"

Grandpa Hanson nodded slowly. "I don't see why not."

"Why?"

"Because God wants us to be happy, even in a sad world. Happiness, I mean real happiness, the kind that comes from pure love, close family relations, and being one with nature, is supposed to remind us of heaven to come. It's sorta like a sneak preview of eternity with Jesus. I believe that's a good reason to be joyful."

Wendy frowned slightly. "I've been feeling kinda guilty whenever I laughed because of someone at school who can't."

"Can't laugh?"

"Yeah. Isn't that sad? If she laughs too hard, she can't breathe because her lungs are bad."

"Oh, you mean Emily?"

"Yeah. I can't even tell her my funniest stories because I don't want to make her have to put on an oxygen mask and lie still on a table in the infirmary. So I just tell her my sorta funny stories."

Grandpa Hanson smiled to himself. "That is a problem, isn't it?"

Wendy glanced at her grandfather then back out at the street. "I was wondering something."

"What?"

"Well, Emily has never been out of Bozeman. Her folks are really poor, and they don't go anywhere. Now, don't get me wrong. I think Bozeman is a great place, a *whole* lot nicer than New York City. I mean, the air here doesn't smell like a truck barfed in your face, the people actually look at you when you pass them on the sidewalk, and the biggest traffic jam we've ever been in is when the high school had a parade and we had to go two whole blocks out of our way. Oh, and the taxi drivers speak English. How wonderful is *that?*"

"Astonishing!"

"Anyway, like I was saying, Emily has never

69

been out of Bozeman, and I know that with Lizzy gone we're kinda shorthanded out on the ranch, but if you think it would be all right, I mean, I could help do stuff like clean clothes and sweep floors and—"

Her grandfather lifted his hand. "We'd be happy for Emily to come out to Shadow Creek for a visit."

The girl blinked. "You would? I mean, can she?"

The old man smiled. "It's not like we've never had young people on the property before."

Wendy chuckled. "Yeah, but that was different. You know, planned and stuff, and Lizzy was helping Grandma and Barry was doing the horse thing and Debbie was doing the nature thing. Now Debbie and Barry are in Mexico, and Lizzy's out on Long Island. Everybody's so busy with schoolwork and chores and stuff—"

"Sweetheart," Grandpa Hanson interrupted again, "it's OK. She's welcome anytime as long as her parents say she can come. And if you're planning for her to stay more than a few days, you'll need to check with Ruth Cadena and Emily's doctor."

"Great! Stop," the girl said.

"Stop?"

"Yeah stop, right here."

The old man steered the vehicle to the curb and set the emergency brake. "What's going on?"

Wendy grinned. "See that house over there,

the one with the little porch and swing set in the front yard?"

"Yes."

"That's Emily's house. I asked her where she lived, and she told me all about her street. I thought it sounded familiar. Then I remembered how you always go to the feed store on this back road, and that's when I figured out where she lived. Right there. We've been passing her house every Friday and I didn't even know it. Amazing, huh?"

Grandpa Hanson chuckled. "And you thought that, as long as we were in the neighborhood, we could stop by and invite her out to Shadow Creek Ranch for the weekend?"

The girl shrugged. "If it was OK with you."

The old man shook his head. "Why do I get the impression that you're in charge of the world and I just work for you?"

"Because," the girl stated while opening the door and slipping out into the cold air, "you want everyone to be happy, same as me."

The rancher watched his granddaughter run along the cracked sidewalk and climb the un-painted steps of the old house on the corner. A rusting car rested on cement blocks in the front yard and an old, abandoned doghouse guarded the pathway leading to the backyard. He heard Wendy knock on the door.

Looking up from her book, Emily saw the outline of someone standing on the porch. Slowly, methodi-

71

cally, she got out of her chair and walked to the door. "Who is it?" she called as loudly as she could.

"The capital of Argentina is Buenos Aires, and its chief export is raw meat, which doesn't do me one bit of good, 'cause I don't touch the stuff."

"I'm coming, I'm coming!" Emily grinned broadly to herself.

Placing a heavy coat over her shoulders and grabbing a small suitcase huddled next to the door, she hurried out into the sunlight. "Is it really OK? Am I really going to your ranch?"

Eyeing the suitcase, Wendy blinked. "Yeah, ah, Grandpa said you're welcome anytime, which is what I knew he'd say. That's why I invited you even before I asked him. I couldn't wait!" She hesitated. "But first we've gotta ask your mom and dad."

"They said it's OK."

"They did?"

"Yup. Then, let's *go!*"

Wendy glanced at the suitcase, then the girl. "Well . . . great. Yeah. Let's go." In a slight state of confusion, she took the satchel from the girl's slender hand and guided her friend down the steps. Arm in arm they strolled at an even, nonhurried pace out to the curb where an old farm truck waited, engine rumbling expectantly. "I take it you're Emily," Grandpa Hanson called, stepping down from the cab and extending his hand. "I'm—"

"You're Grandpa Hanson; I know," Emily breathed, barely able to contain her excitement.

"Wendy has told me all about you. She says you're the best grandfather in all the world and can snore louder than a bull moose in rut."

The old man grinned. "Yup. That's me."

He helped the new passenger up into the cab and fastened her seat belt for her. Then he and Wendy hopped in too and, in a few seconds, they headed down the street once again. "My parents said to tell you thank you for letting me visit your ranch," Emily said politely, smiling up at the driver. "They even got me a bird book from the library, see?" She held up a worn copy of *Field Guide to Western Birds* by Roger Tory Peterson.

Wendy raised her hand. "Wait a minute. When did your folks get you that book?"

"Last Wednesday."

"How did they know you were coming out to Shadow Creek Ranch?"

Emily thought for a minute. "Ms. Cadena came over and talked with them Tuesday night."

"And . . . when did I show up at Lewis and Clark for the first time?"

"Monday."

Closing her eyes, Wendy sighed. "So Ms. Cadena and your folks knew that I was going to ask you to come out to the ranch even before I talked to you about it yesterday?"

Emily nodded. "I didn't want to get my hopes up until you'd actually asked me yourself, which I really, really hoped you would. And you did."

Wendy leaned forward. "And you?" she said, staring at her grandfather. "You were in on this too?"

The man nodded. "Looks like we all know our Wendy pretty well, huh?"

His granddaughter shook her head. "Everyone had figured out what I was going to do even before *I* figured out what I was going to do!" She glanced again at the driver. "Who works for whom?"

Grandpa Hanson grinned broadly. "We all answer to the same Boss," he said with a wink, pointing skyward.

The truck rumbled down the street, leaving swirling leaves in its wake. Emily didn't care who knew what and when and why. All that mattered to her was that she was going to visit the mountains where nature's most wonderful secrets hid among the shadows, and where birds soared high overhead, dancing with the wind and the clouds.

Opening her eyes, Emily stared into the dim, gray light filling the room. Unfamiliar patterns appeared on the wallpaper. A strange wooden lamp rested on a nearby table. Across the small chamber a bookcase marshaled rows of books, some volume boasting bindings bright with color, others dressed in faded leather jackets or worn paper covers.

Where was she? And what were those mysterious sounds filtering through the window?

Slowly she rose on one elbow and waited for her brain to catch up to her senses. This wasn't her bedroom in Bozeman. Nor was this her wallpaper, her bookcase, or her lamp.

Then she remembered, and with the realization came a smile. No, she wasn't home in her bed. She was deep in the mountains, nestled in the arms of Shadow Creek Ranch with Wendy and her dad, Joey and Grandpa and Grandma Hanson and Samantha and Pueblo the dog.

Emily settled back against her pillow, a satisfied sigh escaping her aching chest. Yes, she was at Shadow Creek Ranch. Even the name sounded mysterious and wonderful. Yesterday afternoon, Wendy had snatched her out of Bozeman, away from the traffic and noise, the hustle and bustle of the town, and brought her to a place that had lived only in her imagination.

She'd watched the mountains move majestically toward them as they'd traveled south on the highway. Then the cliffs and towering trees had enveloped them, completely surrounding the truck as it sped along. In a matter of minutes they'd passed from a flat valley to a magical world filled with sparkling streams, granite outcroppings, and pine forests nestled against a hundred hillsides.

And the smell! She'd marveled at the fragrance. No traffic fumes. No lawn fertilizers. No hot, soapy odors spilling from the corner

Laundromat or greasy scents drifting from fast-food restaurants.

No roadside billboards begged for attention. No glaring storefronts or mercury-vapor-flooded parking lots blinded her vision. All of that was gone, replaced by an amazing, body-tingling sensation of freedom, of purity, of absolute nothingness but the presence of nature. The girl had reveled in it, drinking in its energy like a thirsty traveler lost in a desert, allowing the feelings and scents and sounds to swirl about her.

Then had come the evening. No previous experiences in her life could compare with the hours she had spent there between sundown and slumber. There'd been singing, storytelling, gentle laughter, and best of all—silence. Silence in a gathering of people with only the crackling of the logs in the fireplace and the distant whisper of the wind to mark the passing of time. Who would have ever thought that silence could be so beautiful? For minutes on end, no one had spoken. No one had needed to turn on a radio or television to bring entertainment into the cozy den as stars drifted in the night sky. The delicious silence was enough, allowing into each mind the music of creative thought, the conversation of imagination, and the peace of knowing that the week had passed with each having done their best.

Now, as the dawning day appeared in the eastern sky, Emily still couldn't believe that it was real, that she was here in the mountains, among people who treated her with respect and gentle understanding.

Sure, her parents loved her, but she knew her condition worried them. They hurt when she hurt, cried when she cried, and held her during the bad times when her chest ached so much she couldn't sleep or even move. She felt guilty for all the nights she'd kept them awake, for all the money they'd spent for doctor visits and medicines, for the lost hours of work and sleep.

Now, she was in the mountains and they were back in Bozeman. Her parents could sleep all night—and all day—if they wanted to. They could spend time together instead of worrying about her. For a few days they could live life the way it used to be, before the disease struck, before it took her breath away.

A gentle knock sounded at her door. Emily's eyebrows rose. Who'd be calling on her so early in the morning? "Come in?" she said softly.

Wendy's smiling face emerged from the shadows. "You awake?"

"Yeah. Been awake for a few minutes."

The Hanson girl entered quietly and closed the door behind her. "You too, huh? I always get up early—I mean *really* early—except when there's something I don't want to do, then I can sleep 'til noon. But that's not very often. I usually want to get up 'cause there's always something interesting to do around here."

Emily nodded and watched her friend settle in beside her. "I like your ranch," she said.

"Yeah. It's kinda nice, huh?"

The two lay without speaking for a few minutes. "So," Emily said, "what're we doin' today?"

Her companion yawned. "Well, for starters, we're going to church. Then—"

"Church? Really? I haven't been to services for a long time."

"How come?"

Emily sighed. "Well, my dad says that any God who lets a kid like me get TB doesn't deserve to be worshiped. Did God make me get sick? Is that why it happened?"

Wendy frowned. "Nah. God doesn't do stuff like that. Germs and viruses make people sick, and He hates it as much as we do. That's why He's gonna make a new earth that doesn't have any TB or broken bones or hurt birds."

"Well," Emily stated, adjusting her position on the pillow, "I wish He'd hurry up and get with it."

"Yeah," Wendy agreed, "me too."

After another long pause, Emily asked, "How's Feathers?"

Wendy sat up, a smile lighting her face. "He's better. I was just down in the den, and he almost jumped out of his box. I think it's the lettuce. Lettuce must be good medicine—if you're a duck."

Emily nodded. "Maybe I should try eating lettuce and bugs and spiders for a few days. Maybe it would help me, too."

Wendy sighed. "I think you're already on that diet," she stated. "Both of us are. After all, we eat lunch at Lewis and Clark every day, right?"

The other girl grinned. "You have a point."

"Oh," Wendy said, suddenly jumping out of bed, "I almost forgot. After we get back from church and after we eat lunch, Joey and I are going to help you do something really, really awesome, something I bet you've never done before!"

"Yeah? What?"

Lifting her arms, Wendy said, "This afternoon, Emily Wells, we're going to show you how to fly!"

CHAPTER 4

Planet of Joy

Pastor Webley delivered warm smiles and friendly handshakes to each member of his congregation as they exited the church. In the background, the rich, shrill tones of a small pump organ filled the sanctuary and drifted out through the open door, reverberating across the small parking lot where neat rows of pickup trucks and passenger cars waited. Children called excitedly to each other and laughed as their parents chatted with neighbors and introduced themselves to visitors.

Emily stood off to one side, watching the parade of ranchers and country people pass by, reveling in the sensation of being at a place where happiness seemed to be the unspoken order of the day. Since she'd arrived at the little church by the highway, every song, every speech, every greeting had centered on one central theme, a man named Jesus Christ. For some reason, it seemed to have created an atmosphere of tranquillity among the gathered Montanans.

She'd watched preachers on television shout out their sermons, saying "hallelujah" and "praise the Lord" with almost every breath. Some had even uttered words she didn't understand, rolling their eyes heavenward, mumbling like babies from a foreign land.

But this church service hadn't been like that. Sure, the pastor had spoken excitedly, waving his arms sometimes, lifting his Bible over his head, and moving about like a man on a mission. However, the message was different somehow—simple, easy to understand, with lots of Bible texts and interesting stories. Pastor Webley had spoken about Jesus in words filled with reverence as he told how, when a person follows what the Bible says, our wicked world stops being a place of sadness and becomes transformed into a planet of joy. That had even been the title of his speech.

"Pastor Webley was in good form this morning," Wendy whispered as she joined her friend at the far end of the little lobby. "Thought he was going to jump right out of himself."

Emily nodded. "I liked watching him, and listening to him, too. Is it true?"

"What?"

"All the stuff he said about how we're supposed to think of the world as a planet of joy?"

Wendy shook her head. "Sometimes that's not

easy to do. It even seems impossible. Everybody's got problems, everybody's yelling at everybody else. It's a big fat mess. But then I see a really neat sight like a robin feeding a nest of squawking babies or I hear a coyote howling in the night or I smell the flowers in a springtime meadow or," she paused, "or someone sticks up for me at school when a bully is on my case. That's when I say to myself, 'Wendy, get out of the dumps. Forget the homework and the bullies and the mean stuff people do. It's not *all* bad. Really. There are good things in this world too.' Believe it or not, I get to feelin' better. Of course a big dish of Rocky Road doesn't hurt either."

Emily grinned. "Make that chocolate, and I'm with you."

The two girls ambled over to where Pastor Webley stood, his happy chatter lifting the spirits of everyone around him. "Hello, friend of Wendy," he said, extending his hand toward Emily. "I'm happy you visited our little country church. Please come back again soon."

The girl smiled shyly. "I liked your speech this morning."

The man chuckled. "You should see me when I get *really* excited."

Wendy nodded and winked at Emily. "Like when he talks about heaven. The man goes ballistic."

"Ah, heaven," the pastor said, a look of total rapture lighting his face, "land of endless joys and ceaseless activities. I plan to fly to every corner of the universe just to see what's out there. And after I'm done with that, I'm going to pastor a little chapel on the outskirts of the New Jerusalem and have Jesus Himself as my guest speaker. Yup, when it comes to heaven, I could go on and on."

"And sometimes he does," Wendy giggled.

Emily looked into the warm eyes of the minister. "I want to fly, too, like the birds over the mountains."

Pastor Webley nodded knowingly, then leaned close to his visitor. "On one of my journeys, I'm going to visit the sun."

"The sun?" Emily gasped. "You can't go to the sun. It's too hot."

The minister glanced one way then another as if he was about to reveal a long-guarded secret. "I know," he said. "That's why I'm going at *night.*"

After being still for a moment, Emily suppressed a giggle. Wendy rolled her eyes and grabbed her companion's arm. "Let's get out of here. I think Pastor Webley is getting heaven fever again. Next thing you know, he'll have us eating ice cream on Neptune where it's like a million degrees below zero."

The minister smiled broadly and pointed at Wendy. "Now there's an idea. An ice-cream party on an ice-cream planet. Cool!"

The two girls waved and hurried away, laughing at the man's enthusiasm and outlandish ideas.

"I don't know," Emily whispered, "I'm not all that crazy about the sun thing, but that party sounds like fun."

Wendy groaned. "Oh, no. I think you've caught Webley heaven fever too."

Emily paused at the bottom of the church steps and turned to her companion. "Tell me more about it," she said. "Tell me more about heaven."

Her friend thought for a moment. "Imagine Shadow Creek Ranch without weeds, bugs, or Joey Dugan."

"But I like Joey," Emily giggled. "He's funny."

Wendy shook her head sadly and sighed behind a grin. "Girl, you've got a lot to learn."

The two continued out into the parking lot, mingling with the people and enjoying what warmth the late-autumn sun had to offer. Emily glanced up at the mountains towering to the south and east of the little churchyard. High in the deep blue of the sky sailed a hawk, riding the updrafts created by the sloping land, hovering effortlessly over the forests and unseen meadows. She closed her eyes, trying to lock the sight into her memory. *In heaven I will fly,* she said to herself. *In heaven, I will fly higher than the birds.*

At the open door of the church, Pastor Webley stood surveying his congregation. His gaze fell on Emily. He'd heard about the little girl who couldn't run and play like the others, who could only watch the world go by, afraid even to laugh. He, too, glanced toward the bright blue sky and studied the distant form drifting in the void. "Lord Jesus," he prayed softly, "make her wings extra strong. And if You're short a pair, she can have mine."

With that, he stepped back into the church and hurried to join his wife at the organ. She had one more chorus to play, and he didn't want to miss a single note.

As she strode into the den, a big smile lighted Wendy's face. "You ready?" she asked.

Emily opened one eye. "I can't move. Grandma Hanson's 'words cannot describe how delicious it is' potpie has taken over my body. I almost finished my whole plate which, for me, is an accomplishment. I feel like the Goodyear blimp, if the Goodyear blimp can be totally happy and totally bloated at the same time."

"I know what you mean," Wendy said with a grin. "I shouldn't have had that second piece of carrot cake, but I'm a weak human being with terrible vices. Potpie and carrot cake just happen to be two of 'em." She paused, and then let out a deep belch just as Mr. Hanson walked into the room.

"Nice job," he said with pride. "We could'a used you in the choir this morning. Some of those base notes in the offertory were *way* beyond reach."

Wendy reddened. "I'm sorry," she breathed, covering her mouth with one hand and her stomach with the other. "I was planning on saving that one for the pasture."

The lawyer glanced at Emily. "I never had a son. However, I have a daughter who can *sound* like a son from time to time. I guess I should be thankful."

Grinning sheepishly, Wendy continued, "I'm really sorry 'bout that, Daddy. It kinda snuck up on me."

"It's all part of the Wendy Hanson mystic," her father said. "That and getting up before Himalayan monks say their morning prayers. I thought you were going riding."

His daughter nodded. "We are, as soon as ol' blimp girl over there gets her body out of that recliner and joins Joey and me at the horse barn."

"Barn? Horse? Riding?" Emily raised her hands in a defensive gesture. "I don't know how to ride a horse."

"This isn't exactly like riding a horse. It's . . . it's more like riding *behind* a horse."

Mr. Hanson chuckled. "Don't worry," he said, smiling over at the young guest. "Whatever Miss Hanson and Mr. Dugan have planed for you, it won't hurt . . . much."

Stumbling out of her chair, Emily peeked through the window into the bright sunlight. "I see Joey. I see horses. But I'm *not* going to ride?"

"Well, yes and no." Wendy shook her head. "Will you come on so I can show you what we have in mind? Trust me. It'll be fun."

A sudden commotion arose in the cardboard box by the fireplace. A feathered head popped up above the lid and dark beady eyes looked around as if to say, "Hey, I wanna have some fun too."

"Not this time, Feathers," Wendy called as she and Emily headed for the arched passageway into the foyer. "You still need more time to heal."

The bird quacked loudly, then settled back onto his soft towel with a sigh. "Humans have all the fun around here," he seemed to say.

Wendy paused. "That reminds me. We've got to finish registering Feathers on Monday and get that form turned in."

"Registering Feathers?" Mr. Hanson asked. "For what?"

"School," his daughter called over her shoulder.

"School?" the man repeated. He watched the two young people leave the den, then settled back into his chair, mumbling softly to himself, "And they say *lawyers* are crazy."

Joey looked up from his work to see Wendy and her young friend crossing the footbridge. "Almost ready," he called as he headed back into the barn. Emily saw him emerge a few seconds later pulling on what looked like a set of long, carved boards. Then a large wagon appeared, sporting four tall, spoked wooden wheels and a seat hovering high over the whole apparatus.

"What's that?" the girl asked.

"This," Joey announced, placing the wagon

tongues on the ground and gesturing with unrestrained pride, "is a genuine, original buckboard complete with leather seat, steel-spring platform, and brass harness attachments. You're lookin' at a perfectly restored piece of American history brought back to like-new condition by yours truly with the help of Samantha and Pueblo the dog."

"What did Samantha do?" Emily asked, admiring the clean lines and smooth, polished surface of the wagon.

"She watched a lot and spilled wood preserver on Pueblo the dog."

"Oh."

"Actually, Sam did perform a great service," Joey admitted. "Whenever I got really hot and thirsty, she'd go into the house and get herself a cool drink."

"Very thoughtful. And Pueblo?"

"Well, he may not've done a whole lot of work directly on the wagon, but his coat now has a nice sheen to it."

Emily chuckled softly. "Sounds like you three were quite a team."

"This buckboard is classy and practical," Joey continued, motioning toward the wagon. "You can extend the bed for hauling stuff or just ride around in it for fun. So, how 'bout it? Are you up for a trip into the mountains?"

The girl beamed. "Oh, yes! I can ride in this just fine."

"Great," he said, reaching for the long wagon tongue at his feet. "Just stand back and I'll have everything hitched up before you know it."

Glancing over at Wendy, Emily smiled eagerly. "I can't believe this is happening to me. Last week I could only stare at the mountains. Now I'm actually going to ride up into them. I mean, right to the top. Oh, Wendy, thank you. Thank you *so* much!"

Her companion grinned. "Hey. What're friends for? Besides, we have to humor Joey. He did work hard on the wagon, so we should at least agree to take a ride. I just hope this contraption doesn't fall apart under us."

"I heard that," Joey called over his shoulder as he wrestled a set of straps under the wide belly of his powerful horse.

Soon all three sat side by side up on the lofty bench seat. With a whistle and a flip of the reins, the young wrangler guided the horse and wagon over the footbridge and headed down the long driveway leading away from the Station. In a matter of minutes they were deep in the forest, following a road that soon began to climb.

Even before the dust had settled on the driveway, a car turned off the gravel road that ran past the Station and a horn honked its arrival at the ranch. Mr. Hanson glanced out the window and smiled when he saw Ruth Cadena slip from the driver's seat and start for the broad veranda. He met her just as she reached the top step.

"Hey, you," he said with a warm grin. "We missed you at church."

The woman nodded. "I'm sorry, Tyler. But I got a call from the hospital right before I left. One of the kids I'm working with fell off a skateboard and banged up his knee pretty bad. He'll be OK."

"So, why are you looking so sad?"

Ms. Cadena pressed herself into the man's waiting arms. "While I was there, I had a talk with Emily's doctor. The lab results from her last exam are in."

"And?"

"And they don't look good. She's not responding to the most recent medication and treatment. One of her lungs has almost shut down, and the other isn't very far behind."

Mr. Hanson sighed and squeezed her harder. "Oh, Ruth, I'm so sorry."

The two held each other for a long moment, allowing the cold breezes to wash over them as they tried to come to grips with the dismal diagnosis. "You see, she was born with genetically defective lungs, and the TB isn't exactly helping her condition," Ms. Cadena said. "She's growing more and more resistant to drug therapy. They told me there's really nothing else they can do for her here in Bozeman and suggested that her case be transferred to a specialist in Chicago."

The lawyer nodded. "Then that's what you should discuss with her parents."

Ms. Cadena glanced up at the man. "One problem. Her parents have no insurance. None. And they've spent every penny they have trying to beat this thing, but it just keeps getting worse."

"How 'bout a transplant?"

The woman shook her head. "There've been a few lung transplants in conjunction with heart transplants in the past, but they're still too much in the experimental stage." She closed her eyes as tears spilled down her cheeks. "Oh, Tyler, Emily is dying and I can't do a thing about it. I can't give her any medicine, I can't take her someplace to make her well, I can't speak magic words that will cause her lungs to be healthy again. I've just gotta stand by and watch it happen, and it's tearing me up inside. I feel so helpless, so useless."

Mr. Hanson cupped his hands about her chin and lifted her gaze. "Ruth, you are doing something. You're loving her. You're being her friend at a time when she needs friends. And you brought her and Wendy together. Now, I know my youngest has a few problems of her own. She may be rough around the edges, but she knows how to love people. Wendy knows how to give of herself. That's something she's learned since living here on the ranch, something that's been cultivated in her by coming in direct contact with kids like Emily and all the other young people who've stayed with us. So you see, you're really helping two kids at once here. Emily and Wendy need each other, and you made it happen. You did it, Ruth. You."

The woman nodded slowly. "Yeah, but it's not going to make Emily well, is it?"

Mr. Hanson thought for a long moment. "There're two kinds of healing. Sometimes our bodies need help. Other times it's our minds. Seems to me both are important, and both types of healing can change a life for the better."

She gazed into his eyes. "Tyler," she said, "that's what you do for me."

"What?"

"You heal me. You heal my mind when it's sick with worry and grief over one of my children. Did you know that?"

Smiling, the lawyer rested his chin on the dark hair that had fallen over the woman's forehead. He held her tightly, gazing out over the pasture to the mountains beyond. Up there, somewhere, was a girl who was slowly dying and, hopefully, learning to live at the same time.

Joey reined in his horse and brought the buckboard to a bouncing stop. Beside him, Wendy and Emily sat without speaking, staring out at the endless cascade of mountain ranges stretching to the horizon, their summits piercing the low clouds that drifted through the valleys far below.

"Oh my!" Emily breathed, her face radiant with joy. "Look, Wendy, look at that!"

The girl next to her nodded wordlessly. She'd seen this particular vista many times before, but her reaction was always the same. No words could describe what lay before them. Even Tar Boy stood silent as if drinking in the vastness of the scene, letting its grandeur fill every cell of his powerful body.

Finally, Joey sighed. "Ain't no place like this in New York City."

Wendy chuckled. "No place like this anywhere else in the world as far as I'm concerned."

"Look," Emily exclaimed, pointing skyward. "There's a bird up there, a big one. Do you see it?"

The others nodded. "Probably a red-tailed hawk," Wendy stated. "Might even be an eagle."

The three of them watched the creature glide through the cold air, using the air currents to keep him aloft. The bird moved silently through space like a satellite drifting in earth orbit.

Suddenly, Wendy snapped her fingers. "Hey. That reminds me. Joey and I have a surprise for you. Wanna know what it is?"

Emily nodded. "Sure."

"Well, you gotta do something kinda hard, and it might be a little scary."

"What are you talking about?"

For a second Wendy hesitated. "Remember what I told you this morning, about what we were going to do after church and stuff?"

"Yeah. You said something silly about teaching me how to fly."

"So, you wanna try it?"

The other girl frowned. "How can I fly when I can't even run?"

Joey pointed at the horse. "He'll do your running for you."

"But I can't ride horses."

"Don't have to."

Emily shook her head. "What are you guys talking about?"

Slipping from the seat, Wendy stood on the wagon platform. "Get up and climb into the back and we'll show you."

Her frown deepening, Emily said, "You want me to stand in the wagon?"

"Yeah. Just stand right here behind us with your feet on the platform. Spread 'em apart so you won't lose your balance. Then loop your belt through this metal railing that runs across the top of the seat back. See? Like this." Wendy demonstrated with her hands what she had in mind. "That way you're attached to the wagon and won't fall off in case we hit a bump."

Carefully Emily followed the directions, making sure that she securely fastened her belt to the seat back in front of her.

"Now," Wendy cautioned, "you've got to breathe normally. There's no need to huff or puff 'cause you won't be doing any work. It'll just *seem* like you're working, but you're not. You'll just be standing there, OK? Remember to breathe slowly, in and out and in and out no matter what happens."

As she realized what her friends had in mind, Emily began to grin broadly. Ahead of them stretched the relatively smooth surface of a meadow ringed with small windblown bushes and encircled by a grassy road.

Wendy took her place beside Joey and glanced back at her friend. "Are you ready?"

Emily shook her head, trying to keep her breathing steady. "Ready," she whispered.

"Tar Boy," Joey called, his voice bringing the horse to full alertness. "I want you to run like you've never run before." With that he shouted a loud "Heee-yaaa!" and the animal lunged forward, propelling the buckboard and its occupants ahead with neck-bending acceleration. The animal seemed to know the importance of what he was doing, for he put every molecule of energy into his shoulders, flanks, and thundering hooves.

Faster and faster and faster they sped, creating a blur of the dry grass and strewn boulders as they charged across the meadow. Emily felt herself rushing through the air at a dizzying speed. Never in her life had she known such explosive power.

All she could feel was the blast of wind and the incredible sense of freedom that seemed to lift her higher and higher, taking her away from the fears she lived with and slept with day and night. Without even realizing what she was doing, she let go her trembling grip on the seat back and lifted her arms, allowing them to float winglike beside her, her palms held aloft by the icy rush of wind that howled by her ears and face. She felt weightless, totally separated from the wagon, drifting effortlessly across the meadow like the hawks in the mountains, like the clouds high overhead, like the great birds of her dreams. Closing her eyes, she imagined herself gliding among the trees, drifting over streams and rivers, leaping great canyons in effortless glee.

How she'd longed to feel such freedom, to experience movement without pain. Always she'd wanted to race around the bases at school, following the shouts of her classmates as she headed for home plate. She'd longed to speed up the never-ending staircases that faced her day after day and arrive at the top with breath to spare, to jump over sidewalks, to run just for the sake of running. Never had she been able to act like other kids her age who had healthy, fully functioning lungs. The past 12 months had been unrelenting agony as she'd felt the life forces in her chest draining away.

But right now the screaming wind and the headlong rush across the meadow pushed all of those thoughts, all of those fears and sadnesses and embarrassments, aside. For one delicious moment, she could run, she could jump, she could *fly!*

Joey glanced over at Wendy, whose gaze remained fixed on the girl's face. She smiled and nodded, her eyes encouraging the young wrangler to hold Tar Boy just a few more seconds at full run, allowing Emily to enjoy the sensations she was feeling a little longer. The boy obeyed, keeping the reins loose in his hands, watching the world flash by amid the thunder of hooves and surge of the wagon.

But even horses like Tar Boy have limits, and Joey and Wendy both knew that it was time to bring the experience to a close. Slowly, smoothly, the horse abated his headlong lunge across the autumn meadow, shifting from a full run to a gallop, from a gallop to a canter, from a canter to a trot, and finally settling comfortably into a fast walk, his thick, black coat shimmering with moisture in the sunlight.

As the rush of wind diminished, Wendy saw Emily's body relax, her shoulders drooping slightly as her arms fell back to her sides. When Tar Boy eased to a slow walk, she heard the girl crying softly, her face wet with tears.

Wendy stood and wrapped her arms around her friend, feeling the girl's quiet sobs rock her body. Had she made a mistake? Had the ride been too much for her? Had she hurt her friend terribly? Then Emily's arms encircled her and she heard a weak, frail voice whisper in her ear, "It was better than my dreams. Oh Wendy, you let me fly!"

Joey turned his face away, tears stinging his own eyes. Around them the meadow shone brightly in the cold afternoon sun and the sky hung deep blue overhead. The wagon had performed flawlessly, and he knew that the many hours he'd spent restoring it had been worth every second. *Every* second.

Night stars hung in the darkness like candles adorning the windows of a million distant cottages. Shadow Creek ran cold and silent beside the pasture, slipping under the footbridge and continuing down the valley unseen. Inside the Station, light from the flickering fireplace cast long shadows over the den, creating a mysterious warmth that brushed against the faces of those relaxing in its glow.

Wendy wrinkled her nose and studied the game board thoughtfully. If she moved her piece to the left, Grandpa Hanson would jump her best chance of getting a man crowned. But if she shifted it to the right, she'd place her backup pieces in jeopardy. Yet if she stayed where she was, he would most certainly begin an end-run around her guard and invade her home row in three moves. After that, her rear defenses would be toast.

"I never did like this game," Wendy mumbled, chin resting on a clenched fist, feet slowly fanning the air behind her prone body.

"You always say that when you're losing," Grandpa Hanson stated.

The girl frowned. "I'm not losing. I'm just . . . regrouping."

"You're losing," the old man repeated. "I've got you so hemmed in by my mighty warriors that if you tried to make an escape I'd eat you for supper."

"Shush, old man," Grandma Hanson called from her spot by the window. "It's just a game."

Her husband shook his head. "Yeah, like Everest is just a mountain. I've got her beat and she knows it."

Wendy pursed her lips slightly. "What if I did this?" she asked, motioning as if she was moving a piece forward.

"I'd get you in two moves."

"And this?" she continued, feigning another move on the other side of the board.

"I'd take out your left guard and your backup man," Grandpa Hanson smirked.

"Well, then, what if I moved this piece from here to here?"

The old man hesitated. "I'd . . . I'd do something terrible to it very shortly."

A grin creased her face. "Ah-ha! You didn't see that one, did you? You were so sure of yourself, so positive that you were going to wipe the ground with me that you forgot about my mighty warrior sitting over here minding his own business, just waiting for you to weaken. Well, my friend, my worthy enemy, my old but still cuddly grandfather, just watch this." With a flourish, Wendy pushed her red piece forward one square and smiled broadly. "This game is *not* finished. I am *not* defeated."

Wordlessly, Grandpa Hanson picked up a black piece and jumped three of her pieces.

Wendy blinked. "I'm finished. I'm defeated." She laid her head down on her folded arms. "I hate this game," she moaned.

The old man grinned as he rearranged the pieces on the board. "Wanna try for a best of seven? I'll go easy next time."

Her head jerked up. "Yes. *Yes!* Again to the front lines. Again to arms. The battle may be lost but the war—oh the war, it is far from over. Set them up again and prepare to feel the cold, heartless steel of defeat." She paused. "Want some popcorn?"

"Buttered. No salt."

The girl jumped up and ran toward the kitchen. As she passed Emily who was sitting by the bookcase with Feathers nestled in her lap, she grinned. "He's such a pussycat. If I get him munching on popcorn, he'll lose concentration. That's when I'll nail his hide to the wall!"

Emily grinned. "Go get 'em, tiger," she called.

Feathers lifted his head and looked around. He too had smelled the corn popping in some distant corner of the Station. It reminded him of warm days spent in a land far from this valley, where among cornfields he'd felt the summer sun touch and soothe his feathers like a gentle breeze.

His strength was returning slowly, although it still hurt to move his legs and wings. By now, his fear of people had lessened greatly, replaced by a strange, incomprehensible trust. Humans had always been the one species his kind had feared the most. They could hurt you in ways unimaginable, pick you right out of the sky and send you plunging to your death. He'd seen it happen many times.

But here, surrounding him, were humans who didn't have death on their minds, creatures who touched him with gentleness and kindness, bringing him food and providing a soft shelter in which to hide. Even their voices sounded harmless as they mumbled and whispered words he didn't understand.

The duck glanced up at Emily. This creature, like the one with the golden plumage, seemed especially kind, stroking his bent and broken feathers endlessly, showering him with attention and tasty things to eat. Maybe the flock had been wrong to fear humans. Perhaps those that tore his kind from the sky were different, not as advanced as these. Maybe, just maybe, those who brought death weren't even human at all.

Emily sighed as she continued to run the back of her fingers over the soft curve of the mallard's neck. "You're getting better, aren't you?" she said softly. "You look healthier. Even your eyes shine a little brighter than before. Soon you'll be flying away, heading south to catch up with your family.

Well, I don't blame you. They probably miss you and have been looking in every pond and river for you, wondering why you're not around anymore."

Emily rested her head against the leg of the small table rising by her side. "Just be patient," she whispered. "Just wait a little longer and you'll fly again. You'll see. You'll flap your wings and off you'll go, across the forests and meadows and mountains, flying higher and higher until you find your family and can travel with them again. That's what you want most, isn't it? That's what you dream about. I know it is."

Wendy reentered the den, balancing bowls of popcorn in her outstretched arms. "Here, Emily," she called. "This one's for you and Feathers. The one in the green bowl is Grandpa's, and mine's red." Emily accepted the offered container piled high with freshly popped kernels. "Now, if you'll excuse me, there's a war to be won."

As her friend scurried across the room and took up her position at one end of the checkers board on the floor by the fireplace, Emily heard someone call her name. She glanced up as Ms. Cadena settled in beside her, a bowl of popcorn cupped in her hands. Outside, beyond the tall windows fronting the den, the stars continued their silent journey across the sky.

"How'd your wagon ride go this afternoon?" the woman asked. "Joey said you guys had a lot of fun."

Emily grinned broadly. "Oh, we did! It was

great. We went clear to the top of a mountain and it was *so* beautiful. I've never seen anything like it in my whole life."

Ruth Cadena smiled. "I'm glad you had a good time. The Hansons are wonderful people and love it when teens come out to the ranch for a visit. They want you to return as often as you'd like. In fact, they've even named the room you're staying in as 'Emily's Room.' It's yours for the whole winter."

The girl beamed. "Wow. That's really neat."

The woman's expression turned more serious. "I was at the hospital today. One of my kids bummed up his knee pretty bad. After I made sure he was going to be OK, I had a talk with your doctor."

Emily's smile faded. "You did?"

"Yeah. He, uh, he said he wants you to come in for a few more tests."

"That bad, huh?" The girl lowered her eyes.

"I'm afraid it is. He said you're not responding to the medication and wants to try some other drugs and stuff. I'm sorry, Emily. I wish I could tell you good news instead. I stopped by and spoke with your parents and brought them up-to-date."

"I wish you hadn't done that."

"Why?"

The girl sighed. "I cause them enough grief as it is. I've spent all their money, wiped out their savings. Dad can't even fix the car because of my stupid hospital bills."

"Emily, they're not worried about that. They just want to help you get well."

"Mom and Dad can't even go out on a date anymore. They can't eat at a restaurant or go someplace romantic. They have to stay around and take care of me when they're not working their heads off. I hate it."

Ms. Cadena leaned forward. "They don't mind, Emily. They love you. You're their daughter."

"Yeah, well, I'm also the jerk who makes their life miserable. They'd be better off without me."

"*No!* No, they wouldn't! Your mother and father adore you, bad lungs and all. They told me that they can't stand having you away for the weekend because they miss you so much and are counting the hours until you get home after school on Monday. In fact, they're even planning a welcome home party that night with a cake and everything. Emily, your parents love you very much."

The girl stared out the dark window for a long moment. "I hear my mother crying at night because she's so tired from working two jobs. My dad can't help her because he's totally zonked out from his 12 hours at the industrial park cleaning toilets. That's what he does, you know. He cleans toilets and mops floors because he can't get any other job and he can't get any other job because he doesn't have a car that runs. And why doesn't he have a car? Because he's paying doctor bills and lab bills and medicine bills for me, that's why."

The social worker turned the girl's face with her hand and stared into her eyes. "It doesn't matter, Emily. They don't look at it that way. Just this afternoon, your father asked if there was something else they could do, some piece of equipment they could buy, that would help you breathe better. Love doesn't operate only when everything's going well, when lungs are healthy and bodies are free from disease. True love kicks into gear when tears flow and hearts break. Your parents aren't worried about the money they don't have for an outing to Taco Bell. They're far more concerned that you're getting the best care possible. And," the woman hesitated, "that care may be in Chicago."

"Chicago?"

"Yeah. Your doctor suggested that it might be time to take you over there for some more tests. They've got better instruments and more up-to-date procedures, to say nothing of experts in respiratory care. Maybe you and your parents should check it out."

Emily shook her head. "But that costs money."

"Let us worry about that," Ms. Cadena said. "We've made it so far, haven't we?"

"I guess so."

"Then we'll find a way in Chicago too. You've got more friends than you know, Emily."

The girl nodded slowly. "But . . ."

"But what?"

Turning, Emily stared through the window to

the dark forms blotting out the horizon, their summits fingering the stars. "I can't go to Chicago," she whispered.

"Why? Why, Emily?"

She remained silent for a long moment. Ms. Cadena studied her face, trying to catch a hint of the emotions raging within the girl. In the past Emily had always been open to any thread of hope, any plan centered on a new treatment or drug that might ease her relentless pain and debilitating condition. She'd welcomed them with firm resolve, believing each time that finally her battle would be over, that she would gain a normal life in which breathing wasn't a struggle and the future was waiting bright and hopeful just around the corner. But this time, Ruth Cardena saw no such determination or feeling of purpose. The girl had only silence and a terrible emptiness to her expression.

Emily closed her eyes, as if reviewing something in her thoughts, as if she saw some vision more meaningful than the words she and the social worker were exchanging. "I can't go to Chicago," she said, "because in the city ... there aren't any mountains."

She glanced at Ms. Cadena for just a moment, then let her gaze fall on the sleeping duck.

The woman's heart suddenly felt heavy and afraid. She'd seen that look before. It had been on the face of a young boy she'd held in her arms as his life had slipped away, the result of a self-inflicted gunshot wound.

CHAPTER 5

Kidnapped!

Sunday morning stirred gray and foreboding as the sun slipped unseen from behind the mountains to the east, creating only a faint glow to mark its rise. During the night storm clouds had marched through the valley, depositing a thick carpet of snow on every forest glen and pine-bordered meadow, transforming the world, removing all color from its upturned face.

Emily sat by the still-glowing embers of last evening's fire, staring out through one of the den windows at the bleak half-light of dawn, listening to the sounds of the Station as those who called it home drifted from sleep into consciousness. Wendy had just stopped by on her way to the front door, looking like a comical cloth monster under layer upon layer of clothes. "Gotta check on Early," she'd said, her voice muffled by the scarves wrapped tightly about her face. "He likes an extra helping of oats on Sunday morning. Besides, he doesn't like snowstorms. I've gotta calm him down a bit."

Emily had nodded and smiled, knowing that she couldn't follow her new friend through the drifts. The effort would be far more than she could endure. She also understood that it wasn't necessarily Early who felt unsettled by the passing storm. Stories that had echoed about the hearth the night before had recalled another time, another moment in Shadow Creek Ranch history, when a deadly blizzard had caught the Hansons and several of their friends in a terrifying grip, forcing some of them to the very edge of survival. No, Wendy hadn't been afraid of the storm that passed during the night. She'd been frightened by the memories that whispered in its winds.

The girl watched her classmate struggle through knee-high drifts, leaving a crumbling wake behind her as she moved slowly away from the broad porch in the direction of the footbridge.

"Let me guess," someone called, startling Emily. "She's worried about Early, so she's risking frostbite to go from this warm house to that cold barn to make sure he's OK."

Joey sat down in the big chair by the frost-framed window and peered into the gray world beyond. "I told her that mule of hers was fine. But does she listen to me? Noooo! She has to trudge out there through the snow to see for herself. That's one stubborn dame."

Emily giggled. "She loves Early. That's why she's doing it."

He nodded. "Yeah. I know. But I gotta complain about her. It's part of my job description."

The boy pulled his thick bathrobe tighter about him, trying to ward off the early-morning chill. "I suppose you want a fire in there," he said, pointing at the fading embers in the big hearth.

She shrugged. "Would be nice. Is that in your job description too?"

"*Everything* is," he chuckled as he stumbled to his feet. "Actually, Debbie is the best fire builder in the family. She can make one that's really pretty, you know, with the front logs burning and flickering like you see in movies or magazine pictures with a man and woman sitting on a rug drinking hot chocolate and gazing into each other's eyes like two nearsighted optometrists. I don't know how she does it." Kneeling by the hearth, he started collecting kindling from the bin resting nearby. "Now me, I can build a fire that'll make you sweat buckets. Heats up the whole house. But it looks more like a furnace than a movie prop. Guess I don't have that special touch."

"You sure have a special touch with horses," Emily said. "They do exactly what you tell 'em to do."

Joey nodded. "They just know who's boss, that's all. And I give them treats from time to time. Guess they don't wanna bite the hand that feeds 'em. Smart critters."

Emily watched him crumple sheets of newspaper, then arrange a small, neat pile of split logs over the top of them. She noticed that the boy hummed softly to himself as he worked.

After a few moments the girl broke the stillness. "You found it, didn't you?"

Joey blinked. "Found what?"

For a moment she glanced out the window at the gray dawn. "That planet of joy Pastor Webley was talking about yesterday. You found it right here at Shadow Creek Ranch."

The young wrangler paused in his work as he tried to recall the enthusiastic minister's words. "Oh, yeah. I guess I have. Beats living in New York City, that's for sure. I'll take a blizzard over a mugging any day."

Emily was quiet for a long moment. "You're lucky," she said finally.

Joey blew gently on the embers, igniting the paper almost instantly. "I am lucky," he responded, sitting back on his heels as the dry kindling began to crackle. "But luck's a funny thing. I know guys who love the city. Wouldn't leave it for the world. They'd hate Montana with its mountains and rivers and horse manure. Instead, they feel lucky right where they are. Put them on a working ranch in the middle of the Gallatin National Forest and they'd be miserable.

Of course, I think they're absolutely bonkers."

The girl sighed. "I don't know how to find it. You must gotta have lots of breath to live there, and breath isn't exactly something I've got a lot of."

"Maybe, maybe not," Joey said softly, stirring the kindling with a metal poker. "I don't believe breathing is the most important thing in this case. Maybe *thinking* is. You gotta *think* you've got it made even if other people don't agree, like some of my buddies back in New York. They actually feel sorry for me out here in the wilderness with no cable TV or fast-food restaurants or other fancy city stuff. 'Poor Dugan,' they say. 'He's living a miserable life.' And I'm out here on the ranch feeling sorry for them at the same time."

She leaned forward. "So you're saying that people can make any place a planet of joy?"

Joey frowned. "Well, yeah, I guess I am. It really isn't a place, I suppose. It's more of an attitude or a choice you make." He glanced about the softly lit den. "Some choices are easier to make than others. I think I was born to live on Shadow Creek Ranch. Heaven's gonna be just like this, but without all the death and pain. I won't be running down any ducks with my truck."

With a grin Emily glanced over at the cardboard box resting by the bookcase. "I think ol' Feathers would like heaven too," she said.

Joey stood and walked to the far wall. "How is our little friend today?" he asked, pulling back the soft blanket covering the container. "He looks pretty good to me."

The animal stirred and glanced up at his early-morning visitor.

"Hi guy," Joey said.

Feathers quacked sharply and tucked his head back under his wing. The wrangler flinched. "I think he knows I was driving the truck," he whispered, replacing the blanket and smoothing out the wrinkles. "Maybe I'd better just leave him alone."

Emily shook her head. "He forgives you. I know he does."

Joey frowned. "He looked kinda mad if you ask me. Let's just say I won't be getting an invitation for his next family reunion down in Florida this Christmas. They'll probably have my picture tacked up on a tree and throw darts at it."

The girl burst out laughing, then composed herself, working to control her breathing. "Oh, you're just being silly. They all know it was an accident."

He nodded. "I sure hope so 'cause I love animals, even ones with feathers." Then he paused. "And speaking of animals, I'd better get out to the barn before Wendy overfeeds the entire herd. She thinks dumping oats down them will make them stronger and faster. Well, in the winter months all that eating only makes them fatter." Joey turned and hurried from the den. "See ya later," he called over his shoulder.

Emily waved and sighed as deeply as her lungs would allow. It would be so easy to believe in a planet called joy if you lived on Shadow Creek Ranch. But out there, beyond the den's warm embrace, were endless storms and days and nights filled with pain and uncertainty. Perhaps Pastor Webley and Joey were wrong. Maybe there existed hidden places unseen by others where joy could never find a foothold. Most discouraging of all to the young girl sitting by the window listening to the fire crackle at her feet was the thought that it might be possible that she was forever destined to live in one of them.

Closing her eyes, Emily envisioned a hawk flying freely over the mountaintops, far from the choking snowdrifts, far from the hidden places, far from the painful presence of reality.

The hallway of the Lewis and Clark Elementary School fairly trembled under the wet, snowy tread of dozens of noisy students. Overhead, the morning bell clanged, announcing that in five minutes another chime would remind everyone that they should be sitting quietly in their classrooms. A feeling of familiarity about the chaotic scene left Emily strangely comforted. It was loud, it was breezy, and it was Monday morning.

Wendy exited the registrar's office with an amazed expression spread across her face. "What happened?" Emily asked as her friend joined her by the lockers.

"You're not going to believe this," Wendy stated, "but as of now, Feathers is officially, legally, and totally registered at this school. He's in first grade, has his own lunch ticket, an 'I LOVE LEWIS & CLARK' notebook, a box of new pencils courtesy of the office supply store at the Bozeman mall, and a sheet of instructions on how to get his picture taken for the yearbook."

"You're kidding."

"No, I'm not. I even said to the woman, 'Listen, ma'am, I need for you to understand something important. Feathers is a duck. A *duck.*' She didn't even look up from her work. Chuckling, she just said, 'That's all right. For the first seven years of his life, my nephew thought he was a goat.'" The girl spread her hands. "What am I supposed to do now?"

They looked at each other, then at the box at their feet. Slowly, they knelt and pulled back the cover. "Feathers," they chorused, "welcome to Lewis and Clark." With that pronouncement formally delivered, they stood and joined the current of young people as it flowed toward their classroom. The school's newest first grader peered at the world from his open box. He seemed proud of his new standing in life.

Miss Elrod smiled down at her students as the second bell rattled from the emptying hallway. "Good morning, all," she called. "I see everyone

114

made it through the first storm of the season OK." Wendy noticed the woman's hair was no longer pulled back from her face and held in place by stiff combs, but now lay soft on her narrow shoulders, giving her a much kinder, approachable appearance. "I was snowbound for a time," the instructor declared, "but my new neighbor, Mr. Anderson from Seattle, came over and shoveled my driveway for me. It's nice to have a neighbor who's so handsome with a shovel." Miss Elrod paused, her face suddenly flushed. "Did I say handsome? I meant handy. Mr. Anderson is handy with a muscle. I mean *shovel!*"

Wendy glanced at Emily and rolled her eyes. Her friend suppressed a giggle with her fingers and blinked as if portraying a damsel in distress.

The teacher leaned against her desk, trying to regain her composure. "So . . . uh . . . I see everyone made it through the first storm of the season OK," she repeated, a little out of breath. "That's . . . fine. Good. Now we must get to work. We can discuss the storm later."

Everyone in the room reached for their geography book and exchanged knowing glances. The short-lived blizzard had done more damage than they'd imagined. Apparently, it had knocked the combs right out of Miss Elrod's hair.

For the first time since joining the ranks of the student body at Lewis and Clark, Wendy felt like she belonged. The classroom had a warmth she hadn't noticed before, a kind of friendliness that drifted with the hum of activity and buzz of voices as knowledge was being dispensed and absorbed. No, it wasn't as nice as the den on Shadow Creek Ranch, and Miss Elrod was certainly no Lizzy Pierce, but there was something to be said about going to school with a few hundred other young people. A weird type of security came with being jammed in a room with other students her age while snow covered the parking lot and playground beyond the windows.

Wendy looked over at Emily and nodded slowly to herself. Now she knew why she felt that way. She had a friend. For some reason, it made all the difference in the world.

Sensing someone staring at her, Wendy allowed her gaze to drift a little more to the right. Her eyes met two others set within a scowling, slightly puffy face ringed with brown curly hair and a receding chin. Oh yes. The school did have one unfortunate flaw that didn't seem to go away. Among the student body was a sixth grader with a problem. His name was Garwin Huffinger. And she seemed to be his problem.

The boy held her gaze as he lifted his finger and pointed at the box by the bookcase. Then he drew his hand past his throat as if slicing his neck with a knife. Wendy felt her own hands tighten about her geography book. She looked away quickly, not wanting to give him the satisfaction of knowing that she'd noticed or understood the meaning of his gesture. Before returning to her studies, the girl slipped a quick glance at the box. Feathers stood with his head held just above the top of the container, watching the activity that swirled about him. Her eyes narrowed. Not only was Garwin threatening her injured friend Emily, he was also acting unkindly toward Lewis and Clark's newest fully registered first grader. Wendy would tolerate neither. She knew she'd have to deal with Garwin Huffinger again—probably very, very soon.

Unlike the mornings she'd endured during her first week at the new school, today sped by quickly for Wendy, her mind bouncing between South America, old English literature, fractions, and space travel. She was even surprised when the dinner bell clanked in the hallway.

As Grandma Hanson put it, it was time to get some "fuel for the body pumped in one spoonful at a time." Today's fuel of choice was tacos and burritos smothered with hot sauce and ringed with salty chips. Wendy and Emily stood in line with their classmates, waiting for the surprisingly skinny cook who stood at the serving table to dish out the food onto their plates.

The man smiled broadly as the two sixth graders approached. "And how about you young ladies?" he asked warmly. "One or two burritos?"

"One," Emily responded.

"Three," Wendy announced.

"I'm sorry," the cook said. "I'm only allowed to serve either one or two burritos on each tray."

Emily frowned. "Well, then, I changed my mind. I'll take two. But I don't want my plate to get so full that everything mixes together, so would you kindly put one of my burritos on my friend's plate? She doesn't mind her food getting all mixed up, and she can keep my second burrito safe and sound for me."

The man nodded. "Of course. I'll just . . ." He paused and stared at Wendy. "That means you'll have three burritos on your plate, but you're only allowed two."

"Hey, one of those will be hers," Wendy replied. "So, officially, you're only giving me two burritos. I'm just carrying that other one for her. How many tacos can we have?"

"Two each."

"Great. But I think I'd better carry all of my friend's tacos for her because, as she said, she doesn't like it when her food gets mixed up, so just put them here on my tray and we'll work everything out later. Do you have chocolate milk?"

The cook frowned. "Chocolate milk with Mexican food?"

Wendy nodded. "Mexicans like chocolate. I have this friend, Miss Cadena, and do you know what her favorite ice cream is?"

"Chocolate?"

"Well, no, her favorite is strawberry, but once we were at Charlie's in Bozeman and they were out of strawberry, so do you know what she chose?"

"Chocolate?"

"Not exactly. She got fudge ripple but, as you know, it has chocolate in it. Miss Cadena sat right there in front of me and ate it. A genuine Mexican eating chocolate. It really happened. You can ask my dad."

The cook stared at Wendy for a long moment, then wordlessly fished around in the small cooler at his elbow and withdrew a carton of chocolate milk.

"I'll have one of those too," Emily declared, smiling sweetly.

The cook repeated his search and retrieved another carton from the cooler. He was about to place it on Emily's tray when Wendy cleared her throat. With a tired nod, he dropped the second carton on her tray and waved the two girls away.

"Thank you, sir," Wendy said. "Everything looks delicious. Really it does." The man didn't answer. He was too busy studying Wendy's tray piled high with three burritos, four tacos, and two cartons of chocolate milk.

"Oh, by the way," the girl added, "may I have some extra chips? I love chips and . . ."

The cook fixed her with a cold stare.

"Never mind." She and Emily backed away

from the counter. "This will be fine. Yeah. This is great. Thanks. Goodbye."

They hurried out of the cafeteria, casting nervous glances over their shoulders. A minute later they settled in at their desks. Between chews, Wendy stated, "I coulda got more sauce, but I didn't want to press my luck."

Emily nodded, slowly enjoying the single burrito adorning her plate.

The two friends suppressed their giggles while enjoying their meal.

Before long, Emily had picked her plate clean and Wendy's dishes looked like they'd passed through a dishwasher. "I *love* Mexican," Wendy breathed, rubbing her somewhat bulging tummy. "But this still isn't as good as Ms. Cadena's burritos. That woman can do stuff with flour and refried beans that would make a conquistador cry like a baby."

Emily nodded. "Tomorrow we're having Chinese. I think the cook's on an international kick. Get ready for lots of noodles and eggs."

Her companion patted her stomach again. "I'll be ready. My dad can't believe how much I eat. Says I must be hollow inside. Mr. Dugan insists that all my food goes to my head 'cause there's lots of empty space for storage up there. He's a regular comic."

Emily giggled, then pointed at the covered box. "Hey, we didn't leave anything for Feathers."

"Not to fear," Wendy stated, reaching into her

desk and withdrawing a slip of paper. "Duck has got his own meal ticket, remember? I'll just go and get his food for him."

"Ah, maybe I'd better do that," Emily said, stumbling to her feet. "That cook will be on the lookout for you. If you ask for more food, *you'll* be the main course tomorrow."

"Yeah, I guess you're right," Wendy agreed, handing the meal ticket to her friend. "Get lots of salad stuff and bread. I don't think beans would suit a duck's taste buds."

"OK. I'll be right back."

As Emily walked to the door, Wendy leaned over and tugged on the blanket covering the box. "Hey, Feathers, you hungr—" The word froze in her throat. Emily glanced around just as her friend jumped to her feet. "It's empty," Wendy breathed. "He's gone." She looked wildly about the room, then at her friend. "Someone has stolen Feathers!"

Garwin Huffinger was sitting alone at the farthest table in the cafeteria when he suddenly found himself surrounded by two angry classmates. "What'd you do with him?" Emily asked.

"Him who?"

"Him. Feathers. Our duck!"

The boy frowned. "I killed him, cooked him, and now I'm eating him for lunch."

Wendy snatched the food from the boy's hand

and ripped it open. "Don't say that," she commanded, examining the contents of the half-eaten burrito. "There's nothing in here but beans and onions. Where's Feathers?"

"You guys are crazy," he stated, grabbing back his lunch. "That stupid bird doesn't belong in a school for people. He should be in a zoo or a stew. Now leave me alone."

"Not until you tell us where you hid him," Wendy continued. "This isn't funny. That animal is hurt and needs to be fed right now."

Garwin grinned. "Well, well. You do like that duck, don't you?" He leaned back in his chair and intertwined his fingers behind his head. "What's he worth to you?"

"What do you mean, what's he worth?"

"How much would you pay to have him back?"

Wendy leaned over the boy, almost causing him to fall out of his chair. "I might let you live," she said coldly.

Garwin shook his head. "I sense a lot of hostility coming from you today. May I suggest some therapy might be in order?"

Wendy's right fist tightened along with her stomach. She held her position over Garwin, not exactly sure what to do next. All of her life she'd responded to such situations with decided action, attacking her problems physically when necessary. But here, away from the safety and support of the big Station in the valley, she was on her own. Not only that, she was supposed to be a Christian. She was supposed to be different, to act different, to talk different. Grandpa Hanson had told her that life would contain people who would watch her, waiting to see if she had the ability to live her convictions.

She edged closer to the sweating boy, her eyes locked on his. All those sermons, all those late-night talks with her dad, all those confrontations with Joey were supposed to teach her something important, to prepare her to face the Garwin Huffingers of the world. But she didn't feel like a Christian right now. Nor did she feel like being nice and forgiving and tolerant and kind. Instead, she felt like punching the boy's lights out, and she could do it. She knew that. But what would that prove? That she was the better bully? That she could flatten an overweight jerk with one swing of her ranch-hardened arm? Oh sure, that would get Feathers back really fast.

Wendy withdrew slowly, her gaze still frozen on his face. "Five dollars," she breathed. "I'll give you $5."

"Twenty," Garwin said.

"I don't have $20," Wendy retorted, her words measured and even.

"Then you're out of luck." The boy lowered his chair onto all four legs and adjusted the napkin jammed in his shirt. "Now, if you'll excuse me, I've got a lunch to finish. Come up with the cash, I'll

123

give you your bird."

Wendy and Emily looked at each other, sighed with frustration, then walked slowly out of the cafeteria. When they were in the hallway, Emily spoke quietly. "What're we gonna do? Garwin might hurt Feathers, or keep his promise to do even worse. Oh, Wendy, what're we gonna do?" Tears began to sting her eyes as she spoke.

Wendy remained silent for a long moment. Finally she said, *"We're* not going to do anything. Feathers is."

"What do you mean?"

"You'll see."

Returning to the classroom, they lowered themselves onto their desk chairs. Emily frowned and studied her friend's face. What was Feathers going to do that would enable them to find him? She closed her eyes. More important, if Wendy's idea didn't work, what was she going to do without the duck?

While the morning had sped by almost without notice, the afternoon slowed to a crawl. Wendy couldn't concentrate, no matter how hard she tried. She kept glancing in the direction of Garwin's desk, eyeing him thoughtfully, trying to keep her anger in check.

She'd even considered telling Miss Elrod what had happened, but thought better of it. Adults certainly had their place in the world. But in her mind, some things were better left in the hands of those who had a vested interest in the situation. The last thing she wanted was a roomful of laughing sixth graders running all over the school looking for her bird. While it was bad enough to bring a duck to school, it was another matter to lose it to someone like Garwin.

Wendy looked at Emily. The girl wasn't doing so well. She'd formed a powerful bond with the creature, a connection of shared pain and a feeling of hopelessness. Wendy knew that wild animals, even injured ones, could withstand a lot of rough treatment at the hands of human beings. After all, Feathers had been blindsided by a truck and survived. He could probably defend himself against the likes of Garwin Huffinger, at least if things didn't get too far out of hand. But Emily was a different story. She wasn't as strong. Her injury was deeper, affecting not only her body but her mind as well. Wendy didn't understand everything that was going on in Emily's world, but she knew enough. They had better find that duck, and it had better be soon.

By the time the final bell rang, the two girls had about reached the end of their patience. Garwin had made no attempt to return the creature or reveal where he'd hidden it. Feathers wasn't in the classroom, that was for sure. They'd searched every place big enough to hold their bird while trying to go about their studies and not draw attention to themselves. Now, Wendy was counting on one fact that she believed would reveal where Garwin had hidden the missing animal. Feathers had been kidnapped at the beginning of the lunch break while she and Emily were in line getting their burritos. It meant that the animal, whose appetite had been growing by leaps and bounds during the past two days, hadn't eaten since breakfast. What Garwin Huffinger didn't know was that a hungry duck was a grouchy duck and, hopefully, a noisy one as well.

After waving goodbye to her students, Miss Elrod headed immediately for the parking lot. It seemed she had an appointment that afternoon with someone who was both handsome and able to shovel tall driveways with a single bound. As Garwin exited the classroom with the other students, he suddenly discovered that he had a two-girl escort.

"Leave me alone," he ordered, pausing in the hallway.

"Give us back our duck," Wendy countered coldly.

"You got the money?"

"Nope."

"Then you can kiss your stupid critter goodbye."

"I'm not going to kiss anything, much less a duck," she retorted. "We just thought we'd follow you around for a while. You're such a warm, wonderful person that we can't help being attracted to you. We're drawn to you like butterflies to a

126

cow pie."

"Very funny," Garwin declared with a shove. "But it's not going to do you any good. The duck isn't even here."

"Oh?" Wendy responded, falling in again beside the fast-walking boy. "Whad'ya do, FedEx him to Florida where he belongs?"

"Just leave me alone!" Garwin demanded. "I don't like you following me around like this. The guys will start talking."

"Yeah? What about?"

"About you following me around. I hate girls—all girls—and you are girls, both of you."

"Thanks for noticing," Emily said, her breathing becoming a little labored as she fought to keep up.

Garwin stopped and held up his hand. "Look. I've gotta get home, so *bug off!*"

Wendy nodded. "OK. OK. We'll stop. But just remember, we warned you."

"Fine. Great. Now *leave me alone!*"

The boy started down the hallway when he suddenly stopped and turned. "Warned me about what?" Wendy and Emily were nowhere to be seen. They'd disappeared in the throng of students scurrying by.

"Warned me. Yeah, right," Garwin said under his breath. "They don't know what they're talking about."

When he reached his locker, which was located about midsection in the long passageway, he paused and looked first one way and then another. Yes, the two girls were nowhere in sight. Bending low, he studied the numbers on his combination lock. First he twisted the knob to the left, then to the right, then back to the left again. With one final, nervous glance up and down the hallway, Garwin pulled the door open a crack and peeked inside.

The locker seemed to explode in a cloud of dust, notebook paper, discarded candy wrappers, and feathers. Garwin saw what looked like a thick arrow with a beak shoot from the top shelf and slam into his forehead, sending him reeling into a group of astonished classmates. He felt powerful wings pummel his nose and chin before beating him mercilessly about the shoulders while an ear-splitting racket of squawks and quacks roared in his ears. Then his attacker disappeared as quickly as he'd appeared, leaving Garwin gasping for breath.

Wendy and Emily, who'd been hiding just around the corner from the locker, watched in amazement as Feathers, finally freed from his dark metal cell, blasted past them, half running, half flying as he shot down the hallway, sending students diving for cover amid screams and shouts.

The animal finally lifted himself off the ground on unsteady wings and ricocheted his way toward the wide front doors guarding the far end of the long, broad passageway. He would have made good his escape except that, at the last moment, the registrar burst from her office to see what all the commotion was about. Wendy screamed,

"Watch out!" but it was too late. In the next instant, the fast-moving duck and horrified woman slammed into each other, the impact sending them and several students sprawling across the smooth, polished tiles just inside the exit. The woman wound up in a crumpled pile in the corner with Feathers sitting on her chest, quacking loudly into her fear-contorted face.

Wendy and Emily rushed past the prone figures of their classmates and skidded to a stop over the disheveled mess that moments ago had been Lewis and Clark's highly professional registrar. "Are you all right?" Wendy asked, hurriedly retrieving the squawking duck and passing him on to Emily. "Are you hurt? Should I call a doctor or something?"

The woman tried to straighten her now-smudged and twisted blazer. "What was that awful monster that attacked me?" she gasped, looking about with a terrified expression. "It was horrible! I came out into the hall and before I could do anything, it was on me, beating me, yelling into my face."

"Well, to be totally factual, it wasn't yelling," Wendy corrected, helping the trembling woman to her feet. "It was quacking . . . like a duck." She pointed at Emily. "Like *that* duck." The registrar stared at the animal now resting peacefully in Emily's arms. "He didn't mean to hurt you," Wendy continued. "He was just trying to escape Garwin Huffinger, who had kidnapped him and

129

held him for ransom in his locker, which, I might add, is against the law."

"Kidnapped? Escape? Against the law?" the woman sputtered.

"I'm really sorry about all this," Wendy stated, brushing down from the woman's hair. "You have every right to be upset. Here, let me help you back to your office where you can . . . can do something like write a report on your typewriter. We'll just get Feathers out of your way so you won't have any more trouble, OK?" Even before she finished the sentence, Wendy flinched, realizing what she had just given away.

The registrar nodded. "Yes. My office." Then she paused. "Feathers?"

Wendy tightened her grip on the woman's elbow and began walking a little faster. "Don't think about this right now. You've had a bad accident. Not every day you get run down in a hallway by a duck, huh? That must've been awful. Just awful. Let's get you back in your office before anything else bad happens."

"Feathers?" the registrar repeated.

"Now there you go reliving the terrible accident again," Wendy warned, opening the office door. "Mustn't do that. You come in here and sit down . . . or file something. You'll feel better really fast. Honest. Just put the whole thing out of your mind."

"Where have I heard that name before?" the woman breathed.

"You hear so many names. It's easy to get them mixed up. There, you look much better now. I've gotta go. You just rest for a while. Sharpen a pencil or something. 'Bye."

"Have a nice day," the woman said weakly.

Hurrying from the room, Wendy found Emily still standing by the front exit, holding the duck. "Let's get outta here," she whispered, motioning for her friend to follow her down the hallway. "We've gotta get Feathers in his box and away from the school right now. The registrar is about to put two and two together and when she does, we're in big trouble. Let's get our coats and *go!*"

Slowing her pace, Emily called, "Wait. Did you see it? Did you see what Feathers did?"

"Yeah, he dive-bombed the registrar of the Lewis and Clark Elementary School."

"No. Just before that. He . . . he . . ."

"Yeah," Wendy grinned. "I saw. Neat, huh? Ol' Feathers is getting better and better."

Emily looked down at the bird. "He can fly." Then she looked up, sudden fear shadowing her face. "He can fly."

"Well, he *is* a duck."

"I know, but now . . ." The girl paused.

Wendy waved her hand. "Come on, Emily, we can talk about this later. Let's get out to the parking lot *now*. Joey should be waiting for us."

With a nod Emily followed her. But she didn't hurry. Her tread was slow and hesitant. What

131

she'd seen had hit her almost as hard as the duck had struck the registrar. Feathers could not only eat and quack, he could do something more wonderful, more frightening. He could fly.

CHAPTER 6

Fly Away

Joey shook his head and chuckled. After a few moments, he did it again. Wendy glanced at him and smiled shyly. "It was kinda funny."

"Kinda?" the boy laughed. "I just wish I could've been there. I mean, it's not every day you get to watch a duck beat up a bully and then dive-bomb a school registrar." He changed gears and pressed on the accelerator, propelling the old truck along the highway at a little faster clip. "So, tell me again why this Garwin creep stole the bird?"

Wendy sighed. "Who knows. He's just a jerk with a bad attitude. Guess he wasn't getting enough attention from the rest of the school, so he decided to bother Emily and me for a while. Boy, he made me mad, too."

"You? Mad? That's never happened before."

The girl grinned.

"So," Joey continued, "where's Feathers now? How come he's not going back to the ranch with us?"

Wendy glanced out the window. "Emily was kinda freaked out about what happened at school, so I asked her if she wanted to keep Feathers overnight at her house. You should have seen how excited she got. Thought she'd jump right out of her skin. Her bus had just pulled away when you got there and rescued me from the future wrath of the registrar, which I'm sure is not going to be a pretty sight. I don't wanna be in the same county with her when she suddenly realizes she signed up a duck for first grade."

Joey laughed again. "How do you do it?" he asked.

"Do what?"

"Get yourself into so much trouble? If you're not being thrown off a mountain by a horse or getting caught in a snowstorm in a house with no electricity or falling headfirst into a hole in the ground, you're busy supervising the education of a waterfowl. What's next? An earthquake? Or maybe you'll get hit by lightning!"

Wendy shook her head. "I don't know why weird things happen to me all the time. Guess it's just nature's way of making up for the boring life you lead."

He smiled. "Boring's fine with me. You can have all the adventures. I'll be happy to stay on Shadow Creek Ranch forever and live a perfectly sane, uninteresting, run-of-the-mill life."

Suddenly, Wendy pointed. "Oh, can we stop there for a minute?"

They were just about to pass the little country church that the ranch family attended each Sabbath. Joey could see a familiar car parked by the front door and footprints leading from the vehicle up the steps to the entrance. "I don't think Webley does confessions on Monday afternoons," he said, guiding his truck into the parking lot, "but he might make an exception in your case."

His passenger rolled her eyes. "Very funny, Mr. Dugan. I just wanna talk to him for a minute." As soon as the truck slid to a stop on the freshly packed snow, she slipped out of the seat. "I think I hear Mrs. Webley practicing the organ. You wanna come in and listen? I won't be long."

"Sure," Joey agreed, unbuckling his seat belt. "But if I burst out singing, it's your fault."

Wendy paused. "Maybe you'd better wait in the car."

"Come on," he chuckled, "I'll keep it down just for you. Besides, I smell wood smoke. They've got the stove lit up. The heater in my truck isn't all that great as you probably already know."

The two stumbled up the steps and entered the small, dimly lit foyer. The rich, full tones of the organ wrapped around the new arrivals like strong, welcoming arms. Joey headed directly into the little sanctuary while Wendy walked down a flight of steps to the basement office of her friend Pastor Webley. She knocked gently on the door.

"I have a visitor?" a voice called out.

"It's me, Wendy."

"Wendy who?"

The girl grinned. "Cold, tired, and I-have-another-question Wendy."

"Oh her. The girl with the duck. Come right in."

Entering the small office, Wendy smiled at the man seated at a computer by the desk. Bookshelves lined the walls of the room. Where there were no books, she saw trinkets and figurines, all with a decidedly religious theme, such as the clay oil lamp from Israel, a crown of thorns fashioned from a prickly bush that grows in Arizona, and a handmade leather sling similar to the one David might have used to kill the giant.

Pastor Webley finished the sentence he was typing, then swung around in his chair. "Have a seat," he invited, pointing at a faded couch resting by a scale model of the sanctuary in the desert, a creation he had built with his own hands. It was his pride and joy.

"You like my new altar of burnt offerings?" he asked, pointing. "I think a mouse ate the old one. Who knew I was building a tasty model?"

Wendy admired the small structure resting in the courtyard of the meticulously constructed visual aid. "Nice," she said.

The man sighed. "Eighteen hours I work on that altar and all I get is nice?"

The girl blinked. "*Very* nice?"

"Ah. That's more like it," he said with a grin.

"Now. What brings you to the church on a cold and snowy Monday afternoon?"

Wendy frowned slightly and glanced about, trying to organize her thoughts. "I've got a question."

"OK."

"It's kinda serious."

The man nodded. "Then I'll do my best to give it a serious answer."

Wendy took in a deep breath and held it for a second or two. Then she let it out and spoke slowly, deliberately. "Are you still a Christian," she asked, "when you don't *feel* like one?"

Webley's eyebrows rose just a little.

"Know what I mean?" the girl continued. "Sometimes I know what I should do, and I even do it because I'm supposed to. But I don't *feel* like doing it. What I really want to do is punch someone right in the nose."

Pastor Webley suppressed an unexpected grin. Then he studied his hands for a long moment before speaking. "Little lady," he said, "you've stumbled upon a problem that every Christian faces at one time or another."

"Even you?" Wendy gasped.

The man nodded. "The apostle Paul got all tongue twisted one day trying to explain that the things he wanted to do he didn't do and the things he didn't want to do he did. He finally gave up and moaned, 'What a wretched man I am! Who will deliver me from this body of sin?'" Pastor Webley thought for a moment. "Yes, I must admit that I've sat in meetings when it was all I could do not to stand up and tell a church member what I *really* thought about his or her actions. I just wanted to grab 'em by the shoulders and shake some sense into 'em."

The girl's eyes widened. "So, whad'ya do?"

"I smiled and nodded my head and said something like, 'You know, my good brother or my good sister, I see that you feel very strongly about this matter, that it's important to you. So I'm going to give you my undivided attention until we figure out how to resolve this situation.' Then I go home and mow the lawn . . . twice!"

A grin spread across Wendy's face. "Yeah. Or you ride your horse way up into the mountains and race across the high meadows and yell at Mount Blackmore until your throat hurts."

The pastor blinked. "Wow! I see you've come up with a stress-reducer of your own. 'Course, the best thing for any Christian is not to get upset in the first place. That's where you've gotta work the hardest. Gettin' mad is easy. *Not* gettin' mad takes real determination and guts."

Wendy sighed. "I know what you mean. I don't like feeling angry. And I don't like wanting to punch someone out. But sometimes things happen and *bang,* I'm all tensed up inside and just wanna explode." She paused. "So does Jesus still love me when I get that way?"

The minister smiled. "If He didn't, we'd all be in a lot of trouble. There'd be no hope for us because we've got thousands of years of sin in our bones, thousands of years of ancestors who've passed down to us bad habits and evil tendencies. Problem is we're sin-weakened human beings, vulnerable to anger and lust and selfishness and a whole bunch of other nasty stuff. But God knows that. After all, Jesus was a human being once. He learned first-hand what it's like to feel like we feel."

"So what're we supposed to do?" Wendy asked, leaning forward in her chair.

"We're supposed to mow lawns and ride horses and shout at mountains until we learn how to handle our frustrations in more constructive ways."

"What ways?"

Pastor Webley reached over and picked up the crown made out of thorns resting on a nearby shelf. He held it in his hands for a long moment. "Do you know what killed Jesus?"

Wendy shrugged. "Sin?"

"Nope. Sin may have put Him on the cross. Sin may have made the people laugh at Him and spit on Him and drive nails through His hands. But that's not what killed Him. It was love—love for us imperfect, angry, unforgiving, selfish human beings. That's what made Him do it. That's what drove Him to that spot outside of Jerusalem where shouting mobs tortured the life right out of Him. Jesus turned His frustration and anger into something wonderful—sacrifice. He allowed Himself to be crucified so that He could earn the right to stand by our sides when we feel angry and offer help, support, and strength as we fight to overcome our feelings." The minister paused. "So let me ask you a question, Wendy. What makes you a Christian? Your feelings? Or is it realizing why Jesus died and then allowing Him to help you deal constructively with your feelings?"

Wendy sat in silence for a moment as the harmonies from the distant organ drifted in through the open door. What Pastor Webley had said made sense. It meant that even when she was facing the likes of Garwin Huffinger, even when she was working hard to control her anger, she was being loved by the same God that she felt so far away from at that particular moment. Jesus had died for angry people. He had died for her.

The girl nodded slowly. "I understand," she said quietly. "And I think it's neat."

Pastor Webley smiled. "Yeah. It is neat, isn't it?"

Joey looked up to see Wendy walking into the sanctuary. He watched her head for the front of the room and look for a long time at the big wooden cross hanging behind the podium. Then she turned. "We can go now," she said.

The boy stood and waved at Mrs. Webley, who returned his farewell with one hand while continuing to play with the other. As the two young people buckled themselves into the truck and Joey was pumping the accelerator in preparation for starting the engine, Wendy said, "Do you know what?"

"What?"

"I don't want to feel mad anymore."

Joey blinked. "OK."

"But," the girl continued, "if I do sometimes feel mad, I'm still a Christian."

Her companion nodded. "OK."

She glanced over at him. "So the next time you think I'm getting mad at you, just tell me to go and yell at Mount Blackmore."

"Mount Blackmore?" He stared at her in puzzlement.

"Yup."

He shrugged. "OK."

"Good."

Together they drove away, leaving behind the little church by the highway and the beautiful music filtering through its timbers and spilling out across the snows.

Fading afternoon shadows crept amid the cold snowdrifts piled against a little brick house on a back street in Bozeman. Winter chill had chased all the children who lived on the street into homes where warm soup waited and televisions heralded the evening news from living rooms and dens.

Frost-tinted windowpanes framed images of laughter and contentment, creating crystalline mosaics of life in a small western town set within the foothills of the Gallatin National Forest. However, one of the images was unlike the others. Beyond this particular wooden window frame sat a young girl, face damp with tears. She rested at the end of her bed, head bowed forward as if the very weight of it was more than she could bear. Her hands lay motionless in her lap, and her quiet sobs carried within their fabric the rough texture of a breaking heart.

Across the room sat a large cardboard box, its lid open to reveal a male mallard duck standing straight and tall, flapping its wings again and again as if the animal were rehearsing the movements of a dance he would soon perform. The brush of stiff feathers, the power of the wind being swept aside by their rhythmic motion, the *flap, flap, flap* of the exuberant exercise filled the small room with sound.

It was a familiar ritual in nature, a common spectacle seen beside a thousand lakes and rivers across the North Country. For centuries, ducks had performed this dance as they prepared to follow some unseen, unheard directive buried deep in the cortex of their brains. The animal didn't know why he stood in the box flapping his wings again and again and again. He just knew he should, that for some reason it was important, necessary, even vital.

Emily closed her eyes as if to shut out a sight

she'd never seen before. She understood the dance, knew what it meant and how quickly it could leave her without the friend she'd come to love during that past week. Into her world had fallen a true kindred spirit, a creature just like her, unable to fly, unable to soar away from the dangers and sadness of life. Now that same friend was listening to another voice, another summons that all nature hears.

The girl allowed her gaze to lift to the box. She saw the proud head of the duck rising above the rim, its eyes clear and focused, its body gaining strength and vibrancy.

As the last remnants of the day faded beyond the windowpane, as the room settled into darkness, Emily spoke, her words riding the rough edges of her breath. "Feathers, please, don't go. Please don't go."

Up and down the street a cold wind moaned as if sharing her sorrow—and her fear.

"Wendy Hanson, may I speak to you in my office?" The registrar glared down at the girl as she gathered her books from her locker.

"Yes, ma'am," Wendy responded politely. "I think Miss Elrod will let me leave math class a little earl—"

"Now."

"Now's good," Wendy nodded.

The two walked quickly through the crowd of students to the big office by the front entrance. Wendy soon found herself standing before the school official whose face stared back at her with a dark, stony expression. The girl decided that it looked just like some great and terrible monster had grabbed the registrar and sucked all the humanity right out of her.

"What did you want to see me about?" Wendy asked, trying to sound cheerful.

The woman didn't answer. She just picked up a pile of papers and dropped them with a quiet *splat* on the counter separating them. The first line on the first page of the first form contained a familiar name. "Feathers."

"Are you aware," the registrar began, her words as cold as the snow clinging to the windows by the file cabinets, "that I registered into the Lewis and Clark Elementary School a duck? That I placed him in first grade? That I gave him a meal ticket and a box of pencils? That I provided precise instructions on how he can have his picture included in our fine, award-winning yearbook? Has any of this come to your attention at all?"

Wendy was about to answer when she noticed a certain look in the registrar's eyes. She stared at the woman for a long time, trying to make sure she was reading the situation correctly. Finally, she answered, "I can't imagine you doing anything like that, ma'am."

144

The woman nodded. "Good."

With that she picked up the pile of forms, letters, and grade-report sheets and dropped them with a muffled *thud* into the large plastic trash can by her legs. "Now," she said, "I think you'd better hurry off to class. I've got work to do."

Wendy turned and walked to the door. Before leaving, she stopped and smiled back at the registrar. "Ma'am?"

"Yes?"

"You have a nice day, OK?"

The woman smiled ever so slightly. "I will."

With a nod Wendy exited the room, closing the door quietly behind her.

The last bell rang just as she reached the classroom. Students hurried to their desks and settled in quickly, preparing to discover even more fascinating facts about South America. As Wendy took her seat she glanced over at Emily's desk. It was empty. So was the spot where Feather's box usually rested by the bookcase.

H'mm, the girl thought to herself. *She musta missed the bus. Guess I'd better call her during the first break to make sure everything's OK.* Wendy realized there was actually no cause for real concern. Emily had told her that she missed a lot of classes while visiting clinics for tests, going to different hospitals for examination, or simply fighting the potential of a common cold by staying in bed for a day or two.

But try as she might, Wendy just couldn't concentrate on her studies. She kept remembering the look on Emily's face the day before as they had hurried to leave the school. Desperation had lurked in her smile, an uncomfortableness in the way she was acting as she climbed the steps of the bus and waved goodbye from the window. Something was happening to Emily, and Wendy wasn't quite sure what it was.

"Miss Elrod?"

The teacher looked up from her grade book. "Yes, Wendy?" the woman responded with a kind smile.

"I . . . ah . . . I need to make a phone call."

"Who to?"

Wendy motioned toward the empty desk in the center of the room. "Emily," she said. "I'm a little worried about her. She was kinda down yesterday, and now she's not here today."

Her teacher frowned. "Should we be concerned?"

The girl shrugged. "I don't know. If it's OK, I'd just like to call her so I can see if she's home and stuff. May I?"

"Yes. By all means. Why don't you go down to the nurse's office. That way you'll have someone nearby if you need help with Emily."

"Great. I'll be right back."

Hurrying from the classroom, Wendy ran down

the empty corridor leading to the office of the pretty nurse she'd met the week before. After explaining the reason for her visit, she dialed the number Emily had scribbled on a scrap of paper before the weekend. She heard the phone ring three times, then a weak voice answered.

"Emily?" Wendy said, "are you OK?"

A long pause. "I'm OK."

"Why didn't you come to school?"

"I . . . I didn't want to."

"Why?"

No answer.

"Is Feathers OK? Did you give him a big breakfast?"

"I tried to."

Wendy frowned. "So, do you need anything— any medicine or stuff?"

"No."

Wendy glanced at the nurse, then at the oxygen bottle resting in the corner of the room. Something in the way Emily talked, in the way she breathed, worried her, made her feel extremely uneasy. "Listen, Emily, I'd like to come to your house if it's all right."

"You don't have to."

"I know. But you sound kinda sad and . . . and I just want to talk to you. I won't stay very long if you don't want me to."

"Sure. Do whatever you like. I don't care."

Wendy's eyes narrowed as a feeling of fear rose

in her throat. "I'll be there soon. I gotta tell you what happened this morning at the registrar's office. You're gonna love it."

"Fine. Whatever."

The phone went dead. Wendy paused for only a second before quickly dialing another number. When an adult voice answered, she said, "Miss Cadena please." Pressing the receiver closer to her ear she added, "Hurry. This is an emergency."

The newly plowed street seemed deserted as the social worker's car slowed and headed for the curb fronting a small brick house near the corner. Wendy was out the door even before Miss Cadena brought her vehicle to a complete stop. The girl raced up the sidewalk, boots crunching in the hard-packed snow. At the door, she pressed the bell and waited, stabbed the button again, and then again. "Emily? Emily?"

Nothing.

Glancing back at Ruth Cadena who was walking quickly up the driveway, she ran around to the side of the little dwelling. "Emily? It's Wendy. Can you hear me?"

Stopping at a low window, she peered inside. She could just make out a threadbare couch and end table. Continuing around to the back door she began pounding on the wooden frame. "Emily. It's Wendy. Open up. Let me in."

Miss Cadena joined her on the small porch and added her knock to the pounding. They stopped when they heard the latch rattle. Then the door opened a crack. "Why are you here?" a tired voice breathed.

"Emily. Open the door, please," Wendy called. "I just want to talk to you, that's all. Open the door so we can come in. Miss Cadena came with me. We're worried about you."

"Yes, Emily," the woman called, "we were thinking you'd like another visit to the mountains. What do you think? Up for a wagon ride with Joey?"

The door slowly opened to reveal a girl who looked as if she hadn't slept for a long time. "I . . . I can't."

"Why not?"

"I gotta go away."

Wendy pressed in close to her friend. "Go away where?"

Turning, Emily walked slowly into the kitchen. "My mom and dad told me this morning. We're moving to Chicago, to some big hospital where they can treat my disease better—at least that's what they say." She glanced back at her friends. "I don't want to go. I want to stay here in Montana."

Ruth Cadena nodded slowly as Wendy stepped forward. "Oh, Emily, I'm sorry. But, after you get well, you can come back. Then we can—"

"No," Emily interrupted, looking down at the floor. "You don't understand. I . . . I won't be coming back. Not ever."

Wendy's breath caught in her throat. Suddenly

149

she couldn't speak, couldn't think. All she could do was stare at the gaunt, ashen face of her friend, trying to fathom the full meaning of Emily's words. She wanted to scream, to shout out her defiance to the news she'd just heard. It couldn't be true—it just couldn't. Her friend was sick, that was all. And sick people got well. They eventually crawled out of bed and wandered around coughing and sneezing, perhaps even limping on injured limbs for a while, but they didn't go to Chicago and never come back again. That wasn't right—that wasn't fair!

It was Emily who broke the silence. "Feathers can fly now," she said. "He can fly south, because he's all better."

Wendy nodded.

"So," the girl continued, "I think we should take him outside and let him go. It's the right thing to do."

Miss Cadena stepped forward. "It's OK, Emily. We can wait a few more days."

"No. That's the worst thing—keeping an animal from doing what it wants. Feathers doesn't belong here—doesn't belong in a box. He should be out there, high in the sky, flying to his family, to their pond far away from here." Motioning toward the cardboard box in the narrow hallway leading to her bedroom, she said, "I tried to give him a big breakfast, lots of lettuce and stuff, but he just flapped his wings and looked at me as if he was saying, 'Why don't you let me go? Why are you keeping me here?'" Emily wiped a tear from her cheek with a trembling hand. "So let's just take him outside so he can do what he wants to do."

Wendy glanced over at Miss Cadena, then shook her head slowly. "It wasn't supposed to be like this," she said to her friend. "You were *both* supposed to get well."

"I know," Emily stated. "But sometimes bad things happen even on a planet of joy. Isn't that what Pastor Webley said?"

Closing her eyes tightly, Wendy fought to control her emotions. "I'm sorry," she whispered. "I'm so very sorry, Emily."

The girls wrapped their arms around each other, crying softly, holding onto each other tightly, unable to find the words to describe the feelings that burned in their hearts. They'd come into each other's worlds riding the injured wings of a wild animal. Now they were about to watch those same wings, grown stronger, fly away, leaving behind the stark reality that not all stories have a happy ending.

Miss Cadena picked up the box and together the three made their way through the house and out the front door. The yard and street were empty, completely devoid of cars and people. In the distance, past the leafless trees, beyond the low roofs of the houses, rose distant mountains, their summits white and glistening in the morning sun.

The social worker placed the box on the snow-covered sidewalk and looked over at her companions. "Just take off the blanket," Emily said. "He'll know what to do."

Wordlessly, Miss Cadena bent and slipped the cover off the container. Immediately, Feather's head popped up above the rim and he looked around, a little confused. For a moment he studied the thin branches high overhead, then glanced back at the girls. "It's OK," Emily called softly. "You can go now. It's what you want to do. It's what you have to do."

The bird hesitated, still unsure of what was happening. For a solid week he'd been at the mercy of human hands, allowing them to bring him food and offer comfort as his body healed. Now those hands remained at a distance. No smiling face hovered over him. No soothing voice called his name and spoke sounds that calmed his racing heart.

Suddenly, the mallard turned as if hearing a distant call from somewhere far away. This voice he understood. It spoke his language, inviting him to rise above the earth and seek the horizon, to leave the hands to which he'd become accustomed and fly free, following his own thoughts, going his own way.

The duck's head began to bob up and down in short, quick movements as he became nervous, excited, even fearful. He didn't belong in a box, didn't need human hands to care for him. Instead, he was a wild animal, a creation of nature, a feathered spirit made to race the winds that streamed south, away from the cold and the mountains and the presence of people.

With powerful flaps of his wings, he rose quickly from the box like a ball shot from a cannon, and raced away, skimming over the snow, gaining speed and confidence, feeling the rush of icy air as it whistled past his beak and eyes and outstretched neck. Up he flew, watching the earth drop away, feeling a familiar urgency drive his every bone, muscle, and feather. He was going to some distant place far to the south. Although he didn't know where or why, he just knew he had to go there. And the mountains, the glorious mountains, would lead him home.

The long winter was just beginning to lose its grip on the land as Wendy walked the distance from the Station to the end of the driveway. She breathed in the crisp air, squinting into the brilliant sky, trying to imagine what the world would look like without the blanket of snow that had covered the valleys for so many months.

When she reached the road, she sat down on a worn wooden bench jutting from the drifts and waited. It wouldn't be long now, if he kept to his schedule.

The girl glanced back at the Station and admired the proud, handsome structure nestled among the sparse pines and open pastures. Early and the other members of the ranch herd stomped about under the cottonwoods, exploring the dead grasses just under the surface of the snow. They too were searching for hints that spring would soon return.

"Imagine finding you here," she heard someone call. Wendy turned to see Joey leading Tar Boy in from their afternoon jaunt on the logging roads above the valley. "Has he come yet?"

"Nope."

A little red minivan approached, following the road that led past the ranch and intersected the long driveway. The two immediately recognized the driver and his passenger and waved. When it reached them, the vehicle crunched to a stop.

"Has he come yet?"

"Nope."

Debbie slipped out of the van and made her way to the mailbox. "Someone needs to paint this thing," she commented.

Mr. Hanson joined her and nodded in agreement. "Sounds like a good job for our ranch's new, official, full-time head wrangler," he said, glancing at Joey.

"Like I told someone once, *everything's* in my job description," the young man said with a smile. "Even mailboxes. Now that Barry's buying and selling horses over the Internet like some kinda cyberwrangler, I guess all the odd jobs belong to me too. I'm such a lucky guy."

Mr. Hanson grinned. "Hey, you get to spend time with the likes of us plus you can have all the horse manure you can shovel."

Another vehicle approached, this one sporting a little yellow rotating light fastened to the top and a license plate that announced it belonged to the United States Postal Service.

"Hey, Mr. Goldstein," Wendy called as the smiling face of the courier stopped in front of her. "Anything for me?"

"Yeah, like there never is," he laughed, reaching beside him and withdrawing a handful of mail. "Enjoy. See you tomorrow."

With a wave, the man drove away, his little light flashing out a warning to whatever deer or wild animal it needed to of his approach.

Wendy grinned broadly as she selected an envelope addressed to her in firm handwritten letters. She passed the other correspondence to her father, who fished through it with enthusiasm. "Yup," he said, "here it is. A note from Mrs. Pierce. This should tell us what day to expect her and what flight she'll be coming in on. This is wonderful. We'll all be together again, just like before. Lizzy's sister's health is back to normal, and soon so will be Shadow Creek Ranch."

With a nod Wendy ripped open her letter. She read it through quickly, then sighed.

"Well?" Debbie said, "are you going to share it with us?"

Her younger sister nodded. "OK. But, I'll leave out the personal, girl-type stuff. Wouldn't want to embarrass Mr. Dugan. He's very sensitive, you know."

Joey nodded. "When it comes to some of the crazy things those two discuss, you're right."

Spreading the paper out on her lap, Wendy smoothed it with her gloved hand. "Dear Wendy," she began. "I really enjoyed your last letter. It made me homesick for Montana and especially the ranch. Every night I go to sleep imagining that I'm riding with you and Joey up in the mountains. It sometimes helps me forget how much my chest hurts and how lonely I am in this big hospital.

"The doctors say I'm doing a little better, but they're always whispering among themselves, which may or may not be a good sign. It really doesn't matter anymore. I'm learning to take one day at a time and not get too discouraged.

"Tell Pastor Webley 'thank you' for that book he sent to me in your Easter package. I've read it three times. It's all about heaven and stuff, and I really like to think about what it's going to be like to live there and run around with you and chase ducks who will never ever fly away.

"You know, I don't think I have to wait to start enjoying heaven. I can go there now in my mind and even in my dreams. Maybe that's what it's like to live in a planet of joy. Maybe that's what I need to do when I get to feeling sorry for myself.

"Well, the nurse with the crooked mouth just came in. She says I've got to get hooked up to some machine for an hour or two. It's supposed to help build up my good lung. Hey, who am I to argue with technology? So be good and WRITE ME AGAIN SOON. You're my best friend, Wendy. As a matter of fact, you're my *only* friend, but who's counting?

"Give Debbie and Wrangler Barry and Samantha and Joey and Grandpa and Grandma Hanson and your dad my love. Oh yes, and Miss Cadena too. I think it's really great that your dad finally asked that poor woman to marry him. She's been waiting forever!

"I love you, Wendy, and I think about you every day.

"Your friend, Emily."

Wendy looked up at her father with a grin. "I told her about you and Miss Cadena. Hope you don't mind."

Mr. Hanson laughed. "Fine with me. And I agree with Emily. I *did* wait far too long. Now I'm eager for June so we can have another wedding by the footbridge. You're all invited, by the way."

Debbie shook her head as she trudged back to the minivan. "I don't know. I might be doing something else that day—washing shirts or sewing on a new dress."

"Yeah," Joey added, picking up Tar Boy's reins

157

and guiding him toward the driveway. "I might have to miss it too. Gotta fix that weak place in the fence at the far end of the pasture."

Mr. Hanson looked at Wendy, his eyes filled with mock despair. "And you, my youngest and strangest daughter? Will you also abandon me on my day of bliss?"

Wendy shook her head. "Not a chance. I'll be there, Daddy. And for you, I might even put on that silly dress again. I'm not making any promises, you understand. But I'll think about it."

"Fair enough," he stated as he hopped into the van. "Now hurry home. We've gotta plan a welcome back party for Mrs. Pierce. And I think Grandma's making pancakes. Why she's making pancakes for supper is beyond me."

"Ah, that's my fault," Debbie said. "I asked her to. I've been having these weird cravings lately. Yesterday it was catsup and pickles. Is that gross or what?"

Mr. Hanson stared at his daughter for a long moment. "You gotta be kidding."

"What?" the girl blinked.

"You gotta be kidding!"

"Daddy, what's the matter with you? Can't a girl get hungry for catsup and pickles on this ranch?"

Wendy watched Joey and his horse trail the little red minivan with its laughing driver as it moved down the long driveway. The Station waited in the distance, rising from the snow like a friendly fort, its face pleasant and inviting. She folded the letter and slipped it into her pocket. "I miss you, Emily," she said quietly. "I really miss you."

With that she stood and began following the snow-covered pathway that led up the valley and ended at the steps of her home. Overhead, the mountains looked down on her, warming themselves in the breezes that now flowed from the south, bringing the promise of new life to the frozen land. She knew, as did all of nature, that winters never last forever. With the spring would come the excitement of rebirth and the rewards of fresh, unexpected challenges. Soon she'd glance skyward and see returning lines of ducks and geese. Once more there'd be wings filling the skies over Shadow Creek Ranch.